GUARDIAN OF THE GULCH

By

CHUCK MORRIS

GUARDIAN OF THE GULCH

By

CHUCK MORRIS

Published by

Crimson Cloak Publishing

ISBN: 978-1-68160-935-5

ISBN: 1-68160-935-5

Cover by Carly McCracken

Edited by Denna Holm

Publisher's Publication in Data

Morris, Chuck

Guardian of the Gulch

1. Fiction 2. Western 3. Mystery

Dedicated to those whose love and support
made this book possible:
Fernando and Lisa Gutierrez
Sergio and Christy Gutierrez
Gene and Kathy Carter
and of course, Debbie Morris

CHAPTER 1

Kicks sat tall in the saddle as he rode into the town of Helena, Montana. A sometimes bounty hunter, he headed for the sheriff's office to take a look at reward posters. Kicks kept a record book of all the names he'd arrested or had to shoot over the years. He also kept a list of the outlaw names currently wanted. Seeing nothing promising posted, he stepped down from his buckskin gelding and stretched his legs. He glanced toward the Golden Nugget Saloon, thinking a drink sounded good. He'd been riding for days and was anticipating a shot of mescal, or three.

Kicks walked his horse over to the hitching rail in front of the saloon and wrapped the reins loosely around it. A few people were walking in and out of the stores and shops along the street and boardwalk. A white shaggy dog lay in the dirt, partly under the raised boardwalk about five feet from the steps of the walkway. Nothing out of the ordinary.

When Kicks put his foot on the step, the shaggy dog raised his head and growled at him. "Listen, pal," Kicks said. "Better be nice, or me and you are goin' to tangle. Ya ain't gonna keep me from wettin' my whistle." At that friendly warning, the dog wagged his tail and laid his head back down on his paw.

Kicks walked up to the batwing doors and peered inside. When he stepped through, he moved to one side to allow his eyes time to adjust to the dimmer light inside.

The scene was one he'd seen a hundred times before. A crowd of drinking cowboys, the smell of whiskey—or rotgut, as some called it—the acrid scent of sweat and tobacco. Jokes and laughter, soiled doves working the bar, hustling the cowboys. A tinny sounding piano played a timeless favorite Christian song: "Amazing Grace," written by John Newton in 1779. Kicks loved that old song, always amazed at how it was popular not only in churches but in most saloons. He got a kick out of how the drunken heathens would tear up and sing as loud as they could whenever the song was played. They knew every word of the popular hymn.

This was his life, and he liked it.

Stepping up to the bar, Kicks elbowed in between two cowboys. The one at his right side was a big man, taller than him. He accidently bumped the big man's arm, spilling some of his drink, and said, "Sorry, friend."

"It's okay, long as you buy me another drink."

The cowboy must be having a bad day, but it still didn't set right with Kicks. Still, he thought back to what his pappy had always told him. 'Son, if you find yourself in a hole, the first thing to do is stop digging.' *Hell,* he thought, *it is what it is.* So, Kicks said, "Alright, partner." He motioned to the barkeep to give the cowboy another drink. This seemed to satisfy the cowboy, and the two struck up a conversation. They were hitting it off pretty well until the big guy asked, "What's your name, friend?"

"Kicks," he replied.

The cowboy threw back his head and laughed. "Kicks! Man, that's crazy. You'd have to be one tough son-of-a-gun to live with a handle like that."

Tough was right. Kicks, at six foot and two hundred thirty pounds, wide shoulders, narrow hips, a shock of black hair and steel-gray eyes, could put the fear of God in any man.

His dusty clothes matched most working cowboys, and around his waist was a brace of matched Colt .44s.

Though normally cool mannered, the laughing cowboy had ruffled his feathers. He narrowed his eyes at the other man, and with a calm voice said, "Before I was born, my ma kept holding her stomach and complaining that I was always kickin'. Sometimes I'd kick so hard that she'd break down an' cry. When I was born, my pappy named me Kicks. He shortened it to Kick. And for my middle name, he just used the letter A. So they call me 'Kick A Burks, and it's caused me to bruise my knuckles more than a few times."

Still laughing, the other cowpoke asked, "What's the A stand for … uh … let's see now, what words could the A stand for? Oh yeah, a- hole?" With that image in mind, everyone at the bar joined in with the laughter.

It wasn't in Kicks' nature to be laughed at, so he hauled off and hit the other cowpoke in the mouth, sending him sprawling down the bar a few feet to crash to the floor. As he was propelled down the bar, the other men jumped back out of the way.

Kicks stared down at the stricken man, who wiped blood from his mouth. "You got the first part right, but you're wrong about what the A stands for. My full name is Kick A Burks, and that's what I do best, kick ass."

The bloody cowpoke climbed to his feet and drew back his fist, smashing Kicks in the face. Kicks flew backwards and landed on his backside. "My name's Muley. Muley Gentry!"

The crowd began to cheer, some for Muley and some for Kicks.

Lying on the dirt floor, covered with sawdust, Kicks looked up at Muley, rubbing his jaw. "Don't tell me. They call you Muley because you got a powerhouse-punch, like being kicked with both hind hooves of a mule!"

Muley laughed as he reached down with a big right hand and said, "You guessed right, friend. Glad to meet you, Kicks."

Everyone had already moved away from the bar, standing back to watch, probably thinking this would be one helluva fight. Kicks reached up and took the hand Muley offered. Even through the blood covering Muley's face, he noticed the respect in his eyes. "Most proud to meet your acquaintance, Muley."

Muley turned to the bartender. "Me and my friend Kicks here will have a fresh bottle of whiskey."

Hands trembling, the bartender set up the order. "Here you go, Muley, this one's on me."

Muley grabbed the bottle in one big hand and said, "Come on, Kicks, let's see how fast we can empty this bottle."

Kicks grinned. "Lead the way, pal!"

Choosing a table in the back of the room that faced the door, Muley said, "How's this?"

Kicks sat down. "Looks good from here. Seems like we have a lot in common. I always sit with my back to the wall."

"Good," Muley said as he sat down and took a drink from the whiskey bottle, then slid it over to his newfound friend.

"Sorry I made fun of your name, Kicks, but I really thought you were pulling my leg."

Kicks shrugged. "Nope, that's my real name. Sorry I punched you in the face."

Muley chuckled. "Think nothing of it. I never call anyone a friend unless he can knock a man down with the first punch … and hit a running target at least five out of six shots with his six-shooter."

Kicks raised the whiskey bottle, took a long pull, then slid it back over. "Tell me about yourself."

Muley took a swig from the bottle. Instead of answering the question, he asked, "Got the makings? Could sure use a smoke."

"Matter of fact, I do," Kicks said as he reached for the makings out of his shirt pocket and handed it across the table to Muley. "Myself, I don't use tobacco much."

"I don't use it much either, but sometimes I just get a craving." Muley took the tobacco pouch and papers and rolled himself a cigarette. He licked the edge of the thin paper carefully and ran his finger over it to cause it to adhere. Then he twisted the end so no tobacco could fall out. He held it up and observed it for a minute. "Now that's a dang fine masterpiece, by golly." He stuck the finished product in the corner of his mouth and touched the end of it with the flame from a Lucifer.

Watching Muley's big production gave Kicks the urge for a smoke, so he followed suit. They swung their booted feet up onto the table, leaned back in their chairs, and began to blow smoke rings.

"Ain't much to tell," Muley said. "I was found in a pile of hay in the back of a wagon." He took another drag from the cigarette and watched the smoke rings rise and disappear. "We were on the way from somewhere, me and my folks, and going … somewhere. I never knew my folks, or where we were from, because everyone in the wagon was killed but me. I guess the only reason I survived was because my ma hid me in that pile of hay in the back of the wagon, and the killers didn't know I was there." Muley scowled and looked away, obviously done talking about it.

Kicks understood, so he didn't push.

Muley took another long pull from the whiskey bottle and slid it back across the table. "What's your story, Kicks?"

Chuckling softly, Kicks held up the bottle, swirling the dark liquid inside. "My story. Hell, I'm from West Texas. From my pappy's ranch, you can toss a rock into the Conchos River. Pappy was meaner than a wounded grizzly. Why, he'd likely walk through hell with nothing but a bucket of water. I think that's why he named me Kicks. He knew I'd have to be twice as tough as the next guy just to stay alive." Kicks paused long enough to take another pull from the bottle, then he slid it back to Muley. "Actually, my mother's a real jewel, and my pappy's a truly great man. Tough as he is, he cried like a baby when I left home."

Kicks was silent for a moment, and when Muley offered no comment, he continued, "My folks are fine Christian people. I've kinda gone astray, but someday I'll get my b'hind back in church. After another minute of silence, Kicks went on, "Someday, I'll go back home and run the ranch for my old pappy. Then when my folks pass on, I'll settle down there and raise my own family."

Muley and Kicks sat in silence for a while, both thinking about their past life and what their future might hold. Finally, Muley drank the last swig from the bottle, smacked his lips, and said, "Dang, that tasted just like another one."

Kicks leaned forward in his chair and set his booted feet down hard on the floor. "Well, let's go get another bottle of rotgut and see what *it* tastes like."

Muley scooted his chair back from the table and stood up. "Kicks, you're a man after my own heart." The two of them went to the bar and got two bottles and went through the swinging doors to the porch. It was late in the evening and there were a few empty chairs facing the street. They sat down, propped their feet up on the porch's railing, and settled back for some serious drinking.

It had started raining right after Kicks entered the Golden Nugget Saloon, and the street looked almost like a lake. The wagons, buggies, stagecoaches and freight wagons had left huge muddy ruts from one end of town to the other. People out walking were having a hard time keeping dry. Finally, just before dark, the rain changed from a downpour to a slow, steady drizzle with a bit of sleet in it.

"Got a place to stay for tonight? "Muley asked.

"Yep," Kicks answered.

"Where might that be?"

"Right here in this chair." Both men turned silent. Muley glanced over at Kicks. "I'm stayin' at an old, abandoned ranch house about a mile and a half outside of town."

"Room for one more?"

"I guess so," Muley replied. "It's a big old two-story house."

"Well, in that case, do you mind?"

"Nope," Muley grunted. He stood and stretched, then pointed to a big Morgan gelding tied at the hitch rail, midnight black with white socks and a white blazed face. "That's my horse, Morg, right there."

"Kicks laughed. "My horse is that big buckskin right next to your Morgan." The buckskin which Kicks had named Buck, was a beautiful tan color with black socks, mane and tail. He had a white star on his forehead.

Muley stretched again, then moved to the hitch rail. "Then let's go before the storm hits again."

The two cowboys hit the saddles and lit a shuck for the old, abandoned ranch house.

*   *   *

13

Some thirty days prior, Muley Gentry had come thundering down the trail towards Helena, Montana, looking for a place to wait out a storm. The Blackfoot River just north of Helena had been flooding the whole area for days, a mixture of rain and bitter cold. About a mile and a half east of the old Lewis and Clark Trail, Gentry had spotted what appeared to be an abandoned ranch house. Too dark to tell if anybody lived there or not, he rode in anyway, grateful for a dry, safe place to bed himself and his horse down. After off-saddling his horse, he rubbed him down in the old barn.

Muley went inside the house, glad to find several dry logs and kindling left there by the last person who'd taken refuge there. He made a fire in the huge stone fireplace. Poking around in the kitchen for something to eat, he found an old newspaper. While reading it, he learned the town had been established only a couple of years earlier, following the discovery of gold along the Last Chance Creek by four Georgians. They'd named the town Crabtown, after John Crab, one of the four. The main street was called Last Chance Gulch.

Helena's newspaper proudly proclaimed that Lewis and Clark had first discovered it. Its first mayor was James E. Smith, and its first sheriff was Seth Bullock. Bullock had been a businessman, rancher, and sheriff of Crabtown, renamed Helena.

Bullock had left Helena and moved on to become sheriff of Deadwood, and then U.S. Marshal of South Dakota. Helena was a young town; most of its dwellings were tents, slowly being replaced by clapboard houses. Some of the major sites were being laid out and built out of stone. The courthouse, jail and newspaper buildings made the Last Chance Gulch look almost like one of them fancy East Coast main streets.

Muley's coming to Helena had not been by chance. He was a man desperately in search of his past, and his future. He'd told Kicks the truth about being hidden in the hay in the back of a wagon when he was a baby, but Muley had left out the part about his father and mother fleeing from trouble. Unfortunately, trouble had found them anyway, and they were both killed on the trail.

Luckily, strangers had passed by their wagon just minutes after the killers left. Muley's father was already dead, but his mother lived long enough to tell them the baby's name. John and Mary Hicks had raised him as their own but they couldn't tell him much about his real parents.

The first night that Muley stayed in the old, abandoned ranch house, he'd thought about his life's journey thus far. He'd subconsciously drew his Colt .44s, nodding with satisfaction when the sights didn't catch on the leather holsters. He'd filed the sights down, allowing for a smoother, faster draw. He'd also adjusted the trigger mechanism, so it took less than one pound of pressure to fire. He knew the average was three to four pounds. It had saved him more than once when challenged by gunslingers. It also gave him some notoriety as a gunman, which he'd hoped to avoid.

Now, thirty days later, Muley was becoming discouraged. Low on money and patience, this stop at Helena had just about been his last hope. If he couldn't find the answers to his past here, they might be lost to him forever. He'd been in Montana for a month now, and all he'd gotten was soaked to the skin from sleet and rain. At least he had the old ranch house to stay in, and he'd even made a new friend.

CHAPTER 2

At daybreak the next morning, Kicks woke up startled. *Where the devil am I?* he thought. He sat up on the rickety old cot, stretched and yawned. "Ouch!" he said as he rubbed his jaw gently, last night starting to come back to him. *That Muley packs a mean punch.* His clothes were still damp from yesterday's rain, but he stood and dressed, slinging his gun belt around his lean hips. After tying both holsters to his thighs with the leather thongs, he ran his fingers through his hair and stretched the rest of the kinks out of his damp, aching body.

Kicks found his way into the kitchen. Seeing a wooden water bucket sitting on an old stove, he looked out the kitchen window at a water pump. "Hmmm, wonder if it's got any water?" He grabbed the bucket and headed outside. As he walked across the porch and down the steps toward the water pump, he glanced to his right, finding Muley sitting in a big old chair. His eyes were shut, and his mouth hung open, sawing logs like a water-powered lumber-mill.

Kicks stopped and looked down at his friend, chuckling. He kicked the chair and yelled, "Hey, Muley, wake up!" Muley didn't budge or miss a note in his snoring. Kicks went out in the yard and looked up at the sky. The rain and sleet had stopped, but the clouds overhead were dark and heavy with moisture. He walked up to the old pump, afraid it might be rusted shut, or the well dry. Though it squeaked with each pump, out came some rusty-looking water. Kicks continued to pump the handle and soon the water turned clear, fresh, and cold.

A couple of more pumps and the water bucket was full. Kicks took off his hat, hung it on the pump handle, then raised the warped bucket to his mouth and took a long drink. He poured the rest of it over his head. After fingering most of the water out of his hair, he put his hat back on, then pumped the bucket full again. Laughing to himself, Kicks took the bucket and stepped up on the porch, dumping half of it on a sleeping Muley.

Muley jumped up like he'd been shot out of a cannon, sputtering, coughing, and wiping water from his eyes. "What in the Sam hill is wrong with you, boy?" He scowled at Kicks.

If looks could kill, Kicks knew he'd already be buzzard bait. With a straight face, he said, "Sorry, pal. Thought you might be dead. Was tryin' to revive ya." He handed Muley the bucket, which still had quite a bit of water in it. "Here ya go, amigo, have a drink of nice, fresh, cold water."

Muley was so mad he turned red, but he grabbed the bucket and turned it up, drinking the rest of the water. Setting the bucket down, he said, "I'm starving. Let's go into town and get some breakfast."

"Okay by me."

Although the sleet and rain had stopped, the ground remained saturated, and the wind still had a sharp chill to it. Puffs of smokey breath erupted from the horses' nostrils as Kicks and Muley saddled them. Leading them out of the barn, they mounted up, and both horses began to buck, neither of them crazy about leaving their cozy barn. They soon settled and the two cowboys headed toward town.

Burks and Gentry scowled as they rode down the water-logged street of Helena. It looked like one big mud hole. As they rode along, the horses' hooves made a loud sucking sound with each step. Despite the early hour, they could see where a few buggies and farm wagons had already left tracks in the street.

"Where do you wanna eat," Muley asked. "The Golden Nugget or the Silver Spoon Café?"

Kicks shrugged. "Don't matter to me, only we might not be welcome in the Golden Nugget after last night."

Muley grinned in agreement. "Right, then we'll go to the Silver Spoon. Got a pretty waitress works there I like. Name's Cathy. She's new in town herself, so she don't know anything about my situation."

"Lead the way. I'm gettin' hungrier by the minute."

"The Silver Spoon Café is about three blocks up the street," Muley said.

Riding along, they passed a few of the new homes being built and an old cemetery. There was a sign hanging on a post that read: *The Helena Cemetery will be moved to Benton Avenue. It will be called The Benton Avenue Cemetery.*

As they neared the Silver Spoon, Muley picked it up a notch, acting anxious about seeing Cathy. Kicks glanced over at him and chuckled. "Hope she's as pretty as you say she is."

Muley didn't answer, looking preoccupied. A few minutes later, they were stepping inside the Silver Spoon.

The café didn't look like much on the outside, but no worse than most of the other buildings. On the inside, it was like stepping into your mother's kitchen. Clean as all get out, you could eat right off the floor, if you had a mind to. As soon as they stepped inside, Kicks began sniffing the air like a blue tick hound sniffing a rabbit's trail. "I know I smell bear sign," he said, "and I've been craving me some ever since I left West Texas."

About that time, Cathy, the pretty waitress whom Muley had been talking about earlier; came in from the kitchen and stood behind the counter. She was small in stature with auburn hair and blue-green eyes. She was wearing a dress with frills at the neck and sleeves and a large white apron that covered most of her dress. Muley and Kicks were the first two customers of the morning, and that being the case, she took time to talk to them. "Hi there, cowboys," she said with a dimpled grin. "Did I hear someone say they smelled bear sign?"

Kicks grinned back. "Yes, ma'am. Am I right?"

"You sure do, cowboy, and I got a big batch of them coming right up. You know, back east, in places like Saint Louis and Chicago, they call 'em donuts."

Still grinning, Kicks said, "I don't care what they're called, just trot 'em out here with a pot of coffee."

Cathy turned to Muley. "How about you, cowboy? You want your usual steak and eggs, with spuds and frijoles?"

"Uh yes … no! I can't resist the smell of bear sign either. Trot 'em out!"

Cathy faked a confused look. "You cowboys and your sweet tooth. Alright, two heaping helpings of bear sign coming right up." She disappeared into the kitchen. A few minutes later, she came out with a big platter. "Here you go." She set the platter down in front of them and stood back, watching the donuts disappear in record time.

When the platter was empty, Kicks said, "I have to admit, the bear sign was about as good as I've ever feasted on."

"Me too," Muley agreed.

Kicks reached for his money. "It was my idea, so I'm paying. And ma'am, you're not only a darn good cook, but you're the prettiest cook I've ever seen."

Cathy fluttered her eyelashes at him and giggled. "Why, sir," she mocked, "we haven't been properly introduced yet."

Muley laughed. "Sorry, Cathy. This is my friend, Kicks A Burks."

Cathy threw her head back and laughed, then apologized. "I'm sorry … Kicks … is it? It's just that when your friend Muley here first came in, I thought his name was odd." She giggled, then pulled herself together. Clearing her throat, she tried to sound serious when she said, "What does the 'A' stand for?"

Muley shot a glance at Kicks, then began to stammer. "Well, Cathy, uh—"

Kicks interrupted, "No middle name, ma'am. Just the letter A."

Meanwhile, more people had started to enter the café, so Cathy excused herself. "I have to tend to my other customers. Don't want 'em getting upset."

Kicks laid enough money on the counter to pay for the breakfast, with a little extra for a tip. "We need to get going, anyway. We'll see you later, Cathy."

She grinned over her shoulder at them.

On the boardwalk outside the café, Kicks and Muley stopped to roll a cigarette. Muley scratched a Lucifer on a post and lit his cigarette, then held the match out for Kicks."

"You were dead right, Muley. She's a real looker!"

"Just remember, I saw her first."

Kicks grinned as he rubbed his jaw. "Yeah, I remember." Then he changed the subject. "You know, I was just planning to stay a few days when I stopped in at the Golden Nugget to wet my whistle. Now, I ain't in such a big hurry to be on my way. Things around here seem to be shaping up to be mighty interesting. So if you want a sidekick, I just might stick around for a bit."

Muley thought it over for a few seconds. "I never was one for company much longer than a word or two, but you know, it might be nice to have another fast gun around as a sidekick." The two were silent for a while, then Muley added, "You know what I meant when I said another fast gun, right? Someone who's not all talk?'"

"Uh-huh. I 'spect there might be trouble dogging your trail, and you want someone backing you that you can count on." The two men shook hands on their friendship, and that was all there was to it. No other words were needed. Their handshake was their word. A handshake to them was an oath, a bond.

Muley grinned after taking a last drag from his cigarette. He tossed it into the dirt and ground it out with the heel of his boot. "I'm thirsty," he said, and headed for the Golden Nugget Saloon.

When they stepped through the swinging doors, they saw the same bartender from last night. He grimaced at Muley and Kicks, and said, "Oh my." He stopped and pressed his lips together, as though wishing he'd kept his mouth shut. "I mean," he corrected, "nice to see you two gents again. What can I get you?"

Kicks laughed. "We know what you meant, barkeep. We'll overlook it … this time, if you set 'em up for us two or three times."

The bartender sighed as he grabbed a bottle and two glasses. "I'll even serve it at a table for you." he said, heading across the room. He stopped at a table and started to set the drinks down.

"Huh-uh," Muley said. "We want a table with a wall behind us."

The bartender looked around nervously and moved to a table over in a dark corner. "This one okay?"

Kicks lowered his long frame down into one of the chairs. The wall was at his back and he could see the batwing doors swing back and forth as men walked in and out. "This'll do just fine." Then he looked up at Muley. "Take a load off, partner, and have a drink."

Muley sat down, and the barkeep poured the drinks and then started to walk away.

"Hold it," Kicks said. "Leave the bottle." The barkeep set the bottle down and hurried back behind the bar.

The two cowboys drank in silence for a short time. Kicks held up his glass, swirling the brown liquid. He studied the action of the liquid a moment longer, then looked at his friend. "So, Muley, tell me what you've learned? What's our next step?"

Muley picked up his glass, looked at it for a minute, then sat it down and shrugged. "Hell, I've been here for a month now and haven't found out one darn thing. I can say, these people here never miss a good chance to shut up."

Kicks nodded. "Yeah, well, some people are kinda close-mouthed. Like my pappy always says, 'Never kick a fresh turd on a hot day.'"

Muley laughed half-heartedly. "What the deuce does that mean?"

Surprised Muley didn't know, he replied, "Why … it means people don't want to rock the boat, stir up trouble. Might cause a stink, make things messy."

This time Muley's laughter was genuine. "Okay, I get it now." After a moment, his mood turned serious again. "What's got me so discouraged is that this is my last stop, Kicks. My last chance to find the missing link to my past."

"Maybe you ain't asked the right people the right questions."

Muley was about to respond to that statement when a stranger walked up to their table.

"I'm looking for a guy by the name of Muley. Muley Gentry."

*   *   *

Kicks and Muley looked up at the intruder. It was plain as the nose on their faces that the man was looking for trouble, and he was big enough to cause plenty of it. He wore a gun belt with a .44-cal pistol in the holster, and it looked like it'd never been used. He was a huge, barrel-chested man with arms that looked almost as big around as a man's head. He had tree stumps for legs that were about to burst through his tight trousers. This man was not a gunman. At six-foot-eight and about three hundred pounds, he was made for killing people with his bare hands.

Kicks glanced over at Muley, raising his eyebrows in question.

Muley scooted his chair away from the table to stand up. "I'm Muley," he said. "Whose askin'?"

Before Muley could straighten up, the stranger made his move. With surprising speed for such a big man, he put a huge hand in the middle of Muley's chest and shoved hard. The unsuspecting cowboy went crashing back down in his chair. Being a big man himself at six-foot-four, weighing two hundred and forty pounds, Muley came down heavy, and the chair collapsed under the forceful impact. Before he could react, the aggressor again showed amazing swiftness when he grabbed

Muley's splaying left hand. Pulling him close, he heaved Muley up on his shoulders, then tossed him onto the table.

The table collapsed too. Kicks grabbed the bottle of whiskey before it could fall and break. To the onlookers, saving the bottle of whiskey was all Kicks was worried about.

As a stunned Muley was climbing out of the pile of kindling that had once been a table and chair, the aggressor again grabbed him, and this time caught him in a bone-crunching bear hug. It only took about thirty seconds before Muley turned a pretty color blue, desperate to free himself from this mountain of a man.

At this point, Kicks didn't know whether to shoot the guy or club him with a chair. He was soon relieved of that decision though, as Muley managed to free his arms. By turning both of his palms inward, he slammed them together as hard as he could on both sides of the bigger man's head. The aggressor roared in pain, releasing his powerful bear hug as he put his hands to his ears.

Muley gasped for air, shaking his head to clear his vision. Then he shot a quick glance at Kicks, as if to say, *Thanks for the help, partner*. While his opponent was still moaning in agony, Muley waded into him with all the weight and fury he could muster with both big fists. He took a step forward and buried his right fist in the big man's belly. As he exhaled, bent forward at the waist, Muley brought his knee up into the man's face. There was a sickening crunch of bone and tissue as the man's nose and face were pulverized.

The powerful upward action from Muley's knee straightened his opponent to a standing position. Muley took a step back and then rammed the man in the stomach with his shoulder, causing him to fall over his shoulder. He then straightened up and tossed the man onto another table, where the assailant crumpled to the floor in a tangle of busted wood and lay still.

"He dead?" Kicks asked, grinning as he handed Muley the bottle of whiskey.

Grabbing the bottle and holding it over his head, the winded cowpoke opened his mouth and poured half of the whiskey down his throat. With his bandana, he wiped the blood and sweat from his face and eyes. "Ask me if I give a good god damn," Muley answered, staring daggers at Kicks.

Although it might have looked as if Kicks hadn't been interested in helping his friend, it simply wasn't true. During the fight, Kicks kept one eye on Muley and Goliath, to make sure his friend didn't get too banged up, and kept his other eye on the crowd that had gathered. There was something fishy about this whole thing. It was obvious this attacker, this … Goliath fellow, didn't know Kicks or Muley. It was also clear the crowd didn't know him. Putting two and two together could only mean one thing. This fight was a set up so Goliath would kill Muley. What the two cowboys would have to do now is figure out who set it up and why. That's just what Kicks was thinking when he saw two gunmen approaching Muley. *Now we'll find out the who.*

Upon seeing their Goliath defeated, out cold, lying among the broken tables, two gunmen emerged from the crowd where they had kept themselves hidden. They stepped forward. "Hey you, Muley!" one of them called out, using a threatening tone.

Muley rolled his eyes and made an unwholesome gesture with his hands. "Now what?" he muttered, turning to deal with the next threat. Though bloody, sore, and tired from his earlier fight, he exuded confidence as he faced this new challenge. He quickly took in their dress and the way they wore their guns, suspecting they were professional gunmen. Topnotch gunslingers drawing top wages. Goliath had failed, so they were here to earn their pay by killing Muley themselves.

Muley squared off, sneering as he taunted them. "So, you two snakes are the big man's backup, huh?" His hands brushed over the top of his holsters, his eyes widening a moment when he realized both guns were gone. He'd lost them in the fight. For the first time in his life, he experienced a twinge of fear. *Well, Muley, what you gonna do now?* he asked himself.

Facing Muley, both gunmen had already noticed he'd lost his guns during the fight. Speaking boldly, one of the gunmen grinned and said, "So you beat the mountain man, huh? Well, let's see how good you are with your guns."

Still breathing hard, Muley said, "Ain't wearing no guns. Lost them during the fight."

They all three looked down, seeing one of Muley's Colts lying at the feet of one of the gunmen. Grinning, he kicked it across the floor towards Muley. "Well now, I 'spect that belongs to you, don't it?"

"Yep," Muley agreed sheepishly. "I 'spect so."

Silence lay heavy around the room, the crowd waiting with bated breath to see what Muley would do. One of the gunmen taunted, "You can go for it any time you want to."

No one moved or said a word. Muley tried franticly to think of a way out of this.

One of the gunmen spoke again, "Well now, are you gonna go for it or not!"

The other gunmen jeered. "Course, if you wanna take the coward's way out, you could jis' leave town. That'd be okay with us, long as you promise never to come back."

Kicks had been waiting in the background to see if one of the gunmen would say something to give him a clue what this was all about. Didn't seem like that was going to happen.

He figured Muley was about to do something that would get himself killed, so he stepped forward and stood beside him. "Try me on for size," Kicks challenged. "I'm sure you boys wouldn't think of taking advantage of an unarmed man now, would ya?"

"Thanks, partner," Muley said as he stooped to pick up his guns.

The two gunmen had apparently liked the odds better when it was just the two of them against one unarmed man, so before Muley could retrieve his guns, they went into action.

Kicks saw what they were planning and decided to go ahead and start the ball rolling. While Muley was bent over, picking up his six-shooters, Kicks put his size thirteen boot on the seat of his pants and shoved. Muley went sprawling across the floor, though managed to grab one of his pistols as he came up, ready for action.

By then, the lead was already flying.

The two gunmen cleared leather just about the same time Kicks did, but their shots went wild, and he didn't give them a second chance. With both Colts smoking, he got one of the gunmen between the eyes. The man stared for a second through dead eyes, then fell to the floor. Kicks' second shot, fired simultaneously with the first one, caught the second gunmen in the guts. He screamed in agony, then mustered up enough strength to raise his six-shooter again. Kicks cocked the hammer back to finish the man off, but Muley put a slug through his chest before he could pull the trigger, right through the tag from the tobacco sack hanging from his shirt pocket. The man never uttered a sound as he fell over.

By this time, Muley was on his feet and had retrieved both Colts. Grinning sheepishly, he said, "That was some fine shootin', Kicks. Thanks. Next time I get into a gunfight, I'll try to make sure I got my guns with me."

"My pleasure, Muley." Kicks grinned and held out his hand. "Put 'er there, pal."

Muley grabbed Kicks' hand and began pumping it. They stood there grinning at each other, ignoring the fallen outlaws and broken tables and chairs.

"Well," Kicks mused, "Looks like you're nosing around and asking questions has made someone uncomfortable." He shot a quick look over at the busted-up table where Muley had dumped Goliath. To his surprise, he found him gone.

"Dang," Muley muttered, "We shoulda grabbed that sucker while we had the chance. Coulda made him tell us what the hell is going on here."

"Yep," Kicks said. "It's the old shoulda, woulda, coulda, thing. Too late for hindsight now. Ya ask me, what we gotta do is get busy nosin' around, asking more questions. Only this time, we'll be on the lookout for whatever else might come along." He looked around the room, seeing about fifteen, twenty men standing back by the bar. "Good time as any, don't ya think?" he said, lifting his chin toward the crowd.

Muley nodded. "Anyone here know these two dead gunmen? Or the big dude who jumped me?"

When no one answered, Kicks asked, "Any of you ever heard of a family that used to live around here by the name of Gentry?"

Just as the crowd was beginning to loosen up and talk, the law stepped in. Sheriff Cal Tidwell was the boss hog, and he ruled Helena with an iron fist. He stood about five-nine, slender build, though his smaller size didn't interfere with his courage any. He had a reputation for being fast on the draw, and even quicker to make decisions. The town's Boot Hill could vouch for that. Sheriff Cal Tidwell's jeans were worn but clean, and a battered star was pinned to the vest over his plaid shirt. He wore his gray Stetson squared on his head.

"What's going on here?" the sheriff demanded, pushing his way through the crowd. He stopped about four feet from Kicks and Muley. The sheriff looked at the two cowboys, then glanced down at the two dead gunmen. "I said, what's going on here?" He glared at Kicks and Muley. "Who are you and what business do you have in my town?"

Muley grimaced when he started to introduce him and Kicks. Not wanting the sheriff to think he was trying to be funny, he said, "I'm Gentry, and this here is my partner, Burks."

CHAPTER 3

After Sheriff Tidwell questioned everyone in the saloon, and was told that the two cowpokes acted in self-defense, he softened up a little. "Guess there's nothing I can hold you on, so you're in the clear."

Much relieved, Muley said, "Thanks, Sheriff. We sure don't want no trouble with the law." He turned to Kicks. "Fighting ol' Goliath sure was a chore. Made me hungry as a bear. Let's go back to the Silver Spoon and have some lunch."

Before Kicks could answer, the sheriff said, "I said you were in the clear. I didn't say you could leave. Hang around until I can get someone to take these bodies over to the undertaker's office. I need to talk to you two."

Reluctantly, they hung around until Cal had dispersed with the bodies. "Now, just what did you say your business is here in Helena?"

"We ain't exactly got any business here," Muley said. "We're just passing through."

The sheriff looked at them with a raised eyebrow. "So, you're total strangers around these parts, are you?"

"Yes, sir," Muley answered. "I been here about a month. My friend here just rode in yesterday."

The sheriff smirked. "Funny thing, those three men who jumped you were strangers too, 'cording to everyone else I talked to in here."

The two cowpokes looked quizzically at each other, having no idea what the sheriff was implying.

"It's like this," Cal said. "Just seems mighty funny that two strangers, that's you guys, ride into town, and the very next day, more strangers ride in and lock horns with ya. Bang, two of 'em are in Boot Hill, and the third one disappeared." He rubbed his chin. "What I'm saying is, either all five of you guys knew each other, or for reasons I don't know, you two got enemies. I'm leanin' toward the latter. I think someone paid those three guys to kill ya. You sure you never seen 'em before?"

"No, Sheriff," Muley said. "We never saw any of 'em before."

Cal raised his hat and scratched his head, exposing a shock of thick black hair interspersed with a few gray ones. "Well then, I'm afraid we'll never know the answer to this mystery."

"What do you mean by that, Sheriff?" Muley asked.

"Just a rule I got. If you don't live in this town or own a ranch or a business, or at least work on a ranch somewhere around here, then you got three days to move on. That's if'n you don't stir up any more trouble during that time. Three days … no ifs, ands, or buts about it."

"Sheriff," Kicks protested. "That ain't fair. We were minding our own business when those three guys jumped us. I think we oughta be able to stay long enough to figure out who wants us killed, and why. Don't you?"

The sheriff's expression turned hard again. "I totally agree with you. However, if I let you guys stay in Helena, there's gonna be more trouble. That's why I'm sheriff here, to keep trouble away. You've got three days to take care of your business." With that, Sheriff Cal Tidwell turned and walked away, saying over his shoulder, "Don't forget … three days."

Kicks looked at Muley, who was staring a hole right through the middle of the sheriff's back. "Get a grip on yourself, partner," Kicks warned. "And get that notion off your mind. Beating the hell outta Sheriff Tidwell ain't gonna help us one lick."

Muley relaxed a bit. "Yeah, I guess you're right, but I'd like to at least give him a piece of my mind. In fact, I just might do that."

"Not a good idea. Like my old pappy always says, 'Better to let sleeping dogs lie.'"

Muley threw up his arms in exasperation. "What the hell are we gonna do? Blast it, might as well just give up."

"Ain't no way I'm gonna let you give up," Kicks assured him. "Not after all you been through."

"Okay, just what can we do?"

Kicks gave Muley a friendly slap on the back. "We're in a saloon, ain't we? We're gonna get drunk, then we can figure out the sensible thing to do."

"Yeah, well, I guess that's about all we can do."

After the sheriff left, and all the excitement died down, the patrons in the saloon resumed their places at the bar and tables scattered around the room. Kicks and Muley ignored the low murmurs as gazes followed them to the bar, whispering about what had just taken place. They elbowed their way in, and Kicks motioned the barkeep over.

"What can I get for you, my friends?"

It was noticeable to both cowpokes that the bartender was trying to befriend them. They figured he worried about them starting more trouble, afraid they might bust the place up even worse than they already had. Kicks thought a little money might help the friendship along, so he slid a double eagle across the bar in front of the barkeep. "Okay, friend, we'll have a bottle of whiskey and some answers to a few questions. Twenty dollars oughta cover the info too."

The bartender picked up the double eagle, then put a bottle and two glasses on the bar. Instead of putting the coin in his pocket, he turned to the till. When he faced Kicks again, he counted out the difference in change for the price of the whiskey. He laid the bills neatly on the bar in front of Kicks and said, "My name's Sammy Galveston. You can call me Sammy. I don't take bribes, but if you want to ask me some questions, fire away. I'll answer 'em if I can."

Kicks felt a little embarrassed for offering bribe money to a man that was just trying to be friendly. "Sorry, Sammy. Didn't mean to offend ya."

Sammy made a swishing motion with his hand, as if to brush something away. "It's okay. Go ahead and ask your questions, Mister Kicks."

"Just call me Kicks, Sammy. What can you tell us about the sheriff?"

Sammy looked around nervously. "The sheriff's name is Cal Tidwell, and he was appointed, not elected. And I think he's on the take."

Muley jumped in on the conversation. "Who appointed him? Whose payroll is he on?"

Sammy looked around again, then leaned over the bar and whispered, "I can't answer, not here. If you wanna ask me them kinda questions, you'll have to meet me somewhere else."

Muley lowered his voice. "Do you know that old, abandoned ranch house about a mile and a half east of town?"

"Yes. I'll meet you there at eleven tonight. It'll be safe to talk there."

"Okay, and thanks, Sammy."

The bartender left them and moved down the bar to wait on other customers.

"Well," Kicks said, "it's gettin' late. Said you were hungry. Might as well head on over to the Silver Spoon and have something to eat. We can't learn anything until later tonight. By the time we eat, and you get done jawing with Cathy, it'll be time to meet Sammy."

Muley hesitated. "You go ahead, Kicks. Think I'll just ride out to the ranch now and wait there."

Kicks scowled, knowing something must be wrong. "Didn't think old Muley would ever pass up a meal or a chance to jaw with Cathy. What's wrong, pal?"

"Well, to tell you the truth, I'm just about broke. Need to watch where and how I spend my money. Been workin' here and there on different ranches. That's how I been able to keep travelin' around all this time. If I can't find another riding job, or the answers to my questions about my family soon, then…." He shrugged.

Kicks suspected Muley was a proud man, and this had been a hard thing to admit. "Hey, pal, you shoulda told me. I've got enough funds to take care of both of us. Why don't you let me handle the financial affairs?"

Muley's face brightened. "Aw heck, I can't accept that. Nice of ya, but jus' can't do it."

Seeing that approach wasn't working, Kick's laughed and slapped Muley on the back. "Hell, man, I wasn't offering you charity! I'm just offering you a loan. You can pay me back after this is all over with."

"Oh, well, okay, I guess," Muley replied. "But I don't want you to spend all your money trying to help me out. This thing could drag out for a while. Then we'd both be broke."

"Listen, pal, I ain't gonna run out of cash. I've got a pretty large bank account, and it keeps drawin' interest every day."

"So, what are you, a bank robber?"

"No, I'm not an outlaw. Look, I told you I was from West Texas, and my pappy owns a big ranch there."

"Yeah, I remember."

"Well, my pa's ranch is about ten miles outside of San Angelo, Texas, and takes in a pretty large portion of the Concho River. One of the boundaries of his range is a landmark that separates Pa's land from the property of Fort Concho. I don't need to go on the outlaw trail for the money or anythin' else. I could send for any amount of money I want, and I'd get it. I keep my bank account replenished in different ways. Like you, I've worked on ranches. I've been trail boss on a few cattle drives, and every now and then, when I ride into a new town, I go visit the jail and say howdy to the sheriff. While I'm there, I glance over the wanted posters. If I see a face or a name with enough reward money attached to it, I go after 'em. So, you see, partner, we're not goin' to run out of money. Not 'til hell freezes over anyway."

Muley still looked a bit embarrassed. "Okay, Kicks, I'll accept a loan. And thanks. You're a real pal."

"Hell, you'd do the same for me. Besides, the interest I'm gonna charge you will eat you a new rear end, so don't thank me yet."

They left the Golden Nugget and headed on over to the Silver Spoon Café. After dinner and a long talk with Cathy, Kicks suggested they take their horses over to Oatman's

Livery for a good rubdown and some grain. "They'd been grazing on nothing but grass for days."

Muley agreed to that, so they led the horses over to the livery and looked around. Just inside the doors, there was an office with a window facing their way so the hostler could see when someone came inside. Beyond the office were the stalls for the horses.

They could see through the window of the office that the hostler had a card game going on. Kicks whispered, "Let's get in the game, if they'll let us."

Muley shook his head. "I can't afford it."

"Wait! Listen! What if … we get in the game and supply them with all the whiskey they can drink! What do you think will happen?" Kicks could see the bulb light up inside Muley's head. "Get these guys drunk and they might do some talking. Sooner or later, everyone's gotta do business at the livery, so these guys are bound to know just about everything that goes on in this whole town."

Muley looked thoughtfully for a second, then nodded.

"Right, now just follow my lead." Kicks walked over to the door of the office, opened it, and stuck his head inside. "How much for a rubdown and grain for two horses?"

The hostler glanced in Kicks' direction, then back down at his cards. "Dang … and I got a good hand goin' too. Do it yourself," he said. "And when you're finished, bring six-bits in here and give it to me!"

After they finished with the horses, Kicks handed Muley twenty-five dollars.

"That's a lot of money!"

"A card player can't get in the game without a stake. Come on, let's go." They went inside the office and Kicks laid seventy-five cents down on the table in front of the hostler.

"What do you want now?" the hostler asked irritably.

"We'd like to set in on the game."

"We've already got enough players. There ain't no more room."

Kicks pulled a wad of bills out of his pocket. "Well, we've got a big stake here, and it's burning a hole in our pockets. We were fixin' to send someone out to buy some whiskey and play cards." He looked at Muley and shrugged. "Well, guess we'll just have to go somewhere else to spend our money."

When the hostler looked up and saw that big wad of cash, he changed his mind real quick. He stood up and said, "That's different. Sit down and join us. What's your names?"

"I'm Kicks, and this is Muley."

The hostler pointed to each of the card players. "That there's Jinks, and Todd, that's Tim, and that's Cory. And I'm Floyd." In almost the same breath, he waved his hand at two of the men. "Jinks, Todd, you heard the man. Get his money and go 'n fetch the whiskey."

Kicks handed the money to the fellow called Jinks. "Just get however many bottles that'll buy."

Jinks looked at the money. "Oh, hell yeah," he yelled. "This'll buy a bottle for every one of us. Come on, Todd. Let's go make a whiskey run."

"Well," Floyd said, "looks like two seats just opened up. Sit down, gents, 'n let's play cards."

Kicks and Muley sat down in the two vacant seats between Tim and Cory "What's the game?" Muley asked.

Floyd started dealing the cards. "Five-card draw!"

"Hold on there, partner," Muley said.

Floyd hesitated in dealing the cards. "Got a problem?"

"Yep," Muley said. "We like to see *high card* deals first."

Floyd cursed under his breath. "Okay … sure thing. High card deals the first hand." The hostler gathered the cards and shuffled them. Then he placed the deck in the middle of the table. "Pick a card," he said.

Tim was seated at Floyd's left side, so he drew first. "Crud," he said as he angrily threw the card down, face up. "A lousy deuce."

Muley was next. He drew a nine. He tossed his card on the table face up for everyone to see.

Then Kicks drew. "Queen" he said and laid his card down face up.

Cory, being next drew a seven. He tossed it on the table. "Your turn," he said to Floyd.

Floyd carefully drew his card, folded the corner back a little and peeked at it. He grinned and said, "A king. That beats your queen, Kicks. I deal the first hand."

"That's okay," Kicks said. "We just want to keep it straight."

Floyd shuffled the cards again and slapped the deck down in the middle of the table. "Cut, anyone?"

Muley reached over and made the cut. After everyone anted up, the hostler quickly dealt the cards face down to all the players, including himself, and then the betting began.

CHAPTER 4

The game went on for some time, each player winning a hand or two, then losing a hand or two. Finally, Jinks and Todd came back with the whiskey, the two already three sheets to the wind. Kicks gave Muley that ... *I knew it* look, and Muley nodded knowingly.

"Come on," Floyd demanded. "Pass those bottles around." Jinks gave each of the five-card players a bottle, and then the two of them went off to finish drinking themselves into oblivion. As the game went on, Floyd, Cory and Tim began to loosen up and talk more freely.

Kicks and Muley both drew most of the winning hands. However, they wanted to make sure that the hostler and his pal's, Tim and Cory, stayed in a good mood, so even when they drew a pat hand, they would sometimes make a face and curse, then fold.

"Confound the rotten luck," Muley said as he folded in another game. "I think *my* name should be Jinks!"

Kicks tossed in his hand too. "Tell me about it!"

It was Floyd's turn to deal again. As the big winner so far, he was happy.

"Hold on their Floyd," Kicks said as Floyd started to deal. "I've lost a bundle tonight. I think it's time for me to hit the road." Looking at Muley, he added, "You ready, partner?"

Pretending frustration, Muley answered, "Well, I kinda thought my luck was changing, but maybe you're right. We better be on our way."

"No," Floyd insisted. "I don't get to play with real card players that often. Tell you what … why don't we take a break. Then we can start a new game. Maybe your luck will change. Okay?"

"Well," Muley said, "I do feel like my luck is about to change."

Floyd grinned. "Yeah. We'll take a break and make a trip to the privy. I'll go fetch some grub. I'll buy."

"Okay," Muley said. "Sounds good."

Kicks agreed, rubbing his stomach. "I could do with some grub. I'm mighty hungry."

Floyd got up from his chair. "You guys just make yourselves at home. I'll be back real soon with the chow." Without waiting for an answer, the hostler hurried out the door, leaving Kicks and Muley alone with Tim and Cory.

They each took a turn at the privy, Muley going first. As he stepped out of the livery stable office, Kicks told Tim and Cory, "I need a little fresh air; I'll be back in a few minutes." He was hoping it would give the other two the same idea. It worked. When Kicks and Muley came back inside, Tim and Cory went outside, leaving the two cowboys to themselves.

"Well," Muley said. "We've both lost money and haven't found out anything yet!"

"That's true, partner, but I think that's about to change. I 'spect we'll get a chance to ask some questions real soon."

When Tim and Cory came back inside, Floyd had not yet returned, so they all four sat down at the card table to wait on the food. Kicks started the conversation. "I don't know about you, Muley, but I'm getting tired of driftin' from place to place. Been thinking about buying a nice little spread of my own and settling down somewhere."

"Yeah," Muley agreed. "Why don't we see if we can find out who owns that old, abandoned ranch outside of town, the one we stopped at this morning?"

Turning his attention to Tim and Cory, Muley asked, "You guys know who owns that spread?"

Tim shook his head. "Naw, I'm pretty new around here. Just signed on with the Running J Ranch. Only been here fer bout three weeks."

"How about you, Cory," Muley asked.

"I'm new here too. I rode in from Colorado 'bout the same time as Tim."

While Kicks and Muley were still asking questions, Floyd came in with the food. "What's that about the Running J Ranch?"

Muley detected a trace of concern in the hostler's voice, like the conversation did not sit well with him. "We were just asking about that old, abandoned ranch house outside of town. Do you happen to know who owns it?"

Floyd swallowed noisily, his gaze shifting nervously around the room. He looked scared. "I don't know who owns it. Say, let's eat this food and get back to playing cards."

While eating, Muley and Kicks tried to get the conversation turned back to the ranch house, but it didn't work. Felt like pulling teeth from a chicken's beak trying to get any answers. Next, they tried to learn more about the Running J Ranch that Tim and Cory worked for, but that didn't work either. The only thing they did learn was that all the card players except Floyd, the hostler, worked for the Running J, and they'd all been recently hired.

Irritated by the lack of information, Muley and Kicks finished eating, then returned to the game. This time they weren't folding any winning hands.

In a comparatively short time, the two cowpokes had won just about all their money back and then some. Kicks was feeling sorry for Floyd and the other card players, so he glanced over at his friend and gave him the nod. Taking the hint, Muley broke out his pocket watch. "Hey, it's getting late. We better get going. This'll be our last hand."

"Yep," Kicks said. "I sure hate to leave now that I got my luck back, but we got urgent business to tend to early in the morning."

At the rate that Floyd was losing the money he'd won after hours of card playing, he didn't object to ending the game. When that hand was played, Kicks and Muley saddled up and headed out for the old house. When they arrived there to meet Sammy, it was about twenty minutes after eleven. They saw Sammy peeking out a window as they rode up. He rushed out to meet them. "Thank God. Since you were so late, I thought it might be someone else."

"Sorry," Muley said. "But—"

"It's okay," it's just I gotta make it fast. You asked about our sheriff. I already told you his name is Cal Tidwell, and that he was appointed sheriff, not elected. That happened when our former sheriff, Howard Durmhill, a decent man as well as a good sheriff, got shot in the back. Bob Jensen threw his weight around and got Cal appointed as sheriff. Funny thing, though. Cal was on Bob's payroll as a cowpuncher at the time, and everyone knew he was a professional gunman. I think the whole thing was a setup because Cal Tidwell had only been seen around these parts a few weeks before Howard was murdered."

"Wait a minute," Kicks said. "Who's this Bob Jensen guy?"

"Bob Jensen?" Sammy sneered as he said the name. "He owns one of the biggest outfits in the whole countryside. He's a crook and a killer."

Kicks shot a look at Muley, and then back to Sammy. "Would this big outfit owned by Bob Jensen happen to be the Running J Ranch?"

"Why yes, how did you know that?"

"We were in a card game earlier with four guys who said they were riding for the Running J Ranch. You must wanna see the owner, this Bob Jensen, killed, or at least run out of the country, right?"

Sammy's face turned so red he just about glowed in the dark. "You're right, but preferably dead because I'd love to dance on his grave." The bartender paused to catch his breath and then continued, "If you'd like to know why, I'll gladly tell you. Howard Durmhill was my father-in-law, and he was my best friend. I think they had him killed."

Muley shook his head. "Wow, that's some story, Sammy, and I'd love to help you if this Sheriff Cal Tidwell and his buddy Bob Jensen are as bad as you say, but I got troubles of my own, and—"

"Hold on a minute!" Sammy said. "I'm telling you all this for your benefit too. Why do ya suppose I'd put my life in jeopardy to talk to two total strangers, huh? For all I know, you two guys could be newly hired gun hands of Bob Jensen's. Maybe you'll kill me just for saying I thought Bob and Sheriff Tidwell had anything to do with the murder of my father-in-law."

"You're right, Sammy," Kicks said. "But I'd be very interested to learn if that's true myself."

The bartender squared his shoulders and looked at Muley. "I've seen you hanging around here for the past month, and I've heard you say your last name is Gentry. Am I right?"

"That's right. What about it?"

"Well," Sammy replied, "it just might be that I've got some news for you, Mister Gentry."

Muley perked up at the news. "Okay, so you know my name's Gentry, and I been asking a lot of questions. Just what kind of news do you have for me, Sammy?"

"Actually, I don't have the answers you need, but I think Bob Jensen and Cal Tidwell do."

Muley blew softly through his lips, a bit exasperated. "Then you really got nothing I can use."

"No." Sammy admitted, "but I think I know someone who does."

Confused, Muley shook his head. "If you know someone else who knows about my family, then just spit it out."

"Look," Sammy said. "Let me tell you how it is. I'm just a businessman. I own a saloon. I'm not even from around here. I come from back east. It's where I first met Molly Durmhill, Howard's daughter. We got married there, and Howard told us in a letter that if we moved back here, he would set me up in business. Howard kept his word and helped me establish the Golden Nugget.

"Soon after Molly and I moved back here, I overheard Howard talking to his wife, Tilly. Said something like, 'Shame about what happened to the Gentry family.' I understand Howard was doing some investigation into whatever it was that happened to the Gentrys. He got shot in the back shortly after."

Sammy paused, staring between Kicks and Muley. "I don't think Molly knows anything more about it than I do, but I do think Howard's wife Tilly, that's Molly's mother, knows more than she's sayin'. Not long after Howard was killed, I asked Tilly about it, and she said she didn't know anything about any Gentry family, or anything about Howard's death. All she knew was that he was dead." Sammy paused again, then added, "That's all I know to tell you."

"You sure your wife don't know more?" Kicks asked.

"You can talk to Molly if you want to, but I don't think she knows anymore about this mess than I do. You need to talk to Tilly, and of course, Bob Jensen or Cal Tidwell. I'm sure they know *all* the answers. Please don't mention my name to anyone. If it gets back to Bob or Cal, I'm a dead man. I'm concerned for our son, David. He's been staying with his grandmother the last few years. Only fifteen, but he's been a lot of help and company for Tilly."

Muley and Kicks gave Sammy their word they wouldn't mention his name to anyone they questioned. They watched as the bartender left the old ranch house and headed back toward town. As the image of Sammy and his horse faded away into the darkness, Muley said, "Funny, he never even asked us who we were or anything."

Kicks shrugged. "Kinda obvious. Sammy knows your name is Gentry. He knew Sheriff Durmhill suspected Bob and Sheriff Tidwell had murdered a family named Gentry and was investigating it. Sammy just put the two together."

"Yeah, I guess you're right. Sammy didn't really want to know more about the Gentrys or about what happened. He just wanted Sheriff Durmhill's killers brought to justice." Muley paused for a moment, thinking how sad it was that Sheriff Durmhill had been killed. "Well, I can appreciate Sammy feelin' like that."

"That's the best way to look at it," Kicks said. "Besides, now we got somethin' to go on."

"Yeah, I s'pose so. But how we gonna get any answers when everyone's afraid to talk?"

"Well, let's not start off with a negative attitude, Muley. In the morning, we'll go pay people a visit. I think we should start by talkin' to David Galveston. If he's any kind of a loving grandson, he'll wanna see his grandfather's killer brought to justice. And, in the process, if that Gentry family Sammy mentioned turns out to be your family, then we'll find out about them too."

That brightened Muley up some. "Why talk to David first? Why not his grandmother?"

"Well," like my Pappy always says, 'In order to understand what a man really is saying, you gotta listen with your *senses,* not just your ears.' David might be staying with his grandma so he can keep her company and be of help, but I think it goes deeper than that."

"How so?"

"Well, it's not *what* Sammy said about David staying with his grandma. It's the *way* he said it that makes me think David *preferred* staying with her rather than with Sammy, his own father."

Confused, Muley said, "What would make him want to stay with his grandma?"

"Hmmm, can't say exactly." He paced for a few seconds, his expression thoughtful. "Sammy said, 'I'm just a businessman. I own a saloon. I'm not a rancher. I'm not even from around here. I'm from back east.'"

Still puzzled, Muley shook his head. "Yeah, so."

"Well, look at the picture Sammy painted of himself, and then look at the picture he painted of David's grandfather, Sheriff Howard Durmhill. See the difference?"

Muley's eyes widened as it dawned on him what Kicks was getting at. "Yeah, okay, I get it. David's father, Sammy, is kind of a small feller, an outsider, and an easterner to boot, whereas David's grandfather was a rough and tough westerner. A hard-fisted, two-gun sheriff. A lawman who went out and caught outlaws and brought them to justice."

"Now you got it, Muley. You just painted a perfect picture of young David's grandfather … his hero."

"Well, it's too late to do anything about it tonight, so I'm gonna try to get some sleep. We need to get an early start tomorrow."

Kicks yawned. "Yep, that's a good idea. Think I'll do the same."

*   *   *

Early in the morning, Kicks and Muley stepped inside the Silver Spoon Café for breakfast. Cathy had just opened the door, so she was busy getting the stoves heated up and ready to start cooking on. She peeked her head around the corner from the kitchen when she heard them talking. "Good morning, fellas. Coffee and bear sign or coffee with steak and eggs?"

Muley laughed. "How 'bout both?"

"How about you, Kicks?" she asked.

"That'll do just fine for me too."

She came out from the kitchen with three cups of hot coffee. "It'll take a few minutes for the food, I only been open long enough to make coffee and get the stoves going. But we can chat for a while. This is my first cup of coffee this morning, and I need it to start the day."

It was plain to see Muley was lovestruck over Cathy, but Kicks couldn't be sure if the feeling was mutual, or if Cathy was just being friendly. Most waitresses were a might flirty with the customers. It kept them coming back. She did seem to like the big cowpoke, though. Kicks noticed she'd remembered their names, always a good sign, but you never could tell with women.

They talked a few minutes more, and then Cathy said, "The stoves should be hot enough by now. I'll have your breakfast ready in just a couple minutes." She went back into the kitchen, and true to her word, she was back in a few minutes with two plates of steak and eggs and another platter of hot bear sign. "Here you go."

"Wow," Kicks replied, "How did you do all that in just a few minutes?"

Cathy laughed. "Simple. I prepare almost everything at night. In the morning, I just heat up the stoves and throw the customers' orders on to cook, and poof, a couple minutes and it's done."

Muley and Kicks didn't waste much time chowing down. Cathy stood watching, slowly shaking her head as the mound of food quickly disappeared. As they were washing the last bites of the bear sign down with coffee, she asked, "What brings you guys out so early this morning?"

"Well," Muley said as he wiped his mouth with a napkin. "Remember I asked you the first time I came in here if you'd ever heard of a family with the birth name of Gentry?"

"Yes," Cathy agreed. "I remember you said Gentry is your last name, and you wanted to know if I'd ever known of them." She paused a second, her expression concerned. "Have you had any luck finding out about them?"

"Not really," Muley replied. "But we do have a lead now, and if—"

About that time, more people came in and sat at the counter. "Oh, please excuse me," Cathy said. "I have more customers to wait on." As soon as she left, Kicks told Muley. "I don't think we should tell Cathy or anyone else about our findings."

"Why not? That's how you find out things, ain't it, by talkin' and asking questions?"

"Yes, by asking questions," Kicks explained. "Not by talking too much. If word gets out we're on to something, people might get as nervous as a fly in the glue pot. And whoever set them other guys on us will be even more determined to kill us."

A look of concern crossed Muley's face. "You don't think Cathy has anything to do with this, do you?"

"Oh, hell no. At least I don't think she does, but we don't know anything for sure. My old pappy always says, 'Never pass up a good chance to shut up!' If I'm not one hundred percent sure of a person, I keep my yap shut."

Muley sighed. "Yeah, I see what you mean. I guess I was just a little too anxious to share the news with her."

CHAPTER 5

After leaving the café, Muley and Kicks decided to talk to Sammy's wife Molly before talking to Tilly or her grandson, David. By Sammy's direction, he and Molly lived in a nice house on the outskirts of the town. It was a charming place set between a little grove of trees and had a white picket fence around it. After the former Sheriff Howard's death, Sammy had offered to have Tilly move in with them, but she had chosen to live in the hotel where she worked. The name of the hotel was the St. Louis Hotel, named after Charles Broadwater, formerly of St. Louis, Missouri.

Apparently, David helped Tilly by doing odd jobs at the hotel, and around town. As he got older, he also started to work for different ranchers out in the countryside.

As Kicks and Muley walked toward the stable, Floyd, the hostler, stepped out and struck up a conversation. He acted a little friendlier than he had last night. "We're havin' a card game tonight, if you guys want in?"

"Yeah, sure Floyd," Kicks said. "We got some things to take care of, but we'll be here if we can."

After they were out of hearing range, Muley said, "Floyd sure is more talkative than he was the other night."

"Yep." Kicks frowned, glancing back over his shoulder. "Don't exactly fit with his character."

"I was thinking the same thing. Wonder if Floyd wants us there tonight to play poker, or for some other reason?"

"Maybe we should try to make it. Be interesting to find out what, if anything other than poker, Floyd might have in mind for us."

Retrieving their horses, they mounted up, riding down Helena's main street toward Sammy's house. Stopping at the nice two-story house with the white picket fence, they dismounted and tied their horses to the hitch rail. Muley looked back down the street. "House looks kinda out of place with all those tents, and half-finished frame buildings up and down the street.

"Yeah," Kicks agreed. Sammy and Molly's house looked like it came right out of a picture painted on canvas. Sitting there in the middle of a gold-mining camp, it didn't fit."

Sammy must have heard the horses as they rode up. He stepped outside to greet them. "Hello, Kicks, Muley. Didn't expect to see you so soon."

Kicks could see the bartender was a little nervous, so he tried to make him feel at ease. "Hey, Sammy, we came to speak to Molly if it's okay with you. We won't mention anything about talking to you last night. We'll jus' say we dropped in to see if anyone knew anything about the Gentry family, or that old farmhouse outside of town."

Looking relieved, Sammy nodded and said, "Come on in, have a cup of coffee."

Muley stayed right behind Sammy as they entered the house, Kicks coming in last. Sammy, who'd been wearing house slippers, kicked them off inside the door, indicating his wife, Molly, was an immaculate housekeeper. Kicks glanced around quickly and noted that everything was spotless.

Not wanting to offend Molly by tromping across her clean floor with their boots, Kicks hesitated at the door. "Uh,

Muley?" Muley turned to see what he wanted. "Boots." Kicks rolled his eyes and motioned toward the floor, then at Sammy's stocking feet.

Molly must have heard them and came out to see who the visitors were. She smiled at Kicks. "Why thank you for being so considerate, Mister…?"

Kicks smiled back. "Thank you kindly, ma'am. Name's Kicks."

Embarrassed, Muley tiptoed back to the door and began to take off his boots. "I'm sorry, ma'am. Uh, I'm Gentry."

Molly smiled sweetly and replied, "Apology accepted, Mister Gentry." Looking at her husband, she said, "Sweetheart, aren't you going to introduce us properly?"

"Of course, dear," Sammy replied. "Molly, meet Kicks Burks and Muley Gentry. Gentleman, meet my wife, Molly."

As Molly offered her hand to the cowpokes, Kicks noticed she had a very attractive face and beautiful brown hair, but he would later comment to Muley, 'Her but-tocks is about two axe-handles broad.' He was not trying to be disrespectful about it; just telling his observation.

After seating her visitors and serving coffee, Molly sat down. "We don't often get visitors."

Sammy explained to Molly that he had met Kicks and Muley at the saloon and they'd become friends. He hurried the conversation along by saying, "I remember you guy's saying you were looking to buy some real estate. Have you had any luck yet?"

"No," Muley answered. "We haven't found anything yet."

"Have you tried checking with the county courthouse?" Molly asked.

"No, ma'am," Kicks answered. "We figured on checking with the courthouse tomorrow. So far, we've just been asking people around town. Actually, that's one of the reasons we stopped by. We wanted to ask if either of you know who owns that old ranch house outside of town? You know the one about a mile and a half east of here?"

At the mention of the old ranch, Molly became nervous. She tried to hide it by covering her face with her handkerchief, pretending to sneeze.

Kicks offered the usual, "God bless you,"

She dabbed her nose and then at her eyes with the handkerchief, trying to compose herself. "Please excuse me," she said. "Now, what were you saying?"

"Oh, we were just wondering if either of you knew anything about that old ranch just east of town?"

"Yes, I know the one," she said. She paused, as if studying about it. "I have no idea who owns that old place."

"Funny thing," Muley said. "One of the people we asked about that ranch said he didn't know who owned it now, but he thought that a family named Gentry used to. When I asked if he knew how I could get in touch with them, he said he didn't know. They seem to have jus' disappeared."

Molly clutched her kerchief tightly in her fist and covered her face again. Moreover, amidst a fit of faked coughing, she said, "Please … you must excuse me, I have a migraine headache. I have to go lie down." Without further ado, she got up and left the room.

Sammy looked surprised. "I didn't think she knew anything about the Gentry family, but now … I'm not so sure."

Kicks knew what Sammy meant, but he wanted to hear him say it. "What do you mean by that?"

"Oh, come on, man, anyone could tell all that coughing was faked. And, as far as I know, Molly has never had migraine headaches."

"Sorry, I just wanted to be sure!"

"It's okay," the bartender said. "Look, I need to go talk to Molly … if you don't mind?"

"Oh sure, we need to leave anyway. And we're sorry about upsetting her," Kicks said.

"It's okay." Then in afterthought, Sammy lowered his voice and said, "I'll wait a couple days, and then I'll try to talk to her to see what that was all about."

Muley and Kicks nodded, showing their appreciation, then hurriedly put on their boots and left Sammy's house. Outside at the hitch rail, as they untied their horses, Muley said, "Let's go back to the Golden Nugget and get a drink. I need to mull this over."

"I'm with you, partner," Kicks said. Putting a boot in a stirrup, he swung up into the saddle.

*　　*　　*

Sitting at their usual table in the Nugget, the cowpokes downed their first glass of whiskey, then settled back in silence to think about what had happened at Sammy's house. Suddenly, Muley burst out laughing.

"What the devil's wrong with you?" Kicks said. "I ain't seen anything funny today!"

Still laughing, Muley replied, "Damned if you weren't right!"

Expression bewildered, Kicks said, "Right about what?"

"About Molly's but-tocks being two axe handles wide, only I think it might be closer to three!"

Kicks sat back in his chair, chuckling.

"Seriously though, if it wasn't for Sammy, I wouldn't have let her off the hook with that phony coughing spell or the faked migraine headache. She obviously knows somethin' about my family."

"Hmm," Kicks replied. "Probably wouldn't do any good. My pappy always says, 'There are two theories on how to argue with a woman, and neither one works.'"

"So, what do you think?"

"I think we should just pull in our horns where Molly's concerned, let Sammy talk to her for us. I think he was a little surprised and upset by how she acted. Meantime, we keep on doing what we're doing. Looking around, asking questions. Sooner or later someone's gonna give us the right information. Meanwhile, like my pappy always says—"

Muley chimed in with, "'Trust in everyone, but always cut the cards.'" After a few minutes of silence, Muley said, "Kinda feel sorry for Sammy. Appears Molly kinda runs things around their house."

"Yep," Kicks agreed. "Old Sammy was as nervous as a long-tailed cat in a room full of rocking chairs while we were talking to Molly." After a few more drinks, he added, "You know, Muley, I'm getting kind of tired of staying out at that old ranch house. Need me a warm bed and a hot bath."

Muley nodded his agreement. "But where else can we go to bed down for free?"

"There's no place that's rent free." I'm suggesting we go check in at the hotel. We can have that nice fresh bath. I'm kinda tired of washing up under that pump in the yard. That water's cold as ice."

"Sounds good, but dang it, Kicks, you know I can't afford a hotel room."

"Calm down, partner. I told you I'm staking you all through this thing. Come on. Let's go."

*   *   *

It was late in the evening when the two cowpokes arrived in the lobby of the hotel. Muley whispered, "I wonder why it's called the St. Louis Hotel?"

Kicks shrugged. "Hell if I know." He glanced around, noticing a plaque on the wall identifying the name of the hotel's founder as Charles A. Broadwater. "I think someone from St. Louis, Illinois, founded it!"

Muley raised his eyebrows. "How do ya know all this stuff, Kicks?"

Kicks shrugged, smirking.

As they approached the hotel desk, Muley said, "I just remembered. "This is where Tilly Durmhill works."

"Yep, and it's also where Tilly lives."

"And," Muley said, grinning, "her grandson David lives here with her."

"Reason number two for us to be staying at this hotel," Kicks said, patting Muley on the back.

"Is there a third reason?" Muley asked.

Kicks didn't answer as they were now standing at the hotel lobby desk. A young lady was there, ready to help them. "Hello," she said. "Welcome to the St. Louis Hotel."

The young lady was not long out of her teens. However, she looked very mature judging by the way she filled out her gingham dress. She had ample breasts, a slim waist, and well proportionate hips. With her dark eyes and dark brown hair that cascaded across her shoulders and halfway down her back, the young lady was obviously used to the effect she had on men. She grinned and said, "Would you like a room?"

"Uh, yes we would … do," Muley said.

"Okay," she replied, her lips twitching as she struggled not to grin. "Would that be one room or two?"

"One," Muley said. "We'll flip to see who sleeps on the floor."

The hostess turned the register around. "If you'll sign in … and, oh, how long will you be staying with us?"

Muley signed the register and stepped aside for Kicks to sign. While Kicks was signing, he said, "Indefinitely. We'll pay now for thirty days, then if we choose to stay longer, we'll pay again. Meantime, I'd like a schedule of the stagecoach arrivals along with a newspaper delivered to our room. How's that?"

The young lady looked at the signatures. "That'll be just fine, Mister Burks, and I hope you enjoy your stay here in Helena. Is there anything else I can do for you at this time?"

"Yes, there is something, Miss."

"Yes, Mister Burks, what is that?"

"Well, if we're going to be living here, we need to be properly introduced." He gestured to Muley and himself. "Muley Gentry, and Kicks Burks. You can call just call him Muley, and me Kicks. And you are?"

Smiling, she said, "Okay … Kicks. I'm Mary Frances, but you may call me Wendy. That's what everyone calls me."

"Good," Kicks said. "Now I feel right at home. Oh, Wendy, by the way, is there a lady by the name of Tilly that works here?"

"Why yes, Tilly Durmhill. She lives here too, along with her grandson, David. Why? Do you know them?"

"Not personally. I was friends with her husband, Howard Durmhill. I understand he was killed. He was sheriff here at the time of his death, wasn't he?"

"I believe so," Wendy said. "I wasn't here at that time, so I don't know much about that. Only what I've heard, and that isn't much." Handing them the key to their room, she said, "Here you go, room number 9. Just down the hall."

Kicks took the key and said, "Thanks, Wendy."

The two cowpokes picked up their war bags and saddlebags and went down the hall to room number 9. Inside, they found the usual hotel room setting. It had one bed, one bedside table with a lamp, one regular chair, and one bigger, padded chair over by the window. On the wall opposite the window was a washstand with a washbasin and a pitcher of water.

"Not bad," Muley said as he reached in his pocket and pulled out a coin. "We can flip to see who gets the bed the first night. I'll flip the coin and you call it."

"Go for it!"

The coin was flipped, and while it was air bound, Kicks said, "Tails." The coin landed on the bed, tales up, and Muley said, "Okay, you get the bed tonight."

Kicks walked over and stretched out on the bed. He grinned when his feet hung over the end a little. "Sure feels good to lie down on a real bed."

Muley sat down in the padded chair and relaxed his six-foot-four frame, then exclaimed, "That Wendy gal sure is a pretty young thing," putting emphasis on the 'young thing.'

"Yep, she sure is." Kicks knew what Muley was getting at, but he was going to make him come out and say it.

After a moment of silence, Muley said, "I can't say that I blame you, but ain't she a mite young for you to be shinin' up to?"

Kicks laughed. "Shinin' up to? Naw, I wasn't shining up to her. Jus' a little flirtin' to make her feel good. We need to make ourselves known … and liked. Trust me, I have a feeling being liked will be a big help further down the line."

Muley thought about that for a minute. "Yeah, I guess you're right. Probably gonna make a few enemies here before we're done. We'll need all the friends we can get." He paused, his expression thoughtful. "One question though. What are you gonna say if Wendy mentions us to Tilly, about you saying that you knew her husband, Howard?"

"We'll play it by ear. Meanwhile, we'll try to find out as much about Howard as we can."

"Kinda short notice, Kicks. We were plannin' to talk to Tilly tomorrow, and we might even see David then too. Just how are we gonna find out anything about Howard Durmhill by tomorrow?"

"You forget about the card game tonight?"

Muley slammed his right fist into his left hand, grinning. "Hot dang, I clean forgot. Floyd probably knew Howard, and if we're lucky, some of the other card players knew him too."

CHAPTER 6

It was about nine in the evening when the two cowpokes walked into the office at the livery stable. Floyd had just opened a new deck of cards. Muley and Kicks looked around, seeing the same four riders from the Running J Ranch. Everyone acted friendly enough, yet somehow different from last night, more like gunmen than cowpunchers.

Floyd sat down, grinning up at Kicks and Muley. "You remember Tim, Cory, Jinks, and Todd, don't ya?"

Kicks and Muley nodded at them, and they nodded in return.

Floyd continued, "Sit down and get ready to lose your bankroll, cowpokes, 'cause I feel lucky tonight."

Kicks rubbed at his chin, having a bad feeling about this game tonight. Floyd and Tim were sitting in chairs with their backs to the wall opposite the door and window that looked out into the stables. Both men had a view of the big double doors, the entrance to the livery. "Why thanks, Floyd, but where I come from, the house usually gives the guests their choice of seats. I'm sure you wouldn't mind doing the same, right?"

Floyd acted surprised by Kicks' question. "What? You want me to get up so you can sit here?"

"Yep, think I'd like the view from over there better."

Floyd snorted, obviously annoyed. "Who the hell you think you are? Number one, this ain't no regular gambling house where you just come in and pick where you want to sit! Number two, where you from, anyway?"

Kicks narrowed his eyes at Floyd until the hostler finally looked away. "I'm from West Texas, where they shoot tinhorn gamblers just for fun. And my pappy always told me, 'Never kick a fresh horse turd on a hot day.'" That line of his pappy's had nothing to do with what they were talking about, but insulting Floyd was Kicks' way of unnerving him … pushing him harder, calling his bluff.

It worked. Floyd had started to stand, his hand moving toward his six-shooter, but he quickly decided against swapping lead with a man like Kicks. Abruptly, he sat back down, scowled, then scooted his chair back from the table and stood up. "You know, Kicks, I like your style. Sure, you and Muley can sit anywhere you want. We're all just here for a friendly game of cards, ain't we?" Floyd motioned to Tim. "Come on, Tim, let's accommodate our guests." They moved to the other side of the table, and the two cowpokes sat down in their places with their backs to the wall.

Muley looked around and grinned. "Yeah, this is much better."

Kicks looked over at Muley and dropped his chin while raising his eyebrows. He knew they were both thinking the same thing. Playing cards was not the only thing going to happen tonight. From habit, they unconsciously reached to their gun belts and moved aside the leather thong that looped around the hammer of their pistols.

The table, large and square, was set in a corner of the room. Muley was seated at Kicks' right, Floyd to his left, then Tim, Cory, Jinks, and Todd with their backs to the double doors. Floyd began shuffling the cards, glancing around the table. "Seven players, so looks like we're playing low ball."

It was both a statement and a question, and since no one objected, he set the deck in the middle of the table and looked at Kicks. "Cut anyone?"

Kicks cut the cards, and the hostler dealt two cards face down to each player. Then he dealt one card face up to each player. They all looked at their down cards and the betting began.

About an hour into the game, Todd folded. He threw his cards down on the table, cursed his luck, and then said, "I haven't won a hand yet." He stood up and stretched. "I'll go get a couple bottles of whiskey. Maybe if I get half-drunk my luck'll change."

As he started for the door, Floyd said, "Don't bring back any of that cheap stuff! And hurry up!"

At this stage of the game, everyone except for Todd was about even. After Todd left to get the whiskey, Cory seemed to be getting a lucky streak. Kicks had been watching closely and couldn't see that Cory was cheating, so the game continued in a friendly manner.

Finally, Jinks began to complain he was getting 'damn thirsty.'

Another hour passed, and Muley was the big winner. Suddenly Kicks heard a noise outside the office. He looked past Floyd, out the window into the stables, and saw Todd coming through the stable doors with the whiskey. He had someone with him that looked vaguely familiar to Kicks.

The man was about six feet tall and slender in build, wearing a confederate soldier's uniform jacket. That in itself wasn't strange because the Civil War was not long been over. In fact, many people on both sides still didn't think of it as over. Nevertheless, Kicks knew he had definitely seen this man somewhere before. He nudged Muley under the table with his boot to draw his attention to Todd and the stranger coming in.

Muley didn't look up from his cards; he just nodded slightly to let Kicks know that he saw them. Besides the confederate jacket, the man wore a red plaid shirt and black trousers with the legs tucked inside knee-high boots. A battered hat was resting atop his rust-colored hair. He also wore a fancy pearl-handled .44 in a hand-tooled leather belt and holster, tied down low.

As Todd stepped inside the office with the stranger, it became clear that everyone except Kicks and Muley knew him. Stomach tightening, Kicks fought not to react, still struggling to remember where he'd seen the man before.

Todd set three bottles of whiskey down on the table. "Look who I ran into over at the Nugget."

Floyd looked up from his cards. "Howdy, Jim." He nodded toward Kicks and Muley, introducing them. "Think you know everyone else."

The two cowpokes looked at Jim and nodded. The man returned their gesture and then sat down in Todd's chair between Jinks and Muley. It was Kicks' turn to deal the cards, and he looked at Jim. "You in?"

"Hell yeah, deal me in."

Kicks dealt cards around the table, all the time studying the man called Jim. As the game got underway, silence fell pretty much around the room except for the betting and usual small talk. Finally, Floyd said, "So, Jim, have you seen Charley Heart lately?"

"Yeah, just came from talkin' to him. He gave orders to finish the job."

Kicks listened intently. He knew this wasn't just small talk. They were communicating something he wasn't supposed to know about. Suddenly, it hit him like a ton of bricks. Charley Heart was a pseudonym that William C. Quantrill often used. That reminded him who this stranger called Jim was. He used to ride with Quantrill and a gang known as "Quantrill's Raiders."

This was one of Quantrill's top gunmen. While in Lawrence, Kansas, Kicks had visited the local sheriff's office and seen a wanted poster for *Jim Bonner*. Jim was from Lawrence, Kansas, where Quantrill and his Raiders did most of their raiding and terrorizing. One time they'd surprised and killed ninety Union soldiers at Baxter Springs, Kansas. There was a big reward for their capture, dead or alive, for Quantrill or any of his gang. At the time, Kicks had grabbed the poster of Jim Bonner and dogged his trail for a bit. Then he got word one day that one of his own brothers had gotten busted up in a cattle stampede. So Kicks hightailed it for home. Luckily, his brother recovered, but somewhere in all the commotion, he'd lost the urge to ride all the way back to Kansas to pick up Jim's trail again.

Kicks didn't think Jim Bonner could possibly recognize him. He'd never gotten close enough to actually see the outlaw in person, or to be seen by him. He only recognized the man from the poster. In fact, Kicks was thinking he might still have that wanted poster of Jim in his saddlebag. He wished he could figure out a way to let Muley know what the situation was. Could be disastrous if this gunman was here to assassinate him. Kicks wondered if Jim was still connected with Quantrill.

Even with all those questions going on in his head, Kicks remained focused on the game. As the night grew late, he decided he didn't like the overtones of the conversations. "Well, gents, I reckon I'm about ready to call it quits for tonight."

It was Jim's turn to play. He had to bet or fold, so he threw his cards in. "That's it," he said. "I'm out. I'm calling it quits too." He got up and took a couple of steps towards the door, then stopped and turned around. "Oh, by the way…"

It would have seemed natural to most anyone else for him to do that, except Kicks knew who he was, so he'd also stood. "Oh, by the way … what?" he said.

Something in Kicks' look and cynical tone gave a signal to the gunman. His hand moved slowly towards his hip. The leather thong that held the pearl-handled .44 in its holster had already been thumbed off the hammer to make for a quick draw. Jim remained pretty cool, acting natural and friendly. "I was jus' gonna say that I'd heard you were asking a lot of questions around town about the old sheriff." He paused a moment for effect, and then continued, "Just wanted to give you a friendly warning." He paused, as if waiting to see if Kicks would draw.

It wasn't a big stretch to guess this gunman had shown up tonight to learn who they were and what they wanted, possibly even to kill them.

Muley stood, looking between Kicks and the gunman, his expression hardening.

Keeping his eyes on the gunman, Kicks stated, "I know who you are. I recognized you straight away from the wanted poster ordering your capture. Jim Bonner, dead or alive."

The outlaw drawled, "So you won't take a warning and ride out, huh?"

Kicks knew Jim did not want them to ride out. He wanted them dead. That's what he'd meant earlier when he told Floyd that 'Charley Heart said to finish the job.' He was just pretending to give them the choice to leave town.

"I don't take kindly to warnings," Kicks said. "Like my pappy always said, 'Never throw your gun down to hug a grizzly.'"

The outlaw laughed. "Your pappy taught you well."

"Hombre," Kicks drawled, "you came here to kill me. If you've still got the nerve to try, you better fill your hand, 'cause one of us is gonna be carried out of here feet first."

That was like saying sic 'em to a guard dog. The outlaw was fast and got off one shot, but fast was not good enough. His bullet punched a hole in the floor about three feet in front of Kicks' right boot. Kicks drew a split second faster and fired, but his bullet found its mark … right through the left eye. The outlaw flew back against the wall and slid down to the floor without so much as a whisper, leaving a trail of blood and brains all the way to hell.

Floyd must have fancied himself a top gun too. As soon as Kicks and Jim made their move, Floyd reached for his gun, aiming to kill Muley. He did not even clear leather. Floyd's eyes widened as he saw it coming. Muley's slug caught him right through the heart. Meantime, Tim, Cory and Todd attempted to get in on the action, but Kicks' and Muley's .44s stopped them short. They ended up on the floor with Jim and Floyd, in a pool of their own blood.

The room was about a fourteen by eighteen, making it mighty close quarters for a shootout. When the gun smoke cleared, the two cowpokes stood side by side, their four guns smoking. Jinks was the only one of the opponents left standing. His gun was on the floor and his left hand was holding his right arm, his shattered elbow dripping blood. Luckily for him he was left-handed. "You sumbitches," he screamed. "You broke my arm."

"Just feel lucky that it's not your gun arm," Kicks said.

Muley laughed. "Feel lucky you ain't dead like your pals on the floor there."

Jinks whined in fear. "You … you ain't gonna kill me?"

"Naw," Kicks said. "Not if you answer some questions … and they're the right answers!"

His face pale, Jinks nodded, looking ready to answer any and all questions they asked him. "What you wanna know?"

"That's better," Muley said. "Who put you guys up to gunning for us? And why?"

Jinks opened his mouth to answer, but just then, the office door flew open and in walked Sheriff Cal Tidwell and three of his deputies. They all had their guns out, pointed at Kicks and Muley.

Cal had a twisted grin on his face. "Don't try it, cowpokes. You ain't got a chance."

Muley started to try to explain to the sheriff what had happened, but Cal cut him off. "You fellas just keep your lips buttoned. I'll tell you when to talk." He narrowed his eyes at Jinks. "What's that you were about to say when we walked in?"

Jinks began to shake, obviously more afraid of Cal than he was of Kicks and Muley. "Uh, nothing, Cal. I wasn't gonna say nothing … honest."

The twisted grin appeared on the lips of the sheriff. "Shut up, Jinks. It's plain to see what happened here. Poor old Floyd there, being neighborly, invited these two gun hawks in for a friendly game of cards. Someone probably caught 'em cheating, and when they got called on it, they started shooting. Old Floyd and these Running J Riders never had a chance, shot down in cold blood. Right, Jinks? Ain't that what happened?"

"Yeah, Cal, that's exactly what happened."

Cal motioned toward the two cowpokes with his pistol, and then spoke to one of his deputies. "Dutch, go relieve the killers of their guns."

Dutch was a big lumbering guy who was mostly just fat, his clothes dirty and sloppy. Kicks could see he was dumber than a fence post, but he'd still be loyal to Cal. He approached him and Muley cautiously and took their gun belts.

"Good," Cal said. "Now get back over here."

The deputy did as he was told, then Cal motioned to one of the other deputies, who was carrying a shotgun. "Oscar, take Jinks over to Doc's and get him fixed up." Oscar appeared to be a little smarter than Dutch, and Kicks suspected he might be a fair gunman too.

"Doc'll be in bed," Oscar said. "And you know how he hates to be woke up late."

Cal shrugged. "Well, if Doc won't get up, you fix old Jinks up yourself."

Oscar laughed as he guided Jinks out of the room. "I sure as hell know how to do that."

Kicks narrowed his eyes as the two left the stables.

Cal looked at his other deputy. "Come on, Buford, let's get these dangerous killers over to the jail and locked up." Just as they stepped out of the door of the office, they heard a shotgun blast coming from somewhere down the street. No one needed to say anything. They all knew what had happened. Oscar shot Jinks because he'd known Jinks would eventually rat them out. Jinks had been too big of a risk to be allowed to live.

"So that's the way it is, huh?" Muley said. "We don't get to say anything. You're just goanna send us up the creek without a paddle. I'll bet you're in on this setup too, right, Cal? And you're gonna kill us, just like Oscar killed Jinks."

"Keep moving," Cal replied, his expression cold.

Kicks and Muley both knew then they would never leave that jail alive … if they even made it to the jail. Could be they'd end up in the same hole as Jinks.

CHAPTER 7

Sammy Galveston was working a late shift at the Golden Nugget Saloon, taking the place of one of his bartenders. He pulled his pocket watch out and checked the time. "Late," he said. His relief should have been here twenty minutes ago. He was a little concerned because José Martinez was almost never late. José was a young Mexican man who lived with his parents. They owned a small spread outside of town. José had wanted to leave home and do some traveling around before he settled down. There was a pretty *señorita* that he intended to marry when the time was right. However, for now he was helping take care of the place until his father recovered from a sickness that had put him in bed for a spell. He worked for Sammy as a bartender in his spare time. About ten minutes later, José arrived. *"Lo siento que llego tarde a jefe de trabajo."*

"It's okay, José, you don't have to apologize for being a few minutes late."

José insisted on giving a reason in his broken English. "Walk by livery … hear shots. Scare me … duck behind building. Hear gun … down street. Hear … scream. Sheriff, deputies … out stables … two men. They … Muley and Kicks? Why I … late. José wait … sheriff no see."

Sammy knew what had happened. There'd been a shootout. Someone else had tried to kill Kicks and Muley, then somehow the sheriff and his deputies got the drop on the two cowpokes. They were going to be murdered, just like Sheriff Howard Durmhill. "Well," Sammy said, "it's a good thing I have some pull with the authorities around here." In a flash, Sammy had his apron off and his coat on, and was out the door. On his way out, he was going over the conversations he'd had with the two cowpokes earlier. He had mentioned to them that the people of Helena disliked the way the new sheriff upheld the law around here. He was lenient with crooks and gunmen, and harsh to good, honest citizens.

Sammy wasted no time in banging on the doors of Mayor Levi Harper, and then Judge Cleveland. They both protested wildly, but liked and trusted Sammy, so they hurriedly got dressed and followed Sammy to the jail. That's where Sammy figured the sheriff would take Kicks and Muley. They'd say they arrested them, then were forced to kill the two cowpokes when they tried to escape.

*   *   *

Shotguns at their backs, Muley and Kicks knew their fate as they walked along the dark streets towards the jail. Neither one expected to come out of this alive, but neither would they go down without a fight. Kicks didn't plan to die with his tail tucked between his legs, and he suspected Muley felt the same.

When they reached the jail, Cal ordered them inside. "Now," the sheriff said to his deputies, "step back outside and make sure no one is in sight."

As the deputies did as ordered, Kicks knew this was their only chance. Cal was still holding them at gunpoint, but he was only one man with one pistol. Kicks glanced quickly at Muley and could tell he was thinking the same thing.

An instant before Kicks or Muley could make a move to jump the sheriff; the deputies came running back inside the jail. "Cal, there's a bunch of people headin' this way, and they're in a hurry."

"Dammit," Cal cursed. "Who are they and what do they want?"

"Don't know," Buford whined. "It's dark out there. I couldn't see who they were."

"Well, we'll just wait and see if they're coming here."

Seconds later, Sammy, followed by the mayor and judge, came charging inside the jail.

"What the hell's going on here?" Cal demanded.

"That's what we want to know," Sammy said.

"Me and my deputies here just arrested these two gun hawks. They were over to the livery playing cards with Floyd and some of the boys from the Running J outfit. They got caught cheating and shot up the place. Killed Floyd and the others."

Kicks could tell Sammy didn't believe the sheriff's version for a second, but he would have to wait till later to find out what really happened. "Well," Sammy said, "someone happened to be walking by and saw the whole thing. According to them, the story you just told won't hold water in court."

"You say I'm lying?" Cal jeered.

Sammy ignored the challenge. "According to the witness, there was also another shooting. Someone got hit with a shotgun. Know anything about that?"

The sheriff hesitated. He knew as well as Kicks did that they would find Jinks' body and guess what had happened. "Oh, well, it turned out that fellow named Jinks, another

Running J rider, was there too. He tried to run away, who knows why, and one of my deputies had to shoot him."

At this point, the judge looked over at the two cowpokes. "This true? You kill those men?"

Kicks answered, "Judge, it was a setup from the start to kill us. An outlaw name Jim Bonner was brought into the game. He was supposed to do the killing. Turned out I outdrew him, and then everyone got into the action. As a result, all those men were killed. Then this … sheriff and his deputies walked in with shotguns and arrested us. If you guys hadn't showed up just now, they woulda shot us too." Kicks looked at Sammy. "If it weren't for you, we'd be dead right now, friend." Turning back to face the Judge, Kicks said, "Look, your Honor, I can produce a poster that shows Jim Bonner was a wanted killer."

Cal exploded, "That's a goddamn lie. These—"

The judge cut him off. "Hold on. We'll have to settle this in court. For right now, I demand you let these two men go."

"Fine," he said, wanting to have the last word. "They can leave the jail. But I'm giving 'em two hours to get the hell outta town. Don't need this kind of trouble here in Helena."

Kicks smirked. He knew the sheriff would just have his deputies trail them for a few hours, until they were a good way from town, and then shoot them down.

"How do you figure you can force them to leave town?" Sammy asked.

Cal grinned. "Because they don't have a residence here in Helena." He nodded at Muley. "That one came in a month ago. Been causing trouble ever since. The other one caught up to him a few days ago. Gives me the right, as peacemaker of this town, to order them both to leave. Right, Judge?"

Judge Thaddeus shrugged, frowning. "Yes, 'fraid that's the law. If a person doesn't live or work in the town or county, the law can demand they leave after a certain period of time."

"So," Cal said. "I'm ordering you—"

"Can't do that," Kicks said.

"What the hell you mean?" Cal said. "You just heard the judge—"

Muley cut him off, laughing vigorously. "That's the third reason why we're staying at the hotel … proof of residence."

Cal looked angrily at the judge. "What the hell are these guys talking about?"

"Yes," the judge asked. "What are you talking about, Muley?"

Still laughing, Muley said, "Okay, I'll explain. When we checked into the St. Louis Hotel, I told Kicks then it was cheaper to stay at that old, abandoned ranch house out east of town. But Kicks said, 'Reason number one for checking in at the hotel was we could have a good place to sleep and bathe.' After we checked in, Kicks asked for a schedule of the stagecoach for mail purposes. That was to verify we have an address. Reason number two." Muley chuckled. "I asked then if there was a third reason, and Kicks didn't answer, but now it's clear, the third reason is … to show proof of residency."

Now, everyone except Cal and his deputies were laughing. The sheriff was fuming. "That's nonsense, Judge! That won't hold up in court, will it?"

Mayor Levi Harper managed to stifle his laughter long enough to say to the two cowpokes, "That was an ingenuous plan, gentleman." To the sheriff, the mayor said, "It sure as blazes will stand up in court. That residency thing is a standard rule in almost all towns. It is there to help keep out the riffraff. However, if these gents are permanently living at the hotel and have the paper delivered to them, then they have a residence established here in Helena."

Kicks looked at Cal. "We'll take our guns back now, Sheriff."

Cal was not pleased with this outcome, to say the least, but he had no recourse. He turned around and stalked out of the jail, saying over his shoulder, "Give 'em their goddamn guns, Buford!"

Within the hour, Kicks and Muley were back in their hotel room, after buying a bottle of Sammy's best to celebrate. Muley sat down in the chair by the window and took a big drink from the bottle before he handed it to Kicks. "It's just like the mayor said, that was an ingenious idea you had, Kicks. I woulda never thought of it. How'd you know we'd even need a proof of residency?"

Kicks had to admit it was shrewd on his part to think ahead like that, but at the same time, he did not want to appear to brag about it. "My ma always says, 'An ounce of prevention is better than a pound of cure.' My pappy always says, 'Looking ahead is better than looking at hindsight,' and I knew our three-day time limit was coming up, and that Cal could, by law, run us out of town.'"

*   *   *

Sheriff Tidwell had no idea why those two cowpokes were hanging around town, but he knew they were investigating something, which made them trouble. He worried they might be territorial marshals. Was his past finally catching up with him? At one time he'd been a decent man, and when the Civil War broke out in eighteen sixty-one, he'd contemplated joining up, like so many other young men. But Cal could never figure out just what the cause was he'd be fighting for.

One party said that the war was over politics. Another said the war was over slavery, to keep it alive or to end it. Another party said it was over taxation, and tariff, and other such matters. Which in reality, he supposed, it was all those things. Nevertheless, as a youngster, Cal was not interested in any of it. He simply didn't care, so he chose not to join the army, as did many other like-minded men.

During that period, with so many men going off to war, much of the country was shorthanded in other areas. Which left the door wide open for a young man like Cal Tidwell to seek a position as a law officer. Cal landed his first job as deputy under Sheriff Dory Holmes in Chloride, Arizona. Dory was a good man and one of the best of sheriffs. A good-natured man, his close friends sometimes called him Hunky Dory Holmes. He taught young Cal to be like him. Unfortunately, somewhere down the line, like so many other lawmen, Cal turned rogue, and later became an outlaw with a price on his head in some parts of the country.

Cal got fired from the last town he was sheriff, right before he drifted into Helena, Montana. He nosed around and became acquainted with Bob Jensen, owner of the Running. J Ranch, one of the biggest outfits in the area. Both being crooks, they teamed up, and Bob got Cal appointed as sheriff after Sheriff Durmhill was found murdered.

The murder of Sheriff Howard Durmhill had been Bob Jensen's first order of business for Cal, and he carried it out with no questions asked, nor any remorse. As sheriff, Cal pretty much kept the peace in town. Though harsh on the honest people of the town, he tended to be much more lenient with gunmen, specifically the riders for the Running J. Being both crooked and curious, Cal had nosed around and found out a few things about Bob Jensen, things like, he used to be one of Charlie Heart's Quantrill Raiders. He also found out that Bob had done a lot of shady deals in and around Helena, and since Sheriff Durmhill's murder, most all the town's people were scared to death of the man and his riders—who were for the most part nothing but gunmen. Now the town had one more gunman to worry about, Sheriff Cal Tidwell.

After Kicks, Muley and Sammy left the jail, along with the mayor and judge, Sheriff Tidwell sat in his chair behind his desk, thinking about how he could get rid of those two meddling cowpokes. He'd had the two of them as good as dead. He stared with disgust at his three deputies, all three milling around with a cup of coffee in their hands. "Sit down, dammit, all three of you," Cal shouted.

Dutch and Buford sat in two of the three chairs that were by the door. Oscar grabbed the third chair, sliding it over by Cal's desk, where he turned it around and sat straddling it with his arms resting on the back of the chair. "Boss, what are we gonna do about those two cowboys?" Oscar asked.

Cal pondered the question for a moment. "Think we got more here than just a couple meddlesome cowboys, Oscar."

"So who are they ... lawmen?"

"Maybe, but I don't think so."

"Why not?" Buford asked.

Cal hesitated, scratching his nose. "They're both wearin' two guns. The sights been filed off for a faster, smoother draw. Wear 'em low on their hips, tied down. Just two of 'em against Floyd, Cory, Tim, Todd and Jinks, not to mention Jim. I've seen Jim in action before. He ain't no slouch. Gotta be gunfighters, but why are they here?"

"Bullshit," Buford said. "Can't be that good. Why didn't they take down old Jinks?"

"I can answer that," Oscar said. "They were gonna let him go so he could ride back to the Running J and tell Bob all what happened. We stopped him from doing that."

"That's what I think too," Cal said. "They were counting on him to get back to Bob, to get the ball rolling."

"So what do you think those two will do now?" Oscar asked.

Cal sat back in his chair, biting at his lower lip. "Wish I knew." He paused a second, then said, "Need to know just how much they know about what's going on around here, and what they're after." He wouldn't mind knowing more about what was going on around here himself.

"What do you want us to do, boss?" Buford asked.

"Nose around, find out what you can, and stick close by. I might need your help, because—"

The office door flew open and Bob Jensen stormed inside with four of his gunmen. "Just what the hell's going on here, Cal? I heard some of my boys got shot up in the livery by two lone gunmen. Where the hell are they, those gunmen? Are they in jail? Hell no. They're out walking around, aren't they?"

Cal wasn't afraid of Bob Jensen. During his years of being sheriff, and his years of being on the outlaw trail, he had gone up against a lot of bad men like Bob Jensen, and he was still alive. On the other hand, he was tired of being near down and out, and wanted to keep this easy setup as sheriff, especially with a powerful man like Bob to back him. "Take it easy, Bob," Cal warned. "Didn't have a choice. Had to let 'em go."

"Well, spit it out. What the hell happened?"

Cal pulled a bottle of mescal and two glasses from his desk drawer. He glanced over at his deputies. "Go find out all you can about those two guys, and remember, be careful. We don't want word to get back to the mayor or the judge that we're out to get those two."

Cal waited for his deputies to leave the office, then poured Bob and himself a glass of mescal. He handed one of the glasses to the rancher, then sat down in his chair behind his desk. "Take a seat, Bob, have a drink. I'll tell you all I know."

Bob sat, taking a sip of the smoky-flavored drink, then he told his riders, "Go on over to the Golden Nugget, boys, have a couple of drinks. Tell the barkeep to put it on my tab." To Cal, Bob said, "I hope your story is as good as your whiskey."

Ignoring the warning, Cal downed his glass of mescal and poured them another one. "I knew the second I saw 'em that those two characters weren't just ordinary cowboys."

"You found out why they're here?" Bob asked, sounding impatient. "They lawmen?"

Cal shook his head and gave a definite, "No. I don't see them as lawmen. One of 'em claimed he's here to find out about his family. Thinks his parents were murdered somewhere around here. He's not sure. Guess he was just a baby at the time."

"You get a name?" Bob asked.

"Yeah, the one who says his parents were murdered is Muley Gentry. The other fella's name is Kicks Burks." When Bob froze, his features hardening, Cal asked, "Why? You know 'em from someplace?"

The expression on the rancher's face said yes, but he answered, "Nope." He hesitated. "Find out everything you can about both those guys, then get back to me." After another pause, he changed the subject. "What happened at the livery, Cal? Tell me about the shootout?"

Cal took his time telling about the incident, leaving out nothing. "I did everything I possibly could to get those two killed. I set 'em up against six good gun hands. Jim was one of your best. You and him rode together with Quantrill."

"I remember, Cal. By the way, since you brought up Jinks' name, why was he shot by one of your deputies?"

"I gave Oscar Bates the okay sign to do that. When me and my deputies walked in with the scatterguns, it looked to me like Jinks was about ready to talk."

"Hell," Bob said. "Jinks didn't know enough about our operation to tell the law anything. Never mind, it's all over and done with. I just want those two troublemakers taken out. Maybe you should take care of it personally?"

"If it comes down to that, I will."

They had another glass of mescal before Bob left with a parting order to Cal, "I want those two dead, and soon."

When the door shut behind Bob Jensen, Cal shoved the glass aside and took a long swig straight from the bottle. He wiped his mouth with the back of his hand and said aloud, "Something big's goin' on here with Bob, and I'm gonna find out what and cut myself in on it." He never could figure out why Bob had wanted the former sheriff, Durmhill, gunned down. Now he wanted this Kicks fellow and his partner Muley killed. He thought about it a while longer. *Hmm*, the former sheriff had a wife, daughter, and a grandson. All he had to do was trump up some charge against one or all of them. Haul 'em off to jail and interrogate 'em."

Enthused about the future, Cal left the jail and walked over to the Golden Nugget, where he quickly found his deputies. "Here's what I want you to do … start tailing Tilly and that grandson of hers, David. Watch every step they make and keep me informed."

Oscar looked confused. "Why Tilly and David? Ain't they the old sheriff's wife and grandson. What about Tilly's daughter, Molly? Want us to watch her too?"

Cal hesitated. "Yes and no. Molly is Tilly's daughter, but for now just keep an eye on Tilly and David. Should be easy enough. The two of 'em stay at the hotel." Where Burks and Gentry were staying.

"But why?" Oscar asked."

"Don't ask questions," Sheriff Cal snapped. "Just do what you're told."

CHAPTER 8

After Bob finished talking to Cal and left the jail, he felt the need to drink … alone, so he could think. He didn't want to go to the Golden Nugget, where at least a dozen people would know him. Therefore, he mounted up and rode to the edge of town and entered a little Mexican cantina just on the other side of Helena. That is where he visited when he wanted to be alone … or felt the need for female company.

When he stepped inside the cantina, it was dimly lit and cool. He felt better already. He stepped up to the bar and was waiting to be served, but before the bartender could work his way down the crowded bar to him, the owner of the cantina, a woman named Maria, came over and said in Spanish, "*Hola, Señor* Bob Jensen, it is much good to see you again. Would you like Rose to come and sit with you? She can make you much happy, no?"

Bob's Spanish wasn't that good, but he could understand her pretty well, even speak it on some level. "No thanks, not tonight. I need to be alone. Got a little problem I need to solve."

Marie smiled and said as she turned to walk away, "*Muy bien, Señor* Bob Jensen, but if you change your mind…?"

"I won't change my mind, Maria, but thanks." As he watched her walk away, he pondered what might have happened if he'd told Maria to send Rosa his way. Here in this cantina, he was thought of and treated as a decent man. They didn't know him for being an unscrupulous killer, always just one fast horse and faded trail ahead of the law.

Bob had grown up and spent the first part of his outlaw years in and around Kansas and Missouri, which is where he'd met and joined up with William C. Quantrill, also known as Charley Heart. Quantrill had been a Confederate guerrilla fighter during the Civil War. Born in Canal Dover, Ohio, he became the leader of a guerrilla band on the side of the Confederacy. In Kansas and Missouri during American Civil War, Quantrill taught school in Ohio and Illinois before moving to Kansas in 1857. It was there he began his life of crime. Within three years, Quantrill had put together a gang of about four hundred and fifty gunmen. They robbed towns that held with northern sympathies. He was given the rank of captain by the Confederate army, and raided up through Lawrence, Kansas.

In August of 1863, he and his Raiders killed one hundred and fifty people. They later surprised and killed ninety Union soldiers at Baxter Springs, Kansas. After that, things got pretty hot for the gang, especially for Bob, because Bob had been known in that region by too many people.

One night, after a drunken celebration, when his comrades were asleep, Bob packed his war bags and left them and that part of the country behind. After months of traveling, he started drifting west, and eventually heard about the four Georgians and how they had discovered gold in Montana at a place called Last Chance Gulch. By this time, Bob had been tired of drifting around and decided to head for Montana to check it out.

Besides being a fast gun, he was also a master at cards. So Bob moved into a tent among the many other tents and buildings being built all along the banks of Last Chance Gulch.

The gulch was becoming a real town, judging from the number of people coming in. The town officials would eventually rename the town *Helena*.

When Bob Jensen first arrived at the Last Chance Gulch, several good-sized buildings had already been erected, replacing the tents, and were being used as a saloon and gambling hall. Later, when the town became more heavily populated, another building would be erected for the use of drinking and gambling named the Golden Nugget Saloon.

One of the buildings being vacated would be used as the Town Hall, for the courthouse, office spaces for the mayor and judge and other officials. Meantime the newer building, the Golden Nugget, was filled night and day with miners, ranchers, gamblers, and soiled doves.

Bob felt it was the perfect place for him to settle in and get hold of his fortune. After just a few weeks of doing business at the gambling hall, drinking and dealing at the faro table, he finally managed to meet the four Georgians. Polite and businesslike, he did not mention anything to them about their finding gold that night. However, he learned they liked to play blackjack and draw poker.

A week later, they were at his faro table again. He waited until they were ready to leave, and then said, "If you gentleman would like a private game of draw poker or blackjack, I can arrange a game for tomorrow night?" They eagerly agreed, and the game was arranged for six the next night.

During the game, Bob found the small-talk amusing. The four Georgians were John Cowan, D. J. Miller, John Crab, and Reginald (Robert) Stanley. Only one of the four was really a Georgian, John Cowan. Miller was from Alabama, Crab from Iowa, and Stanly from England. They told Bob they were not named the Georgians because they were all from Georgia, but rather because they practiced the Georgian method of placer mining.

They explained to Bob how they'd left the Alder Gulch prospects of Virginia City, Montana to head north to find richer prospects. After prospecting the Little Blackfoot River, they crossed the Continental Divide to Prickly Pear Creek. Finding little in the way of color, they moved further north. After six weeks of hard work, they returned south to a place they had earlier named Last Chance Gulch—so named because the group had decided if good gold could not be found there, they would give up on the whole area.

Although Bob found this information interesting, it was not any use to him. He didn't really care about who discovered the gold or how they did it. He just wanted a piece of the action. However, in his talk that night with the four Georgians, he offhandedly mentioned, "I sure hope you fellas filed title with the proper authorities to the land on which the gold was found."

To Bob's surprise, they answered, "Naw, we're not interested in owning land, or gold mines, for that matter. We just like to discover them. We discover them and work them until we get tired, and then we move on. Hell, we got so much money now, we'll never be able to spend it all."

Bob tried to sound concerned, saying, "You mean you never even filed on the claim?"

"Nope," they answered. "We just put up wooden stakes to mark the boundaries and sketched out a map of it on a piece of paper."

"Well," Bob coaxed excitedly, "what happened to the paper? That in itself would be proof of ownership. Have you got it locked up safely in your personal belongings?"

"Naw, we never kept it. We sold it for few hundred dollars in gold to a friend of ours who helped us with the mining."

"Surely that friend of yours has recorded it by now ... hasn't he?" Bob was trying to sound concerned for their friend, but he was really hoping the paperwork had not yet been recorded.

They laughed. "Well, old Isaiah Gentry was not one to trust banks or anyone else. He said he was just going to hide it for a while until they got a better banking system in Helena. Then he would see about having that paper recorded."

There it was. Bob had gotten the information he'd hoped to get. All he had to do was get that paper and go have it recorded in his name. If he could do that, he would not only have the gold mine, but also the gulch where the gold was discovered. In addition, whoever owned the gulch and mine would own and control the whole town of Helena!

That same night, after the private game with the four Georgians, Bob went to work at figuring out how to get possession of that paper. Over the years, being a card dealer and a gunman, he had become acquainted with a few other gunmen with somewhat tainted reputations. One was a fellow called Jinks, and three more named Cory, Tim and Todd. They later became riders for Bob after he got ownership of the Running J Ranch in a crooked game of cards.

Leaving the gambling hall, Bob had gone straight to the Golden Nugget Saloon, where he knew he would find his four new gunmen friends, and he hired them to go with him that night to Isaiah Gentry's ranch. Isaiah had used some of the gold from the mine to buy a ranch, the Triangle G, which was normally just called the Triangle. Bob and his outlaw friends were not able to obtain the paper that would give him ownership of the land that the gulch and the mine were on, but they did manage to chase the Gentry's from their home. In fear for their lives, they ran.

Bob and his four riders caught up with the couple a few miles outside of town. They killed Isaiah and his wife, Geneva, never aware they'd hidden a baby in the back of the wagon under some hay. When they couldn't find the map on the couple's bodies, Bob and his friends went back to Isaiah's Triangle G Ranch the next day and searched there, with no luck. Bob continued to go back and search from time to time, but he never did find it.

Feeling sure the paper must be in the house or outbuildings somewhere, Bob tried to get Mayor Harper to help him get possession of the property. Failing that, he tried to get Judge Cleveland involved. He would not agree to help Bob either. All it did was raise their suspicions. So they'd asked Sheriff Howard Durmhill to see what he could find out about Bob Jensen. Meantime, the mayor and judge put a lien against Isaiah Gentry's property. No one could buy it until they released it.

The lien did not really bother Bob. He figured as long as no one else owned it, he could go out there and search for the paper anytime he wanted to. Meanwhile, between himself and all his other cohorts, he could keep watch on Isaiah's place in case it ever did go up for sale. But then he ran into more trouble. Sheriff Durmhill started digging too deep into Bob's past, so a few weeks later, they found the sheriff murdered, shot in the back. One of Bob's new friends, a gunman named Cal Tidwell, took care of that problem for him.

By then, Bob, being the owner of one of the biggest ranches in the county, had become both powerful and popular. Using that power, he got Cal Tidwell voted in as Howard Durmhill's replacement as Sheriff of Helena. As the years passed, Isaiah Gentry's Triangle G Ranch became rundown. No longer called the Triangle G, most folks just called it the old, abandoned ranch house.

Bob sighed as his thoughts slowly began to drift to a new set of problems, ones that came with the names of Kicks and Muley.

"*Hola*, Bob Jensen. Rosa es very happy to see you again. Why you look so sad? Rosa can make happy again. You like, no?"

Bob smiled as he turned to face Rosa, drawing her into his arms. He decided to forget about his problems for the night. Tomorrow would be the start of a brand-new day.

*　　　*　　　*

Tilly Durmhill had once been considered a beautiful woman. She'd been excited about life, and everything in it. They were young and had a baby girl. She had everything to look forward to. That was before her husband, Sheriff Howard Durmhill, was murdered. Or assassinated.

Since Howard's murder, the only thing that kept her going was her daughter Molly and her son-in-law Samuel Galveston, and her grandson David.

Fourteen years she'd been working at the hotel. This morning seemed no different to her from any other day. She got up and dressed, making sure her white blouse was tucked in neatly to her long black skirt before she walked down the stairs. She patted her black hair, which she always kept pinned up in a bun, to make sure it looked neat. A minute later, she was behind the lobby desk and ready to start the day.

The first thing she noticed was one of Cal's deputies. He was sitting in one of the big lounge chairs with his dirty boots propped up on a table. His spurs were making ugly scars on the polished tabletop. This angered her, but she smiled sweetly and said, "Hello, may I help you?"

The deputy looked over at her and shook his head. "Nope."

She waited a couple minutes to see if he would move, or at least take his boots off the table. To her dismay, the deputy didn't move. She smiled sweetly at him again, and said, "Would you please not rest your boots on the table? Your spurs are scratching the finish."

The deputy stared at her a moment, keeping the same position. She grew uneasy, afraid to say anything else. Tilly had heard bad things about Sheriff Cal Tidwell and his deputies. She hoped he was just waiting for someone and would be gone soon.

The deputy did leave at lunchtime, but he came back an hour later. Tilly had been relieved when he left again at the end of the day, thinking that would be the end of it. However, when she came down to the hotel lobby the next morning, another one of the deputies was setting in the lobby chair with his boots propped up on the table.

They were watching her. But why? Were they planning to kill her too? She became more frightened for her grandson than for herself. What would happen to David?

What can I do? Who can I turn to?

*   *   *

Sheriff Tidwell's deputies, Oscar, Buford and Dutch, didn't really fancy the idea of wasting their drinking time watching the widow Durmhill and her grandson. Nevertheless, there generally wasn't much else to do in Helena, so they took turns hanging around the hotel. Not a hard job, if a bit boring.

After a week of nothing happening, the deputies began to complain to Cal.

"Hell's bells, Cal," Buford said. "That woman just stands there all day long, staring daggers at us. Makes us feel plumb uneasy."

"Yeah," Dutch whined. "It'd be different if she worked the night shift when there's not so many people coming and going. Might me and her could get better acquainted."

Buford agreed to that.

"I don't know," Oscar said. "I don't much cotton to messing around with the likes of her. She's too uppity."

"Now look here, you guys," Cal said, pointing a finger at each of his deputies. "So far, we got this town eating right out of the palm of our hands. Just like a pet dog. But if any of you start trying to mess around with a respectable woman, these people will rip off you're … well, you know what, and shove it you know where. You eggheads get to feeling too love-struck watching the widow Durmhill, you can go over to the red-light district and see Madam Josephine Airey."

Oscar smiled at the thought. "Hey, did you guys know Josephine's real name is Mary Welch?"

Not to be left out of the conversation on such a popular profession, Dutch interjected with, "Hell, Mary Welch ain't all that much. She was working in Chicago during the Civil War. Known there as Chicago Joe."

"Forget about Mary Welch, or Chicago Joe, or whoever she is," Buford whined. "No point in sitting in that hotel watching the widow day after day. She ain't gonna do anything or go anywhere."

"Forget the widow," Oscar yelled. "We got another problem. Old Oatman, over to the livery, says he's gettin' tired of shoveling horse apples and pitching hay for all those horses. Said he's looking for a new hostler, someone to replace Floyd. Said since we caused Floyd to get his rear-end shot off, we oughta get someone in to take the job. He said no one that he asks wants to be a hostler."

"Dammit, Oscar," Buford said. "You go tell that old son of a—"

"Hold on there a minute," Cal said, snapping his fingers together. "That's it!"

"That's what?" Oscar asked.

"Oscar, you done put a good idea in my head."

"What, boss? What idea?"

Cal explained. "We know David, the widow Durmhill's grandson, has been looking for a job. He works part time for the ranchers around here."

"Yeah, that's right!"

"Well," Cal explained, "you guys make sure David hears about that job as hostler at Oatman's livery, and make sure Oatman hires him. You got that?"

"We got it," Oscar agreed. "If David takes that job as hostler at Oatman's, then we can figure out how to frame him with something. Might even give us a reason to bring him in, or even kill him. Hell, we'll plant him so deep, they'll never find him."

"You got it right, Oscar," Cal agreed. "But don't be killing anybody unless I tell you to. I could be wrong, but I figure Bob wants them all dead: Howard Durmhill's widow, her grandson David, and those two cowpokes, Kicks and Muley. Then there's Howard's daughter, Molly, and her husband Sammy. Bob might want them put out of the way too. I don't care if they are eliminated, or who does it. I just want to get some answers out of them *before* they get killed."

Cal's deputies didn't waste any time setting things up. The next morning, while Buford went to the hotel to keep his eye on the widow Durmhill, Dutch and Oscar went to the livery stable to talk to Oatman about hiring David as hostler. Oatman owned the only livery in town, so if you wanted to board your horse, you went to his stable. And for that reason, Oatman got a lot of business.

When the deputies arrived at the stable, the owner was sitting in the office drinking coffee.

As soon as they stepped inside his office, Dutch quickly shut the door behind them. "Damn, Oatman, this whole place reeks!"

Oatman curled the tip of his long, dirty mustache as he growled at Oscar, "What the hell ya expect. I can't keep up with cleaning all these stalls. I need help here."

"That's why we're here, Oatman. We got someone in mind. All you have to do is go ask him."

The stable owner perked up as he agreed to ask David if he wanted the job.

The next morning, Tilly was busy at work behind the hotel lobby desk, helping David sweep the floor. Oatman peeked inside the window, then stepped inside when he saw David.

Tilly knew who Oatman was even though he had never been in the hotel before. Whenever they passed each other on the street, he never spoke to her. However, she had heard talk about him, so she wondered what he wanted. She smiled and said, "Hello, Mister Oatman! How can I help you today?"

"You can't," he snapped. "I've come to talk to this here young'un. David, I believe is his name?"

Hearing his name mentioned, David walked over to the man. "You wanted to talk to me, sir?"

Oatman curled his lip and twisted the end of his mustache. "That's why I came in here. I heard you was looking fer a job?"

David perked up at the question. "I sure am, Mister Oatman. Are you looking to hire someone?"

Oatman looked at David a few seconds. "Now that's a stupid question, young'un. But yeah, I'm looking to hire a hostler to take care of my livery stable. Seems my other hostler, Floyd, got hisself killed, damn fool. You interested?"

"I sure am, Mister Oatman. When do I start?"

As soon as Tilly heard David's answer, she interrupted angrily, "No, David, I won't allow it!" Immediately, she knew she'd stepped over the line by talking to him like that in front of Oatman. She'd embarrassed the boy and put him on the defensive. She should have waited until Oatman left, then tried to discuss it with David.

David gave her a hurtful look, anger in his eyes. "It's my decision, Grandma," he said. Then looking at Oatman, he said, "When do I start?"

"Taint an easy job, boy. It's cleanin' out all the stalls throughout the whole stable. Shoveling horse apples for hours most every day. Bucking hay bales and liftin' heavy sacks of grain. It means taking care of a lot of horses. And taking complaints from customers that jus' plain likes to argue. Some of the men come in there are gunmen, mean as a lion that just got a backside full of buckshot."

"You don't have to go on with all that," David said. "I'll take the job."

Oatman lowered his voice as he said, "Sure you can manage it, boy?"

David replied, "I sure can, only…"

"Only what?"

"You have to pay me a fair wage, and my name is not *boy!* You call me Dave! Do you understand?"

Oatman eyes widened in surprise, though he answered without hesitation, "Okay, sounds like a damn good deal to me, boy … uh, Dave." Oatman smirked at Tilly as he twisted the end of his long mustache with his thumb and forefinger. "Be there by five in the morning, Dave, and I'll talk details with you then." Oatman swaggered from the hotel lobby out onto the street.

Later, in their hotel room while eating dinner, Tilly tried to speak with David about why she didn't want him to take that job at Oatman's livery.

"I understand, Grandma, but I'm a grown man now, and I'm gonna take this job. I've heard all the talk, and I can take care of myself." He wanted to tell her that he had been sneaking his grandpa's gun out and practicing with it for a long time now and was getting to be a pretty good shot. However, he knew it would just worry her more than ever, so he didn't mention it.

Tilly sighed, her proud shoulders slumping a bit. "Okay, take the job. Only be very careful, David. Some of those men are very dangerous."

Dave felt good about the talk he'd had with his grandma, but now all he could think about was going to work for Oatman. He would be free to talk to other men who might have known his grandfather. Maybe now, he could finally start to learn what had happened all those years ago, when he'd been just a little boy, and his grandfather killed.

CHAPTER 9

At five-foot-nine, Dave Galveston was not a big man. Much like his father, he was muscular with brown hair and eyes, and was considered quite handsome by the young women in town. Though he'd been a little boy when his grandfather Howard was murdered, he remembered everything that his parents and grandmother had told him about it, and vowed that someday he would track down those responsible for his death and avenge him.

For the past year, he had been helping around the hotel and taking odd jobs at different ranches in the area. He had been warned by some of the ranchers to be careful around Bob Jensen of the Running J. They would never say much else, only to '*be careful.*' He'd heard the talk around town that Bob Jensen had Sheriff Cal Tidwell on his payroll. So David kept shy of him too. He figured with everything he'd heard about the Running J rancher and the sheriff, that maybe they were the ones who'd killed his grandpa. While working around the other ranches, he would start conversations, talk about his grandfather. It seemed like everyone who'd known Howard had liked him, but no one knew who murdered him. Or they weren't saying.

Dave always gave a part of his wages to his grandma to help with the finances. He also bought himself a good horse which he kept at Oatman's livery stable. Behind his grandma's back, he'd bought several boxes of shells for his grandpa's Colt .44. Because his grandpa had lived and died by the gun, his grandma and parents would never allow him to have one. A few months after Dave started to earn his own money, he bought shells for his grandpa's gun and began to go out to the woods to practice. He practiced until he became a pretty quick draw.

Dave was up before daylight, got dressed, and went into the kitchen. His grandma was already up. She looked worried as she fixed them breakfast, which they ate in silence. Finally, when he was ready to leave, they talked, but not about the new job. She told him to be careful and that she would have supper ready when he got home.

Not wanting to worry his grandmother, Dave had wrapped up his gun in his big mackinaw and carried it through the hotel lobby. He'd planned to put it on once he got out of sight but decided against it. He'd just keep it close in case he needed it.

When he got to Oatman's livery, he went inside the big double doors at the entrance of the building and looked through the window of the office. Oatman was there but fast asleep, sitting in a chair at the table that doubled as a card table and whatever else they might need it for.

Dave figured the old man had probably been up all night, so instead of waking him, he hung his gun belt on a wooden peg that was protruding from a post by the door of the office, then hung his coat over the gun belt, keeping it hidden. He checked his horse first to make sure it had plenty of hay, adding a bit of grain to its manger, then rolled his sleeves up and began taking care of the other horses.

The stalls took a while to clean. He had to take each horse out of its stall and tie it up, clean its stall, then put the horse back inside and feed it. In the meantime, he'd have to stop to take care of any new horses as customers came in.

It was near noon when he finally finished, and his stomach told him it was time for lunch. He looked in the window of the office, finding Oatman still asleep in his chair. David figured it was time for the old man to wake up, so he opened the door and then shut it again. Oatman didn't budge. So he opened the door again and slammed it shut.

Oatman jumped like he'd been shot. "What … what's going on?" Then he saw Dave standing there. He looked at his pocket watch, which had been placed on the table. "Gawl-dammit, boy! You just now gettin' here? Why, I oughta fire you right now!"

Dave looked him straight in the eye. "Dave, its *Dave* … old man, and I've already cleaned all the stalls and fed and watered the horses. Now I'm going to lunch." Dave turned and started toward the door.

"Hey, wait a minute," Oatman yelled. "Who's goin' take care of things while you're gone?"

Dave just kept on walking, "You!" he yelled back, slamming the office door behind him.

Oatman jumped up from his chair and walked out into the stables to look around. When he saw that every stall was clean, and all the horses had been groomed and fed, he grinned, twisting the end of his mustache. "Well, I'll be damned. Place ain't never looked this good before. Why, I could eat right off the floor."

*   *   *

The night before, in their hotel room, Kicks and Muley had ended their celebration when the bottle of the mescal was empty. Muley had already stretched out in the big chair by the window, and in five minutes was snoring away. Kicks stretched out on the bed, feet hanging over the end of the mattress. He'd cursed himself then, wondering if the big chair might not be more comfortable than the bed.

The two cowpokes woke up late the next morning and discussed everything that had happened over the last few days. They didn't leave the hotel until almost noon. When they sat down at their usual table in the Silver Spoon Café, Cathy came over to take their order. While they waited for their food, a young man came in and sat down at the counter. Kicks looked at Muley to see if he'd noticed. "Ain't that David Galveston?"

"Yep, I think yer right."

Just then Cathy brought their food out and placed it on the table, "How's that, fellas?"

"Just fine, Cathy," Muley said. He lifted his chin toward the counter "That young man that just sat down, ain't that David Galveston?"

Glancing over, Cathy said, "Sure is. Why, do you know him?"

"No," Muley said. "Just wondered." As they were talking, Sheriff Tidwell's deputy, Buford Turner came in and sat down at the counter beside David.

Cathy left Kicks and Muley's table to go wait on her two new customers. She approached them with a smile. David had sat down at the counter first, so she asked him, "What can I get for you?"

Before Dave could answer, Buford spoke up, "Look, sister, I'm in a hurry. You can wait on this pup later."

Cathy smiled politely. "But he was here first. That's the way we do things here. First come, first served."

"That's okay, ma'am," Dave said. "I'm in no hurry. You can wait on him first."

Without giving him a glance, Buford said, "Shut your trap, pup. I'm doing the talkin' here." Then to Cathy he said, "You gonna take my order or not?"

David stood up and looked the deputy in the eye. "Look, mister, I don't care if you are a deputy sheriff, you shouldn't talk to the lady like that!"

Buford stood up too, towering over David. "Who's gonna stop me? You?"

"Yes, me!"

Kicks could see the boy was trying to act brave, even though he didn't have the faintest idea what to do. "He's goadin' the boy into a fight," he said to Muley. "Probably end up beatin' the kid to a pulp."

"Yeah, or killin' him," Muley grumbled.

Kicks stood with a cup of hot coffee in hand and walked over to the counter. He bumped into Buford and spilled the hot liquid down the front of the deputy's shirt.

Buford yelped as the hot coffee soaked through and began to burn him. "Watch out, you clumsy, no-count drifter!" He jumped back and started to brush the hot coffee off himself.

Kicks stepped back, his expression cold. "Them there's fightin' words, deputy. Choose your weapon, fists or guns. Don't make a damn bit a difference to me."

It took a few seconds for Buford to react, but then he recognized Kicks and wanted no part of him. He was willing to do anything just to get away from him. "You ... you challengin' me?"

"Damn straight I am. You started the music, now yer gonna dance ... or bow out and run." Kicks was prepared to draw if the deputy found enough courage to draw first, but he was hoping it wouldn't come to a shootout. He could almost read Buford's thoughts. *This is one of the two men that gunned down six gunfighters in a close-quarters shootout at the livery.*

His expression fearful, Buford said, "Look, Mister Kicks, I was just surprised when you accidentally bumped into me. Sorry fer what I said. I was just upset. How 'bout I buy you another cup of coffee."

Muley grabbed Kicks' arm, making sure he knew it was him. "Aw, come on, Kicks," he said, "you don't want another notch on your gun, do ya? Let the man go." He turned to Buford. "Just let him walk away."

His expression angry, Kicks pretended indecision, then slowly relaxed. "Yeah, I guess you're right. Thanks."

Buford saw that as a window of opportunity and split as fast as he could. Once he was out of sight, Cathy sighed with relief, and everyone laughed.

Everyone except David. "Why'd ya do that? He was trying on purpose to goad me into a fight."

"Exactly, kid, and you'da lost."

David sighed, his expression depressed. "I guess I owe you one, mister." He held out his hand. "I'm Dave Galveston."

Kicks shook his hand. "I'm Kicks, and this is my partner, Muley."

"You're the two cowpokes who's been the talk of the town," David said. "I heard about the shootout over to the livery the other night." David turned to Muley and shook his hand. "Glad to meet you guys."

"Same hear, David."

"Dave. Name's Dave. I took Floyd's place as hostler over at Oatman's livery, and if I can help you in any way, just let me know."

"Appreciate that," Muley said. "There is something we'd like to talk to you about, when you got time."

Cathy brought out Dave's food and set it on the counter in front of him. He ate while they made small talk. "Well, I gotta get back to work now, but we can talk more later if you want. When and where do you wanna meet?"

"Well, David ... Dave," Muley said, "since we're all staying at the hotel, why don't you just stop by our room sometime tonight? It's on the first floor, room number 9."

"Okay," Dave said. "I'll see you later then."

CHAPTER 10

It was late in the evening by the time Dave got back to his room at the hotel. Oatman had grumbled at him because *he* was going to have to stay another night at the livery. "What the hell do you think I hired you for, so you can work the day shift? Hell's fire, boy, the hostler is in charge and responsible for the livery stable period, twenty-four hours a day."

"Hold on there," Dave came back at him. "You didn't say that when you came to me to ask me if I wanted to work for you. I can't just *live* there."

"Well, I'm telling you that's what's expected of a good hostler."

Dave thought it over for a minute. "Okay, here's the deal then. If you want me to work for you as your hostler, I'll move in and take care of the livery on a twenty-four-hour basis. However, when I want time off, like a day or two here and there, I'm takin' it. You can take it or leave it."

Oatman grinned and twisted the ends of his mustache. "You drive a hard bargain, Davy boy, but it's a deal. You can move into the stable office in the morning."

"It's Dave, not Davy boy."

Oatman just grunted and waved him away.

Tilly had dinner ready when Dave got to their room at the hotel. "David, you're so late. I was getting worried thinking about you working for that horrid old man."

Dave knew his grandma would struggle to understand what he had to do. "Look, Grandma, I know you still consider me to be a child, but I'm a responsible adult now, and there are things I gotta do."

"What things, David?" Tilly asked.

"I'm not a little boy anymore, Grandma. People call me *Dave* now. I gotta move into the office at the livery stable. Oatman's putting me in charge of the whole thing." Dave knew it would be hard springing this on her suddenly, but it had to be done.

Dave put his arms around his grandma when her eyes filled with tears. "I promise to be careful, Grandma. I'll come see you often. I'll only be a few blocks away." He felt her tremble. "Grandma, please don't cry."

She shook her head. "I always knew you'd leave me someday. I think I'm prepared. Just watch out who you hang around with, okay, David. I mean … Dave."

Dave felt humbled seeing his grandmother struggle to let him move to his own place. "You can call me David if you want to, Grandma."

"No, I'll respect your wishes, just like you respect mine. From now on I'll call you Dave."

During dinner, he told his grandma about meeting Kicks and Muley. He didn't know how much she knew about the two cowboys, and she didn't offer to ask about them, so he just told her they were new friends of his and that he was going to meet them after dinner.

When they finished eating, Dave went downstairs and knocked lightly on the door of room number 9. Muley opened the door. "Come in, Dave. Take a seat. I think we might be a big help to each other."

After talking for a couple of hours, comparing what Dave knew from memory to what the two cowpokes had learned since they'd been hanging around town, they gained a bigger picture of who their foes were, but they still didn't know why or how it was all tied together.

"Seems Bob Jensen is the big cheese around here," Dave said. "Cal Tidwell is supposed to be the sheriff and in charge of things, but everyone knows he's in Bob Jensen's pocket."

"Does seem like Jensen is the biggest spoke in the wheel around here," Kicks agreed. "But there just might be someone bigger than Bob that's behind all this."

"Well," Dave said, "sooner or later everyone comes around Oatman's livery, seeing how it's the only one in town. I'll keep my eyes open and my ears tuned in, try to keep you informed when, or if, anything happens. Next time I have a run-in with that deputy, I'll have my .44 with me." He noticed the look Muley gave Kicks. "Don't worry, I'm no amateur with a six-shooter."

After he left their room, the two cowpokes talked over what they had learned from Dave. They decided it would be a good thing for him to be on their side in this mess. Dave could possibly learn who'd killed his grandfather and why, while Muley could find out who killed *his* parents. What had the two worried at this moment was Dave talking about wearing his six-shooter. Likely to invite unwanted trouble.

"Well," Muley said, "he claims to not be an amateur with a .44. Guess we'll probably find out sooner or later if he's right."

"If he's gonna pack a gun, he better know how to use it," Kicks replied. "Like my pappy always says, 'A man's only as good as his word … and the size of his gun.'"

Muley pressed his lips together as he nodded. They were both worried for the boy.

By eleven the next morning, Dave had already moved all his gear into the livery stable's office and had his responsibilities as manager completed. About eleven thirty, the two cowpokes came to see how he was doing.

Dave greeted Kicks and Muley, inviting them in for a cup of coffee. "I just made a fresh pot."

They returned the greeting, both their gazes moving to Dave's hips, where he wore his .44. "You wear'n your gun low," Kicks said. "You a fast draw?"

Dave gave one sharp nod, then poured coffee all around. He looked over his shoulder when he heard a group of horses ride up. "Got customers. Looks like some boys from the Running J."

Dave stepped out of the office as the riders dismounted and led their horses through the big double doors inside the livery. "Howdy, gents," Dave said as he approached them. "How are things goin' out at the ranch?"

Ignoring his friendly greeting, the spokesman for the four men said, "So you're the hostler took Floyd's place, huh." It was more of a statement than a question, so Dave didn't bother to answer. "Don't seem the same without ol' Floyd being here."

"Well, from what I hear, Floyd and his cohorts got what they asked for. You wanna leave your horses here or not? I got work to do."

"Naw, we'll tie up over to the Golden Nugget." The man hesitated for a few seconds as if deep in thought, then shook his head. "I'd sure like to get them no-good drifters that done in Floyd and my partners in that gunfight."

Dave grinned and turning around, facing the office. He pointed through the window at the two cowpokes. "That's them no-good drifters right there. Be my guest."

Kicks and Muley stepped out of the office and walked over to where Dave and the Running J riders were. "I hear my name being mentioned?" Kicks said, narrowing his cold eyes at the man.

Caught off guard, the gunman swallowed and licked his lips, while his three comrades slowly moved a couple paces to either side of him, making them a harder target to hit if lead started flying. It gave the speaker a few seconds to recover from his surprise.

Kicks broke the silence, "Name's Kicks Burks, and this here is my partner, Muley Gentry." His eyes moved between the four gunmen as he continued speaking, "We're the no-good drifters that sent Floyd and five of his buddies to Boot Hill. You fellas like to join 'em there? I'm sure we can arrange it."

"Art Boswell's my handle," the man said coldly. With a jerk of his thumb, he motioned to either side of him. "That's Jake Terrell, Billy Thompson and Blackjack Ketchum."

To Kicks' surprise, Dave stepped forward, lining himself up with him and Muley, leaving about ten feet of distance between the three of them and the Running J gunmen. "My name's Dave Galveston," he said.

Just might get to see how gun savvy the kid is, Kicks thought. There was a pause of about ten seconds, and then

Kicks said impatiently, "My coffee's getting' cold, fellas! Let's move this thing along."

The gunmen stared at Kicks for a moment, each one waiting for the other to move, or even flinch. Kicks wasn't really trying to get a gun battle started. People tended to get hurt or killed. But, his philosophy was, *if it has to be, than bring it on.* "I hate cold coffee!"

Art, apparently caught off guard by the statement, hesitated. During that time, Kicks took a quick assessment of the other three men. The Running J riders weren't in range clothes, so it appeared they'd come to town just to have a good time. Although, all four riders chose then to open their coats to expose their guns.

The tension grew for a minute, then Art laughed. "Well, it would be downright impolite if I caused you to have to drink cold coffee." He touched the brim of his hat with two fingers in a parting gesture. "See you fellas around."

As Kicks, Muley, and Dave watched the gunmen mount up and ride off toward the Golden Nugget, Muley said, "We ain't seen the last of those hard cases."

Kicks nodded. "Got that right, partner. And Dave, thanks for throwing in with us, but you better be on your guard from now on, 'cause you just made four badass enemies. Probably be more of 'em comin' when they see they can't scare us off."

Dave, who appeared unaffected by Kicks' statement, said, "Yeah, I guess you're right. "Come on inside and I'll warm up that cold coffee."

The trio went inside the livery office and sat down at the table. Muley took a sip from his cup. "Well, what do you think, Dave? You've worked at all the ranches around here, right? You know anything about those four Running J riders?"

"I've seen 'em around quite a bit. Art Boswell and Blackjack Ketchum are the two guys to watch out for. Billy

Thompson and Jake Terrell are just sidekicks. Followers, if you know what I mean."

"What about the rest of Jensen's crew?" Kicks asked, wiping his mouth.

Dave thought about it a moment, his expression thoughtful. "Their pretty much the same as Billy and Jake, I guess. Bob Jensen, the owner of the Running J outfit, he's the tough one. He runs the whole town except for Mayor Harper and Judge Cleveland. That's two good things in our favor."

Kicks laughed. "Yeah, after the shootout the other day with Floyd and his buddies, your pa, along with the mayor and the judge, saved our bacon."

Dave's eyes widened with surprise as he looked from Kicks to Muley. "My pa saved you guys?"

"Sure did," Muley said. "After the shoot-out, Sheriff Tidwell and his deputies busted in and got the drop on us. They covered us with scatterguns on the march to the jail. Know they planned to kill us, claim we were trying to escape, but then your pa busted in, leading the judge and the mayor, and the sheriff had to let us go."

"Wow," Dave said. "I, well … I always kind of thought…"

Kicks could see Dave was at a loss for words, and now knew he'd been right in his calculation about why Dave chose to stay with his grandma rather than his parents. "You probably thought your pa wasn't very tough, huh, maybe even a coward?"

"Well, yeah, I guess so," Dave admitted, refusing to look him in the eye.

"Look here, son, your pa is different from me and Muley, and you and your grandpa. But he's no coward. He's an easterner, and eastern ways are different from ours. I'm telling you, when it comes right down to it, your pa will fight. I guarantee you that. You shoulda seen him when he busted in on us down at the jail with the judge and mayor at his heels. No fear at all in him. Your pa didn't even have a gun, and Cal and his deputies were holding shotguns."

Dave was silent for a moment, easy to see he couldn't picture his pa coming to the rescue of Kicks and Muley. Suddenly, he grinned and looked up. "Damn, sure glad you guys shared that with me."

"Never got the opportunity to know my own pa," Muley said, putting his hand on Dave's shoulder. "Just think a man should get to really know his father, share a strong bond with him if he can. They can be proud of each other."

"Come on, guys," Kicks said. "Don't go gettin' mushy on me. We need to keep diggin' around town, find out what's goin' on around here. Just remember, keep your guard up at all times."

"That's for sure," Muley said. "And Dave, I think it's a good idea you keep our horses ready and easy for us to get at."

Dave looked surprised. "Why? You thinkin' about pulling out?"

"Not before we get what we came here for," Muley replied, grinning. "The only way we're leaving is to be carried out feet first."

"Yeah," Kicks agreed. "Keepin' the horses ready is just a precaution."

*   *   *

Bob Jensen left Maria's Cantina feeling good. Rosa had given him the full treatment that night. First a full-body massage, then finished up with what she did best. He'd been exhausted by the time he left. However, he felt somewhat recovered when he reached his ranch, so he decided to stop by the bunkhouse and pay the boys a visit. With most of his crew being hired gunmen, there was almost always an all-night card game going on.

As he rode into the yard, he heard the metallic click of a pistol being cocked, and a voice calling from out of the dark. "Hold it right there. Identify yourself."

That's what Bob liked about this crew, always careful to have guards posted, because most of them had warrants out for their arrests. "Coleman, it's me … Bob."

"Oh. Sorry, boss, just being careful."

"It's okay, Coleman. I like it when the lookout is alert. There a game going on now?" He looked toward the bunkhouse but could not see any light coming from the window. Of course, they usually kept the windows covered after dark so no one could see inside. Safer that way. One never knew when some nosey ranger might come snooping around.

Coleman holstered his gun. "Yeah, there's a game going alright. Pots nigh up to two hundred dollars now. I went broke, so I came out and relieved the guard."

Bob dismounted. "Take care of my horse, will you? I'm going to get in the game. I feel lucky tonight."

Coleman took charge of the horse. "Sure, boss, and good luck."

Bob walked over to the bunkhouse. He paused at the door and rapped softly before opening it. "It's me, Bob."

"Come on in, boss!" he heard Blackjack Ketchum say.

He stepped inside, crossed the room to the card table and sat down. "Deal me in."

The game got underway, and after an hour of 'win some, loose some,' Bob's luck began to change, making him the big winner.

About that time, Coleman rapped on the door. "Forgot to tell you, boss . . . three men rode in earlier. One of 'em said to tell you Charlie Heart was here and would be back later tonight. Said you'd know who he is." Coleman offered Bob a single nod, then stepped out and shut the door.

Great, his luck was turning bad again. "Well, let's finish up this game, boys," Bob said.

"An hour later, he finally quit and went into the main house. He figured Charlie Heart, or William Quantrill, would be showing up soon, and he'd probably want a drink while they talked. A few minutes later, the coffee was done, and Bob poured himself a cup. He got a bottle of whiskey from his stock and was about to pour a double shot in his coffee when he heard horses galloping into the yard. A second later, Coleman called through the door, "Boss, it's Charlie Heart and two of his riders."

"Thanks, Coleman." He poured three more cups of coffee.

A few minutes later, he heard a knocking at the door. He opened it to find Quantrill and two other gunmen outside. Quantrill shook hands with Bob as he stepped inside, and they exchanged some small talk.

"Coffee?" Bob offered. "Thought you and your riders might like a hot cup with a jigger of whiskey."

Charlie took a cup and nodded to his two riders. They each took a cup, then one of them went and stood to the right side of the doorway. The other followed suit but stood at the left.

Bob grinned inside. *Still acting the soldier, huh.* To Quantrill, he said. "Have a seat and let's talk."

Quantrill took a sip of coffee, set the cup down and poured in more whiskey. He took another sip. "That's better. Now, Bob, I hadn't planned to ride back here again this soon, but I heard about those two cowpokes keep causing you trouble in Helena. What's the deal with them?"

Bob Jensen and Quantrill went back a long way together. He and Jim Bonner had been two of Quantrill's top gunmen at that time, and pretty close comrades. Although the war was now over, Quantrill believed in his crazed mind that he was still Captain William C. Quantrill of the Confederacy. Moreover, he trained and commanded his gang of outlaws in the same manner.

"Well, I don't really know that much about them yet. The one who calls himself Muley Gentry rode into town a little over a month back. The other one, called Kicks Burks, showed up a few days ago. Maybe a week. Near as I can tell, they met in the Golden Nugget Saloon and teamed up. Both seem to be top gunmen, fast and dangerous. Killed six good gunmen that I set against them. Don't you worry, I'll find out what their cause is, and I'll put an end to 'em. I have Sheriff Tidwell on it even as we speak." He didn't want to tell Quantrill any more at this time. Best to get rid of him, the sooner the better.

Quantrill poured himself more whiskey and scratched his chin, a habit that seemed to help him think. "Gentry, that name sounds familiar."

"Well, yeah, sounded familiar to me too. Gentry was the name of that couple me and your men killed. You remember, back when we tried to get the ownership papers to the Last Chance gold mine. I think it's just a coincidence. Gentrys didn't have a kid. Just the two of 'em in that wagon."

"Yeah, I remember. You're sure there was no kid?"

"Yep."

Bob and Quantrill talked long into the night, Bob trying to convince him that everything was under control. Sheriff Tidwell would take care of the two strangers. He'd find out through Tilly, Molly and Sammy, or their son David, what they were looking for in Helena. And eventually, Bob would get hold of the papers to that gold mine. He shouldn't have even involved Quantrill in that. He hadn't needed anyone's help, and he sure didn't intend to share the mine or the property with the outlaw.

Quantrill finally left the Running J Ranch with the last word, "Well, Bob, I'm running a bit low on finances. I need money to keep my army going. If I don't hear from you within the next couple of months, I'll come back. This time I'll bring Captain William Anderson with me. You remember Bloody Bill Anderson, don't you?"

Bob's eye twitched at the mention of Bloody Bill, an image of the man flashing through his mind. Bloody Bill always wore a six-gun on his left side outside of a gray duster. He sported a mustache and full beard. If there was a man Bob Jensen feared, it would be Captain William Bloody Bill Anderson, also one of Quantrill's Raiders. Bob remembered that Bill carried a long red silk cord with him, used to tie a knot in it for every Yankee he killed. Before he moved over with Quantrill's gang, Bloody Bill used to ride with Jesse James and the Younger Brothers. Bob always figured Bloody Bill would break loose from Quantrill too. Just like he planned to do when he finally laid claim to the Last Chance gold mine, and all the property that went with it. Bob would own the town of Helena, lock, stock, and barrel, and he didn't plan to share with anyone.

It was early morning by the time Bob went to sleep. By then, he'd put Quantrill and Bloody Bill Anderson completely out of his mind.

CHAPTER 11

Dave Galveston was happy with the way things were going. He figured with this job at Oatman's livery and his new friends Kicks and Muley, he could finally get to the bottom of who murdered his Grandpa Howard. A lot of sheriffs were killed in the line of duty. Bad enough just to get outgunned, but to get shot in the back … well, that was a different story, and Dave figured he would dig and dig until he found out who'd done it and then make them pay for the cowardly act.

It was growing late, and his work for the day was finished. He'd cleaned all the stalls and fed the horses, so he spent the rest of the evening relaxing in the stable office. Tired after the long day, he decided to turn in early.

He'd just left the office, planning to check on the horses one last time, when he felt a tug at his shirtsleeve just below the shoulder. At the same time, he heard the report of a shot. Luckily, he was close to an empty stall. Dave pulled his Colt and squeezed off a shot in the direction of his assailant as he dived into the stall. The shooter was hidden by the shadows just inside the doors of the livery, but Dave thought he recognized Buford Turner. And he'd heard a grunt when he squeezed off that shot, so he figured he must have scored a hit. As he tried to get into position for another shot, Dave heard the man's fading footsteps as he ran away.

By the time Dave made his way to the door, the man had disappeared into the shadows outside. He lit a lantern and walked over to where the shooter had stood and examined the doorframe. The wood was splintered from his shot and showed the shine of wet blood. "Well," he said, sighing. "Guess I can't do much about it tonight." Tomorrow, he'd try to find someone with a bandaged arm. He finished checking on the horses and went back inside the office.

Worried he might have another visitor during the night, he opened the loading gate of his Colt and replaced the spent shell, then spun the cylinder and dropped the pistol back in its holster. He set the lantern on the corner of the table, but instead of going to bed, as he'd intended, he settled himself in a chair behind the table so he would have a clear view of the stable doors through the office window. He blew out the flame of the lantern and propped his feet up on the table. A few minutes later, he was asleep.

The next morning, Dave woke at dawn and made a fresh pot of coffee. Holding his cup, he stared around the back of the office, and found a sign that read:

*Be back shortly, you can feed
and water your horse. Prices are as follows:*

Under that was a list of prices that covered everything.

While reading, a thought struck Dave. Last night was the first time he'd ever been in a gunfight. Oddly, he hadn't been afraid or nervous. All that practice drawing and shooting had given him confidence. He smiled as he thought back to when he'd squared off with Kicks and Muley against those four gunmen. He hadn't been nervous then either, though there hadn't been much time to think about things.

After placing the sign on the office door, he headed for the Silver Spoon Café for breakfast. When he stepped inside, he spotted Kicks and Muley sitting at a table. It being so early, they were the only two customers in the café, and Cathy was at their table, waiting to take their order. The two cowpokes saw him come in and waved him over.

"Good morning, Dave," Cathy greeted. "You're just in time to order with your friends."

Muley put a boot on the bottom rung of a chair and scooted it away from the table. "Sit down and take a load off."

Kicks nodded. "Morning, Dave!"

"Howdy, partners. Morning, Cathy." As Dave sat down and greeted his friends, he thought, *Feels good to be counted a man by these good men.*

"Well, what'll it be, cowpokes?" Cathy asked.

"Same as usual, I reckon," Kicks said, lifting his chin toward Muley.

"Yep, sounds good to me too," Muley replied.

Looking at Dave, Cathy said, "What about you, cowboy?"

"Me? Whatever their usual is, that's good enough for me."

"Okay!" Cathy said. "By the time you all finish your first cup of coffee; I'll be back with your breakfast."

When she came back from the kitchen, she had three big platters of beefsteak, eggs, fried potatoes, and hotcakes. "There!" she said, setting the platters of food on the table. "I'm getting pretty busy with other customers now, so when you're ready for your bear sign, just give me a whistle."

"Wow!" Dave exclaimed, looking at all that food. "I haven't eaten like this since … well, I guess I've never eaten like this."

"Just stick with us and we'll show you how to pack it in," Muley said.

They all three laughed, then got down to some serious eating. The café was crowded by the time the three cowpokes finished and sat back for a last cup of coffee.

"You know," Dave said, looking at the scraps he'd left on his plate. "That food doesn't look quite so enticing now."

Kicks belched and patted his stomach. "Like my pappy always says, 'Acorns are always bitter when a hog gets his belly full.'"

"Yep," Muley said. "Your pappy might have something there. Ain't that right, Dave?"

But Dave wasn't listening. He was looking toward the counter.

"What is it, Dave?" Muley asked.

"That man at the counter, the one with his back to us. Third one from your left. That's deputy Buford, ain't it?"

"That's Buford alright," Kicks said. "That's one of the deputies we had a squabble with the other day. Why? Did you two get into it?"

"You bet we did," Dave said. "He took a shot at me last night. Came close to killing me too, put a hole in my shirt right at the left shoulder. A little further to the right and I wouldn't be here."

"Someone took a shot at you last night?" Muley asked, raising his eyebrows. "What happened, and how do you know it was Buford? Did you get a good look at him?"

Dave told the two cowpokes what had happened. "I'm sure it was him. I winged him, saw blood on the doorjamb that he was hiding behind." Dave stood. "And I'm gonna settle the score with that deputy right now."

Just then, the man in question got up from the stool at the counter and was paying for his food.

"Hold on, Dave," Kicks said. "Wait until he gets away from all those people at the counter. Let him come back here by the door."

Dave sat back down and waited, clenching his fist. Finally, Buford turned from the counter and started walking toward where the three cowpokes were seated.

Kicks watched impatiently as the deputy came closer and closer. He noticed the man had his shirtsleeves rolled down and was favoring one arm. At that point, Kicks became a little more wary, but decided to let Dave call the shots.

When the deputy came within five feet of them, and Dave had not made a move yet, Kicks thought maybe the kid had lost his nerve. However, just as the deputy got within arm's reach, Dave stood and bumped into Buford's arm, making it look like an accident.

"Aw, damn, man!" Buford yelled, grabbing at his arm.

"What's the matter, Buford? That wound I gave you last night hurt some?"

The deputy recovered quickly. "What the hell you yappin' on about, boy?"

Dave lifted his chin toward the deputy's sore arm. "I put a bullet in you last night when you tried to gun me down. Ain't that right, Deputy?"

"I don't know what you're talking about, kid. I got this wound from a bullet alright, but it weren't from you. I didn't shoot at you last night."

"If that wound ain't from my bullet, then who shot you?"

"I ... I busted up a drunken fight last night over at the saloon. One of the drunks drew against me."

"Well," Dave demanded, "who was it? He in jail?"

"Naw, I didn't jail him. I just ran him outta town."

"Deputy, you're a damn liar," Dave said.

"Now hold on, kid. I can't draw against you with this bad arm."

Kicks knew if he didn't do something to stop Dave, he would push the deputy into a gunfight for sure. Either way, shoot or be shot, Dave would be the loser. There was no way to prove it'd been Buford who shot at him last night; no way to prove how the deputy came by that wound.

"Dave," Kicks said. "Better let him walk away from this. We'll find our proof and then go after him … okay?"

Dave's eyes sparked with anger as he glared at Buford, but then he appeared to rethink his position and his shoulders relaxed. "Yeah, you're right, I'll let it go for now."

Buford, seeing he was going to be allowed to slide out of this one, smirked as he turned to walk away. He looked over his shoulder and said, "This ain't over yet, kid. I'll be coming for you."

"Let it go," Kicks said, motioning toward Dave's chair. "He's right. This ain't over, not by a long shot."

At the jail, Buford told the sheriff about the incident with young Dave Galveston. "I swear to God, Cal … boss, I don't see how the kid could've seen me last night. I was hidden in the shadows behind the door. I just wanted to make him jumpy by taking a potshot at him. Figured he'd be ready to tell us everything he knows when we put the squeeze on him and his kinfolk."

Dutch and Oscar burst out laughing at Buford. "You thought the kid would turn yellow and run, didn't ya?" Oscar said. "Instead, he took a shot at you. Outgunned ya, didn't he?"

Buford turned red in the face and started to curse at the other two deputies, but Cal cut him off. "Shut up, you fool. This goes for all of you. Don't you ever try to do anything on your own again. You got an idea, you run it by me first. I'll be the one to decide whether or not to follow through with it." He paused, then added, "You understand?"

"Yeah, boss," all three said.

"Good, now let's see if I can make this clear. Why are we keeping a tight surveillance on Dave, his ma and pa, and his grandma?"

After a moment, one of the deputies said, "Because we know there's some connection between Bob Jensen and the ex-sheriff, Howard Durmhill. Ain't that why Bob had you kill 'im. That's why we're after Dave and his kinfolk, to find out why Bob had you to kill Howard."

"And what's the reason why I want you guys to keep an eye on Bob Jensen?"

"To find out why Charlie Heart comes to see him. Always has at least two gunslingers with him."

"Good," Cal said. "That's all I want you to do. Observe, and report to me." After eyeballing his three deputies for a minute or so he said, "Now get the hell out on the street, and keep out of trouble."

*   *   *

Dave wanted a day off, so Oatman allowed him to hire another person to help watch the stable when Dave was gone. The person they hired was on old prospector named Whiskers, and also the town drunk. He got the name because no razor had touched his face for many a year. Consequently, he had a full beard and mustache. He wore a ragged, blue-checkered shirt with jeans and an old leather vest. He always packed a Colt Dragoon revolver, .31 caliber, five-shot cylinder, on his hip. He wore an old battered floppy hat and worn boots that were run down at the heels. He owned a mule that looked to be on his last legs that he called Tumbleweed. Dave liked the old prospector, felt sorry for him. That's why he'd talked Oatman into hiring the old man.

The old prospector had wandered into town from another gold camp years ago, when Helena had first been established, and he'd been here ever since. Whiskers would wander from place to place, sweeping floors for a meal and a drink. He jumped at the chance to work at the livery, getting paid every week, so he wouldn't have to wonder about his next meal. When he proved to be a good worker, Dave offered to let him bunk in the stable office with him.

"Well," Whiskers said, "don't sleep so well at night, so sometimes I just get up and go walk around town. When I get tired, I find a place to lie down and go back to sleep. If it's alright with you, Dave, I'll jus' find a nice empty horse stall and sleep there."

"Suits me just fine, Whiskers. We won't be in each other's way."

About midnight on the first night the old prospector spent the night there, Dave woke to the sound of muffled voices. At first, he'd thought some riders must have come in late to stable their horse and Whiskers was taking care of them. However, he didn't hear any noise made by new horses, and he was only hearing one voice.

When Dave went out to check, he found Whiskers talking in his sleep, a half-empty bottle of whiskey lying next to him. "Well at least you blew out the lantern before you passed out," Dave muttered, shaking his head. He could have burned down the whole stable.

That same scene happened just about every night.

*　　　*　　　*

Restless one night, Muley dressed and left Kicks asleep in their room. He walked over to the livery, figuring to chat with Dave for a while if the boy was still up. Upon entering the stable, he saw there was no light in the office, so he turned to leave. That's when he heard a man's voice coming from out of the darkness.

Unable to see well, Muley moved cautiously forward. He narrowed his eyes, seeing the silhouette of a post with a lantern hanging from it. As he lit the lantern, he heard the voice again, but this time he recognized it as someone talking in their sleep. He relaxed when he saw the still form curled in an empty stall, sure he'd just found some drunk sleeping one off. As he turned to leave, he heard the sleeping man mumble, "Check … the Guardian."

Muley turned back to look at the old man. "What did you say?" But he was still asleep, so Muley started to leave again. Then, he heard the old man repeat. "Check … the Guardian."

Bewildered, Muley said, "Check what guardian, old timer? To his surprise, the old man answered. "The Gulch, check the Guardian of the Gulch."

Muley laughed. "You better give up the booze, old timer, before you start seeing snakes." After a few minutes of silence, Muley figured that was all the old man was going to say, so he blew the light out and hung the lantern back on the post and left the livery.

The next morning, Dave was up and had coffee made by five thirty.

Whiskers came in the office, his nose lifted, sniffing. "Coffee smells mighty good."

"Just in time, Whiskers. Sit down and I'll pour us a cup."

The old man wiped his mouth on his shirtsleeve. "Thanks."

Dave poured them both a cup, and they sat down at the table. Whiskers pulled a pint bottle out of his pocket. "You want a little nip in your coffee?"

"Sure." Dave pushed his cup across the table.

Whiskers poured him a jigger, then poured himself a *healthier* jigger. Taking a big swig, he made a face and said, "Man, that's what I call good coffee."

CHAPTER 12

Kicks and Muley were sitting in the Silver Spoon doing some serious damage to a breakfast of salt pork, eggs and taters, with sourdough biscuits and gravy, topped off with Arbuckle's coffee, black and steaming hot.

Between bites, Muley asked, "What you think about the way Dave braced Buford yesterday, Kicks?"

"Well, I think if we hadn't been there, they woulda carried one of 'em out feet first."

Muley nodded. "Yep, that kid sure ain't afraid to yank that hogleg out of leather."

Kicks washed a bite of food down with a sip of coffee. "That's for sure. But that's what worries me … him becoming trigger-happy."

"Yeah, I know."

They finished their breakfast in silence. They had just paid Cathy for their breakfast when they saw Bob Jensen walk in, flanked by Art Boswell and Blackjack Ketchum.

"Wow," Muley said. "Look what the cat just drug in."

"Yep, and you know what my pappy always says about that, don't you?"

Muley laughed. "Go ahead, Kicks, tell me."

"'When the cat's away … the mice will play.'"

"And that supposed to mean…?" Muley asked.

"It means," Kicks replied. "While Bob and his two main watchdogs are here in town, we're gonna be out snooping around his doghouse."

"Darn good idea, Kicks."

"After Bob and his cohorts eat breakfast, they'll probably go over to the Golden Nugget and try to drink the place dry. Come on, partner, let's ride."

The two cowpokes left the Silver Spoon and walked over to the stable to get their horses. When they got there, Dave was in the office working on paperwork. He looked up from his desk when they stepped inside. "Hey, cowpokes, got the coffee pot on. Sit down and have a cup!"

"Love to, Dave, but me and Kicks are headed out to the Running J spread to do some looking around. We just stopped to say howdy and get our horses."

Dave laughed. "Did you get permission from Bob?"

Kicks chuckled. "Saw Bob come in with Art and Blackjack over to the café. Figured it was a good time to go out to his place and do some snooping around."

Dave shoved his papers aside. "I can have my new helper take care of the place for a while. Could you use an extra gun? You never know how many hornets you might stir up when you go poking around in their nest."

"Damn," Muley said. "You musta been talking to Kicks' pappy." He shrugged as he glanced over at Kicks. "I don't see a problem with you taggin' along, if it's okay with Kicks."

Kicks gave one nod. "Okay with me. In fact, might even save some time since Dave knows the country around here."

Dave got up from his chair and hurried to the office door. He opened it and hollered, "Hey, Whiskers, come in here a minute." While they were waiting for Whiskers, Dave grabbed his gun belt and slung it around his waist, buckled it, then adjusted it in place.

"What's up?" the old-timer said, peeking his head through the door.

"I want you to meet some friends of mine, Kicks Burks and Muley Gentry. Cowpokes, meet my helper, Whiskers."

Muley greeted the old prospector with a handshake. "Howdy, Whiskers." He recognized him as the old man he'd seen talking in his asleep in the horse stall, but decided to keep it to himself.

"Howdy, gents," Whiskers said. "Say, ain't you two the cowpokes who shot it out with those Running J gunmen?"

"Yeah, well," Muley said, "neither me nor Kicks ever killed a man that didn't need killing. Or at least wasn't trying to kill us."

Whiskers chuckled, wiping his hand down his full beard.

Dave said, "Whiskers, I'm gonna take a ride with my friends here. Think you could take care of things here while I'm gone?"

"Sure, Dave, you go on ahead. I can handle things jus' fine."

A few minutes later, the three cowpokes were mounted up and headed south out of town. They followed the winding path of Alder Gulch. After a few minutes, the street narrowed down to a trail. A short distance farther, they came to a huge, twenty-five-foot-tall wooden structure with a large bell in the tower. Looked a bit like a church. Kicks pulled his horse up and stared at the structure.

As Dave and Muley rode up beside him, Kicks motioned towards the building. "What's that for, Dave?"

Dave pushed his hat to the back of his head and shaded his eyes so he could look up at the top of the structure. "Well, you can see the mountains here are covered with trees. About six months ago, we had a forest fire, lost about a third of our town to it. We just recently finished rebuilding."

"Wow," Kicks said. "Fire did a lot of damage to Helena, huh?"

"Yep, terrible thing, but I guess God was with us because we didn't lose a single life. People were hurt, and some folks lost everything they owned, but we came out in pretty good shape. That there building is to help make sure it don't happen again."

Just then a man stuck his head out over the railing of the structure and waved. Dave waved back, "This is manned twenty-four-hours a day. We call it the Guardian of the Gulch."

"That's it!" Muley said. "Check the Guardian ... of the Gulch,"

"What are you talking about, Muley?" Kicks asked.

Muley explained what Whiskers had said in his sleep last night in the horse stall. Then he asked Dave, "Do you have any idea what Whiskers could have meant by it?"

Dave chuckled. "No, can't say as I do. Coulda been dreaming about the fire. It was a terrible thing to see. Impossible to keep it out of your mind."

"Yeah," Muley agreed. "Could explain it."

"We better get moving," Kicks urged. "We're burning daylight."

As they rode past the fire tower, the scenery began to change from densely wooded areas to bare ground with large boulders on both sides of the trail, and prickly pear growing over the hillsides. As the trail narrowed, they rode single file, with Dave in the lead. When the trail widened again, they rode abreast, hard and fast. It was a long ride out to the Running J Ranch. A half-hour later, they stopped for a few minutes to give their horse a rest.

Kicks dismounted, noticing the landscape was changing again. "Looks like some pretty good grassland once you get past the rocks and prickly pear."

"Yeah," Muley agreed. "Reminds me of Kentucky bluegrass."

"Yeah, kinda," Kicks agreed. "I see some bear grass and timothy too." He looked over at Dave. "We're getting real close to the Continental Divide, ain't we?"

"Here in Montana we call it the Great Divide, but yeah, we're getting' close. How did you know?"

"Just have a good sense of direction," Kicks replied. "Never crossed the divide from the Montana side, but I've crossed it from Wyoming, Colorado, and a few other places." He motioned towards the range of mountains that seemed to have no end. "I knew we were close because of the mountain range over there, and by the way the landscape changes from flat prairie to hilly terrain."

Kicks mounted up, and they rode in silence for a few minutes, then Dave pulled his horse to a stop again. They stood abreast as Dave pointed to a densely wooded area a hundred yards up the trail. "That's Helena's heaviest wooded area. The trees start again along the trail here and go all up through the mountain range of the Great Divide. You can see where the trail splits up ahead about a hundred yards or so. We want to follow the trail that veers to the left around the edge of the forest. You can't see it from here because of the trees, but this terrain will get hillier, and you'll see a lot more rocky cliffs."

As they moved forward, Dave continued to explain, "This trail will wind around and through those hills. You'll be able to see the Running J Ranch house and outbuildings on the other side, down in the valley."

The three cowpokes started up the trail again, following the winding trail in and around the boulders and cliffs. They stopped on a summit overlooking the valley where the Running J Ranch sat.

"Pretty nice layout," Muley said.

"Yep," Dave agreed. "Sits in a nice grassy meadow, well protected on all sides by the hills and rocky cliffs."

Kicks dismounted and opened his saddlebags. "I wanna get a good look at this ranch and its surroundings." He opened the flap and pulled out a long brass cylinder from a leather sheath.

"That an old pirate's spyglass, isn't it?" Muley asked. "Should do the trick."

Dave acted surprised. "Almost looks like a surveyor's hand level."

"Yep," Kicks said. "They work the same way, serve the same purpose. I think this old telescope came first though, invented in 1606." Kicks put the telescope to his eye and carefully viewed the ranch house. "Like my pappy always says, 'When the cat's away, the mice will play.' I don't see a living soul moving around anyplace." Kicks handed the spyglass to Muley, who looked through and then handed it to Dave.

Dave looked through and then handed the glass back to Kicks. "I didn't see anyone stirring down there either. Some horses running loose in a big corral, and two saddled horses tied at a hitch rail by the house."

Kicks raised the glass to his eye again to check their back trail. "Yep, that's all I saw too, but I think we got company coming up behind us. I see … a lot of dust rising up back there." Kicks closed up the telescope and put it back in its sheath, replacing it in his saddlebag. Mounting up, he nudged his horse forward. "Probably best if we get off the trail and take cover behind some of those boulders. We really got no excuse for being here on the Running J. Don't know how many riders are in that bunch either."

Dave and Muley followed suit, reining their horses away from the trail to get behind some huge boulders. They dismounted and made ready to quiet their horses in case they tried to nicker.

About ten minutes later, they heard the rumble of approaching horses pounding against the rocky trail. A few minutes more and the riders went thundering by. After the dust settled, the trio emerged from behind the rocks and boulders. Kicks again took the telescope from his saddlebags and viewed the situation. "That's Bob Jensen, and let's see … eight … no, ten riders with him." Kicks handed the glass to Dave. "See how many of those fellas you recognize."

Looking through the glass, Dave said, "There's Bob, Art Boswell, Blackjack Ketchum, Jake Terrell, Billy Thompson. But I don't recognize the other five guys." Dave handed the glass back to Kicks, and he put it back in its sheath.

"I'm not positive because I didn't get a good look at their faces," Kicks said, "but I think one of them is Charlie Heart. Another one is his right-hand man, Bill Anderson, also known as Bloody Bill. And if I'm right about that, those other three men are followers of his."

"Who's Charlie Heart?" Dave asked.

Kicks blew softly through his lips before he answered. "It's not well known, but Charlie Heart is another name for William Clark Quantrill, one of his aliases."

"You really get around, don't you?" Muley said.

"Yeah, well, like my pappy always says, 'A rolling stone gathers no moss.' And I sure don't aim to have no moss growing from my but-tocks."

"If it is Quantrill," Dave said, "what do you think he's doing around here ... with Bob Jensen?"

Kicks shook his head. "Darned if I know, but now I'm sure glad we rode out here and saw 'em ride in. We don't need any big surprises like that jumping out of the woodwork at us."

Frustrated, Muley asked, "What do we do now?"

"First thing," Kicks said, "we need to get back to town and put our heads together, try to come up with a plan. We need to find out what these guys are up to, where it's goin' to happen, and why. And probably more importantly, *when* it's goin' to happen."

"Yeah," Dave said. "We'd better get back to town, I don't want to leave old Whiskers by himself too long."

Kicks and Muley agreed. The trio led their mounts out of the rocks and back onto the trail where they mounted up and started back for town.

CHAPTER 13

Oscar Bates rode into town hell-bent for leather. He pulled up at the hitch rail in front of the jail, dismounted, and ran inside the sheriff's office. "Boss," he shouted. He stopped short when he noticed there was a woman present, and Bob was engaged in conversation with her. Oscar stammered, "Ah … sorry, ma'am, sheriff, you go ahead. My business can wait."

Cal narrowed his eyes at Oscar a moment, then hurried the woman along, "Yes, ma'am, I'll certainly check into it." He took her gently by the elbow as he walked her to the door. "Now don't you worry. I'll take care of it."

The woman gathered up her skirts and scurried out the door.

As soon as she was out of sight, Cal turned to Oscar. "Now what the hell do you mean by busting into my office and interrupting a conversation between me and a citizen?" Then he laughed. "Thank God you came in when you did, Oscar. You saved the day."

"Boss, you know how you told us to keep a watch on Bob Jensen, to observe him and report to you?"

"Yeah, go on."

"Well, me, Dutch and Buford, we been taking turns every couple days to ride out to Bob's ranch. We hide in the rocks above his place to keep watch. Well, I was out there bright and early this morning, and guess what? We ain't the only ones watchin' old Bob." The deputy paused, as if Cal would actually try to guess who else might be out there.

"Well, out with it, Oscar," Cal demanded. "Finish your report."

"Okay, it's like this. I just got there and settled in to watch the ranch, and well … I saw dust rising up from the trail behind me, so I moved up in the rocks where I could see better. I saw ten riders come burning up the trail. Bob and four of his men were in the lead, and right behind them were five more riders. And guess what? I ain't for sure, but I think the other five riders were Quantrill and four of *his* men."

This surprised Cal. "Are you sure about it being Quantrill? Do you even know him?"

"Only by seeing a reward poster of him one time, but I'm sure it was him."

Cal nodded, knowing Oscar was probably right. He knew Bob had once rode with Quantrill and his Raiders. "Good job, Oscar. Now get out of here so I can think."

"Wait, boss, there's more. I saved this part till last. Right before Bob and those riders came through, I saw three other riders leave the trail and hide in the rocks. It was Kicks Burks, Muley Gentry, and Dave Galveston. They was watching Bob and the riders too. They didn't see me, but I was close enough to hear what they was saying. They knew it was Quantrill, and they said one of the men with him was the gunslinger, Bloody Bill Anderson."

Cal began to swear, then lapsed into a moment of silence." He looked over at Oscar. "Damn good job. Now get the hell outta here."

Oscar left, looking quite pleased with himself. Cal reached into his desk drawer and got out a bottle of whiskey and a glass. After filling the glass, he took a sip of the brown liquid, then reached inside his vest pocket and took out a cigar. "Something about a glass of whiskey and a good cigar," he murmured, his expression thoughtful.

*   *   *

Kicks, Muley, and Dave rode straight to the livery stable after they got back to town. Whiskers came out to meet them, taking charge of their horses while they talked for a few minutes. "We need to do some planning," Dave said. "Come on in the office and I'll put the coffee pot on."

"Sounds good," Kicks agreed. "But I need somethin' stronger to wash the trail dust out of my mouth. How bout we mosey over to the Golden Nugget and get a drink? I'll buy."

Muley agreed to that, but Dave declined. "Sounds good, fellas, but I gotta stick around here for a while to make sure Whiskers got everything cleaned up."

"Okay," Kicks replied. "Muley and I will be over to the saloon if you wanna join us later. If we don't see you there, we'll drop by later tonight for a friendly game of cards, and we can talk more then."

"Sounds like a winner, but either way, I'll see you guys later."

*   *   *

Bob Jensen, as well as most of the other ranchers, usually stopped in at the telegraph office when they came to town. Bob had been keeping in touch with Quantrill by wire, and the last time he had gotten a wire from him, it read as follows:

Bob Jensen.

"I'll be in Helena in three days. I am only bringing four men with me, so I want you to meet us at the livery stable around two o'clock. Bring four of your men with you in case there is trouble. See you in three days."

Charlie Heart.

Bob had not liked this news one bit, but he didn't have a choice. Three days later, at the appointed time according to the wire he had received, Bob met Quantrill with four of his best men. Art Boswell, Blackjack Ketchum, Jake Terrell, and Billy Thompson.

With Quantrill was Bloody Bill Anderson, Frank Beard, Walter Miller, and Morgan Maddox. Counting Bob and Quantrill, there were ten men meeting at the livery.

Ten gunmen strong, they thundered boldly out of town and along the trail through the prairie and the hills and rocks, never thinking that anyone would have guts to try to trail them. When they rode into the yard of the Running J Ranch, a couple of Bob's ranch hands came out and took charge of the horses.

Bob and Quantrill dismissed the men to do whatever they wanted while they went inside the house to talk. Some of the men went in the bunkhouse to get the cook to fix them some chow, while others threw their bedrolls out on the ground and went straight to sleep.

All the men got along except for Bloody Bill Anderson, Quantrill's top gun, and Blackjack Ketchum, Bob's top gun.

These two chose to check their weapons and keep an eye on each other.

Inside the house, over a bottle of mescal, Bob and Quantrill began their talk. Bob patiently explained that he had never been able to locate the document that was needed to proclaim him the owner of the Last Chance Gulch gold mine. He had turned Isaiah Gentry's old ranch house inside out and could never find it. "I ordered Sheriff Tidwell to have his deputies watch everyone in town who is related to, or had been friends with, Isaiah Gentry. I even managed to get Dave Galveston, Howard Durmhill's grandson, a job at Oatman's livery stable so I can keep an eye on him too."

Quantrill slammed his fist down on the table. "Dammit, Bob, that's not good enough. Not *nearly* good enough."

"What the hell do you expect me to do?"

After a moment, Quantrill took a deep breath and slowly exhaled. "In all fairness to you, Bob, I realize your hands are kind of tied here. Everyone around here knows you, so you can't get really tough with anyone. Same goes for your sheriff, Cal Tidwell." He paused again while lighting up a cigar. After offering one to Bob, he continued, "That's why I'm here, and brought some of my best men. I'm gonna take over this operation. We'll get results. You and I will own that gold mine within a month. The whole damn town will be under our control."

Bob remained silent for a minute. It was him who'd learned the four Georgians had sold the claim to Isaiah Gentry for a lousy fifty bucks. It was only right that the gold mine and town should belong to him alone. However, Bob figured he could let Quantrill and his men do the dirty work to find the paper he needed, then somehow figure out a way to cut Quantrill out of it. Bob didn't plan to share with him or anyone else.

"Okay," Bob said, "here's the deal. You and your men can stay here and see what you can do to get hold of that document to give us ownership to the claim. However, you need to run anything you do by me first. My name needs to be kept out of it completely. Agreed?"

Quantrill scowled, obviously not pleased by the terms. "Okay, Bob, it's a deal. I'll need a headquarters to work from. In fact, I'll want to set up two places, just in case someone gets nosey and tries to watch our movements. Here and somewhere near town. That old, abandoned ranch house outside of town will do." He stared hard at Bob, as though daring him to disagree.

"Fine by me, Quantrill. I like my privacy, though. You and your men can use one of the bunkhouses. It has all the pleasures of home."

The two agreed and sealed the deal with a drink and a handshake.

Quantrill spent the rest of the afternoon getting himself and his men settled into the unused bunkhouse, then filled them in on his plans. The bunkhouse was a perfect setup. It would allow him and his men to keep an eye on Bob and his men. Wouldn't be long before he took full control of this operation.

*   *   *

A week after Quantrill had moved into his headquarters at the Running J Ranch, he sent two men into town to nose around. One of the men was his top gunman, Bloody Bill Anderson. The other was Bob's top man, Blackjack Ketchum. It would keep Bob happy, and Ketchum was no stranger to the town's people. They feared him, which would work to make them more cooperative.

It was midmorning when Bloody Bill and Blackjack rode into town and pushed their way through the swinging doors of the Golden Nugget Saloon. They stopped just inside the door, expressions cold as they looked around, noting how many men were in there and where they were seated or standing. That was the custom of most gunmen, especially those with a price on their head. José Martinez and Sammy Galveston were behind the bar, waiting on several men who were lined up to get their first drink of the day. There were men seated at four of the tables. Two working girls were also at one of the tables, trying to make a deal with a couple of cowpokes.

Whiskers stood at the far end of the bar where no one would notice him, having a drink. He'd retired from being a drunkard when Dave took an interest in him, giving him a job at the livery stable and a warm place to stay. He watched as the two gunmen elbowed in at the bar. José moved down to wait on them. They ordered whiskey and began asking questions.

Sammy motioned for José to go wait on the men at the tables while he moved down to take care of the two gunmen.

"This town called Helena?" Bloody Bill asked, as if he didn't already know.

"Yep," Blackjack answered. "I really don't know much about it. Not been here long. Spend most of my time out at the ranch. Sammy here could probably tell you everything there is to know about this town. Right, Sammy? Oh, by the way, Sammy, this is Bill Anderson. New hand out at the Running J."

Sammy nodded. "I been around here for quite a spell."

Bill took a drink of whiskey and wiped his mouth with the back of a gloved hand. "I heard someone struck gold around here, and that's how this town got started. That right?"

"Yep," Sammy said. "Gold was discovered in that gulch right out there in the middle of Main Street. It's called the Last Chance Gulch. Where it all got started. Guys called the four Georgians struck gold there, right smack dab in the center of town. Gold mine is still being worked."

"Who owns it?" Bill asked.

Sammy shrugged. "No one knows."

The conversation went on for some time, with Sammy skirting around the direct questions that were being asked. Finally, the two gunmen took a bottle and went to a table to talk.

Sammy moved down the bar to where Whiskers was standing. "Why don't you go see if you can get close enough to hear what they're sayin', Whiskers."

"Give me a bottle of whiskey," Whiskers said, nodding. Pretending to be drunk, he took the bottle and a glass, then staggered over to a table next to Blackjack and Bill and sat down. When he noticed the two gunmen glaring at him, he turned the bottle up and took a big drink, then fell face forward across the table, pretending to be passed out.

"Well," Blackjack said, "we didn't learn anything from the bartender."

"Yeah, you're right about that," Bloody Bill sneered. "We don't get some answers 'fore long, we'll turn up the heat. When people start dying around here from lead poison, you can bet their tongues will loosen up purty damn quick."

Whiskers lay there on the table in a supposed drunken stupor, until the two gunmen got up from their table and left the saloon, then he went over to tell Sammy what he'd heard.

Sammy rubbed the back of his neck. "Sounds like big trouble coming our way. Sure glad Kicks and Muley are here. They're just about our only hope. You better go find them and tell 'em what you heard."

"Yep," Whiskers said, and headed over to the livery stable.

Dave had just finished cleaning up around the stalls and was sitting in the office taking a break when Whiskers came in. He could tell something was wrong just by looking at the old man. "What's up, Whiskers?"

Whiskers sat down and told him about the conversation he'd overheard between the two gunslingers.

"Who were they?"

"One of 'em was Blackjack Ketchum, Bob's man. I never saw the other one before, but his name's Bill Anderson. Blackjack said he was one of Bob Jensen's new hired hands. Sure weren't no cowhand though. Had all the markings of a real gunslinger."

Dave thought momentarily about what to do. "We need to let Kicks and Muley know about this." He tapped his fingers on the desk a moment. "They weren't at the saloon?"

"Nope."

"Okay. You stay here. It's lunchtime. I'll go on over to the Silver Spoon and try to catch them there." Dave knew this situation could get bad real quick. He left the stable and headed for the café, but then changed his mind. He'd go to the hotel first and see if they were there. That would give him a chance to check up on his grandma, make sure she was okay.

CHAPTER 14

ave entered the hotel lobby and noticed Mary Frances was behind the lobby desk. He hesitated when he saw her, his face growing warm. She always affected him this way.

Mary Frances smiled at him brightly. "Hello, Dave. If you're here to see your grandma, she's upstairs in her room. I've come in to relieve her for lunch."

"Um, thank you, Miss Mary. I'll go right on up." Despite his best efforts to get away, she managed to stop him.

"Why don't you stop by and see me sometime?"

"Why, I'd like that, Miss Mary."

"Dave, please call me Wendy. Everyone else does."

"Okay, Wendy, I sure would like that." He stood there awkwardly for a moment. "Well, I'll see you later." He tipped his hat to her and was gone in a flash. He made it upstairs to Grandma Tilly's room in record time and rapped lightly on her door. "It's me, Grandma. Dave."

She opened the door and hugged him. Only then did he realize he'd left his gun belt on. When she stepped back to get a good look at him, he felt awkward and embarrassed. He knew she hated guns. Grandpa Howard had lived and died by the gun. Instinctively, he began to apologize. "Sorry, Grandma, I—"

She held up her hand to quiet him. "Shush, Dave, just stand there and let me look at you."

He stood there with his hat in his hand, wondering what she was doing. After a long minute that felt like an hour, she smiled at him. "My, but you look just like your Grandpa Howard. I used to call him Howie." She laughed, "I was the only one allowed to call him that." She shook off the moment. "I'm sorry, Dave. Come in. I'll fix you something to eat."

"No, I don't have time to eat, Grandma. Look, I know you don't like guns, but—"

She shushed him again. "Yes, Dave, I do hate guns. However, I think I was wrong to disallow you to have one. I guess I'm glad to see you disobeyed me. It takes men like you and your Grandpa Howard to rid this country of evil men like those that killed him. You make this country safe for decent folks. Only … please be careful."

Dave nodded, then changed the subject, asking how she'd been doing since he went to work at the livery. Before he left, he told her he would drop in from time to time to visit, and she knew how to reach him if she ever needed anything.

He went next to Kicks and Muley's room and knocked on the door. When he got no answer, he figured they were probably at the Silver Spoon. It was past lunch time, and his own stomach was beginning to gnaw at his backbone.

Kicks and Muley were not in the café either, but Dave was hungry, so he sat down at the counter. When Cathy delivered his food, she lingered to talk for a minute. "You seen Muley or Kicks today?" Dave asked.

"Why yes," she replied. "You just missed them by about twenty minutes."

"Thanks, Cathy, they're probably over to the Golden Nugget."

She smiled and nodded. "Probably."

After eating, he paid for his food and went over to the saloon. He stepped inside and immediately spotted Kicks and Muley at their usual table over in a dark corner. He walked over and sat down.

After exchanging greetings, Muley caught Sammy's attention and motioned for him to bring over another glass.

"Thanks, Sammy," Dave said. "Did you tell these guys about Blackjack and Bill yet?"

"No, haven't had time. But if you talked to Whiskers, then you know the whole story, so you can tell them yourself."

"Okay."

Sammy left their table then and went back behind the bar.

"What was that all about?" Kicks asked.

"This morning, Blackjack Ketchum … you guys know who he is, don't you?"

"Yeah," Muley agreed. "We know Blackjack. He's one of Bob Jensen's top gun hands."

Dave nodded, his lips pressed tight together. "Well, he came in here this morning with another gunman he introduced as Bill Anderson. He told Sammy that Bill was another hired ranch hand of Bob Jensen's, and the two of them started asking Sammy all sorts of questions, most of which were about the gold strike here in Helena. Sammy didn't share much. When they didn't get the answers they wanted, they took a bottle and went to a table away from the other people. Whiskers sat at a table near enough to overhear them and pretended to be passed out drunk."

"What'd he hear?" Muley asked.

"Blackjack said something about turning up the heat if they didn't start getting some answers. Said folks' tongues would loosen up real quick when the lead started to fly."

Muley blew softly through his lips, sitting back in his chair. "Sounds to me like they've already turned up the heat."

"Yep," Kicks agreed. "Gonna get a lot hotter when *we* get involved. Like my pappy always says, 'When you put that branding iron in the fire, make sure it's hot enough to burn deep so the hair won't grow over the scar.'"

Dave smiled. "Your pappy sounds like a right smart man. Sounds like something my Grandpa Howard would say."

There was silence for a while, then Muley said, "Seems to me like we're in a game of chess with these crooks, and we're the pawns."

Kicks laughed. "You know, Muley, you're exactly right. Pawns are the least powerful pieces on the chessboard, but if I remember the rules of the game, they also have the potential to become equal to the most powerful pieces. We put our heads together, we'll not only become equal, but more powerful than our opponents."

"That's well and good," Dave agreed, "but how are we gonna do all this maneuvering. We can't even keep track of each other. I had to run all over the place to catch up to you two guys today."

Kicks nodded. "You're right, Dave. We need to get organized. Can do that by setting up a headquarters, a place where we can meet and talk. We need to know where each other are at all times."

"How about my office over at the livery stable? That can be our headquarters," Dave said.

Both Kicks and Muley agreed. "Yeah," Muley said. "If anyone starts nosing around, we'll just be there havin' a friendly game of cards."

"Then it's settled," Dave said. "Our official meeting place will be in the office at the livery. I need to get back over there now, so I'll see you guys later … at my office … our headquarters." He grinned.

*   *   *

Bloody Bill Anderson and Blackjack Ketchum stood on the boardwalk and rolled a cigarette. After touching his smoke with a Lucifer, Blackjack took in a long pull and inhaled deeply, then slowly exhaled. Blackjack, being a Yankee, could see Southerner written all over Bill. He bet he even still carried confederate bills in his pocket, just in case. "You're south of the Mason-Dixon line, right?" Blackjack said.

Bill took another drag from his cigarette. "Yep."

Irritated, Blackjack asked, "You like riding with Quantrill?"

Bill tossed his smoke to the ground and stepped on it. "You got a problem with that, Yankee man?"

Blackjack ground his cigarette out. "No. We're both riding the outlaw trail, so I guess it don't make no difference." Neither of these men trusted the other, but for now, they knew they would have to get along. Blackjack looked up street, seeing few people walking up and down the boardwalk. A couple horses were standing three legged at the hitch rail in front of the saloon. "Well, we're supposed to be gathering what information we can. But so far we've drawn a blank. You got any ideas, Bill?"

Bill grinned. "The sheriff's on our side, right?"

"Yep."

Bill laughed. "Follow me." They walked down the boardwalk past a couple doors. Bill stopped and pointed to a farmer who had just pulled his wagon up to the hitch rail. "See that sodbuster standing by his wagon?"

"Yep," Blackjack replied.

Bill laughed again. "See the sheriff standing over there on the other side of the street?"

"Yeah."

"Well, this is where we're gonna start to turn up the heat. Hey, sodbuster!" he called to the farmer.

The farmer looked up, "You talkin' to me?"

"Yeah, I'm talkin' to you. Do you see any other sodbusters standing around?"

"Look, mister," the farmer said, "I ain't here for any trouble. I just wanna get my supplies and get back home."

Bill pulled a six-gun from the back of his waistband and laid it on the end post of the hitch rail. "There you go, sodbuster. Pick it up."

"No. I ain't got no beef with you, mister."

"I said pick it up. I can see in your eyes you hate me, don't you?"

"No! I don't hate you. I don't even *know* you!"

"Sure you do, sodbuster. Bet you wanna kill me."

The farmer was getting alarmed. He knew this gunslinger wanted to kill him, though he didn't know why. Blackjack stood watching, fascinated. He didn't care if Bill killed the farmer or not, though he didn't understand why he'd want to waste a bullet on a worthless piece of trash like this.

The farmer looked around, catching the attention of Sheriff Cal Tidwell standing on the other side of the street. "Sheriff!" he shouted. "Can't you see this man is gonna kill me?"

Sheriff Tidwell turned his head and ducked into the doorway behind him, ignoring the scene being played out.

Bill laughed, and one could hear the sadistic humor in it. "No one here to help you, sodbuster. Better pick up that gun."

"No! Please, mister!"

Without looking away from the farmer, Bill said, "Blackjack, count to three, slowly." To the farmer, he said, "I'm not gonna go for my gun till my partner here says three. Just to show you I'm a good sport, you can go for your gun any time after he says one."

Blackjack smiled and said, "One." He could see the indecision in the farmer's eyes. He knew if he didn't go for the gun, he would certainly die. If he did go for the gun, he might have a slim chance.

"Two!"

With trembling hands, the farmer reached out as fast as he could to grab the gun. Blackjack was surprised to see that Bill kept his word. The farmer's hand was on the gun. Bill just stood there, motionless.

"Three!"

The farmer had the gun up and pointed at Bill, his face determined as his finger tightening on the trigger. Suddenly, in a hundredth of a second, Bill's hand flashed to his side. That big Smith and Wesson .44 was out of its holster and roared once, then five more times. The first bullet hit between the farmers eyes, and would have been enough, but as Bill was reloading, he laughed and calmly explained, "The last five slugs were just for target practice."

Blackjack laughed, thinking about how the sodbuster's body had jerked after the impact of each bullet before he hit the ground.

Immediately, a few people came running over to see what was going on. One of them said, "I saw the whole thing. That poor farmer didn't have a chance. A couple more people chimed in, agreeing with him. About that time, Sheriff Tidwell stepped out of the doorway he'd ducked into. He elbowed his way through the gathering crowd.

"What's going on here? What's all the shooting about?" He looked at the two gunslingers as though he didn't recognize them. "Which one of you did the shooting?"

"I did, Sheriff," Bill answered.

Cal looked at Blackjack. "You saw the whole thing?"

"Yep, the sodbuster challenged Bill. Bill tried to talk him out of it, but he went for his gun. Bill had to kill him. Had no choice."

"That's not true, Sheriff," someone yelled.

Cal and the two gunmen look at the crowd. "Who said that?" Cal demanded. With all three gunmen looking menacingly at the crowd, everyone fell silent. Cal paused for just a second, and then said, "Well then, I have to take your word for it. Self-defense. You're free to go."

Blackjack walked over and picked up the gun. After spinning the cylinder, he gave Bill a surly look. "Hell, Bill, I really thought you was givin' the sodbuster a chance. This gun ain't even loaded."

Bill shrugged, then laughed. "Purdy damn good trick, ain't it? Can't lose, even if that farmer had managed to get the gun up and pull the trigger." The two gunmen sneered at the crowd and walked off, laughing. When they got to the hitch rail where their horses were tied, Bill took a long red ribbon from his saddlebag and began to tie a knot in it.

"What's that for?"

Bill held the ribbon up so Blackjack could see it, "Oh, that's how I earned my nickname, Bloody Bill. You see, each one of these knots stands for a Yankee I killed."

"You are one sadistic bastard. Hope you don't try to add a knot on there for me."

After tying a knot in the ribbon for the killing of the farmer, Bill calmly replaced the red ribbon back in his saddle-bag. "Oh, I have a *few* Yankee friends. You'll know if, or when, your time comes."

This didn't scare Blackjack, but it did put him on his guard.

CHAPTER 15

icks and Muley finished their meal at the Silver Spoon about three in the afternoon, then headed over to the Golden Nugget for a drink. It was a bit early yet, so the saloon didn't have much of a crowd. The two cowpokes went to the bar, where Sammy stood waiting.

"Been able to find out anything about my family or Sheriff Durmhill's murder from your wife, Sam?" Muley asked the bartender.

Sammy shook his head. "No, every time I try to bring up the subject about her pa's death, or anything about the past, Molly clams up. I think she's too scared to talk about it. Anything new happening with you guys?"

Kicks ordered a drink. "Heard about that poor farmer getting shot earlier. You know anything about it?"

"Yeah, people say it was those same two gunmen who came in here this morning. Way I heard, they shot him for no good reason. Sheriff let 'em go too. No one's sayin' much though. Too scared."

Kicks downed his drink. "Guess there's no use talking to the sheriff then. We better get on over to the livery. Dave will be waiting for us."

"Yeah," Muley agreed, then downed his shot of whiskey. "Let's go."

"If you hear anything more, you'll know where to find us," Kicks said, following Muley out the door.

A few minutes after Muley and Kicks left the saloon, Mayor Harper and Judge Cleveland entered. They looked around, then walked straight up to Sammy. Sammy moved them down the bar a way to give them some privacy. "Howdy, Mayor, Judge. Something wrong?"

In a lowered voice, the judge said, "A few people came in who saw that shooting earlier. We need to do something about this before it gets outta hand."

Sammy shook his head, not sure how he could help. "What do you need me to do?"

"Well," the mayor replied, you know Sheriff Cal sure ain't gonna do anything about this. We figured we'd try to talk to Kicks and Muley, see if they can help."

Sammy smiled, chuckling softly. "Yeah, if anyone can keep the peace around here, it'd be those two fellas. In fact, I think they already have that in mind. You'll find 'em over to the livery stable."

"Thanks, Sammy," the judge said, then they nodded before walking out the door.

Muley and Kicks had barely stepped into Dave's office when the mayor and judge walked in behind them. Surprised to see the two city officials, the three cowpokes greeted them with handshakes.

"Welcome to my office," Dave said. "What can I ... *we* do for you gentleman?"

"We're here on business, fellas, if you got the time to talk," the mayor said.

"Of course," Dave replied. "We were just about to have a cup of Arbuckle's. Care to join us?"

"That'd be great," the mayor said. They each accepted a cup, and then they all sat down to talk business. "I suppose you guys heard about the shooting earlier today."

"Yeah," Muley acknowledged. "We heard about it from Sammy a few minutes ago. Said a farmer got shot down in the street."

"Well, here's what happened," Judge Cleveland said. "Two gunmen from the Running J outfit came into town. They shot the farmer down in cold blood."

After relating a blow by blow detail of the incident, Mayor Harper added, "One of the witnesses saw one of the killers take a red ribbon from his saddlebag and tie a knot in it. Then put it back in his saddlebag."

"That's strange," Dave said.

"Hmmm," Kicks said. "Did anyone know who the two gunmen were?"

"Yes," the mayor said, rubbing his jaw. "Blackjack Ketchum and Bill Anderson."

"That'd be Bloody Bill Anderson," Kicks said. "One of Quantrill's Raiders." He went on to tell about Bloody Bill Anderson and the story behind his red silk ribbon.

Muley filled them in about what they'd seen out at Bob Jensen's ranch.

"This is much worse than we expected," the judge said. "We need to get down to business about why we came here."

"Okay," Dave said, raising his eyebrows.

Mayor Harper shifted himself in his chair, acting nervous. "We've known for quite some time now that our sheriff is working for Bob Jensen. We were going to talk to you about what we could do about him. But now, if Quantrill and his killers are somehow involved, it appears we have a bigger problem than the sheriff."

"Might be that it's all connected," Muley said. "Bob Jensen has the sheriff in his back pocket, and he's also connected to Quantrill. We think this might all have something to do with Sheriff Durmhill's death and the Last Chance gold mine."

The judge cleared his throat. "Well, I don't know how we're supposed to cope with all this."

"Can't you kick Cal out of office, elect someone else?" Dave asked.

"No," the mayor replied. "Whole town's afraid of Bob Jensen and Cal Tidwell. If we try something like that, there'd definitely be more killing of innocent people. We think that's what today's shooting was all about. To scare people so they'd do what they're told. If they find out Quantrill is in with Bob and Cal, there'll be an all-out panic in Helena."

"Well, I know one thing we could do," Kicks said. "Fort Harrison is less than ten miles away. We can send a wire. Have a troop of cavalry soldiers here in just a couple days."

"Actually," Mayor Harper replied, "we already thought of that. We sent a wire to the captain at Fort Harrison. He said by military law, they couldn't do anything for us. There'd have to be a major outbreak of lawlessness before they could intervene."

"Then what would you have us do?" Muley asked.

The judge hesitated, biting at his lower lip. "Like we said earlier, we can't just kick Sheriff Tidwell out of office. That would take time, and in the meanwhile, they would really start terrorizing the people of this town. However..." He looked over at Kicks and Muley. "...we can swear one of you into office as U.S. Marshal, and the other as a Deputy U.S. Marshal. You could work undercover ... if you wish, and if push comes to shove, you guys, as U.S. Marshals, could override the sheriff's power and take charge of the situation no matter what the case might be."

Dave became excited. "Yes, I believe that's the answer! There was a pause for a minute where no one said a word. "Well? You guys are gonna accept the office, aren't ya?" Dave insisted.

Kicks and Muley exchanged a look. "Guess that's one way to handle it," Kicks agreed. "What do you think, Muley?"

Muley nodded, his expression thoughtful. "Would give us some authority, all right. Guess I vote we accept. Kicks, you take the position of Marshal. Since you did a stretch as sheriff one time, you know more about the law than I do."

"Okay, I accept."

Both the mayor and judge grinned, looking relieved. The mayor reached in his vest pocket and produced two U.S. Marshall badges. "Here we go, gentleman. We might as well make it official. As of right now, let the ceremony begin."

"How did you know we'd accept?" Kicks asked.

"Because we know what kind of men you are, and we also know you're damn good with your guns. If anyone can do this job, it's you two guys."

Kicks and Muley accepted the marshal badges, and Judge Cleveland performed the ceremony, with Mayor Harper and Dave Galveston serving as witnesses.

"One thing, though," Kicks said. "We don't want the news of this to get out yet."

"That's okay with us," the judge said. "The badges and the ceremony are official. It's up to you as to when you want it to be public knowledge."

*　　　*　　　*

The next morning, after they finished an early breakfast, the two cowboys stepped into their headquarters at Dave's livery stable. "We have to organize ourselves and make plans about how we're goin' to manage this situation," Kicks said.

"This is why I suggested you be the marshal, and I'll be your deputy," Muley said, chuckling. "We're in this thing together, the three of us, so how do you suggest we play this out?"

Dave said, "Well, I'm impressed and flattered, fellas, but I don't see how I can be of service."

"Muley's right, Dave," Kicks said. "You've lived here your whole life. You know this town and everyone in it. And you can help us later if we need it with your gun."

Dave grinned. "Okay, I'm in! Sit down and I'll pour us some coffee. We can start making plans."

"For now," Kicks said, "we take turns patrolling the streets in town. At night, we should patrol in pairs. That's gonna get tiresome real fast because there's only the three of us."

Suddenly a voice from behind them spoke up, "Four, there's four of us." They all jerked around to see Whiskers standing there. "Count me in on this, fellas. It's my town too."

They all nodded their agreement, so Kicks said, "Okay, Whiskers, welcome to the club." The old man sat down at the table, and Dave poured him some coffee.

"Now," Whiskers said, "let's get on with the business at hand."

The foursome patrolled the streets of Helena for four days without any problems. They decided at night, Dave or Whiskers would team up with Muley or Kicks, since they held the badges.

On the fifth night of their patrol, Kicks and Dave were on duty. They could hear the usual sounds of laughter coming from the Golden Nugget, and a woman singing accompanied by a tinny- sounding piano. As they approached the batwing doors, a shot rang out.

"Okay, partner," Kicks said, glancing over at Dave to see if he could detect a hint of fear. "Sounds like we got trouble. You ready?"

Dave's voice was steady as he answered, "I'm ready. Let's go."

Kicks pushed the swinging doors open and stepped inside with Dave on his heels. With the first glance, Kicks recognized a scene that he'd witnessed many times before. Just prior to their entering the saloon, there had been several men lined up at the bar. Two of the men had got into an argument, and shots were fired. One man now lay dead on the floor, and the other man stood holding a smoking six-shooter.

The other men at the bar had stepped back to give the gunmen room, and to get out of their line of fire. To Kicks, the one thing odd about this scene was that the fellow holding the gun didn't look the part of a gunslinger. He was a young man, barely out of his teens, wearing bib overalls, had blond hair and blue eyes, about six-foot tall and slender in the waist. Looked more like a farmer than a gunslinger.

As Kicks and Dave walked up to where the action was, no one paid any attention to them. For all anyone knew, they were just two curious cowpokes.

Suddenly, one man stepped away from the crowd that had gathered, and said, "You stinkin' sodbuster. You shot my partner." Three other gunmen stepped up behind him and began cursing the young man too.

Kicks knew if he didn't interfere, they were going to kill the young man. "Okay," he said, "that's enough. Nobody move till we get this straightened out."

The spokesman for the group—who was hell-bent on killing the young man—turned to Kicks. "Who the hell are you, drifter? Think you can stick your nose in on something that ain't your business?"

Ignoring the question about his authority, for he was not wearing his badge. Kicks said, "You know who I am, and I know who you are. You're one of Bob Jensen's gunmen." Turning to the young man, Kicks said, "Howdy, stranger. You mind telling me who you are and what happened here?"

The young man holstered his six-gun, a Colt .44. "Name's Caleb, Caleb Jackson, and I was just standing here having a drink when these dudes came in and started making jokes about me. When I told them to shut up, the one on the floor there drew down on me. That's what happened."

Kicks looked around. "Anyone else see what happened?" No one from that side of the bar spoke up, so Sammy said, "We all saw it. Happened exactly how the boy … that is Caleb, said."

The Running J gunmen were starting to get more rowdy, acting like they wanted revenge. The spokesman cursed at Kicks, "Stand out of the way, drifter, or go for leather."

"Don't have to end like this," Kicks said. "Let's talk about it, get things straightened out." Kicks barely finished speaking when the man went for his gun. Kicks' .44 came out and up quicker than a wink of the eye, and one bullet sent the gunman crashing to the floor beside his dead comrade.

They didn't have to look to know he was dead. For multiple reasons, Kicks turned his back to the dead gunman's comrades to talk to the young man. He trusted Dave was fast enough and dependable enough to watch his back. Plus, he knew Sammy already had his hands on the sawed-off shotgun that he kept under the counter and would blow away anyone who tried to shoot him.

As Kicks turned, he had a clear view of everyone behind the bar in the mirror. Just as he figured, one of the men went for his gun. However, before the back shooter could clear leather, Dave's six-gun bucked in his hand and that gunman joined the other two dead men on the floor. Slowly and calmly, Kicks turned back to face Dave, the kid looking a little pale. "Good job, Dave, I knew you'd cover my back."

Dave just grinned and nodded.

About that time, Sheriff Tidwell and his deputies walked in. "Hey, what's going on in here?" His gaze landed on the three dead gunmen on the floor, then he looked up at Kicks and Dave. "Guess I'm gonna have to arrest you again, cowboy."

Before he could finish his threat, Sammy brought the sawed-off shotgun up on top of the bar. "Hold on there, Sheriff. One of those dead Running J riders started the whole thing. He picked a fight with this young man, Caleb, and Caleb outdrew him. Kicks and Dave here just tried to calm everyone down. But that other gunman pulled a gun on Kicks, and Kicks shot him. Then, while Kicks' wasn't looking, the third gunman drew and was about to shoot him in the back, so Dave shot him. It was all fair and square on Kicks' and Dave's part."

As Cal looked around, several men from the crowd yelled, "That's right, Sheriff."

Cal grimaced, knowing his hands were tied for now. "Okay, the rest of you Running J men clear outta here. And that goes for you and your pal, Kicks."

Kicks wasn't ready to blow his cover yet, so he thanked Sammy, then turned to go. "Come on, Dave, let the sheriff clean this mess up." He motioned for Caleb to follow them. "I think you 'bout wore your welcome out here, son. Better come along with us."

As the three of them walked out of the saloon, Dave turned to look back at his dad. Sammy grinned as he watched them go, touching two fingers to his forehead in a goodbye salute.

Dave grinned back, returning the salute.

As soon as Kicks, Dave, and Caleb left the saloon, Cal and his deputies got the three dead Running J gunmen over to the undertaker's office. After banging on the man's office door a few times and not getting an answer, they dumped the bodies on the porch and pinned a note on them, saying:

Come see me in the morning.
Sheriff Tidwell.

That taken care of, Cal told his deputies, "I'm tired. I'm going over to my office and crash for a few hours. First thing in the morning, I want one of you guys to hightail it out to the Running J. Tell Bob exactly what happened. Tell him I need a couple more men. Good gunfighting men."

CHAPTER 16

Whiskers had the coffeepot on the stove when Dave and Kicks came in with Caleb. They introduced Caleb to Whiskers, then sat down at the card table. Whiskers poured them a cup of Arbuckle's, and over hot coffee, they talked about what had happened at the Golden Nugget.

Kicks looked at Caleb for a second, then said, "If you don't mind me asking, what's your story? I mean, you look like a farmer, but you handle that hogleg like it was a part of you."

Caleb laughed. "Naw, I don't mind. You see, my ma and pa died of consumption a few years back. Since then, I been staying with this old sheep herder. I hate sheep, but I figured I owed the old man something for taking me in, so I stuck around to help him out. The only fun I ever had was practicing with my six-gun. And, well, a couple days ago, the old man sold out and left to go back east to live with his kids. I had no place else to go, so I came to town hoping to land a job with some cattle outfit. That's what I was trying to do in that saloon when those guys started cracking jokes 'bout me. I was sure glad you guys showed up when you did."

Kicks grinned. "Now there are five of us."

Dave shook his head. "Six if you count my pa."

Caleb grinned too as he asked. "What's going on here? What does 'six of us,' mean?"

"It's like this, Caleb," Kicks said. "You said you were looking for a job. Well, I'm offering you one, so how about it? The work is a bit dangerous, but easy, and the pay is good. I'll pay you top gunfighter wage."

"Let me get this straight," Caleb said. "You're hiring my gun?"

"Yeah, I reckon I am … along with your guts." Kicks had a few good reasons why he'd offered the young man a job. One, Caleb would now have a place to stay, and two, if he hadn't grabbed Caleb first, sooner or later Bob's outfit would have … one way or another. He'd rather have the young man on their side than against it. "You can bunk right here at our headquarters. So, what do ya say?"

Caleb looked around at his new friends and grinned. "From farmer to gunfighter. Hell yeah, it's a deal."

Kicks and Caleb went to the bank the next morning, and Kicks drew out some money and gave it to Caleb as an advance on his salary. Next, they went to A. J. Grimes' General Store, and Caleb bought new clothes so he wouldn't look like a farmer. When they got back to their headquarters, they made some adjustments in their plans. Kicks looked over at Caleb and said, "Caleb Jackson. Hey, did you know how Stonewall Jackson got his name?"

"Nope," Caleb replied.

"Well, one time the lieutenant led his men into battle, and they were so outnumbered that it seemed they would surely fall. Afterwards, his men said Jackson refused to quit fighting. Said he just stood there like a stone wall, never budging an inch. From then on he was known as Stonewall Jackson."

"That's an interesting story, Kicks. What made you think of it."

Kicks grinned. "Yesterday, when Dave and I walked into the saloon and saw you standing there facing all those Running J gunmen alone, it reminded me of old Stonewall Jackson." Kicks paused for a second, then continued, "Some men are mighty particular about what other people call them. I know I am. But I think that name would fit you perfect. Would you mind if I tagged you with that handle … Stonewall?"

Caleb laughed. "I'll get used to it. In fact, I kinda like it."

*   *   *

Whiskers woke up in his usual place in the horse stall. He was in a cold sweat, as often happened since the town had caught fire. Remembering the sight of that raging wall of fire had singed a lasting picture of destruction in Whisker's head. He had not been drunk since Dave hired him, so that wasn't the reason for the sweats. It was that recurring dream of the town fire, and the fire tower.

It was time for him to get up anyway. He could smell the coffee brewing, so he stashed his bedroll and went on in the stable office, where Dave had just poured himself a cup.

"Morning, Whiskers, sit down and I'll get ya some coffee."

Just as Whiskers was taking a seat, Kicks, Muley, and Stonewall stepped inside. "Burrrr," Muley said. "It's freezing out."

"Yeah," Dave agreed. "September's the beginning of fall, and it gets pretty chilly here in Helena. Won't be long before the snowstorms set in." He laughed as he got out more cups. "I could start my own coffee shop here."

Soon all five of the cowpokes were seated and drinking hot coffee.

Muley frowned as he glanced over at Whiskers. "Something up, Whiskers? Look like you got somethin' on your mind."

The old prospector grimaced, rubbing at his whiskered chin. "Now that you mention it, there is. You remember that time you overheard me talking in my sleep?"

"Yeah, sure do. You kept saying something like 'Check the ... Guardian, or 'check the gulch.'"

"Yeah, that's it. I keep havin' that same stupid dream." He shook his head. "It's nothin'. I don't wanna bother you guys with my dreams."

Kicks didn't dismiss them. "Like my pappy always says, 'Dreams are like visitors from your past, and generally they're telling you something that could be linked to the future.' So if this is a recurring dream, maybe we should talk about it."

Whiskers scratched his head. "Okay, but what's there to talk about?"

"Well, do you remember in your dream where you were? Did you see any images or anything like that?"

"Hmmm. I recall a fire, and an old building. A tall building. And sometimes I see people, but I can never make out their faces."

"Does it help any to talk about it?" Kicks asked.

Whiskers shook his head. "Nope, not really."

"Wait a minute," Dave said. "A tall, old building. And fire? Watch the Guardian. Watch the gulch? The Guardian of the Gulch is that old fire tower at the edge of town. Remember, we rode by it the other day."

"Wow, Whiskers," Muley said. "You dreaming about that old fire tower?"

"Yeah, guess I am. It's spooky, and it's wearing me down. I have that same dream most every night."

"Well," Stonewall said. "Maybe we should go check that old fire tower out. Might be holding some sort of secret."

"Good idea," Kicks agreed. "But right now, we all need to be here in town. I have a feeling something big is about to happen."

"I agree with that," Muley said. "After that useless shooting of the poor farmer the other day, then the three shootings in the saloon when you and Stonewall had that run-in with the Running J crew. Yep, I'd say something big is about to happen."

*　　*　　*

It was mid-morning, and Bob was sitting at his kitchen table, having a cup of coffee laced heavily with whiskey, and wishing he'd never allowed Quantrill and his men to move onto his property. He heard a knock at his door and yelled, "Come on in!"

Dutch opened the door and stepped inside.

Bob looked over at him. "Dutch Simmons? You're one of Cal's deputies, ain't ya?"

"Yep, Mister Jensen, Cal sent me out here with a message for you."

"Well, spit it out."

Dutch looked longingly at the coffee and bottle of whiskey, probably dry after the long ride from town. He cleared his throat. "Yesterday, a farmer came into town and went into the Golden Nugget. Three of your riders was in there, one of 'em got into it with the farmer. Farmer was packing a .44, and he outdrew him. Killed your man dead."

"What? A farmer outdrew one of my men. He musta been drunk."

"I don't know about that," Dutch stammered. "They said the farmer was damn fast on the draw. And that ain't all, Mister Jensen. Them fellers, Kicks and Dave Galveston, they was there too. They got into it with two more of your riders. Killed them too."

"Three of my men got killed, huh?" Bob paused, growing thoughtful. "I been losing men ever since those two saddle-bums drifted into town." Bob grew silent again, until Dutch began to shift nervously on his feet. "Well, is there more, or is that it?"

"Yeah," Dutch whined. "Cal said to tell you to send more men. And they'd better be *good* gunmen."

Bob began to curse. "You go back and tell your boss I'll send more men, but if I have to come in there and take over his job, he just might have to take up a new residence … in Boot Hill."

Looking suddenly fearful, Dutch said, "Yes, sir, Mister Jensen! I'll go right now." He cast one last look at the bottle of whiskey before he hurried out the door.

Carrying his cup of coffee, Bob walked over to the window and watched as Dutch hurriedly mounted up, wheeled his horse away from the hitch rail, and raced off toward town.

*   *   *

William Clarke Quantrill was too much of a military man to allow anything or anyone to slip past him. Although Bob never saw the need to keep a guard posted during the daytime, Quantrill kept several of his men posted twenty-four hours a day. On this day, when Dutch Simmons rode into the ranch yard to talk to Bob, two of Quantrill's guards had watched from strategic locations.

After Dutch went inside, one of the guards moved up close enough to overhear what was being said through the open window.

As soon as Dutch was back on the trail, they went into the bunkhouse and reported about the visit to their commander. "So," Quantrill said, "old Bob's let things get out of control, huh? Might be time for me to take over."

Quantrill had agreed to use Bob's second bunkhouse as his headquarters, along with the old, abandoned ranch house outside of town. What he hadn't told Bob was his plan to bring in even more of his men. There were now six staying in the bunkhouse with him at the Running J, and six more staying at the old ranch. Five more gunmen were on their way, due to arrive any day.

These seventeen gunmen were just a small number of the men under Quantrill's command. However, these guys were also some of the *best* gunmen he had. Of the most notorious of his men—which included the James and Younger brothers, Bloody Bill, and the Wild Irishman, Arthur McCoy—he only had McCoy and Bloody Bill with him.

Thinking it over for a few minutes, Quantrill called Bloody Bill and the Wild Irishman to his side. "Bill, I'm putting you in charge of a detail. I want you and the Irishman to ride out to the old ranch and pick up Tom Pickett and George Shepherd." He paused.

"Yes, sir. I understand," Bill acknowledged. "What do you want us to do after that?"

"I want the four of you to go into town and start terrorizing the folks there. Guerrilla style. You know what I mean, don't you?"

"Sure do, Captain. We'll hit that town where it hurts. Rob the bank first, then wait a night or two and knock off the mercantile. We'll get the saloon next."

"Don't let 'em see ya. Don't wanna draw attention to us. Come back in a week or so and we'll decide what to do next."

"Is that all, Captain?"

"Not quite. You can't stay at the old ranch. Do you have a place in mind where you and your men can camp out?"

"Yes, sir. The Missouri River runs parallel with the Blackfoot River not too far outside of Helena. There's an area on both sides of the Missouri River where these limestone cliffs rise about twelve hundred or so feet. They call that area the Gates of the Mountains. On the other side of those Gates is a nice wooded area, lots of wildlife, bighorn sheep, bear, and the like. It's a perfect place to hide out. That's where we'll be camped."

Pleased, Quantrill said, "Excellent. Okay, gentleman, carry out your orders. I want a weekly update. Dismissed."

It didn't take long for Bloody Bill and the Wild Irishman to gather up their gear. They stopped at the old ranch house to pick up Tom Pickett and George Shepherd. Some of the other men became argumentative, so Bill agreed to take a few more with him. He told the rest to hang tight. It wouldn't be long before they were needed.

Just before nightfall, after riding alongside the Missouri River and through the Gates of the Mountains, they camped deep inside the forest, close to the river. It was cold out, so they built a big fire, then fixed a good meal. Afterward, they settled back to relax, drinking hot coffee laced heavily with whiskey. Later, they put the coffee aside and just drank the whiskey.

"Sure beats being cooped up inside that old rundown ranch house, don't it?" Juan said, one of the men they'd picked up along the way.

"Sure does," his brother Arturo agreed. "I was gettin' sick of sitting around there twiddling my thumbs all day."

"You guys need to get some shuteye," a half-drunk Bill said. "Me and the Irishman will take first watch."

Once everyone was asleep, Bill and the Irishman made plans for how they'd hit the town. For the bank job, they decided it would be just themselves, Tom Pickett and George Shepherd. They'd set the others up with something else.

The Irishman laughed. "Better take out Kicks Burks and Muley Gentry first. Think they'll be our biggest trouble."

Bill leaned back against his saddle, coffee cup in one hand, rubbing his chin thoughtfully with the other. He wasn't afraid to draw against either of those two men, but he'd be stupid not to carry doubts. "Let's send Arturo and those other four men after them. They're all damn good gunmen. The five of 'em together oughta be able to take out Kicks and Muley. Just need to figure out a way to set it up.

"Tomorrow night, we'll knock off the bank. The following night, we'll all ride into town together. You and I will go over to the Silver Spoon Café while the rest head over to the Golden Nugget. Our men can take care of Muley and Kicks there. They can take out that barkeep too. Heard he was given' our men trouble. Quantrill wants to put the fear of God into this town, and I think that oughta take care of it."

"The Irishman chuckled. "I'd say so."

CHAPTER 17

The next morning after breakfast, Bill informed the men of their plans. "Me, Mccoy, Tom and George will rob the bank today. Tomorrow, we'll all go to town. You guys can take out Kicks and Muley at the Golden Nugget. Start an argument with 'em there. Take out them two cowboys and anyone else who gets in your way. A couple days after that, we'll make further plans to terrorize this town."

No one objected, so Bloody Bill, the Wild Irishman, Tom Pickett and George Shepherd rode into town, arriving about two hours before the bank closed. It gave them time to set everything up.

"Normally we'd rob the bank right before it opens," Bill told his companions. "But in this case, we purposely want to draw attention to the bank getting robbed. Anybody gets brave and tries to interfere, we can take them out then. Just don't get yourselves killed in the process."

An hour later, they saw the time was right. The four men pulled their bandannas up to hide their identity and stepped inside the bank. There were two bank tellers and three customers. Before anyone could do anything, the outlaws shot the three customers and one of the tellers. Bill pointed his gun at the remaining teller. "Hurry up, give us the money from the tills and then open the safe."

The teller didn't move, staring fearfully at the four people shot dead on the floor. Knowing he'd get shot no matter what, he refused to open the safe. Bill snarled as he shot the man in the back of the head.

"Hurry up," one of the outlaws said. "We need to get outta here."

"Not till I get the loot," Bill said. He applied some prepared explosives to the front of the safe. "Stand back," he said. "This won't take long."

"Oh hell," McCoy muttered, looking around for cover. A moment later, the explosives went off and the safe was blown open.

"Let's go!" Bill yelled.

The outlaws ran outside with the loot. Just as they'd figured, there were a few people running towards the bank. "It's a holdup," one yelled. "The bank's getting robbed!"

The outlaws shot them down in cold blood, then jumped on their horses and made their getaway. Not one shot was fired in return. Outside of town, they split up, later meeting up at the camp in the wooded area behind the mountain Gates.

The Sanchez brothers, Arturo and Juan, were the greediest of the five men left behind. "Hell's fire," Arturo said as he watched the loot from the bank being counted. "We're not gonna turn all that cash over to Quantrill, are we?"

Bill laughed. "What do you mean by *we*? The four of us robbed the bank. We'll take a cut and then give the rest to Quantrill. That's the way it's done."

"What about us," Juan demanded.

"Hold on there. You won't get left out. The four of us did the bank job, so the five of you will do the next job. That's the way I got it planned out. Tomorrow night, when you guys finish your job, you'll take your cut."

"So you got the jobs already figured out, huh?" Juan said.

"Well, yeah … with a little help from Quantrill." Bill knew he was stretching the truth a little, but the mention of Quantrill's name worked to shut them up.

Juan glanced over at his brother and shrugged. "Okay, so what's our job gonna be?"

Bill grinned. "You lucky gents get to take out Kicks Burks and Muley Gentry."

One of the other outlaws spoke up, "Yeah, I heard tell of 'em. Jus' a couple drifters supposed to be purdy fast on the draw. Never seen 'em in person though."

"Yep," Bill said. "They've been nosin' around too much. Quantrill wants 'em taken out. Think you guys can handle it?"

"Hell yeah, but how is that gonna get us any money?" Arturo asked.

"Glad you asked," Bill said. "After you kill them two cowpokes, and anyone else trying to act the hero, you rob the Golden Nugget. Make sure you kill that pesky barkeep too. Me and the Irishman will ride into town with Tom and George first. We'll be over at the Silver Spoon if you get into trouble."

"That's it, huh? Juan said. "We just walk in there, shoot those guys, and rob the place. We get a cut of the money, right?"

Bill shrugged. "Yep, simple as that. You don't even have to worry about the sheriff. He's in with Bob and Quantrill."

After a brief pause, Arturo said, "Okay. Sounds easy enough, but there's bound to be other people in the saloon, ain't there?"

"Yeah, might be some local farm or ranch hands in there having a drink. If they give you trouble, shoot 'em. Not gonna bother Bob or Quantrill any. Should be an easy enough task for five good gunmen."

"Okay," Arturo said. "When do we head for town? I wanna get my hands on some of that money."

"We'll leave late tomorrow afternoon. By the time we get there, it'll be dark out. Perfect time to pull off your job."

*   *   *

Tilly Durmhill and Wendy Frances were at their station behind the lobby desk when Muley and Kicks came down for dinner. "Did you hear?" Tilly said, looking nervous.

"Hear what?" Kicks asked, looking between the two women.

"Bank's been robbed."

"Shit," Kicks mumbled under his breath. "Come on, Muley, let's go check it out."

They got to the door of the bank just as Sheriff Tidwell and his deputies arrived. Acting his part, Cal stood in the doorway, yelling over the noise of the crowd. "Alright, folks, everyone go home. I got this under control here."

The two cowpokes saw the bank manager, Allen Prescott, standing inside the bank, wringing his hands nervously. They wanted to see what information they could get from him, so they started to step inside. Cal stopped them at the door. "I said *everyone* go home. That means you guys too."

Kicks didn't want to reveal his authority as a marshal yet, but he needed to investigate this robbery. "Look, Cal, I got a lot of money in my account in this bank and—"

Cal cut him off. "I don't give a good goddamn what you got! You need to get outta here."

At that time, Mayor Harper came running inside the bank "Hold on there," he said. Giving Kicks a knowing look, he turned to Cal. "Look, Sheriff, I know you and these two guys don't get along very good, but Kicks used to be a lawmen himself, so I figure we might need their help."

Cal bristled. "So what? I don't need their help."

The mayor didn't back down. "I'm giving them the authority to help investigate this crime."

Cal grew red in the face. "Well, they better not get in my way."

Muley and Kicks nodded at the mayor, then began to examine everything in and around the bank to see if they could find any clues. After Cal left the bank, they asked the bank manager a series of their own questions.

"Anyone see who the robbers were?" Kicks asked.

"Nope," Allen replied. "Not anyone left alive anyway. Killed two tellers and three customers who were inside the bank, then they killed three other people outside. Eight people killed during this robbery." Allen shook his head in disgust. "Why all the questions? You see something that'll help us catch the robbers?"

"No," Kicks answered honestly. "I'm just trying to visualize the crime scene. Could tell us something about the robbers."

"Oh, okay."

Kicks continued to ask the manager questions as Muley began to examine the blown safe. "They obviously used explosives to blow the safe. You find anything interesting about that, Kicks?"

"Like my pappy always says, 'You can't put a puzzle together unless you first examine each piece carefully. Gotta make sure all the pieces are there.' He paused, his expression thoughtful. "Why you suppose no one heard the explosion when it blew. No loud boom. The whole town shoulda heard this, us included, but we didn't."

Muley looked around and shook his head. "Whoever they were…" He leaned over to examine the safe. "…I gotta hand it to 'em. This stuff they used, don't appear to be gunpowder. I don't know what it is."

"Hum," Kicks mused. He touched the residue around the safe with his fingers, smelling it. "Wow, these crooks are really smart. Until a few years ago, black powder, or gunpowder, was the first known explosives. But, back in '46, something called nitroglycerin was discovered. Used to be too unstable to use safely, but they've figured out a way around that. Now it's the modern explosives. That's what this is, Muley. These crooks used nitroglycerin."

"So," the Mayor said, "what does that tell us?"

"Why not just use dynamite?" Muley asked. "Seems like that woulda been a whole lot easier than making this stuff."

"A couple reasons," Kicks replied. "Number one, they can make nitro themselves. Won't draw any attention that way. Number two, it only takes a little nitro to get the job done. Won't blow the whole safe apart. Less noise. Less mess."

Dumbfounded, Muley said, "The hell you say."

"I'm impressed," the mayor said. "Does all of this information tell you anything else?"

"Yeah," Kicks answered. "And I'm not at all happy about it."

"We're listening," Allen, the manager, said.

"A month or so ago, when I first came to town, some strange things began to happen around here. Me, Muley, and

Dave Galveston, got the idea that Bob Jensen and Sheriff Tidwell were both behind it."

"That's right," Muley agreed. "We figured the sheriff is on Bob's payroll. They set me and Kicks up to get killed in that card game with Floyd and those other gunman over at the livery, including Jim Bonner. Woulda killed us too if you and the judge hadn't stepped in with Sammy."

"I remember," the mayor said. "Go on."

Kicks began to pace, rubbing at his brow. "A week or so ago, we spotted Quantrill and some of his men riding into Bob's ranch."

"William Quantrill," Mayor Harper said in a whisper. "Charlie Heart. You figure this bank job is the work of Quantrill and his Raiders?"

"That'd be my guess," Muley replied.

"I thought Quantrill and his Raiders were over around the Missouri-Kansas area?" the mayor said, his expression shocked.

"Why!" Allen Prescott almost yelled. "Why would someone like Quantrill want to come all the way out here just to rob my bank?"

Muley and Kicks exchanged a look. "It's our guess," Muley said, "that robbing your bank ain't the only deal Quantrill has planned for your little town."

"No, there's something bigger going down here," Kicks added. "The bank robbery could just be to throw us off the track. You know, a deterrent to keep us guessing while they prepare for the big one, whatever that is."

"What are we gonna do?" Mayor Harper asked.

Muley sighed. "I haven't known him long, but Kicks and I have both survived some hellish gun battles. We ain't about to tuck tail and run over this one, but we're gonna need some help. Unless I miss my guess, this is shaping up to be a war. I think it's time to wire the cavalry again. Fort Harrison ain't that far away."

"I wired the fort three days ago, got the same answer as before. They can't intervene or use any kind of military force in matters pertaining to civilian townships, not unless the town comes under siege by enemy forces."

"In spite of the seriousness of the moment, Kicks grinned. "I think I can get us some help."

"Why don't you let us all in on the secret," Allen urged.

"Okay, here's the deal," Kicks said. "You all know about the Dragoon Soldiers, don't ya?"

"I don't," Allen said, shaking his head.

The mayor held up his hand, nodding. "They're a regiment of soldiers specially trained to fight both off and on horseback. They go into battle first, and then the foot soldiers come afterward. The Dragoon Soldiers are supposed to be the best trained and toughest fighting men there is."

"That's right," Kicks agreed. "And I happen to know two men who are Dragoon Soldiers. Sam Ford and Frank Mullen. Guess where they're stationed?"

"Fort Harrison," Muley said, grinning.

"Yep. I sent a wire there myself, found out where they were. We happen to be good friends, and they both owe me a big favor. But I won't call on 'em unless I need to. In the meantime, let's keep this under our hats. Is that clear?"

Mayor Harper nodded. "You think these two friends of yours could win in a showdown against Quantrill and his murdering Raiders?"

Good question, especially with men like Bloody Bill Anderson in the bunch. "Well," Kicks admitted, "I'm sure my two friends will bring some friends of their own along too." His grin widened.

The Mayor sighed with relief. "Okay, good. I think I can rest a little bit easier now. Sounds like you know what you're doing."

"Like my pappy always says, 'Too many cooks spoil the pot, but sometimes a few more cooks make the pot boil better.'"

Muley laughed. "Yep, most times it's good to have a plan B all worked out ahead of time."

"Now you're talking," Kicks agreed. "Okay, we'd best get on over to headquarters and let the rest of our crew know what's going on."

Mayor Harper agreed. "I'll go let Judge Cleveland know about your plans. We don't want to get our wires crossed. How will we keep in touch?"

"That's the beauty of having our headquarters at the livery stables, Mayor," Muley explained. "Every day or so, you or the judge can drop by to check on your horses. Someone will always be there to let you know what's goin' on."

The mayor nodded. "Good thinking, boys. Okay, I'll talk to you soon." He took one last look around the bank, shook his head in disgust, then walked out.

CHAPTER 18

It was late the next evening, and Muley and Kicks were sitting at the livery, talking with Stonewall, Whiskers, and Dave.

"Heard any more about the bank robbery?" Stonewall asked, acting excited. "I've heard 'bout Quantrill and his Raiders, and now I might actually get to see him in person."

Muley frowned at Stonewall. "You might think you'd be happy to see Quantrill, but if and when you do, you'll likely be swapping lead with the man, and maybe nigh on the twenty or more trained outlaws and killers riding with him. I wouldn't be too anxious about it if I were you, kid."

It didn't appear Muley's warning had any effect on Stonewall. "What's the story on him, anyway?"

Kicks could see Muley was getting upset with the kid, so he intervened. "It's good to know about your enemies, Stony, so I'll brief you on the man. Have you ever heard of the Missouri Partisan Rangers?"

"Nope, sure haven't."

"Well, The Missouri Partisan Rangers were the Irregular Cavalry units of such commanders as William Clarke Quantrill, Bill Anderson, George Todd, John Thrailkill, and more. These men rode hard and defended the innocent citizens of Missouri from the slaughter and carnage that had been committed by Federal occupational forces sent by Abraham

Lincoln. Although many northern sympathizers consider the Partisan Ranger to be bushwhackers, they were only waging the type of war that had already been committed against them and their southern families. See, when the Federal occupational forces invaded Michigan and Wisconsin, they raped, pillaged, burned and destroyed much of West Central and South West Missouri. At the time, the people of Missouri's only defense were the Partisan Rangers. They were given no quarter when they were captured. And in return, none was ever given to them."

"So," Stonewall inquired, "doesn't that put Quantrill in the right and the Union in the wrong?"

"No, not necessarily." Kicks replied. "Depends on which side you rode on. In the beginning, neither the North or the South were right or wrong. Both sides fought for what they thought was right. But war is war, and someone has to win. Quantrill wound up on the losing side. Guess that sorta drove him crazy, made him killing mad, so he kept on fighting even after the war was over. Almost got himself killed several times over. Now it looks like he's here, and we're gonna have to deal with him."

That seemed to satisfy Stonewall. "Okay, so what do we do, go after him?"

Kicks laughed. "That's the spirit, but for now, I think we better sit tight. Wait to see what he's got in mind. I don't know how many men Quantrill's got. Could be thirty or forty by now. It's something we need to figure out before we stick our necks out. We also need to know just how far Bob Jensen will go along with Quantrill. What's their connection? Could be those two will end up in a fight over the Running J outfit too. We just don't know."

Stonewall sighed. "So we don't really know anything so far. Is that what you're trying to tell me, Kicks?"

Kicks chuckled, shrugging. "Fraid so.

"We think it might have something to do with what happened to my ma and pa years ago," Muley said. "Something to do with the Last Chance gold mine."

"Also," Dave added, "since we've been poking around, I think Bob and that sheriff of his had something to do with my Grandpa Howard getting shot in the back. He used to be sheriff here."

"Well," Stonewall said, "I don't know anything about Muley's ma and pa, or your grandpa, but ain't the Last Chance gold mine the one that's right smack in the center of town? Ain't it still gettin' worked?"

"That's the one," Dave agreed.

"Okay," Stonewall continued, "If that mine is registered all legal like and everything, then what possible business could Bob or Quantrill have nosing around here about it?"

Muley and Kicks shot a quick glance at each other, as though a light bulb had been lit up in their heads; Muley slapped the young man on the back. "Stonewall, you just brought to mind something worthwhile to check up on."

"Yeah, what's that?"

Kicks laughed. "I don't wanna be jumping the gun or anything, but what you just said about the mine being registered kinda makes sense. Bob's been here in Helena almost since the day it was founded. Bet he knows a lot more than we do." He frowned, tapping his fingertips on the table. "Think we need to go have us a talk with the mayor and judge about this. But it can wait till tomorrow."

Muley frowned. "Why wait?"

"I don't wanna draw attention to 'em," Kicks said. "Won't do to go knocking on their door in the middle of the night. Bet Sheriff Tidwell's got deputies watching them like a hawk. He knows they're on our side. Don't want any more people getting' shot in the back." He nodded at Dave. "Like Dave's grandpa. Mayor said he or the judge would drop by every day or so. We'll wait until they check in to question them."

"Yeah, I guess you're right," Muley said. The other three nodded in agreement.

"Meanwhile, we got five of us now," Kicks said. "We'll double up on our rounds about town. Muley and I will keep our room at the hotel, but we'll be stayin' here at the livery so we'll all be together if trouble strikes. Stonewall and I will make the afternoon rounds now. We'll plan to change off every four hours. That okay with everyone?"

They all agreed, so Kicks and Stonewall left the livery and stepped out onto the boardwalk. They walked the streets and alleyways for about two hours. Nothing unusual happened. Just before dark, they stopped and rolled a cigarette. "Hungry?" Kicks asked.

"Getting there,"

Kicks grinned. "That makes two of us. Let's walk on over to the Silver Spoon and grab a bite."

Stonewall grinned back, already walking. "Suit's me fine. Let's go."

The café wasn't very busy, only four men sitting at a table close to the counter. They were talking and laughing, but when Kicks and his partner walked by their table toward the counter, they grew quiet. As Stonewall and Kicks sat down, the four men stood and paid for their food.

"Hello, Kicks," Cathy said, coming back to the counter to take their order. "Who's your new partner?"

"Kicks smiled, "Newest member of our gang, Cathy. This is Stonewall Jackson. Stony, meet Cathy. Prettiest gal around, and the best cook this side of the Rockies."

Stonewall stood up and reached over the counter to take her hand. "Mighty pleased to meet you, ma'am."

Cathy shook his hand. "You can call me Cathy, Mister Jackson."

"It'd surely be my pleasure, ma'am. Uh, I mean Cathy. And I'd be pleased if you called me Stonewall, or Stony for short."

Laughing, Cathy said, "Okay, Stony, what'll you guys have?"

They gave Cathy their order. She hesitated, biting nervously at her lip. "Umm, did you happen to get a good look at those four men when you passed by their table?"

"Yeah, we sure did, why?" Kicks said.

"Umm, they were sitting real close to the counter when they first came in, and I could hear what they were saying. They used terrible language, so I went into the kitchen. I guess they thought I couldn't hear them from in there, so they kept on talking. Kicks, they said they were going to rob the Golden Nugget tonight, and kill the bartender, shoot up the place."

Stonewall jumped up. "You sure about that?"

"Wait," Cathy said when Kicks also stood. "That's not all. They said they aimed to kill as many people as they could, but especially that pesky bartender. I think they mean Sammy."

"Why," Kicks murmured, more to himself than Cathy, but Cathy answered.

"They said something about the sheriff, that he'd told them Sammy pulled a sawed-off shotgun on him the other day. Stood up for some farmer that came in the saloon. The sheriff couldn't arrest the guys that shot those Running J riders."

Kicks tossed some money down on the counter. "Thanks for the information, Cathy. If you hear anything else, you can find us over at the livery. That's where we'll be staying." He started for the door. "Come on, Stony, business just picked up."

Stony followed Kicks to the door.

"What about your food?" Cathy yelled. "You still want it?"

"Save it for us," Stony answered. "Maybe pray we get to come back for it. If we don't, throw it away."

As they hurried over to the Golden Nugget, Kicks was thinking about their situation. "I know you're not afraid, Stony. Saw you outdraw and outshoot that one outlaw, but this is different. We're gonna be up against at least four gunmen, maybe more. Just keep your eyes peeled and follow my lead."

"What if I see someone going for his gun before you do?"

"Good question. I don't want you to be too jumpy or too quick to draw, but I don't want to see either of us dead either. If you see someone going for a gun, and you're sure about it, then put a bullet in his brisket. If you're wrong, you just say, 'Oops, sorry.'"

Before Kicks and Stony entered the saloon, they looked over the batwing doors and quickly scanned the room. The place was busy, as usual, the bar lined with men, and most of the tables full. "Nothing's happened yet," Kicks said. "I don't see those four guys from the Silver Spoon in there."

He pushed the doors open, and they stepped inside. It was dark outside, but inside, every candle and lamp in the place had been lit and turned up, and the huge chandelier with its five tiers of oil lamps was shining brightly.

Kicks, with Stony close on his heels, elbowed themselves a place at the bar. José Martinez moved down the bar to wait on them. "*Hola, Señor* Kicks, what can I get for you and your friend?"

"Howdy, José," Kicks said. "Give us a bottle of mescal and two glasses." When José set their order on the bar top, Kicks told Stony, "Take the bottle and go find us a table somewhere we can watch the door."

Stony picked up the bottle and glasses, and Kicks turned back to the bar. He caught Sammy's eye and motioned him over. Sammy moved down to him, and Kicks whispered, "Keep your shotgun close at hand. You're gonna need it tonight."

Sammy pressed his lips together and nodded.

Kicks walked over to the table where Stony was sitting. They sat there and sipped their drinks for a few minutes, watching the batwing doors swing open and shut with no sign of the four gunmen they had seen leave the Silver Spoon. The doors swung open again, and five heavily armed men stepped inside. Kicks leaned forward to get a better look at them. Not the men they were looking for.

"Not them," Stonewall murmured.

"You're right about that," Kicks agreed. "But I bet that's part of their crew. Get ready, the dance is about to start."

"You sure?" Stonewall whispered, "What can we do against five gunslingers? And what if those other four show up?"

Kicks laughed, then under his breath whispered, "Pick your partner, and when the music starts, you'd better not miss a step."

"What the hell does that mean?" Stonewall asked, his gaze never wavering from the five armed men. They'd placed themselves carefully from opposite ends of the bar, three on one side, and two on the other.

Kicks answered Stonewall's question without looking away from the gunfighters. "It's like this, Stony. It's gonna be the two of us against the five of them. Sammy will probably help if he can. We'll walk over to the bar like we're just gonna order another drink. Try to squeeze in beside them, or at least get as close to them as possible. As soon as any of them make a move for their guns, act fast cause there won't be any second chances. I'll take the three at the right end of the bar. You take the two at the left. See you later, Stony. Good luck."

As Kicks made his way toward the end of the bar, he was thinking, *Sure hope Stony don't freeze up, and I hope he's a fast as I think he is.* Those thoughts passed in a hurry, and all that remained in his mind was the business at hand. When Kicks reached the end of the bar where his three adversaries were standing, Stonewall moved up on his left side.

José moved down to wait on Kicks. "What you need?"

The five gunmen turned their backs to the bar and faced the room. As they turned, the three on Kicks' side all drew their guns. It was plain to see they intended to open fire on the crowd without giving any warning.

Kicks saw the movement. Before the gunmen could fire, he turned his back to the bar and drew his gun. At the same time, he lunged into the closest gunman, which caused a domino effect and threw them all off. Before they could recover, Kicks had them covered with his .44. "Hold it," he shouted. But he could see there would be no stopping them. Kicks dove to the floor and began rolling and firing at the same time.

Seeing that all three gunmen were down and out of action, he rolled over one more time and came up on one knee, ready to open fire on the two gunmen at the other end of the bar. A quick glance told him that probably wouldn't be necessary. Stonewall already had them down.

It was all over in a matter of seconds, and when Kicks stood up, the first thing he said was, "You all right, kid?"

Stonewall, still standing there with his gun in the firing position, nodded slowly.

Kicks looked over at Sammy, "You okay, partner?"

Sammy nodded. "Yep!"

Kicks looked around the room at the shocked faces. "Anybody hurt?" The few people still in the saloon all signified they were okay.

Kicks and Stonewall stood at the bar while Kicks explained to everyone exactly what had happened.

Sammy said, "People, if it had not been for Stony and Kicks here, most of us would not be alive right now. So everybody, belly up to the bar, the drinks are on me." Sammy and José poured drinks for everyone in the saloon.

"Thanks, Sammy," Kicks said as he placed his empty glass back on the bar. "Now, guess we gotta get these dead bodies over to the undertakers."

"Not so fast, drifter," Sheriff Tidwell said as he and his deputies stepped inside the saloon, "I got some questions to ask you. And you ain't going anywhere, 'cept to jail."

Really tired of Cal trying to slap him behind bars, Kicks pointed a finger at him. "Listen, you poor excuse for a sheriff. Do your damn job for a change. I'm walking out of here right now." Kicks motioned toward the five dead gunmen, now laid out side by side. "I thought I'd make these five dead men here my limit for tonight, but if you don't step aside, I just might change my mind." Kicks could tell Cal wanted to draw against him in the worst way and felt sure he could beat him.

Cal glanced around the room, stiffening. No doubt he could tell everyone in the saloon was against him. This was not the time for a showdown. Nevertheless, he had to get in the last word. "I don't have time to fool around with you right now, drifter. Go on, get out of here. I'll deal with you later."

Kicks brushed by Cal and grabbed the almost full bottle of mescal from their table. "Put it on my tab, Sammy." Over his shoulder, he called, "Come on, Stony, drinks are on me. My pappy always says, 'If there's a skunk in the watering hole, you better not drink till you get downstream from him.'"

Stonewall grinned mockingly at the sheriff, then nodded a goodbye salute to Sammy before he followed Kicks out the door. Kicks knew the kid was pumped up after the shooting, and he figured it wouldn't hurt to heap on a little praise. There were not a whole lot of men that could have withstood a shootout with five gunmen and live to tell about it.

After they stepped out onto the boardwalk, Kicks stopped and pulled a tobacco pouch and papers from his vest pocket. After he rolled a smoke, he tucked it in the corner of his mouth and handed the makings to the kid. "Here, Stony, have one. I need a smoke."

"Thanks," Stony said, and began to build himself a cigarette. After they lit up, Kicks asked, "You did a damn fine job back there. If you don't mind my asking, how many shootings have you been in?"

"I don't mind talking about it to *you*. The first time was the other day in the saloon, when I had it out with that gunman from the Running J. The second was just now."

Kicks noticed that Stony had put emphasis on the word 'you.' That pleased him, so he continued, "Well, you did good, kid. How do you feel after shootin' it out with four more men in a couple of days?"

Stonewall paused, as if not sure how to answer that question. So, Kicks relieved him of the decision. "Feeling a little off your feed because you just killed two men? It's nothing to be ashamed of. I felt a little queasy myself after the first few times I got into a shootout. It's nothing to be proud of … killing a person. Every life is sacred. Should be treated with respect. And, well, I just wanted to let you know that you did good and I'm proud of you."

Kicks didn't expect any thank you for the talk, and he didn't get one. They crushed out their cigarettes with the heel of their boots and walked on over to the office at the livery stable to report about the gunfight to the rest of their comrades.

CHAPTER 19

Cal watched Kicks and the farmer kid walk out of the saloon, knowing there was nothing he could do legally to stop them. Of course, that had never stopped him in the past, but sometimes he had to put up the pretense of doing things legal. He wasn't fooling anyone. Cal knew who the dead gunmen were, and everybody else in the saloon knew it too. "Anyone know who these guys were?" He pointed at the five deceased men.

Sammy shook his head, shrugging. "Nope."

"Well, does anyone know who started the fight? What was it all about?"

Sammy put both his hands on the bar, narrowing his eyes at Cal. "Kicks and Stony came in, said they'd heard some gunmen were planning to rob the place, and kill as many people as they could. They mentioned my name specifically."

"Hmm," Cal muttered. "Why would they want to come in here and kill you and a bunch of other people?"

"Don't know," Sammy replied. "I'm just glad someone was here to protect Helena's citizens tonight."

Cal glared at Sammy, his lip curling with disgust. "You know, you oughta be more respectful to your law officers. Might come a time when the great Kicks Burks ain't around to protect you or your families." Cal turned his back to Sammy before he could reply. "Come on, Buford; lend Oscar and

Dutch a hand with these stiffs. Let's get 'em on over to the undertaker."

It was one in the morning by the time they got all the bodies handled. "I'm beat," Oscar whined. "Think I'll go crawl in my bunk now and get some sleep."

"That's what we're all gonna do," Cal said. "Come daybreak, we need to be in the saddle. Gotta head out to the Running J to see Bob Jensen and Quantrill, find out what the hell's going on around here."

"Oscar, Buford, and Dutch showed surprised. "Quantrill?" Oscar blurted out. "So I was right about it being him riding in with Bob Jensen the other day. Was it some of his men got kilt tonight?"

Cal shrugged. "Probably. They've been layin' low out at Bob's ranch for a while now."

"Damn," Buford whined. "Wonder what Quantrill and Bob got cooking up?"

Annoyed at the stupidity of his deputies, Cal snapped, "That's what we gotta find out. Now let's stop jaw-jacking and get some rest. Tomorrow's gonna be a big day."

*   *   *

It was midmorning when Quantrill stepped out of the bunkhouse at the Running J. He walked to the main house, planning to have lunch with Bob Jensen. Time to start pushing the outlaw rancher to act.

They were just sitting down to eat when Blackjack Ketchum stuck his head inside the door. "Boss, four riders coming in. Looks like Sheriff Cal Tidwell and his three deputies."

Bob started to get up but changed his mind and sat back down. "When they get here, tell Cal to come on in. His deputies can wait outside."

About ten minutes later, they heard horses come galloping into the yard, then a knock on the door. "Come on in, Cal," Bob called.

The sheriff opened the door and stepped inside. He acted surprised to see Bob and Quantrill together. Neither of them offered to shake the sheriff's hand, though Bob did get up and pour him a glass of whiskey. "Sit down, Cal," Bob said as he refilled his and Quantrill's glass.

Quantrill said, "We was just about to discuss you. Need to know what's going on with that damn document on the Last Chance gold mine."

Looking puzzled, the sheriff sat down and picked up the glass, taking a drink. "Tastes good after a long ride." He sat back and wiped his mouth with the back of his hand. "Is that what this is all about, the Last Chance gold mine?"

Quantrill chuckled. "I'm guessing you don't have a clue about the missing papers."

Bob laughed, though he looked irritated. "I told you, Quantrill, no one knew about those papers but me and you."

Quantrill's laughter ceased as he narrowed his eyes at Bob. "And now there's three of us that know," he said sternly. "Wasn't lookin' like you were getting anywhere with it, Bob."

Bob threw both hands up in the air. "Guess it doesn't matter now. I figured I'd have to tell Cal about it sooner or later. Only way to get him to take his job seriously."

Cal's face twisted with anger. "Are you tryin' to insinuate I'm not doing my job? Mighta helped if you'd told me what you were after in the first place, Bob. I've been working blind."

"Well," Quantrill mused, "Cal does got a point there, Bob."

"Damned right I do," Cal said. "Why don't we stop playing games here and lay the cards out on the table. Maybe we can get something done."

No one spoke for a minute, then Bob said, "I suppose you'll want a cut?"

"I already killed Howard Durmhill for you. As Sheriff, I'm in a good position to poke around and find things out. You shoulda told me what you were after sooner. It's me and my men who'll be doing the dirty work, so yeah, I think I deserve to get a cut."

Surprisingly, it was Quantrill who said, "Bob, I think it'd be wise to make this partnership a threesome." He allowed a hint of a smile to form as he raised his eyebrows at Bob.

Bob grimaced. "Fine. Let's get some solid plans on the table and put the wheels in motion."

"All right then," Quantrill said. "Cal, there's a missing map to the claim for the Last Chance gold mine. We need that map to get it registered. The Gentry family bought it from the four Georgians for fifty bucks years ago. Old Bob here killed 'em, but he couldn't find the map. Durmhill started doing some checking around, which of course, Bob couldn't have, so he had you get rid of him too. We need that map, Cal. You say you know how to get things done, so prove it. Bring us back that document."

Cal laughed. "I already got it covered. I'm sure Durmhill's wife and daughter know something, maybe even where the map is." He straightened in his chair, rubbing his jaw. "Anyone ever actually see this document? How do you know it's real?"

Bob answered, "It's real. Talked to the four Georgians myself."

"Where have you looked?"

"About tore Gentry's old house apart, that abandoned ranch out east of town. Always figured Isaiah woulda hid it there, but he musta put it somewhere else. Weren't in the wagon with him and his wife when they were killed. Figure we might have to terrorize the town to get some answers. That's why I brought Quantrill and his men into it. Somebody's gotta know where that map is."

Cal listened intently. "Well, at least things are starting to make sense. You said Sheriff Durmhill was starting to ask questions around town?"

"Yes," Bob replied.

"He probably talked to his wife then. Daughter might know something. Not sure about the grandson, but I'm keeping an eye on him too. Anyone else Durmhill mighta talked too?"

Bob thought for a moment. "Sammy, the daughter's husband. Owns the Golden Nugget."

"Yeah, I know who he is."

"What are you gonna do with the women?"

Cal shrugged. "Put some pressure on 'em. If they don't talk, or don't know anything, I'll kill 'em. Ain't got no problem killing a woman."

"Okay then," Bob said, then poured the three of them another drink. He held his glass up in a salute. "Here's to our new plan, and to our health and wealth."

They all saluted with their glasses, and then Cal set his glass down on the table. "Well, men, guess that settles it. I'll take my leave now so I can get to work. I'll keep in touch." He stopped at the door and turned around to face Bob and Quantrill. "Oh, guess you probably already heard. Five men got shot down at the Golden Nugget last night." He narrowed his gaze on Quantrill. "Didn't know 'em personally." He shrugged. "Anyway, thought you should know." When Quantrill didn't react, he turned and left.

"Your men?" Bob asked.

Quantrill didn't answer. Instead, he got up and walked to the window, watching Cal through the window as he and his deputies rode off. "Well Bob, what do you think? Can he do it? Can he find the map?"

"I think he'll get the job done now that he has a stake in the deal."

Quantrill wasn't so sure. "You think Cal will try to double-cross us, claim the document for himself?"

"It's possible," Bob said. "If he does, I'll kill 'em myself."

Quantrill nodded, then turned and walked out.

*   *   *

The sun was just starting to set when Cal and his deputies got back to town. He reined in at the front of the jail and started to dismount, then changed his mind. "We might as well stable our horses. I don't expect we'll be doing anymore riding tonight."

It was quiet around the stable. As they approached the big double doors in front of the building, they could see through the office window. "Looks like we got a crowd in there," Cal muttered. Kicks and Muley, Dave and that drunken old fool they called Whiskers … and that farmer, the kid they called Stonewall.

"Wonder what they're doing?" Buford muttered. "Looks like they're having some kind of a meeting?"

Cal and his deputies dismounted and led their horses inside their designated stalls. While off saddling and brushing the horses, the foursome kept watching inside the office through the window. Curious, Cal peeked his head through the office door when they were done.

Dave waved him in. "What can I do for you, Sheriff?"

Cal pushed the door open farther and stepped inside. "Umm, just wanted you to know that we put our horses up and brushed them down ... so you don't have to worry about it." He noticed the card game going on the table and relaxed a bit.

Dave gave the sheriff and his deputies a big grin, "Why thanks, Sheriff, appreciate that. We're just sitting down to a friendly game of cards. You all can join us if you want. We got coffee on."

Cal hadn't expected the warm reception. Although he knew he wasn't really welcome, he figured, what the hell, why not. Maybe he'd learn something worthwhile by playing cards with these pesky men. "A hot cup of coffee and a friendly game of cards sound mighty good right now. Thanks." He stepped inside the office and motioned to his deputies, "Come on in, men, we're done for tonight. May as well be neighborly and enjoy the company."

As everyone sat down around the card table, Dave poured the coffee.

Kicks and Muley exchanged a look. Kicks grinned, shuffling the cards. Dave had been smart to invite Cal and his deputies to play cards with them. They were all about as slow as molasses in December. They might actually learn something useful.

The cards were cut and dealt, and the small talk began. Cal cleared his throat. "Think we mighta got off on the wrong foot, boys."

"Yeah," Dave said. "We walk the same streets, drink from the same trough. Might as well try to get along."

"Yep," Buford agreed.

About three hands into the game, Kicks asked casually as he shuffled the cards, "Cal, I was talking to a fella the other day. He told me about a gunman shooting a farmer down in the street for no good reason. You know anything about that?"

"'Fraid not," Cal lied. "Hadn't heard. Why?"

"Well, this fella told me there was quite a crowd witnessed the whole thing. Kinda surprised you didn't hear about it."

"What else this fella tell you?"

"Said there were two gunmen. One did the shooting while the other just stood there and watched."

Cal laughed and motioned toward Stonewall. "Too bad that farmer wasn't as handy with a six-shooter as your friend here. Make it self-defense, wouldn't you say?"

Kicks laughed. "Yeah, in a case like that, I'd have to agree with you. But this fella who saw it happen said he was just a poor farmer, didn't even have a gun. Said the gunman put a revolver in reach of the farmer and then forced him to try for it. When the farmer made a move, the gunman shot him down."

"Hum," the sheriff mused. "Seems a bit farfetched, don't it? Why would they do that?"

Kicks studied his cards a moment. "Oh, I don't know. I've seen it happen the same way before. But that's not the really interesting part about this story." Kicks paused to see if Cal would be interested in hearing the rest of the story. Cal didn't say a word, so Kicks shrugged. "This same fella, the one who told me about it, said he definitely saw you there.

Said you didn't do anything to try to stop it." There was silence for a full minute. "Well, what do you think?"

"I think," Cal said slowly, gritting his teeth, "that this fella you been talkin' to is lying."

"Hmm, s'pose anything's possible, but I never knew this fella to be partial to lying before. It'd pain me some to think he would. Oh, you might be interested to learn this. Said he caught the names of the two gunmen. Blackjack Ketchum was one of 'em. Think he's one of Bob Jensen's gunmen. But the one that did the shooting was a noted gunman named Bill."

Cal squirmed in his seat, beginning to sweat. "Lot of men named Bill in this world. Don't mean anything to me."

"Well, I heard this particular man's name is Bill Anderson ... Bloody Bill Anderson."

Cal's face turned red with anger. "I don't know anyone by that handle," he snarled. "And even if I did, what the hell difference would it make?"

"Oh, I think you know who Bloody Bill is. Maybe not in person, but certainly by reputation. He's one of Quantrill's Raiders. You know what else I heard, Sheriff?"

Cal didn't answer, his posture stiff.

"Heard tell that Quantrill is hiding out somewhere around here."

Obviously nervous now, Cal laid his cards face down on the table and stood up. "Haven't got one good hand during this whole game. Might as well quit. Oh, by the way, I don't like what you seem to be implying here, cowboy. People have got themselves killed for less than that."

Kicks grinned. "Oh. I didn't mean to imply anything, Sheriff. Just making conversation. Thought you'd like to know those things, being as you are the town's sheriff."

"Toss your cards, boys," Cal said, then turned to go. "We're leaving."

As Cal and his deputies reached the office door, Kicks called out, "Oh, Cal, that gunman who shot that farmer down in the street, it was Bloody Bill Anderson all right. Took a red ribbon out of his saddlebags and tied a knot in it. Ring any bells?"

Cal had stopped without turning when Kicks had called his name. He cursed under his breath. "You son of—"

The last words of his comment were lost to Kicks' ears as Cal stomped out, but he laughed at the thought of making Cal nervous.

As soon as the door slammed closed behind the sheriff and his deputies, Kicks reached over and picked up the cards that Cal had placed face down on the table. "'Haven't got one good hand during this whole game.'" Kicks looked at the cards. "Anyone care to guess what cards Cal threw away, claiming they were no good?" Silence. "No takers, eh?" Kicks laid the cards face up on the table. "Aces and eights."

Everybody said in unison, "Dead man's hand."

"Why would Cal toss in a hand like that?" Muley said. "Think it was because he had a dead man's hand, or was Kicks makin' him nervous?"

Kicks shrugged. "Like my pappy would put it, 'Nervous as a long-tailed cat in a room full of rocking chairs.'"

Stonewall acted fascinated with the whole thing. "Bet old Cal thought he was gonna trick one of us into telling him all our plans, but you sure cooled his heels on that thought, didn't ya?"

Never one to boast, Kicks laughed. "Yeah, well, old Cal kinda let the cat out of the bag, all right. He knew about

Quantrill staying out at the Running J spread, and he knew about Bloody Bill gunnin' down that farmer."

"Say," Stonewall asked. "Why do they call him Bloody Bill? And what's that talk about tying a knot in a red silk ribbon?"

"Oh," Kicks said, "that's how he earned his nickname Bloody Bill Anderson. Every one of those knots represents a Yankee he's killed."

"How'd he know that farmer was a Yankee?"

Kicks shrugged. "Guess it don't matter no more."

CHAPTER 20

Sheriff Cal Tidwell was fuming by the time he left Kicks and his *amigos* at the livery. You could have lit a match on his red face by the time he and his deputies reached the jail. When they stepped inside the office, Buford made the mistake of whispering a little too loudly, "We sure didn't learn anything from that Kicks fella, did we, Dutch?"

Cal whirled, his fist pulled back, ready to slug the deputy. "Shut up, Buford, and git the hell outta here. All of you git, now!" As the three deputies scurried out of Cal's office, he sat down at his desk and reached in the bottom drawer for a bottle of whiskey. He took a long swig straight from the bottle, then spewed out a long string of cusswords. Taking another long swig, he muttered, "That blasted drifter. I gotta do something about him, and fast."

After a couple of hours of drinking and cussing, Cal passed out in his chair with his head resting on his arms on his desk. About nine the next morning, his deputies came sneaking in the office, afraid to wake him.

As they whispered back and forth, Cal slowly lifted his head, rubbing his bleary eyes. "Well, don't just stand there gawking, get the coffeepot on to boil!"

"Okay, boss," Dutch said. "Gettin' on it right now."

A few minutes later, after the sheriff had splashed some cold water on his face and had a couple cups of coffee under his belt, he felt a little better. "Sit down, men, we got some planning to do."

It didn't take long for Cal and his three bungling deputies to figure out a plan. "This is what needs to happen," Cal said. "We gotta grab those two women, Molly Galveston and Tilly Durmhill. Gotta get someone else to do it though, so we ain't recognized. Town folks might object to us kidnapping two of their women. Once we get them in a safe place, I can question them about this document we need."

"What document?" Oscar asked.

"Don't worry about it. Right now, we just need to worry about gettin' them gals without anyone tyin' it back to us."

"Clever," Oscar said. "What'll we do with 'em after you get what you need? Can't turn 'em loose again. They'll tell."

Cal shrugged. "Have to kill 'em, I guess. Won't have a choice," He narrowed his eyes at the three deputies, as though daring them to disagree. Although a little shy on brains, the idea of killing women might seem a bit drastic for these roughnecks.

"What if they don't know nothin'?" Dutch asked. "You still have to kill 'em?"

"One of 'em has to know," Cal said. "Might need to grab Dave Galveston, or possibly his pa, Sammy. Help loosen their tongues. But for now, we'll start with the women, especially Tilly." Sheriff Durmhill must have said something to his wife about the claim.

"Well," Buford asked, "If we ain't gonna grab them, who is?"

Cal grinned smugly. "One of Quantrill or Bob's men can take care of that problem for us. Come on, boys, let's go get somethin' to eat before we ride out."

After filling their bellies at the Silver Spoon, they walked over to the Golden Nugget to quench their thirst.

"Are we gonna ride all the way out to the Running J again?" Buford asked. "Talk to Quantrill?"

"Hell no," Cal swore. "I ain't stupid. I know some of his men are staying at the old ranch out east of town. We'll go there."

"Quantrill's stayin' at both places?" Dutch asked, acting stumped by the information.

"Yep," Cal chuckled. "Bet they thought I didn't know."

After they finished their drink, the four lawmen went to the stable to get their horses. Cal looked through the office window, seeing Kicks and his four *amigos* inside. "What're them troublemakers up to now?" he mumbled. Why were they even still here, anyway?

About that time, Whiskers stepped out of the office. "Howdy, Sheriff, Deputies. Need help gettin' your horses saddled?"

"Hell no," Cal snapped. He motioned towards the office. "What the hell goes on in there, Whiskers? Why's everyone always congregated in there?" He chuckled. "Take up homesteadin', are they?"

"Why no, Sheriff." Whiskers snickered, "Just havin' a friendly little game of cards. Wanna join us? Yer welcome to."

Cal turned around, ignoring Whiskers. "Come on, men. Let's get the horses and get the hell outta here. Waste of time talkin' to a damn drunk."

He didn't see Whiskers snicker as he turned and walked away.

It took about twenty minutes to reach the abandoned house. Cal looked around uneasily. "Don't appear to be anybody around," he murmured.

Suddenly, the door to the hayloft of the barn opened a crack and a rifle-barrel became visible. "Don't bother to put your feet on the ground, boys. Just sit in your saddles and reach real high."

The four did as they were instructed. "We're reaching," Cal said, "Now what?"

"Who are you and what's yer business here?" the voice demanded.

Cal was a bit surprised these outlaws didn't appear to know him. Might not be a good idea to mention he was the sheriff of Helena. "Name's Cal Tidwell, and these three guys are—"

"Cal Tidwell, huh," the voice behind the rifle interrupted. "You're that sheriff, and these guys must be your deputies, right?"

Cal lowered his hands, feeling a little perturbed. "So, you know who I am. Jus' came back from talking to Bob Jensen and Quantrill," he lied. "They told me to come out here and talk to whoever's in charge. That you?"

"Hang tight. I'm coming down." Shortly, the bearer of the rifle stepped into view; he was a tall, hatchet-faced hardcase with a hooked nose. "Okay, you can put your hands down and climb outta them saddles." The rifleman's cold eyes followed Cal and his deputies as they stepped down. "Go on in the house."

Cal's eyes widened as he stepped inside. He'd been surprised to see so many gunmen. Some were playing cards, some were asleep on the floor, and some were just sitting around talking. Those awake looked up when he walked in, causing the hairs on the back of his neck to rise.

One of the men, a burly redheaded fellow, put his cards down on the table. "What ya got here, Wesley?"

"Sheriff from Helena, Red. Said his name's Cal Tidwell. Other three are his deputies. Claimed they just came back from talking to Quantrill and Bob Jensen. Wants to talk to the fella in charge here."

Red stood. "You're lookin' at him. What d'ya want?"

Cal was getting ticked. "First, if you're in charge, tell your man to get that rifle barrel outta my back."

Red nodded at the rifleman, and Cal heard the man behind step back. Relaxing, Cal stated his business, leaving out a few details, of course. "I need at least two men. Four'd be better. I got an important job needs to be done."

Red laughed. "Well, you can have 'bout as many men as you want." He spread his arms out to encompass the room.

"Four'll be plenty."

The man in charge looked at Wesley. "You wanna go?" he asked, without even asking what kind of job they'd be involved with.

"Hell yeah," Wesley said. "I'm 'bout to go stir crazy out here."

"Then pick out three more men and go with these guys." Red sat and went back to his card game.

Wesley turned to a group of gunmen who were sitting around the room. "Okay, I need three men. Who wants to ride into town with us?"

Ten men stood up.

Wesley pointed and called out three names; "Claude, James, Joe, you three men come along with us."

*   *   *

It was dark out by the time they returned to Helena. They'd stayed out at the old ranch most of the day, making plans. The timing for these abductions had to be perfect. Thankfully, these four men appeared to be a bit brighter than his deputies, who were all three dumber than rocks. Cal was kind of hoping he could talk them into staying once this business was done with. Might have to jerk some strings where Bob and Quantrill were concerned, but he figured he could pull it off.

As they entered the main street of Helena, Wesley read aloud the sign. "Last Chance Gulch. What kind of a street name is that?"

Ignoring the man, Cal stopped and held up his hand, bringing the riders to a halt. "Sign ain't important. You four men wait here for a couple minutes, then ride on in and tie up at the Golden Nugget Saloon. It's straight up the street on your right. Walk down the boardwalk till you get to the jailhouse. Make sure nobody is out watching before you come inside the office."

Cal didn't wait for an answer as he nudged his horse to a walk, motioning for his three deputies to follow him.

*   *   *

It had been quiet in town all day. Kicks hadn't seen hide nor hair of the sheriff or his deputies, which made him a bit nervous. He wasn't the only one either.

Muley, pacing inside the small office at the livery, turned to Kicks and said, "You know, we been nosin' around this town for months now and we ain't come one whit closer to knowing what's going on around here, let alone what happened to my family. I'm about ready to start bustin' some heads. Maybe that'll get the ball rolling. Start with that damn sheriff."

"Yeah," Kicks agreed. "I reckon that would start something all right. Jus' ain't sure it's gonna help get any answers we want."

"I don't know," Dave said. "I'm just about to agree with Muley. I been waiting a long time to learn who killed my Grandpa Howard, and why."

"Look," Kicks said. "I know it's been slow going, but right now things are pretty much going our way. We got the town officials on our side. With Sammy backing us up, we got the town's people on our side. We just need to be patient. Something's gonna cut loose soon. I can feel it in my guts."

Everyone looked at Stonewall for his input.

"What?" He grinned. "You wanna know what I think?" He shrugged. "Wouldn't mind some action, but I say we follow Kicks' lead, do what we've been doing, at least for a while. If things don't improve before long, then we can start bustin' heads."

Kicks yawned, stretching his arms over his head. "It's late, fellas. Let's all get some sleep. We can put our heads together in the morning, take a new look at the situation. Oh, by the way, whose turn is it to patrol the town tonight?"

"I believe that'd be me and Stony," Muley volunteered.

"Okay," Kicks said, "You two guys go start making your rounds. Wake me and Dave up in about three or four hours and we'll relieve you."

"After that," Whiskers added, "I'll team up with someone to make a few rounds."

"Sounds good," Stonewall called as he and Muley left the office. "We'll see you in about four hours then."

The two patrol officers walked the boardwalks, streets, and alleyways for two hours. The saloons were busy, noisy as usual, but other than that everything felt peaceful. Finally, as they were nearing the Silver Spoon Café, they noticed the lights were still on. "My stomach's growling," Muley said. "How about you?"

Stonewall laughed. "Ya hungry? Or you just wanna see Cathy?"

Grinning, Muley replied, "That obvious, huh? Well, I 'spect it's a little of both. Wouldn't mind talking to Cathy for a few minutes, and while we're there, might as well grab a bite to eat."

"Okay, let's do it."

Cathy was about to close the restaurant, but she agreed to serve them coffee and a snack. Stonewall could see the couple wanted a little time alone, and since he'd taken a shine to Wendy, over at the St. Louis Hotel, he told Muley to behave himself and he'd see him over at the hotel.

"Okay," Muley replied. "I'll be over there in a few."

As Stonewall approached the front door of the hotel, he could see through the window that Dave's grandmother, Tilly, was about to leave the desk and go up the stairs. He smiled, glad he'd have some alone time with Wendy. Being bashful around women, he'd been dreading trying to talk to both Wendy and Tilly. As he stepped in the door, Wendy looked up and smiled.

"Well, hello, cowboy. I haven't seen you in a couple of days."

"I ... uh, been busy. Just stopped in to see if everything is all right here."

Turning on the smile again, looking coy, Wendy said, "Why, thank you, kind sir. Everything is just fine … now."

"Uh … well then, I guess I'll be going."

Seeing he was at a loss for words and about to leave, she quickly added, "Everything is fine now that you're here." At Wendy's urging, and her doing most of the talking, Stonewall began to relax. They talked for about twenty minutes.

"Well, I should get back. Muley's probably waiting for me. Hmmm, do you think it would be okay if I came to call on you sometime?"

"I'd like that very much."

He grinned. "Okay then, I'll be seeing you soon, Wendy." He tipped his hat as he left the hotel lobby and started down the street to meet up with Muley.

*   *   *

The four new members to Sheriff Cal's group did as they were told. They rode in and tied up in front of the Golden Nugget Saloon. There were a few strangers in town, and it was after dark, so they went unnoticed as they walked down the boardwalk toward the jail.

"Okay, men," Cal told them once they'd come inside. "I have two simple jobs to get done. Since there's four of you, you can pair up. You shouldn't have any problems."

"Whatcha need?" one of the gunmen asked.

"Here's the deal," Cal said. "There's two people that I want you guys to nab for me. They have information we need. Since I can't incarcerate them legally, it needs to be done in secret, by force."

"Who are they? Where are they? And where are we sup-posed to take them?" the same man asked. Wesley, Cal thought his name was. He appeared to be the one in charge. "You gonna need our help gettin' this in-formation outta them?" He didn't appear to mind the idea.

"No," Cal said. "I can handle that part. Now listen, it's important you get these people without being seen. Grab 'em, blindfold and gag 'em, then bring them here." Cal showed them how the jail was laid out. "Lock them up in that building out back. I'll need at least one of you to stay and stand guard while I'm interrogating them. The rest of you can go over to the saloon or do whatever you want. Do you understand?"

"Yeah," Wesley said. "We understand. Now who are these two guys you need us to nab, and where can we find them?"

"Well," Cal answered slowly. "They ain't guys. They're two women, and—"

"Hey now, hold on a minute," Wesley warned, his eyes hardening. "We ain't gonna kidnap no damn women."

Cal could see the idea didn't sit well with the man. The other three didn't look any happier about it. Kinda of surprised him for hardened outlaws. Though angry, he controlled his temper. "I can understand how you feel, but all I need is a little information. Don't wanna hurt 'em. I'll pay you on top of whatever you're getting paid from your boss, Quantrill."

"I don't know," Wesley murmured. "Don't feel right."

"Look, fellas. I only want a little information from them. What you folks do with them afterward is totally up to you. Long as they don't recognize me, let 'em go if you want."

One of the other men stepped up, Claude, he thought his name was. "You say you're gonna pay us extra for grabbin' these two women? And we can do what we want with them afterwards?"

This was a good sign to Cal. "That's what I said. Once I get what I need, they're yours to dispose of any way you want. Probably be best all around if we just got rid of them though."

Claude thought about it for a second, then shrugged. "Sheriff, far as I'm concerned, you got yourself a deal. Now what are their names, and where can we find 'em."

Wesley pressed his lips together, not looking happy, but he didn't say anything more.

Cal grinned. "Tilly Durmhill and Molly Galveston. Mother and daughter. Tilly works at the St. Louis Hotel here in Helena. Molly lives right at the edge of town. Stays pretty much to herself. You can't miss her house. Fancy place, got a white picket fence." Cal described both women. "Now, don't come near me or this jailhouse, not till you got those women blindfolded. Like I said, I'd rather they didn't recognize me, just in case things go wrong." Because then he'd have to kill them both for sure, personally.

"No problem, Sheriff," Claude said. "Come on, men, times a wastin'. Got a nice easy job to pull off, then we can get to drinking."

"I don't like messin' with no women," Wesley grumbled, but it didn't stop him from following Claude and the other two out the door.

Cal smiled, nodding to himself. Wouldn't be long now.

CHAPTER 21

Muley left Cathy at the Silver Spoon Café at about the same time Stone-wall left Wendy at the hotel. They crossed the street and met midway be-tween the two places. They paused to make plans to finish their rounds. Muley pulled a couple of cheroots from his vest pocket and offered one to the kid. They lit up and were enjoying the smoke and the night air when they noticed four men across the street, acting suspicious.

"Looks like strangers to me," Stonewall said.

"Yeah," Muley agreed. "Somethin' ain't right here." They quickly cupped the cheroots in their hand so the cherry at the end of the cigar could not be seen in the dark. Then they stepped further back into the shadows and watched the four strangers.

They split up. Two went into the hotel, and the other two continued toward the end of town.

"That's strange," Muley said. "You stay here and keep an eye out for the two that went into the hotel. I'll follow the other two." About that time, the two men came out of the hotel and whistled. The other two men stopped and waited for them to catch up with them, and then all four men continued down the street.

"We better follow these guys," Stonewall whispered.

Muley agreed. Suddenly, the four men split up again, going in four different directions. "Shoot, musta spotted us," Muley said. Before they knew it, all four men were out of sight.

"What'll we do now?" Stonewall asked.

"Nothin'," Muley replied. "When you lose sight of someone in the dark, you don't go running after 'em. Good way to get shot."

"Yeah," Stonewall agreed. "Still, I wonder what they're up to. I'm bettin' no good."

"Come on," Muley said. "Let's go back to the hotel and see if they said anything to Wendy."

Stonewall nodded, falling into step beside Muley.

"Yes," Wendy said after they questioned her. "Two men came into the lobby and asked if Tilly was here. Asked for her by name, I figured they knew her. Before I could tell them that she already went up to her room, they went back outside."

"Hmmmm," Muley said. "If they come back in, just tell 'em you don't have any idea where she's at. Try to find out what they want with Tilly."

"What's going on, Muley?" Wendy asked, looking between the two men. "Why would strangers be looking for Tilly?"

"We don't know," Stonewall replied for him. "Be careful of 'em, Wendy. We'll try and keep an eye out for you just in case they come back. Our watch for tonight is over, so we'll tell Kicks and the others about this."

*   *   *

Bob Jensen had mixed feelings about this whole operation. It felt like he was losing control. He did not like dealing with Quantrill. The man was a lunatic. Still thought he was fighting for the rights of the South. Him and his men were even outfitted in gray uniforms, as if they were still in the Confederate army. Bob had been forced to kill in the past, and he knew he wouldn't hesitate to kill again if anyone got in his way, but he did not kill for the simple pleasure of it. Quantrill looked at people like they were animals waiting for the slaughter. He didn't care if his men molested the women after they killed their menfolk either. But this is not what Bob wanted around here.

Still, as bad as Bob hated having Quantrill around, he needed him. He also needed that no-account sheriff, Cal Tidwell. Tidwell was just as much of a killer as Quantrill.

Bob stood, rubbing his brow. He could feel a headache coming on. Maybe he should head over to Maria's Cantina, have a few drinks, lose his troubles in Rosa's intoxicating embrace for a couple hours.

Once he made up his mind up to go, it only took a few minutes in the corral to catch and saddle his horse. What Bob did not know was that Quantrill didn't trust him, and he always kept one of his men on his trail. He left the ranch not knowing he had a tail, Two Bears, a Shoshoni native who'd broken away from the reservation to join up with Quantrill and his gang.

It usually took forty-five minutes to ride to Maria's Cantina on the outskirts of town. He tied up at the hitching post in front of the cantina, still not aware he had a tail.

Two Bears sat outside in the dark, watching, waiting, blending into the countryside.

Much later, at the first gray streaks of early dawn, Bob Jensen left Ma-ria's Cantina, feeling relaxed, invincible, and ready to face his troubles and fears again. He was tired of hunting for that damn document that would give him control over the gold mine. It was time to put an end to this thing, but he needed to get rid of Kicks Burks and his ragtag gang. They were driving him crazy. As a bigtime cattleman in the area, Bob had an image to uphold.

Hungry after his night of debauchery, Bob figured he'd stop and have breakfast at the Silver Spoon, then go over and pay a visit to Cal. He need-ed to check up on the sheriff, still irritated with the man for horning in on his dealings with Quantrill.

There were two seats open at the counter at the Silver Spoon, so Bob sat down and waited to be served. He'd hoped to get a few minutes to talk with Cathy. He found the woman attractive and wanted to get to know her better. However, because of the breakfast crowd, one on one time with Cathy appeared to be out of the question this morning.

After he finished his meal, Bob left the café and walked down to the jailhouse. They'd just started a conversation when a man stepped inside the office, acting upset. Bob didn't recognize him. A rancher by the looks of his clothes, about six-foot, give or take an inch. He wore a tall Texas-style crowned hat, blue shirt, and brown leather vest. His pants were tucked inside of worn brush boots. Worn low on his hip was a Colt .44. He looked angry, not a man you'd want to cross, so Bob stepped aside to let Cal deal with him.

"Sorry to interrupt your conversation, Sheriff, but I need to talk to you ... now!"

Cal held his hand up as if to ward off an attack. "Whoa there, Seth, calm down. What seems to be the problem? You got trouble?"

"Trouble? I'll say there's trouble!" The man paused and looked from Cal to Bob.

"Uh, Seth," Cal said, "this here's Bob Jensen of the Running J outfit. Bob, meet Seth Morgan. He runs a sizable spread out north of town a ways, the S slash M."

Seth gave Cal and Bob both a look that would scare a rattlesnake out of its skin, "I know who Bob Jensen is, Cal." After a brief pause, Seth continued. "Some dirty lowlife coward burned me out last night. Barely got my wife and kids out of the house in time."

Acting sympathetic—though Bob knew Cal couldn't care less—the sheriff cursed the incident. "Any idea who did it? You see any faces?"

"Naw, too dark, and I was busy trying to save my family."

"Well, shoot," Cal said. "I'm sorry, Seth, but if you don't have any idea who's responsible, I can't promise to be of much help."

"Oh, I don't expect nothing outta you, Cal. I'm just here to tell you what happened. I'll find out who's responsible myself. And I'll kill 'em." Without waiting for a response, Seth turned on a heel and stormed out of Cal's office.

Cal looked over at Bob, narrowing his eyes. "About a week ago, someone robbed the bank, killed eight or nine people. Next night, five strangers show up and try to shoot up the Golden Nugget. They ended up gettin' killed instead. Last night, someone burns out Seth Morgan and his family. You know anything about this, Bob?"

"Hell no," Bob replied. "When the man bust in here saying he got burned out, I thought you were behind it."

"Well then," Cal said. "Must be Quantrill's men."

"Yeah," Bob agreed, sighing. "Quantrill didn't mention it to me, but I expected he and his men would terrorize the town and ranches around. Get 'em frightened enough to stick to their own business, at least until we can get our hands on that map."

Bob left Cal's office a few minutes later, stepping up into his saddle, still unaware he was being followed. He started back for the ranch, wondering how he was going to bring up Quantrill putting out orders without running them by him first. The man was becoming a real thorn in his side. Might be getting time to pluck it out.

*   *   *

"Start from the beginning," Kicks said. "Tell us again what happened last night."

Stonewall looked over at Muley, grimacing. "You tell 'em this time."

Muley nodded, going over the story again about the four strangers behaving oddly. "Wendy didn't know what they wanted with Tilly."

Kicks was about to ask another question when they were interrupted by a hard knock at the office door. They looked out the window to see a man with a rifle in his hand.

Dave was closer to the door, so he opened it. "Hello, can we help you?"

The man stepped inside, expression hard, his posture stiff. "Yeah, you sure can. I need to rent me a team of horses, and a wagon."

"Okay," Dave said. "We got a team and wagon for rent."

As they worked out the finances, Kicks sensed urgency in the face of the man. "Is there something else we can help you with, friend?"

"Yep," the man replied. "You could tell me who torched my house last night, damn near killed me, my wife, and kids. I'd like to get 'em in my gun sights."

Kicks blew slowly through his lips. He had always been a fair judge of character and knew this man was dangerous. "Sorry to hear it, friend. Why don't you tell me about it."

"Where's your family?" Kicks asked after hearing all the details.

"That's why I'm here for the wagon. Need to go pick 'em up, bring 'em back to town."

"I'll go with you. Your family might still be in danger."

Within a matter of seconds, they had a wagon hitched up to a team of healthy, sleek-looking bays. The man jumped into the wagon's seat and grabbed up the reins. Before he could yell, "Get up there," Kicks slapped one of the horses on the rump. As the wagon started to pass him, he swung up into the seat next to the rancher.

Kicks yelled over his shoulder at his comrades, "Sit tight. We'll get back when we can."

Once they got out of town, Kicks asked, "Anyone in your family get hurt?"

The man looked over at Kicks and managed a thin-lipped smile as he shook his head. "They were okay when I left them hidden in the woods." He held out his free hand, "I'm Seth Morgan ... and thanks for the help."

Kicks shook the hand. "Kicks Burks here."

They took the left trail, which forked off to the north for about a mile. All the while Seth kept urging the horses to keep at top speed. Finally, as they neared Seth's place, Kicks could see there was nothing left of the rancher's place but a smoldering heap of charred wood and ashes. Almost brought tears to Kicks' eyes to see what must have been a beautiful picture.

Behind the house lay a range of magnificent mountains. On the left was a large, wooded area, while on the right showed miles of top-grade pastureland. As Seth pulled the team to a halt in what had once been the ranch yard, he wrapped the reins around the wagon's brake and leaped from the seat, headed for the wooded area, yelling, "Emily, Hattie, Kevin." Even as he was calling out their names, they came running from the edge of the woods.

Kicks began rummaging through the smoldering debris, picking out what he figured might be salvageable. Presently, he heard Seth calling his name. He walked over to where the little group stood, their faces still stained with ash from the fire last night.

"Kicks," Seth said, "this is my family ... my wife, Emily, my daughter Hattie, and my son, Kevin." He motioned toward Kicks. "Guys, this stranger, and now our friend, is Kicks Burks.

As Kicks shook hands with Seth's family, he sized them up. The wife, Emily, or Em, as Seth called her, was a comely woman with dark hair and eyes. The daughter, Hattie, was an attractive young lady of about nineteen. She had her mother's looks, including the dark hair and eyes. Kevin was younger that his sister. Kicks guessed him to be fourteen or fifteen. After the introductions, Kicks asked Seth, "You got any idea what your next step will be."

"Not really," Seth admitted. "Find a place for my family to stay first. Might have to put 'em on a stagecoach and send them back east to live with Em's folks while I rebuild. I'm not gonna let anyone chase me off my land."

Kicks saw fire flash in Emily's dark eyes. "No!" she said sternly. "We're a family, Seth, and we will not be chased off our land either. We Morgans stick together, dear."

Despite the seriousness of the tragedy that had taken place, Seth laughed. Holding his hands up in defeat, he said,

"Okay, but where do you expect to stay? All we got left is our land and cattle, and I can't just sell them. I don't have a buyer, and I'm not gonna have time to look for one. I gotta rebuild before winter hits."

"We'll put a shelter up in the woods. We can help you rebuild the house, Seth."

Kicks cleared his throat. "Gets mighty cold here in the woods at night this time of the year. Tell you what. I got a large room at the hotel in town that I don't even stay in. You're welcome to it."

"Seth's eyes widened, acting a bit taken aback by the offer. "It's mighty kind of you to offer, but we can't accept—"

"Oh yes we can," Emily said, turning to face Kicks. "You must be our guardian angel, Mister Burks. Thank you. And yes, we accept your offer. Hopefully, we can repay your kindness someday."

Embarrassed, Kicks said, "Just call me Kicks, ma'am, and you're mighty welcome."

Overjoyed, she threw her arms around him in a hug. "Thank you so much," she whispered, choked up. "And please, call me Em."

Bewildered, his face red, Kicks looked over at Seth, who shrugged, rolling his eyes. He lifted his hands, simulating helplessness. Then they all started laughing, the solemn moment lightening up some.

"God is good," Seth said.

Em grinned, nodding. "All the time."

There were more tears from Em and the kids as they searched through the charred wood that had once been their home. With the wagon finally loaded with the few things they could salvage, they started to make their way back to town.

It was getting late when they reached the livery stable. After taking care of the wagon and horses, Kicks introduced the Morgan family to the rest of the guys. Afterwards, he took Seth and his family to the hotel and got them settled in his room. Upon entering the hotel, Kicks introduced the Morgans to Wendy, and asked about Tilly.

"She hasn't come down from her room for a while," Wendy said.

"Okay," Kicks replied, frowning. "Guess they can meet Tilly later." Next, he took them over to the Silver Spoon Café and introduced them to Cathy. They had dinner together, and as they were eating, Kicks told them about the situation here in town that he and his friends were in.

Kicks looked over at Seth. "Maybe we can help each other, friend. I think the people responsible for burning your house are the same people be-hind all our problems."

Seth sat back for a moment, looking thoughtful. "Well," he finally said, nodding, "guess I need to find out who these people are before I start rebuilding. Probably jus' come out and burn me out again if I don't."

"Yeah," put in young Kevin. "I can help ya, pa."

Seth frowned at his young son but didn't reply.

"Okay, guess that settles it. Glad to have you on our side, Seth." Kicks suggested Em, Hattie and Kevin go back to the hotel and start unpacking their things while he and Seth went over to the stable to talk it over with the rest of the crew.

When they got back to the livery, Muley offered his condolences. "Sorry to hear about your house, Seth, but the good news is, you got an outfit of fighting men here to help ya. We'll find out who burned you out, and why, and who's behind it."

"Yeah," Dave agreed. "And now there are six of us. I think things will be coming to a head real soon."

He'd no sooner spoke than Sammy came rushing inside the office. "Quick, we gotta do something. Tilly and Molly have both disappeared."

Kicks jumped up, feeling a tingle of fear rush down his spine. "What do you mean they disappeared?"

"Just what I said," Sammy replied, breathing hard. "Tilly and Molly are both gone. I pulled a long shift at the saloon last night, so I just went to sleep in the back room until morning. I do that sometimes. When I got home, Molly wasn't there. I didn't panic then. I figured she went to see Tilly. She does that sometimes. When she didn't get home tonight, I went over to the hotel to check on her. Wendy said Tilly never came down from her room today. And she hadn't seen Molly at all. They're both just gone!"

CHAPTER 22

Cal was furious. After his four new gunmen managed to lose Muley and Stonewall by splitting up, they came back to the jailhouse. "You guys better not screw this up, you hear?"

"Hey, don't worry about it," Claude said. "We just need to lay low for a few hours, wait for those men to give up."

Later in the night, Wesley and James went back to the hotel. When they peeked through the window, they saw an older woman had taken the place of the younger one from earlier. *This must be Tilly*, Wesley thought. They crept in through the back door and waited until she walked over by the stairs.

She jumped back when she saw them, her hand going to her throat. "You startled me, gentlemen. I didn't see you come in. Did you need to rent a room?"

Wesley shook his head, his lips pressed tight together as he grabbed her. He wrapped his hand around her mouth before she could cry for help. James held up a stained bandana, stuffing it in her mouth when Wesley released her. "Gimme that sack," Wesley growled. He jerked the burlap sack out of James' hand and pulled it over her head, then shoved the old woman down the hall. "Behave yerself and you won't get hurt," he growled.

They stepped outside, checking the boardwalk for people. James leaned over and pushed his shoulder into the old woman's belly, coming up with her over his shoulder. Wesley kept his eye out for trouble as they approached the jail. He pushed the door open to the office, breathing a sigh of relief when they finally got off the street. He didn't think anyone had seen them.

"Knock it off, lady," James said, swatting the old woman on the butt when she started kicking and trying to scream. "Ain't no one can hear you." He looked over at Wesley. "Now what?"

Cal looked up when the two men entered his office, one of them carrying Tilly. His face turned red as he struggled not to yell at them. He didn't really want to have to kill the old woman, but he wouldn't have a choice if she recognized him.

Obviously seeing his fury, the one called Wesley said, "Stop frettin'. No one saw us."

Cal stood, motioning for them to follow him. He led them out the back door of the jail to the building behind it. After they dropped Tilly on the bare cot inside and tied her up, he locked the door, satisfied she wouldn't be able to get free.

Back inside his office, Cal said, "Good job, fellas. Where's the other one?"

"What are you gonna do with 'em once you get what you need outta them?" Wesley asked.

"I don't know yet. Why? That's really none of your concern."

"Hey," James said. "You said we could have 'em once you were done."

Wesley gave the other guy a cold look. "I don't cotton to harming women. Kidnapping one is bad enough, but I don't wanna see either one of 'em hurt."

James snorted, waving him off. He obviously had no problem hurting a woman.

Cal looked between the two men, sensing trouble. "Long as she doesn't recognize me, I don't really care what you do with them. Now, go bring me the other one. And take her around back this time. Don't come in through the jail. Idiots. Lucky you weren't seen."

Cal ignored the angry glares. He watched the two men leave, then sat down at his desk. He'd let the old woman stew for the night, then start questioning her tomorrow morning. Hopefully, those idiots would bring Molly in before then. He'd have that damn document in his hands in no time.

Then he'd see what he could do about cutting out Bob and his murderous partner, take the mine for himself. Cal chuckled, well aware Bob didn't respect him. Might change his mind after this.

*　　　*　　　*

At the same time Wesley and James entered the hotel to grab Tilly, Joe and Claude were headed for Sammy's house. They knew Sammy was working at the saloon, which meant his wife, Molly, would be home alone. Their only problem was going to be in getting her to the jail without being noticed. They had a little further to go. When they got to Molly's house, they walked all the way around it, peeking in the windows to make sure she was alone. There was light coming from only one window in the back of the house, so they went around to the front and opened the unlocked door, walking inside.

"Sit down, dear," Molly said, obviously thinking it was her husband. "I'll fix you a cup of coffee."

Claude and Joe went to the kitchen doorway and stood one on each side of the opening. When Molly stepped inside, they grabbed her from behind and quickly tied her hands behind her back. After gagging her, they put a burlap bag over her head.

The woman was too big to carry easily, so it took a half an hour to push the scared female to the jailhouse. They went around the outside of town to keep from being seen.

Cal was delighted. He put Molly in a separate cell from her mother, leaving both women bound, gagged, and with the burlap sacks over their heads so they couldn't see. He left Claude as guard to the outbuilding. He appeared to be the more cold-blooded of the three outlaws. He wouldn't let anyone get near the outbuilding, not and live to tell about it anyway. The other three men went over to the Golden Nugget to drink.

The next morning, Cal was up at daybreak. As soon as his three deputies walked in, he told them to stay at the jail and take care of things while he went out for breakfast. "Make sure no one goes poking around the building out back while I'm gone." Not that he needed to worry about it with one of Quantrill's men guarding it. He would go out and have a little talk with the women when he got back.

*　　　*　　　*

Molly and Tilly spent a horrifying night locked up. They knew they weren't alone, but unable to see or talk, they didn't know who else was there. Every muscle in Molly's body ached from sitting tied on a hard cot in the freezing cold with no blanket. At least she hadn't been thrown to the floor. She couldn't imagine why anyone would want to kidnap her. She could hear men talking outside, but their voices were muffled. The men who'd taken her had been complete strangers. There didn't appear to be anything she could do but sit here and wait.

It felt like hours passed before she finally heard someone unlock the door.

The door opened, and a familiar voice said, "Okay, men, you can go get yourself some breakfast. Got good chow down at the Silver Spoon. Come back in about an hour."

Molly could tell the man was trying to mask his voice. The next thing she heard was, "Good morning, ladies. If you promise not to try and scream, I'll take your gags out."

Ladies? So it's another woman in here with me. But who?

She nodded, struggling to breathe beneath the burlap sack. Molly heard what sounded like a key being placed in a barred door, then someone reached up beneath the sack and removed her gag. She sucked in a deep breath, grateful for the fresh air. She'd been afraid she might choke on the gag.

"Sorry I can't remove the sacks, ladies. I'm sure you understand why."

"Who are you? What do you want?" Tilly demanded.

"Shut up, old woman," he said harshly. "I'll ask the questions here."

She listened as he walked away, then she heard the key being inserted in another lock. Were they at the jail? She froze, thinking she might know who that disguised voice belonged to.

"Now," he said, "I'm sure you two know each other."

"Ma," Molly said, her voice shaking. "Is that you?"

Tilly felt her heart skip a beat as she replied, "Are you okay, Molly?"

"I'm cold, but I'm okay. Do you know what's going on? Why did they kidnap us?"

"I don't know, sweetheart."

"Information, ladies. I need information, and if I don't get some cooperation from you, I'll have to give my uncouth friends out there a turn at you two. I'm sure I don't have to spell it out for you what that means, right?"

He paused, but Tilly could hear him pacing somewhere in front of them.

"So, ladies, you think you wanna try to cooperate?"

"What do you want? What information is it you think we have?" Tilly snapped.

The man chuckled. "That's the spirit, Tilly. Maybe you two will just get out of this mess unscathed. We can all three walk away happy."

*   *   *

"What do you mean they just disappeared," Kicks repeated, a statement more than a question. "Two women don't just disappear. Someone musta kidnapped them. But why?"

"Ransom?" Seth Morgan said.

"It's possible, I guess," Sammy said. "But I don't have a lot of money. They wouldn't get much. Tilly owns the hotel, but I don't think she has a lot of extra cash either."

Kicks reached out and placed a comforting hand on Sammy's shoulder. He could see the man was about at the end of his tether. "Try to stay calm, Sammy. It won't do us no good to panic. For now, let's just carry on as normal, or at least make it look that way. Don't say anything to anyone about this. Leave it to us. We'll turn this town upside down if we have to. I promise we won't quit until they're safely back home."

Sammy nodded, rubbing at his face with both hands. "Yeah, okay, you're right, Kicks. Can't trust the sheriff. I know you and Muley, and the rest of you men, will do your best to find them. I'm just scared for them. I'll be over at the Golden Nugget if you hear anything."

As Sammy turned to leave, Seth's young son came into the office. He must have been standing outside the door, out of sight. "You can count me in on this," he said. Kevin was fourteen, and already about the same height as his dad.

No one said a word. They just looked at Seth. He cleared his throat. "Does your ma know you're here, and for what reason?"

"Yes. I mean, she doesn't know about this kidnapping, but she knows I want to help figure out who torched our place."

"She okay with it?" Seth asked, narrowing his eyes.

Kevin stepped from foot to foot, obviously uncomfortable at being put on the spot. "She ain't happy about it. But I'm here now, and I wanna be of some help." He looked up at his dad, refusing to break eye contact. "The S slash M belongs to me too, pa, and if it takes blood to keep it alive, then I expect some of that blood to be mine." Kevin paused for a couple seconds, then continued. "Pa, if I ain't able to help, then I ain't worthy to wear the name Morgan, or claim any part of the S slash M."

Seth brushed his hair back with his hands, obviously conflicted. "I understand what you're saying, son, but..." Seth paused and looked at Kicks and the other men.

"Well," Kicks said, interrupting, "As my pappy always says, 'A newborn colt won't ever amount to much unless he can stand up on his own.'"

Seth appeared relieved. "Okay then, what can we have him do? I've been teaching him to shoot, and he's a pretty good shot with a six-shooter. But I don't want my son involved in any shootouts if it can be avoided."

Dave suggested, "He can help me. Horses need fed and watered every day, and I could use the help in cleaning the stalls. Also, seeing as how things are starting to heat up pretty fast around here, I think we should keep a couple horses saddled and tied up at the hitch rail, jus' in case anyone needs them fast. Kevin can help me swap them out during the day." He met Seth's eyes. "If that's okay with you, sir."

Seth nodded, looking relieved. "Sure, sounds good to me." He smiled at his son, who also looked happy to be able to do something to help.

"Smart thinkin', kid," Whiskers said. "How'd you come up with that idea?"

Dave grinned. "It's not really my idea. My grandpa used to tell me stories. Said you always needed to be prepared when trouble might be headed your way."

"Okay, men," Kicks said. "We need to find those two women before something bad happens to them." He didn't have to say he hoped it wasn't already too late for that. They were all thinking it.

"Glad to have you with us, Kevin," Kicks said. "You can start by helping Dave saddle up four horses. Take 'em outside and wait." He took a deep breath, releasing it slowly. "The rest of us can pair up and start the search. We'll knock on every door, search every business." Kicks paused a moment. "Anybody got anything else to add?"

"Yeah, what do we tell folks," Whiskers asked, brushing his hand down his ragged beard.

Kicks grimaced. "I think we need to keep as much as we can to ourselves. Don't want to push the men who took them into doing something rash. Just ask if they've seen Molly or Tilly today. Say you got a telegraph or something for one of 'em. Tell 'em to come by the livery if they hear anything." He doubted they'd be able to keep this quiet for long. People were naturally suspicious, but he didn't want the sheriff involved. He didn't trust the man.

"All right, men," Muley said, "if we're ready, let's get on with the search."

Kicks motioned Seth to him. "Me and Seth will pair up and start at the south end of town by the old fire tower and work our way back. Muley and Dave can start at the other end of the town and work toward us. Check out any old outbuilding you might run across along the way. We'll leave Kevin here to run the livery while we're gone. Whiskers, you're known here in this town. Folks might open up to you easier. You and Stony can start searching up and down the side streets, check out businesses, ask questions. We'll meet up later today over at the Silver Spoon. We won't stop searching until we've looked behind every door in town."

Everyone agreed, and the search began.

When Seth and Kicks got to the old fire tower, Kicks took the time to explain about the history of the town and why the fire tower had been built. After they questioned the guard, finding nothing suspicious inside, they began to work northward. They found no sign of Molly or Tilly, though the trail that led toward Bob's ranch looked to be well used.

Hours later, they rode back to town. Whiskers had shaken his head, looking grim as they rode past him and Stonewall.

Finding the sheriff sitting outside having a smoke, Kicks glanced over at Seth and shrugged. Looked like he wasn't going to have a choice but to bring the sheriff into it. They walked their horses over and stepped down, stretching before they tied them to the hitch rail.

Sheriff Cal Tidwell smirked as he walked inside, leaving the door open for Kicks and Seth to follow him. Dutch Simmons, one of Cal's deputies was already inside. Kicks started to introduce them, but Seth interrupted, "Me and the sheriff already met."

"What do you need?" Cal said. "Already told you there wasn't much I could do unless you saw who set the fire."

"Worthless," Seth said under his breath. He turned to Kicks. "Let's just search the place and be done with it."

Cal jumped up from his desk, looking alarmed. "Now hold on there, fellas. Just what the hell's goin' on here? Search for what?"

Kicks narrowed his eyes as Dutch ducked out the back door. Maybe he had to use the outhouse, but the man had looked a bit worried when he left.

Seth started to follow him, but the sheriff stepped into his path.

"Hold on there a minute, Seth," Kicks said, raising his eyebrows. "We can spare a minute to chat with the sheriff."

"Would someone mind tellin' me what the hell is going on here?" Cal demanded, his face turning bright red.

Kicks stepped up and got right in Cal's face. "Sure, Sheriff. Actin' a bit nervous, ain't ya? You and your idiot deputies been butting heads with me and Muley ever since we got here. I know Quantrill and his outlaw gang's been hangin' around. One of his men killed that farmer, and you just ignored it. One of Bob's men was with him. Don't you find that just a bit odd?

I do." He took a deep breath, releasing it slowly as he rubbed his chin. "Seth's place gets burnt down. And now, two of our women have come up missing. What I find really strange, you bein' the sheriff and all, is that you don't know squat about any of it. Find you just sittin' here on your butts, playing with yourselves." He paused, stepping closer, smirking when Cal backed up. "Know anything about these missing women, Cal?"

The sheriff shook his head. "First I've heard of it. Why didn't someone tell me Tilly and her daughter came up missing? We'd have been out helping you search."

"That's odd, Sheriff," Kicks said, cocking his head to the side. "I don't recall mentioning any names."

By this time, Seth was already down the hall past the jail cells, headed out the back door.

Cal turned to race after him. "Hey, you can't just come in here and start doing as you please. You gotta have permission to go out back."

Kicks was right on Cal's heels. "What's the matter, Cal? Got somethin' to hide back there?"

By this time, all three men were out the back door. Kicks and Cal were striding up the path that led to the privy. Seth was already checking the door to the outbuilding that held spare cells. When he found the door locked, he shouted, "Hey, anybody in there? Can you hear me?"

"Get the hell away from there!" Cal yelled. He pulled his gun. "I swear I'll stick one in you if you try to open that door."

He must have forgotten about Kicks, too focused on Seth. "Drop it, Sheriff," Kicks said coldly, sticking the barrel of his gun against the sheriff's back. "You pull that trigger and you're a dead man."

"You coward," Seth said, pulling his own gun. "You gonna shoot me in the back, Sheriff? You got the guts for a fair fight? I'll face off with you anytime. Right now sounds just fine with me."

In a flash, Kicks weighed the pros and cons of a shootout between these two. He really didn't care if Seth killed Cal, but they had women to worry about. They could get in the line of fire. "Hold on, you two." Kicks said. "Let's get the two ladies taken care of first. You can settle this later."

"Yeah, I guess you're right, Seth admitted, frowning.

"Yeah," Cal agreed, starting to relax. He stuck his gun back in its holster. "Sorry I got a little carried away there. Why don't you fellas go start talking to some of the town folks. Me and my deputies will join you in a few minutes. I'll need to speak with Sammy first. Then Wendy over at the hotel."

"Sounds good, Sheriff." Kicks motioned with his head for Seth to come with him.

Seth looked toward the locked building, then back at Kicks, narrowing his eyes as he holstered his gun. As they turned to walk off, he murmured, "I believe those two women are in that building, Kicks."

Kicks nodded, speaking behind his hand, "Yep, think you're right."

"Well then, why didn't we go get 'em?" Seth asked. "They got the windows covered so no one can see inside?"

"Yep," Kicks agreed. "I saw that too."

"Well then," Seth asked, "What's our next step? You must have somethin' in mind."

"Wasn't ready for a shootout with the sheriff, not with the women so close. Got another problem too. You notice how fast Dutch disappeared?"

"Damn, kinda thought he went into the privy."

"Those idiot deputies aren't smart enough to figure out how to abduct someone and not get caught. I suspect Cal had help, probably from Quantrill or Bob's men. Pretty sure they were somewhere close, watching us. Couldn't you feel it?"

"Oh," Seth said, his expression saying he was beginning to understand. "They'd have killed us if we'd try to get to the women."

"That's right."

Seth scratched his head. "So what do we do next?"

"We can't let 'em move them out of that building. We'll never see 'em again. We need to find who's working for Cal and take them out. It's the only safe way to get the women free. Just wish I knew why they were taken. Doesn't make any sense."

CHAPTER 23

C al followed Kicks and the rancher, watching through his office window until they were out of sight. Then he hurried back to the outbuilding where the women were being held. He banged on the door, disguising his voice as he yelled, "Open up. It's me."

Dutch opened the door, his eyes wide, expression nervous. "They leave, boss?"

"They'll be back," Cal said softly, pulling Dutch out of the building. "Go find Oscar and Buford and bring them back here."

Furious, Cal went back inside and reached up under the burlap sack to remove the gags from the women's mouths. "You ladies ready to talk about that document yet? And don't play dumb. You know perfectly well what document I'm referring to."

Tilly took a deep breath, the older woman's posture slumped. "Molly doesn't know anything about this. I know what you're talking about, but I have no idea where it could be. Why would I?"

Cal wasn't convinced. "I've tried to be patient, ladies. You just don't realize the danger you're in." He paused, frustrated. "Listen, I don't wanna see either one of you hurt. Just tell me where I can find the map. Once I get possession of it, I swear I'll let you go … unharmed. If you don't talk, well,

I'll turn you over to the four men who nabbed ya. I don't think you'll enjoy that much." He suspected they'd take turns using them, then dump their bodies up in the mountains for the animals to feed on.

Cal cursed when they both remained silent. He was running out of time. He suspected they'd heard Kicks' voice and knew there were men trying to find them. *But what if they really don't know anything?*

It didn't matter. He couldn't turn them loose now. He suspected Tilly knew it was him.

"Fine, ladies, I see you've made your decision. Don't say I didn't warn you." He stuffed the gags back into their mouths, then walked to the door, pausing, giving them one more chance. They neither one said anything.

When he opened the door and stepped out, Cal was a bit taken aback to see not only Dutch, Oscar and Buford, but also Quantrill's men. So they had been guarding the building. He'd wondered about that. He turned to his deputies. "You three stay here and guard those women. Kill anyone who comes snooping around." He motioned to Quantrill's men. "You guys come with me. We need to talk."

"Why are we holding these women, Cal?" Dutch asked, looking confused.

Cal cursed. If they hadn't known who he was before, they did now. "Just shut up and do as you're told, Dutch." He led the other four men back into his office. "Take a seat, gentlemen. We need to figure out what to do with those women."

James grinned, though his eyes remained stone cold. "We know what to do with 'em boss. Jus' turn 'em over to us if you're havin' trouble gettin' answers. Why don't you jus' tell me what you want outta them."

Cal hesitated. He couldn't trust these men not to run back to Bob or Quantrill. "They don't know anything. Can't keep 'em here. Those saddle tramps are gonna come back nosin' around. Can't risk anyone finding them." Cal had a good thing going here and didn't want to ruin it. Maybe he should have thought about that before he had those two women abducted.

"So what are we gonna do?" Claude asked. "Where you want us to take them?"

"Gonna be hard to move 'em in the middle of the day," Wesley said.

Cal rubbed his chin, then grinned. "You know where A. J. Grimes' General Store is?"

"Yeah," James said. "A couple blocks from here, but what's that got to do with anythin'?"

"Well," Cal announced proudly, "old man Grimes keeps a team and buckboard tied up out back of his store for when he needs to make a delivery. I think we need to make a delivery of our own. No one will think to question it." He nodded at Wesley. "Go get me that wagon. Bring it around back."

"If Grimes complains?"

"Do what you have to do."

"Where we gonna take the women?" Wesley asked.

"Hunters built an old lodge up in the woods just before the Gates of the Mountains. Heard it was used for a hunter's lodge. I think some of Quantrill's men been up in that area. You take 'em up there. I'll make a map for you."

Claude narrowed his eyes. "How'd you know some of Quantrill's men were up there?"

Cal shrugged. "I got my ways. Don't really matter, does it? We're all on the same side. Now hurry up, fellas. A couple of you need to go get that buckboard. Those two cowboys aren't gonna stay away long."

Claude and Wesley nodded, leaving Joe and James behind with the sheriff.

Cal watched them leave, then he reached in an open drawer and took out a bottle of whiskey, pouring him and the other two men a drink. He pulled over a piece of paper and drew a crude map to the hunter's lodge, stuffing it in his pocket. Throwing the bottle back in the drawer, he said, "Come on, fellas. We need to go get those women ready to go. Grab some blankets out of the cells there. We'll keep 'em covered."

Twenty minutes later, they had Tilly and Molly wrapped up and shoved in the back of the buckboard. They forced them to lay flat, throwing several blankets over them. Cal pulled the map out of his pocket and handed it to Buford. "You go with Wesley, drive the team of horses. I'll be up as soon as things calm down around here." He stepped closer to Buford, out of hearing of the others. "Don't kill 'em. I still think they might know more than they're sayin'."

Though he still looked confused, Buford nodded. He tied his horse to the back of the buckboard and crawled up into the seat, taking the reins.

*   *   *

Kicks was relieved to see the rest of their crew in the office when he and Seth returned. "Any luck?" he asked, suspecting the answer would be no.

"Didn't see hide nor hair of Molly or Tilly," Dave reported. "How about you folks? Any luck?"

"No," Kicks replied. "But I think I know where they are. Check your guns, fellas. I think the sheriff is involved. Think he's got Tilly and Molly in one of the outbuildings behind the jail."

"Damn," Muley said. "You sure, Kicks?"

"Pretty sure. He didn't want me or Seth anywhere near that building. Pulled a gun on Seth. Was gonna shoot him in the back. Ain't much of a surprise, really. Sheriff is bad news, and his deputies ain't no better."

They all agreed on that.

"We better get over there before something else happens to them. If my mom or grandma either one gets hurt, there ain't nothing this side of heaven or hell gonna stop me from killing Cal, or anyone else involved."

"Yep," Stonewall agreed. "And you got plenty of firepower to back you up."

"Need to be careful, boys," Kicks said. "Ain't just the sheriff we're dealing with. I don't know exactly how many men might be involved, but I suspect Bob and Quantrill has men of their own helping out. For all I know, we could be walkin' into a trap."

"So how you want to handle this?" Muley said.

Kicks rubbed his chin, expression thoughtful. "Need to saddle fresh horses. Some of those outlaws might try to make a break for it. Don't wanna waste time running all the way back here to get a ride."

"Kevin, you stay here," Seth said.

"No, Pa. I need to help this time. I ain't stayin' behind."

Kicks didn't interfere. This was between the boy and his pa. He wasn't surprised when the boy won.

"You do what I tell ya, son," Seth said, narrowing his eyes at the boy. "I say get, you get. Understand? It's the only way I'll let you tag along."

"I got it, Pa."

Within twenty minutes, there were seven determined men mounted on fast horses pulling up in front of the jail.

Cal watched from inside his office, having hoped to avoid a gun fight. At least he'd managed to get rid of the women before those pesky cowpokes made it back. He'd sent Buford with Wesley to take care of the women, but that still left his two deputies and three of Quantrill's outlaws. More than enough to take care of these seven idiots, two of them just boys. Cal wasn't bad with a six shooter himself.

Cal grinned. "Things are about to get interesting, fellas." He pointed toward the gun rack on the wall. "Dutch, Oscar, grab a couple shotguns. Joe, James, Claude, loosen those guns in your holsters."

Taking a deep breath, he moved toward the door, opening it before his unwelcome guests could barge in. He stepped out on the porch, his men spreading out around him. "Well, boys, what brings you back so soon?"

Kicks didn't recognize three of the men, but suspected they were part of Quantrill's Raiders. These were the fellas who were watching them when they'd argued with the sheriff out back. Two of the men were carrying shotguns. The sheriff and the other three men were wearin' pistols.

Kicks remained relaxed, looping his reins over the hitching post. "Expecting trouble, Cal? Nice welcoming party. Was kind of hoping we could avoid a shootout. We just want the two women back."

Cal laughed. "Naw, I don't 'spect you guy's will be much trouble. My advice is you hop back up on those ponies and go back to where you came from. Colt ain't much use against a shotgun, not at this range."

Kicks sighed. "Well, Cal, I think it's high time we stop playing games. Just tell us where Molly and Tilly are, and we'll take them and leave."

"What makes you think I know where they are?"

"I'm not here to make small talk, Cal. You got two choices, either give up the women, or start the ball rolling. You got ten seconds to make up your mind, and then you'd better go for leather. Just remember, I'm takin' you down first, then the two with the shotguns. Muley and the boys will finish off the rest of you women-snatching cowards." Kicks had a reason for telling Cal the order. He was letting Muley and the others know who their targets were. "One," he said, starting the count.

Cal's grin disappeared when Kicks started the count. He'd obviously thought it was a bluff. Before Kicks could say two, the sheriff went for his gun. The other five men followed suit.

Though a fearsome gun battle, it only lasted less than a minute. When the smoke cleared, Sheriff Cal Tidwell and four of his men were dead. Dutch Simmons had a badly busted leg and a hole in his chest, the man slowly bleeding to death.

Kicks had taken a slight wound in his right hip, and another to his right shoulder, both little more than flesh wounds. Muley was bleeding at his left side, and had a bullet burn across the right side of his neck, leaving the collar of his shirt soaked with blood. Dave and Whiskers were both down, having taken some buckshot. They were bleeding but didn't seem to be seriously wounded. Stonewall had taken a bullet through the left leg. Looked like it went straight through. He was wrapping a kerchief around it. Seth and Kevin were the lucky ones. They both came out with hardly a scratch.

When Kicks saw that none of his men were mortally wounded, he walked over to where Cal lay dead, shot through the head and the heart. As he looked down at the outlaw-sheriff, he said, "What a waste. Some guys never learn. Then he walked over to Dutch.

The deputy was bleeding from the nose and mouth. Kicks heard the death rattle in his voice as he tried to talk, "Oh, God, it hurts. Am I … dying?"

Kicks stared down at the wounded man, saddened, even though the he'd asked for what he got. "Yes, Dutch, you're dying. And you know where you're going, don't you?"

"Yeah gawldammit, I know."

"Well, I think you oughta do one good thing before you cash in, don't you?"

Through a pained grin, Dutch managed to say, "You … you wanna know where … those women are … don't ya."

"Yes," Kicks said. "You have one last chance to do something decent in your life. Don't pass it up, Dutch."

"Loaded 'em in a wagon … 'bout half hour ago." Dutch began to cough, strangling on his own blood. Kicks kneeled and helped him sit up a bit. "Damn, it … hurts," he gasped. Tears formed in his eyes. "Buford and one of … Quantrill's men took 'em."

"Where'd they go, Dutch?" Kicks asked, knowing there was nothing he could do for the man.

"Hunter's lodge. Near Gates of the Mountains. Could be more of … Quantrill's men there." Dutch coughed weakly, grabbing at his chest before he went limp in Kicks' arms.

Kicks kneeled for a minute beside the dead deputy, thinking, *If the women weren't even here, why did Cal force a gunfight?* It didn't make sense.

A crowd had gathered by this time. Most were spectators, but there were a few who were trying to help the wounded. Wendy came running out of the hotel, the mayor and judge not far behind her.

Kicks stood, grimacing against the pain in his hip. "Okay, men, who can still ride?" His eyes widened when all six pushed to their feet. Stonewall was the one he worried about most, but he left it up to the man to make his own decision. "Okay then, let's mount up. Those women are counting on us." Looking at the mayor, he said, "They got Molly and Tilly, Mayor. We gotta go rescue them. Can you delegate some men to clean up this mess? Oh, and someone needs to tell Sammy what's goin' on. Tell him we'll do everything we can to get his wife and Tilly back."

"Don't worry," the mayor assured Kicks. "We'll take care of everything here. Just get those women back here safely. And be careful. I'll go talk to Sammy myself."

CHAPTER 24

"Come on, men," Kicks called over his shoulder, grimacing as he swung into the saddle. "Time's a wastin'."

Before they could leave, old man Grimes jogged over, his eyes widening behind his glasses as he took in the dead men in front of the jail. "Someone jus' took my team and buckboard. Went out to load an order just now and found it gone."

"You don't know how long it's been gone?" Kicks asked. That's how they got the women out without anyone noticing.

"Sorry, no. I leave it parked out back during business hours. Don't pay much attention unless I need it to deliver an order."

Can't have been too long, Kicks thought. Maybe they could follow the tracks.

It only took seconds for the men to mount up, then Kicks whirled his horse around and kicked it in the side. Riding hard, they left Helena and took the left fork out of town. A couple miles later, Kicks called a halt to let the horses rest while they made further plans.

"Anyone know where this hunter's lodge is. Supposedly near a place called the Gates of the Mountains."

"I do," Whiskers said. "Used to hunt there a few years back. Gotta cross the river, then follow a path up into the woods. Gonna put us out in the open though if someone is waitin' there. Could pick us off like flies."

"Can we ride around and come in from behind?" Kicks asked.

Whiskers thought for a moment, brushing his fingers down his straggly beard. "Yeah, might be able to. Take more time."

"Anyone got a better idea?" Kicks asked. When no one replied, he said, "All right, let's get moving. Whiskers, since you know the area best, you take the lead."

Whiskers nodded, looking determined. He jerked his bay mare around, slapping the reins on her flank as he yelled. Kicks stuck his spur in his buckskin's side and loosened his reins, falling in behind Whiskers. Muley's Morgan started fighting him for the reins, the gelding thinking it was a race. Muley gave Morg his head and let him run, Buck and Morg running side by side behind Whisker's bay mare.

It didn't take them long to reach the river. "Shoot," Kicks said when he saw the empty buckboard, the horses unhitched and gone. "They dumped the wagon."

Whiskers pulled up beside him, his mare's sides heaving after the lengthy run. "They didn't need the wagon once they got 'em out of town. They can move faster without it. Normally we'd take the path straight up on the other side." He pointed toward the towering peaks that made up the Gates of the Mountain. "I think I can find us a way in if we go around to the left. They won't be expectin' that. But it'll put us a few hours behind 'em."

"Nothing we can do about it," Kicks said, easing his buckskin into the cold water. The others followed him. Luckily, the river was fairly shallow most of the way. Kicks stopped on the other side and looked up at the magnificent limestone cliffs. Would definitely be a hunter's paradise. "Lead the way," he said to Whiskers. They didn't have time for sightseeing.

Several hours later, Whiskers led them back onto the original trail, bringing them in at the rear of the hunter's lodge.

*　　*　　*

Leaving the jail with the kidnapped women, Buford drove the team and buckboard like a crazy man, while the new man, Wesley, followed on his horse. Buford did not like what was going on here but didn't know what to do about it.

At the river, Wesley pulled him up. Buford unhitched the team while Wesley got the women out of the back. At this point, he didn't appear to care if they saw them or not. He ripped the burlap sacks off their head and untied them.

"Listen up, ladies," Wesley said, narrowing his eyes at the scared women. "We need to go the rest of the way on horseback. You can cooperate and live, or I'll shoot you right here where you stand. It's your choice."

"We'll cooperate," Tilly said, drawing her daughter into her arms. Both women were shaking with fear.

"Smart of ya," Wesley said. "Bring those nags over here," he ordered Buford.

"Buford?" Tilly said. "What are you doing?"

Buford shook his head, refusing to meet her eyes.

"Hurry up," Wesley snapped. He grabbed Molly's arm and jerked her away from Tilly. They didn't have a saddle, so he boosted them up bareback. "Hang on tight. You fall off, I'll just shoot ya."

Getting back on his own horse, Buford grabbed the reins of the horse carrying Molly while Wesley took hold of Tilly's.

An hour later, they rode into the old hunter's lodge at the edge of the forest. Buford was a little surprised to see four men come out with their pistols drawn.

"We need to get these women inside," Wesley yelled, jumping down from his horse. "Might have some trigger-happy cowpokes on our tail." He turned to Buford. "Get the horses out of sight. I saw an old barn out back."

Buford didn't dare complain, though he wondered what the hell Cal had got him into this time.

"Hey, Red," Wesley said once they were inside. "Thought you were stayin' down at the old ranch." He accepted a bottle of whiskey, taking a long pull before he handed it back.

Red laughed. "Bloody Bill had a few of us move up here. Said there might be trouble." Red glanced toward the women, who were sitting on the end of one of the old cots, holding each other. "Whatcha got here, Wes? Bring us some entertainment?"

"That damn sheriff had us kidnap these two. Not sure what he wanted with 'em. Kept us away while he questioned them. Couple cowpokes showed up, askin' questions, so he needed us to get 'em out of there. Woulda been too close to town to take 'em to the old ranch. So here we are."

"Think Bill or Quantrill knows anything about this?" Red asked, frowning.

They all turned to the door when Buford came in. The deputy closed the door behind him, looking nervous. "Got the horses put up," he said.

"Don't think so," Wesly replied to Red's question. "Might ask this one, but I get the feelin' he don't know much either."

"Know what?" Buford asked.

"Why the sheriff wanted these two women kidnapped?" Wesley said.

Buford shook his head. "He never said. I didn't even know about it until this morning." He turned toward Molly and Tilly. "Why don't you ask them?"

"Well?" Red asked, narrowing his eyes at Tilly.

"He wanted a document, a map of the Last Chance gold mine. I told him I didn't know anything about it, and I don't."

"Wonder why he'd want an old map?" Wesley said, frowning.

"So tell me what went on with those cowpokes," Red said, turning his back to the women.

Buford stammered, "Sheriff had the town under control until that drifter and his buddy showed up."

"Yeah, and who might they be?" Red asked, looking curious.

"Guys by the names Kicks Burks and Muley Gentry. Both are pretty fast with a gun. Faster than anyone I've ever seen before. Killed the livery's hostler plus five of Bob Jensen's gunmen in a card game, including Jim Bonner. You heard of Bonner, ain't ya?"

"Hmm," Red said. "What's this Kicks and Muley fellers look like?"

Buford rubbed nervously at his mouth. "Well, Kicks is about six-foot-two, and probably weighs two-ten. He wears two Colt .44s on his hips. His pal Muley is a tad taller, probably six-four, around two-thirty. He also wears two Colt .44s."

Red paused a minute before he asked. "Burks and Gentry, you say?"

"Yep, do you know 'em?

Red rubbed his whiskered jaw. "Yeah, sort of. I know of 'em by name. Both got a reputation as a fast gun. Didn't know they were runnin' together though. Been wantin' to meet 'em."

Buford chuckled. "Well, you jus' might get your chance. Suspect they won't take kindly to the sheriff abducting these two women. Got a feeling they'll be here soon … if the sheriff didn't kill 'em."

Red nodded, chuckling. "Okay, men, the deputy here seems to think that we're gonna have company real soon. Couple of fast guns comin' to rescue these two. Let's give 'em a warm welcome if they show up. What do ya say?"

Red posted Two Bears out back, knowing the native would be hard to spot in the woods. The redskin wouldn't miss much either. A couple men could be posted out in the barn, but the rest would stay in the house. Even if they had taken a couple of women, Red seriously doubted anyone would be stupid enough to go after some of Quantrill's men, an automatic death sentence.

Two Bears disappeared into the forest, stopping to look up when he noticed several flocks of birds leave the trees. He cocked his head to the side, listening. It didn't take long to pick up the sound of horses snorting. He moved silently forward, counting seven men trying to sneak in the back way. Instead of going back to warn Red, Two Bears decided to collect the scalps for himself. After all, he was Two Bears, a mighty warrior who had ridden with the great Shoshoni Chief, Washakie.

As Two Bears moved through the forest, he checked his weapons, a Smith & Wesson .38 that he'd taken from a Mexican bandit. The .38 was a beautifully engraved pistol with a holster and shell belt. In a scabbard on his belt, he also wore a sixteen-inch bowie knife. He'd killed many men and taken many scalps with these two weapons. Now he would prove himself once again by killing the two feared gunmen, Kicks and Muley. The other five in the party didn't matter. Only one would survive this battle, Two Bears, the great Shoshoni warrior.

*   *   *

"Let's leave the horses here," Kicks said, dismounting. "We'll go the rest of the way on foot. Horses will be too noisy." He glanced over at the two younger men in their party. "You two stay here and guard the horses." He held his hand up when Dave and Kevin started to complain. "It's an important job, men. Kill anyone who tries to take them from you." That seemed to settle them down.

Kicks had spent a few summers living in a Comanche village. He'd learned from them, how to track in silence, how to use his senses. He took out a pair of moccasins from his saddlebag and traded them for his boots. "Follow my lead," he said to Muley and the other three. "Trust me."

"Whatever you say, Kicks," Muley said. "You ain't steered me wrong yet."

Kicks nodded, then took the lead as they followed a faint path. He stopped a few minutes later and whispered, "We're getting close. I wanna try to set up and watch them for a bit, see if we can figure out how many might be there." Kicks stepped away from the path. "You guys work your way closer, but don't let yourself get seen. I'm gonna—" A bird that had been singing to its mate in a nearby tree suddenly went quiet. Something had disturbed it. Could have been an animal, but he didn't think so.

Kicks froze, his head cocked as he listened. Then he heard it … the sound of a dry leaf being crushed under a foot. Kicks motioned for the others to crouch down as he slipped silently into the brush. He slowly worked his way back around, then stood behind a large western cedar tree, all his senses on high alert. After another minute, he caught a slight flash of movement, but it was all he needed. A native was stalking Kicks and his friends.

For a fleeting moment, Kicks thought about just shooting him, because he had no doubt this native would shoot him if he got the chance. However, that was not the way of this Texan, so he called out, "Got ya spotted, friend. Who are you and why are you stalking us?" He suspected this native was one of Quantrill's men and would speak English.

Whirling, the native said, "Two Bears stalks to kill the enemy of my friends. First, I kill you, then I kill your friends, all but one. That one I will scalp but let him live to tell other white eyes about the mighty Shoshoni warrior, Two Bears."

"'Fraid I can't let you do that, Two Bears."

For a moment, the two just stood there looking at each other, then Two Bears went for his gun, but the native was no match for Kicks with a six-shooter. Kicks' gun cleared leather seconds before Two Bears, but he didn't shoot. "Huh-uh, friend. Don't try it." Kicks didn't really want to kill the native. He held a lot of respect for them.

Two Bears tossed his gun down, then stood waiting to see what Kicks would do. When Kicks tossed his own gun down too, Two Bears offered him a hint of a smile, though his dark eyes remained cold. He drew his knife and began to circle Kicks. "White eyes foolish like young squaw. I kill fast."

Kicks drew his knife, keeping his gaze fixed on Two Bears as the native circled him. Maybe he'd been foolish to throw his gun down. Though experienced with a knife, the native probably had the advantage. *Damn fool*, he told himself.

Two Bears moved closer, taking a swing at him. Kicks was slow to react and felt a searing pain in his right arm as the native drew his blade back across it. Blood immediately ran down his arm, dripping from his fingertips. Kicks knew by the numbness that it was probably a serious cut. He didn't have time to dwell on it.

Two Bears laughed. "First blood, white eyes! You much slow."

That gave Kicks an idea. He pretended to be more hurt than he really was, holding his wounded arm to his chest.

The trick worked. Over-confident now, Two Bears rushed in carelessly, hoping for a quick kill. Kicks jumped backwards and grabbed the native by the arm, jerking him off balance. Two Bears tried to spin around, but Kicks swung his arm up, holding his blade to the native's throat. A trickle of blood flowed down his neck, staining his leather shirt.

"It's over, Two Bears, drop it," Kicks ordered. He narrowed his eyes when the native hesitated. "I said drop it!"

Two Bears nodded and whispered, "Okay," then dropped his blade.

Kicks eased up the pressure on his blade at the native's throat. Instantly, Two Bears made his move. His hands darted upward, fingers like steel talons grasping Kicks by the wrist. The unexpected trick worked, and before Kicks knew it, Two Bears was free.

Knife once again in hand, Two Bears grinned and said, "Foolish old woman." He made a straight-arm lunge at Kicks' throat with his blade. Kicks ducked under his enemy's outstretched arm and thrust up with his blade deep into Two

Bears' ribs. The native dropped his knife and clutched at the knife still sunk deeply in his ribcage. Kicks looked into unbelieving eyes as Two Bears sank to the ground and lay still.

Releasing a slow breath, Kicks retrieved his blade and wiped the blood off on Two Bears' leather shirt. He'd hated to kill the man but there hadn't really been a choice. Shaking his head, Kicks started down the path toward his friends. When he caught sight of Muley and the others, they were crouched down at the edge of the forest, staring in at the old hunting lodge. Not wanting to get accidentally shot, Kicks imitated a soft bird whistle, drawing their attention toward him.

"What happened to you?" Muley said, raising his eyebrows when he caught sight of his bloody sleeve.

"It's not as bad as it looks," Kicks told them, and quickly explained the incident with Two Bears.

"How do you guys want to handle this?" Whiskers asked.

"They probably got a couple guys in the barn," Kicks said. "I didn't see anyone but the injun out in the forest. The rest will be inside with the women." He crouched there beside Muley and thought for a moment. "Well, fellas, it's like my pappy always says, 'The only way to deal with a snake is to walk right up to him and spit in his eye, then yank out his fangs. He might still be your enemy, but now he's harmless, and you're the boss. All that's left is to cut off its head.' What do you think, Muley?"

Muley scratched his head. "Guess we just follow your pappy's instructions. Whiskers, you and Stony take out the men in the barn. Me, Kicks and Seth will go up and spit in the eye of the snake." When nobody said a word, Muley grinned. "Suppose that sounds foolish, don't it?"

"On the contrary," Kicks said. "I found out a long time ago that most of what my pappy offers is good advice." Kicks looked at the situation another minute. "We'll go in through the back. Porch is falling down, and the door's stuck open. I'm bettin' most of the men inside are watching out the front. They thought that injun would take care of anyone coming in the back. A mistake."

He rubbed his chin. "Looks like the same people who built that old, abandoned ranch house also built this. Similar design, don't you think, Muley?"

"Yeah, it does look the same. Means the kitchen will be to the right through that back door. Bedroom is on the left. Front room will be straight ahead. Could be someone upstairs. More bedrooms up there. Gotta watch out for the women if there's any gunplay."

"I'll go right when we go in. Muley, you go left. Seth, you go up the middle. Should be a short hall. Stay low and against the wall. We'll take out the men downstairs first, then worry about anyone upstairs. Whiskers, Stony, give us five minutes to get set up, then you take out the men in the barn. Don't hesitate, boys. Shoot to kill. Anyone who'd kidnap a woman don't deserve to live. If they hurt either one of 'em, I'll make sure anyone left alive suffers before I end them."

Everyone nodded, agreeing with Kicks.

Kicks waited for Whiskers and Stony to get into position out by the barn. Luckily, the forest had grown up right next to the broken-down structure, giving them plenty of cover. It would be a little trickier getting into the lodge without notice.

CHAPTER 25

Buford knew these outlaws weren't taking the threat of Kicks and Muley seriously. Their apparent leader, Red, and four other men were sitting at a table drinking and playing cards, acting like they didn't have a care in the world. "You think one injun is gonna be able to handle both those gunslingers?"

"Aw, shut the hell up," Red yelled. "You been saying the same thing now for over two hours. I'm sure my boys and the sheriff took care of those fellas in town."

Several of the men laughed, but Buford knew what Kicks and Muley were capable of. He'd been there when they shot down all of Bob's men at the livery. "Don't say I didn't try to warn you," Buford mumbled.

"Sheriff did seem mighty jumpy around them," Wesley said, shrugging. "Can't see 'em chasing us clear up here though."

Red leaned back in his chair, giving Buford the evil eye. "I already said, ain't nobody gonna get past Two Bears. We got two men watching from the barn too. Now leave us the hell alone. Or better yet, why don't you go outside and keep watch. If you see anyone, just shoot 'em. Save us the bother."

Everyone laughed, including Wesley.

"Fine," Buford said. "I'll be out front." He glanced back at the two women who were still sitting on the cot, wishing he'd never got involved in this mess. What the hell had Cal been thinking? Maybe he'd go back to town since he obviously wasn't welcome here. But he'd have to go to the barn to get his horse, and Red had two men posted guard out there. Doubtful they'd let him saddle up and leave. Course, he'd noticed those two outlaws took a bottle of whiskey with them. He could just wait it out a few hours and they'd be passed out drunk. Maybe he'd get his horse and just leave the state. He didn't want to be associated with kidnappers of women. If these boys got drunk and ended up raping or killing them, it be a hanging offense for him too.

Buford opened the front door, scanning the forest around him before he stepped outside, not that he could see anyone through the thick brush if they were waiting to ambush him. At least he didn't get shot right away. Gave him some hope he might get out of this thing alive.

*   *   *

Everything was quiet outside, almost too quiet. Kicks and Muley stood beside the back door, one on each side, and waited for the signal that Whiskers and Stonewall were in place at the barn. Seth stood on the other side of Muley, his gun drawn. Kicks could hear every word said between Buford and one of the outlaws. He waited for the front door to close, then looked toward the barn. Stonewall nodded that they were ready.

Kicks pressed his lips together, his adrenaline spiking as he nodded at Muley and Seth. They rushed in, Kicks going right, Muley left, and Seth up the middle.

"Don't anybody move or you're dead," Kicks said, not surprised to find five men sitting at a table playing cards. They hadn't taken Buford's warning seriously. No one reached for their gun. In fact, they didn't even drop their cards. They just sat there with dumb expressions, shocked by the intrusion.

"No one in the bedroom," Muley said, walking into the open area of the kitchen and front room. Seth stood at the top of the hall, covering two more men in the front. "Anyone upstairs?" Muley snarled, cocking his gun.

"Nope, this is all of us," one of the men at the table said.

Everyone twitched when they heard two shots coming from outside.

"Is that right," Kicks said, narrowing his eyes. "Then who was that?" He motioned with his head and eyes for Muley to check upstairs, then turned his attention to the women. You okay, ladies?" he asked, not daring to take his eyes off the men at the table.

"We're okay," Tilly said. "Thank God you came. The sheriff is behind this, Kicks. Him and four strangers did the kidnapping."

"Yeah, we know. He ain't gonna be a problem anymore." Kicks listened for Muley to come back downstairs. "Anything?"

"All clear."

Kicks motioned with his head for Muley to come over. "Why don't you relieve these men of their weapons, partner."

"Be my pleasure," Muley said, grinning as he walked over to the table.

"You must be Kicks and Muley. So the coward was right about you coming?" a redheaded outlaw said. "Guess I shoulda listened to him."

Kicks grinned. "You mean Buford? Can't argue the man's a coward, but yeah, you shoulda listened."

"Don't think we're gonna see much of Buford ever again," Muley said, chuckling. "Saw him hightailing it down the trail through the window after he heard those shots. If he's smart, he won't go back to Helena."

A few minutes later, Whiskers and Stonewall came in through the back, Stonewall limping pretty bad from the gunshot he'd taken in town earlier.

"All clear out back, boss," Whiskers said. "Sorry, had to kill those two fellers."

"Don't worry about it, Whiskers. Sure they had it coming. Get some rope and let's get these boys tied up." Kicks turned his attention to the redheaded leader. "Who you ride for? Quantrill or Bob Jensen?"

"Quantrill," the man growled. "And he ain't gonna like it much when he hears about this."

"I 'spect not," Kicks said, "but I also don't give a damn what he thinks, him or Bob either one."

Once Whiskers and Seth got all the men tied, Kicks sent Whiskers to go get the horses out of the barn. He sent Seth after the two boys. "There's a dead injun out back too. We'll need to take his body, and the two in the barn, down to town.

Twenty minutes later, Seth returned with Dave and Kevin, leading their seven ponies. Whiskers brought out two saddled horses from the barn, and two carrying the bodies of those they'd killed. He handed the reins to Muley, then went back for the rest.

Seth walked over to Kicks, looking worried. "Couldn't find the injun, boss. Looks like he weren't killed. Found a blood trail headed away from the lodge."

"Well, ain't nothing we can do about it now. Probably headed back for Bob Jensen's ranch," Kicks said.

Red chuckled. "Looks like you stepped into a real hornet's nest this time, boy. Know you got a reputation for being fast with a gun, but not sure you're gonna be able to walk outta this one with your hide intact."

Dave ran over to his ma and grandma, giving each woman a hug. "You okay?" he asked. "Did any of those men hurt you?" They all knew what he meant.

"No, son," Molly said, tears flowing down her chubby cheeks. "We're okay. I just want to go home and see your pa."

Both women looked exhausted, their clothes rumpled, dirt stains on their faces. Tilly was trying to be strong for her daughter, but Kicks could see her hands trembling. They needed to get them home. He caught Seth's attention. "Why don't you help the women get on a horse. Whiskers got two saddled for them. These outlaws here can walk down the mountain, help keep 'em outta trouble. We'll hitch up the team to the wagon once we get across the river."

"You got it, boss," Seth said. He walked over and held his hand out to Tilly.

*   *   *

It was dark out by the time they rode back into town. Everyone was sore and tired. Dave, Whiskers and Stonewall needed some medical attention. They'd taken the most damage during the gunfight this morning. Whiskers pulled the team of horses to a stop in front of the jail and they unloaded their wet prisoners from the buckboard. They'd been forced to walk, and swim, across the river since Kicks refused to give them horses.

Sammy ran over, helping Molly and Tilly down from their horses. It was an emotional scene as they hugged each other and cried.

"We got this handled," Kicks told Dave and Sammy. "You take your women folk home. They've had a rough time of it. Dave, you need to see the doc soon, get that buckshot taken out. Whiskers, you too."

Dave nodded, his face pale. Whiskers just waved him off.

It didn't take long to get their prisoners locked up. The only sign that there'd been a gunfight at the jail this morning were a few bloodstains left on the boardwalk. The mayor had handled getting rid of the bodies. But Kicks knew this fight was far from over. They still had Bob and Quantrill to deal with, not to mention Two Bears. No doubt the native would run back to his boss and alert him to the problems.

Outside the jail, a crowd had formed. Kicks looked out, seeing the mayor and judge pushing their way toward them. They came in through the door, shaking his and Muley's hands.

"Blessed is the day we were able to talk you boys into being officers of the law," the mayor said. "You're sure cleaning this town up good and proper."

Kicks forced a thin-lipped grin. "I'm not so sure I want to thank you for the honor of being officers of the law, Mayor. This ain't finished yet. Quantrill and his Raiders ain't gonna disappear anytime soon, not till he gets what he wants. Not sure yet what Bob's part is in all this."

"You didn't learn anything from the sheriff before you killed him?" the judge asked.

"No, not really. I learned from Tilly that the sheriff was after some document concerning the Last Chance gold mine. Don't really know what Bob or Quantrill's involvement might be in that, if any, though I suspect Bob wants full control of the town. If he gets his hands on the mine, on the gold, that'll give him what he needs."

The mayor turned to Muley, rubbing the back of his neck. "You think this had anything to do with Sheriff Durmhill getting killed? That's when Bob brought in Sheriff Cal."

"Could very well be," Muley replied. "Nothing would surprise me right now. Makes sense if Cal thought Tilly might know where the document was."

"How many men are we talking about with Quantrill?" the judge asked.

Kicks sat down behind the sheriff's desk and pulled open the bottom drawer. He pulled out the bottle of whiskey he knew Cal had kept there, taking a long drink before handing it to Muley. "Hard to say how many men Quantrill might have brought with him. We got a good number locked up right here, but that means he's gonna try to break them out when he learns about it. Pretty sure they got more men out at the old, abandoned house out east of town. Then we got Bloody Bill and the injun to worry about. Don't know where they are. Maybe out at Bob's place. We're gonna have to stay on guard, day and night."

"All right, fellas," the mayor said. "You just tell us what you need. We'll do everything we can to help you. I'm sure we can get you more men if you need."

"Right now, I need to go out back to the privy," Muley said. "Then we can go get somethin' to eat. I'm starving. We can discuss what we're gonna do later."

"Okay, I'll wait here for you," Kicks said.

Muley had just left by the back door when Cathy came hurrying inside the jail. "Hello, gentlemen," she said, nodding at the mayor and judge. "I just finished helping Tilly and Molly get settled in at the hotel. Molly didn't want to go home just yet. She's understandably scared. They're both pretty shaken up. I can't imagine going through what they did. I can't believe it was Sheriff Cal and his deputies who abducted them. Just terrible. Thank God you boys were here to help bring them back. Who knows what would have happened."

Kicks agreed with Cathy's assessment. "Glad we could get them back safe."

"Umm, where's Muley?" Cathy asked. "He didn't get hurt, did he?"

Kicks grinned. "I figured that's why you came running in here. Muley's fine. Just a mite tired, and hungry. He's out back taking care of business. He'll return in a few minutes."

Cathy blushed. "Yes, I was worried about the big galoot. I've been trying to get his attention ever since I met him. You men are such dummies when it comes to women."

"Guess that's our cue to leave," the mayor said, chuckling. "We'll talk to you fellas more tomorrow morning." He shook Kicks' hand again, then he and the judge left Cathy alone with Kicks.

"Muley's just a little bashful," Kicks said. "He was raised by a decent family, taught to respect women. Suspect he's afraid of offending you by comin' on too strong."

"I guess I knew that," Cathy replied. "But ... you're a decent man too and you aren't bashful, Kicks. At least not around me. Why is that?"

Kicks grinned. "Cathy, you're a beautiful woman, and I admire and appreciate your beauty, but I'm not in love with you, not like Muley. I just wanna be your friend." He laughed. "Hell, my old pappy always says, 'The only things that can take the place of a beautiful woman is a fast horse and a true shooting .44'"

Cathy laughed. "Kicks Burks, I think you're just a mean old man."

"Who's a mean old man?" Muley asked, coming in through the back door.

"Hey, partner," Kicks said, "I'm afraid your gal here has me pegged. So I'm gonna leave you two lovebirds alone and go over to the Golden Nugget, get something to eat and something strong to wash it down with. See you later, Muley."

"What about us?" Red called from his cell. "You gonna feed us anytime soon?"

Kicks scowled and shook his head. "Let 'em starve tonight. I'll bring 'em back something for breakfast in the morning."

After Kicks left, Cathy moved closer to Muley. "I was really worried about you."

Muley grinned. "You ... you was?"

"Of course, I was." Cathy paused a moment, waiting for him to take charge of the situation.

"Really," he said. "Why?"

Cathy moved even closer to him, leaving no space between them. "Yes," she whispered, "Really." She paused again, looking up into his eyes. "Muley, Kicks told me you're in love with me. Is that true?"

Muley's heart was pounding so hard he thought it would leap right out of his chest. He actually reached up to put a hand against his chest. "Why, I guess I do. Yes, Cathy, I love you. Have from the first moment I laid eyes on you."

Cathy stood up on her toes and slid her arms around his neck. "Then put your arms around me. I won't break."

Shaking all over, he put his arms around her, and crushed her body against his own. Their lips came together, and the world began spinning around, leaving them both dizzy.

*   *   *

Kicks walked into the Golden Nugget and elbowed himself a place at the bar. Sammy was tending bar with his helper, José Martinez. When he noticed Kicks, he grabbed a bottle of mescal and went around to Kicks' side of the bar. "Come have a drink with me," he said, then made his way to a corner table with Kicks right on his heels.

Sammy set the bottle of mescal and two glasses on the table as Kicks lowered his six-foot-two frame in a chair, facing the front of the room. It was a struggle not to groan, his body aching where he'd been clipped by the bullets this morning. The native's knife hadn't helped matters. He probably should get it looked at, but he just wanted to sit and have a drink, try to relax.

"Molly and I will be forever grateful to you, Kicks. I didn't … I didn't think I'd ever see her again, not in one piece. Think those men woulda killed them both if you and Muley hadn't gone after them."

"Well, Sammy, weren't just us. There were five more brave men went with us. How's she doing anyway?"

"She's shook up. Tilly too. Wants to stay with her ma at the hotel for a few days. Can't say as I blame her. I feel better with her there anyway, at least until we figure out what the hell is going on around here. Why would Cal think Tilly or Molly would know where an old map of the mine is?"

"It is a puzzle," Kicks said. "Hey, Sammy, think you can fetch me a plate of those delicious ham and beans you keep simmering on the stove behind the bar? I'm starving. My belly thinks my throat's been cut. That'll be thanks enough."

Sammy laughed as he stood. "You got it. I'll be right back."

While Sammy was fixing a plate of food for him, Kicks leaned back in his chair and took a deep breath, relaxing as he watched the crowd. The mescal soothed not only his dry throat, but his aching body. Just as Sammy was bringing the food over to Kicks' table, Muley came in, grinning from ear to ear.

Sammy set the plate down in front of Kicks. "I'm real glad to see you, Muley. You want some of these beans too?"

Muley grinned. "You bet, Sammy, would sure appreciate that."

Sammy left to get another plate, and Muley groaned as he sat down, looking as sore as Kicks felt. Kicks refilled his glass and shoved the bottle across the table to Muley. "Here, have a drink. It's on Sammy. What did Cathy have to say?" Kicks teased. "She sure seemed anxious to see you."

Muley's face turned red. "Aw, hell, Kicks; I think I'm in love."

Before Kicks could answer, Sammy came back with another plate of beans and a loaf of freshly baked bread. He also set a bowl of small red peppers on the table. "Here you go, fellas. On the house. These chili peppers, called tepin, are grown out in the desert. They might be tiny, but they're hot. You Texans are always complainin' my peppers aren't hot enough, so I got these special just for you." He looked up, smiling when Dave, Whiskers, Stonewall, Seth and Kevin came in, heading for the table. "Might as well bring five more plates," he said, chuckling as he left the table again.

Soon, everyone was eating, their sweaty faces turning red from the hot peppers. Sammy grinned. "What's the matter, fellas, thought you Texas boys were tough. Can't handle a tiny little pepper?"

"Good gosh almighty," Muley said. "I have to admit; those little peppers are too hot for me. Can't feel my tongue."

Kicks tipped the bottle of mescal up and drank straight from the bottle, while the other five men said, "Amen to that."

Sammy laughed. "Guess you won't be griping about my peppers any more, will ya? If you need anything else, give a shout." He chuckled all the way back to the bar."

Finally, after everyone had eaten their fill, Kicks pushed away from the table. "Okay, men, we need to plan our next step. Best not talk out here in the open. We'll take turns guarding the prisoners. Whiskers, you wanna go first?"

"Yep. See you boys later." The old man got up and headed out the door.

The other six walked over to the office in the livery stable, where they rolled smokes and enjoyed Dave's coffee laced with a touch of frontier whiskey.

Kicks took a drink from his cup then set it down, sighing. He glanced at his friends around the table. "You fellas know we're goin' to have to deal with Quantrill and his Raiders."

"Yeah, probably Bob and his crew too," Muley said. "The two appear to be working together."

"So what do you suggest we do," Seth asked. "If there's more of 'em hidin' up around the Gates, they'll be dang hard to flush out of there."

Kicks took a last drink from his cup and set it back on the table. "First thing in the morning, me and Muley will ride out to the Running J and snoop around. I doubt Buford headed that way, but that injun I knifed probably will. I shoulda made sure he was dead." He paused, releasing a slow breath as he scrubbed at his tired eyes.

"Maybe we all ought to go," Stonewall said. "Strike while the iron is still hot, so to speak."

"Yeah," Muley said. "Could sit up in them rocks above his spread, pick 'em off like ducks as they ride by. You know, same as they were gonna do with us."

"Okay now," Kicks said. "Ain't gonna turn into no assassins. Need to put our heads together, come up with a plan." He dug a cheroot from his shirt pocket and chewed on it for a second, then struck the head of a Lucifer on the edge of the table. The sulfur instantly burst into flames and he held it up and looked at it for a couple seconds, then touched it to the end of his cheroot. After he got the small brown cigar going, he rolled it over to the corner of his mouth.

"Here's my suggestion," Kicks said. "We're all tired tonight. Let's sleep on it, then meet back here in the morning. I'll go over and sit with Whiskers for a couple hours. Got a cot in there. We can take turns catching some sleep. Muley, you and Dave can relieve us around midnight. I don't expect trouble tonight, but you never know. Tomorrow, me and Muley will ride out and see if we can learn anything at the Running J."

"Okay," Dave said, glancing over at his cot. "Think I'll get a little shut eye here then."

"Yeah," Seth said, looking over at his son. "Me and Kevin are gonna head back to the hotel. We'll come down about four this morning and take over watch at the jail."

"Thanks, fellas," Kicks said, standing. He reached out and shook Seth's hand, then Kevin's. The boy beamed, likely proud to be treated like a grown man. He deserved it. He and Dave had both been brave today. Kicks only hoped he didn't go and get the boys killed before this mess got cleaned up. They'd be lucky if they all made it out alive.

CHAPTER 26

It was just starting to break daylight when Kicks and Muley stopped on the cliffs overlooking the Running J spread. "Looks pretty quiet down there," Kicks said.

"Yep," Muley replied. "Cook will be the first one up."

"Well, let's mosey on down there and question him before the rest of those outlaws wake up." He pulled his spyglass from its sheath and took a slow look around. "Don't see no guards posted. That's kinda strange. A man like Quantrill is usually pretty paranoid."

"Maybe he ain't here," Muley said. "Coulda hightailed it out of here after the shootout with the sheriff yesterday. That injun coulda made it back and alerted him too."

"Yeah, maybe." But Kicks kind of doubted it. A man like Quantrill wasn't easy to spook.

It took them about twenty minutes to work their way down the mountain. Kicks and Muley moved slowly, keeping an eye out for danger. Dawn came fast as the first gray streaks appeared in the sky. They left their horses tied over by the barn, then sneaked through the yard behind the bunkhouse. As they'd suspected, the cook was the first one up. He stepped out of the bunkhouse and walked around the corner near where Kicks stood and relieved himself.

Kicks allowed him to finish urinating, then said in a low but clear voice, "Don't move, friend. Just stand there and act like you're still taking a piss."

The cook jumped, startled, but then did as he was ordered. "Who are you? What do you want?"

"I'm your worst enemy if you don't do exactly what I say. I need answers … the right answers."

"Anything, whatever you wanna know, just ask." His voice broke as he added, "Please don't kill me, mister."

"I got a Colt .44 aimed at your head, but it don't have to come to that. Also got about thirty men up in the hills, got the place surrounded." That was a lie, but it sounded good. "First question, where's Quantrill?"

"He ain't here." the cook whined. "Left late yesterday, almost sundown. I heard some of the men say they were going to a place called … the Gates of the Mountains."

Kicks frowned. "To the hunting lodge?"

"I don't know. I don't know anything about any lodge. They just said the Gates."

"How many men went with Quantrill?"

"I'm not sure, mister, but I think about fifteen, maybe twenty. Most of the men here went with Quantrill, even some of Bob's boys."

"Bob still here?" Kicks asked.

"Yeah, he's probably still asleep. Bob don't usually get up until late, then he has me fix breakfast for him. In fact, everyone on this whole ranch sleeps late 'cept me."

"How many men stayed here at the ranch with Bob?"

The cook took a moment to think. "Let's see now, there's Blackjack Ketchum, Robert Louden—his brother-in-law—

and Bill Chadwell. Then there's a couple men I don't know. Think they were part of Quantrill's riders. That makes six, counting Bob."

"There's one more," Kicks said.

"No, mister, I ain't lying to you. There's just six. Everyone else left with Quantrill yesterday."

"Wrong. *You* make seven."

"No! I'm just the cook. I ain't one of 'em. I don't even carry a gun."

"What's your name?"

"They just call me Cookie. You can too."

Kicks felt sorry for the man. He was a short, bald, fat man who walked with a limp. "Okay, Cookie, get in the barn." The cook didn't hesitate, hobbling over to the open barn door. Kicks grabbed a piece of rope that was hanging close by on a hook. "I'm gonna tie you up so I don't have to worry about you. When this is over, I'll come make sure you get loose."

After he bound the old man, Kicks stepped cautiously out of the barn. He signaled to Muley that there were six men, five in the bunkhouse and Bob in the main house.

"What do you think?" Muley said after he stepped into the barn. "Maybe we ought to go back and get the other guys."

Kicks grimaced. "I say we go take Bob ourselves. We can get him out of here before any of them other cowpokes wake up. Bob will be the one who has answers we need. Cookie here said he's in the house alone. Quantrill and most of his men left yesterday."

"Maybe we'll get lucky again," Muley said, grinning. "We got in that lodge without firing a single shot."

"Yeah, maybe. But my pappy always says, 'Lady luck is great when she's on your side … but sometimes she's fickle.'

Meaning, you got to cover your own rear when you're among enemies." He paused long enough to let that sink in. "Now, you ready, cowboy?"

"Yep." He looked over at the bound cook. "You trust him? Could be Quantrill and his men are inside right now just waiting for us."

The cook shook his head, sweating. "I swear. A whole pile of men took off yesterday. Quantrill was with them."

"And you don't know where they were going?" Muley asked.

"They just said something about the Gates. That's all I know."

What Cookie hadn't told Kicks, because he didn't know, was that Blackjack had gone out before daylight to use the privy, then decided to go on over and have a private word with Bob. He'd gone in the back way, so Kicks and Muley hadn't seen him.

Both Bob and Blackjack froze when they heard the creaking of a loose board coming from the front porch. "Cookie is up a might early, ain't he?" Blackjack said.

Bob just frowned.

When Kicks and Muley stepped inside the room, all four men were surprised. Not a word was spoken as they all four went for their guns. Bob got off a shot just tenths of a second before Muley did. However, Muley's shot was more accurate. The outlaw boss' bullet took Muley's hat off his head, and some hair and a bit of hide with it, but Bob Jensen now lay dead on the floor of his own kitchen.

Kicks and Blackjack cleared leather at about the same time. Kicks couldn't tell who pulled the trigger first. The shots sounded simultaneously, but when the smoke cleared,

Blackjack had two holes in his chest and was staring up at Kicks in disbelief. Ten seconds later, he was dead. Kicks felt no remorse over the death, Blackjack wasn't a good man, though he looked down at the body and thought, *Someday that might be me laying on the cold floor, my blood soaking into the wood.*

"Kicks, you okay?" Muley shouted, both of them a bit deafened by the shots fired inside the house.

Kicks shook his head hard, like some wild shaggy buffalo that had just run head-first into the side of a mountain. He ducked as a bullet crashed through the window. "Guess there are only four out in the bunkhouse. Think we mighta woke' em up?" He grinned over at Muley.

Kicks stood by the window, risking a peek out when he heard the echo of a rifle shot. "Hell, think there's somebody up in them rocks taking potshots down here." Kicks motioned with his hand when he saw a man run from the bunkhouse over behind a water trough.

A second later, the man jerked and fell forward into the water, the report of a rifle shot following a half second later.

"Hmmm, think they're with us," Kicks said. "That leaves three."

Right about then, the back door crashed open. Kicks and Muley didn't hesitate, both pulling the trigger at the same time.

Two of Bob's men were down by the time the smoke cleared. Kicks brushed his hand down his chest, just to be sure he hadn't got hit. So far Lady Luck was staying on their side.

"Got one trying to run on horseback," Muley said.

Kicks nodded, then looked down at the dying man at his feet. "What name should I put on your stone?" he asked.

"B-Bob. Bob Louden." The last had been nothing more than a whisper.

Kicks nodded. "Sorry, friend. Guess you picked the wrong crowd to run with."

"Rather die … this way … than on the …. end of a rope."

"Well, you're gonna get your wish."

Kicks and Muley both twitched at the report of a rifle.

"Guess that last fella didn't get far," Kicks said. He chuckled, moving toward the side of the window and peeking out. "One of our guys musta followed us out. Who do you think it is? Must be pretty good with a rifle."

"My guess would be Seth or Whiskers. Could be Stony though. Those ranchers tend to be a fair shot with a rifle. Lotta practice pickin' off coyotes."

They both looked up when a riderless horse came running back toward the barn.

"Think that's everyone here," Kicks said, rubbing his mouth as he glanced toward Bob's body. "Wish we coulda questioned him first. Still don't know why the sheriff wanted that map of the gold mine, or what Bob's involvement in it was."

"Maybe it was the sheriff working alone on that?" Muley said.

"Could be, but I don't think so. We just ain't got all the pieces to put this puzzle together yet. I have a feelin' Quantrill might have some answers, but he won't be so easy to get at."

"So what now?" Muley asked.

"We go back to town, try to figure out what our next step will be." He looked around at the four bodies, Bob having taken his last breath. "We'll send someone back to help the cook take care of this mess. Bodies will have to be buried here or taken back to town."

"Think it's safe to go outside?" Muley asked.

Kicks looked out the window, narrowing his eyes on the rocky hills in the distance. He caught a flash of movement and picked up a single horse working its way down. "Looks like Seth."

Muley and Kicks went out to the bunkhouse, entering cautiously, just in case they'd missed one outlaw. On one of the cots a blanket had been pulled up over the head of what looked like a body.

"You don't want a bullet put in ya, you'll lower that blanket real slow and put your hands in the air," Muley said. He already had his Colt pulled, the hammer cocked.

The lump didn't move.

Kicks bit at his lower lip as he crept closer. He ripped the blanket down and jumped back at the same time, staying out of Muley's line of fire.

"I'll be damned," Muley said, putting his pistol back in its holster. "That the injun who attacked you up at the hunter's lodge?"

"Yep, Two Bears, dead." There were bloody bandages covering his chest where he had been wounded during the fight with Kicks. Kicks pulled the blanket back over him; "Guess he made it back after all. What we don't know is if Quantrill was already gone."

"What difference does it make?" Muley asked.

"Well, he could be intending to meet up at the hunter's lodge with his other men. He won't know they're already gone. Can't forget Bloody Bill and Thrailkill are still out there somewhere too."

"I say we ride up there and wipe the rest of those outlaws out. Get them before they can organize."

"Not sure it's gonna be that easy," Kicks said. "The bank robbery, that sodbuster getting killed in town, Seth getting burned out; Quantrill is behind it all. He's already organized. We need to get back to town and try to figure out what to do. Quantrill ain't got what he came for yet. He'll be back. You can count on it."

"So you don't think he mighta just hightailed it out of the state? We could let Kansas handle it."

"Nope, he's still here."

After Kicks freed the cook, they walked out of the barn to find Seth sitting on his horse.

"Thought you boys might need some help," Seth said, grinning as he patted the butt of his rifle.

"Appreciate it," Kicks replied, grinning back.

"Where'd everyone go? Was expectin' more trouble than this."

Kicks explained what they'd learned so far, then he and Muley retrieved their horses, mounting up. "We'll send someone back to help you with the bodies, Cookie."

The cook nodded, refusing to meet their eyes. He looked happy to still be alive.

CHAPTER 27

When Kicks, Muley and Seth arrived back in Helena, it was about ten thirty in the morning. They still had most of the day ahead of them. They went straight to Dave's office in the livery stable and took care of their horses—a good rubdown followed by some grain and hay. After filling everyone in on what had happened out at Bob's ranch, Kicks and Muley walked over to the mayor's office, filling him in on what was happening too.

"Let's go get some chow over at the Silver Spoon," Kicks said as they left the mayor's office. "I'm sure you're dyin' to see Cathy about now."

"Not gonna argue with that," Muley said, grinning.

Sitting down at the counter, they ordered their food. Kicks waited until Cathy went into the kitchen to prepare their lunch to speak with Muley about his plans. "So, after we eat, I'm gonna stop off at the Golden Nugget and have myself a good stiff drink. Then I need to go out of town for a bit. Everything goes all right, I should be back in the morning."

Muley frowned. "You're not gonna do something foolish, are you, Kicks, like going out to the outlaw camp by yourself?"

Kicks chuckled, sitting back in his seat. "I've done some pretty dumb things in my lifetime, but I'm not that stupid."

"Then what kind of business you got going that don't involve me, or the other fellas."

"Okay, I wasn't gonna say anything about this to anyone, because I don't want to get your hopes up. Could be making this trip for nothing."

"Well, come on, spit it out! Got me curious now."

"I need this to stay between you and me, partner. Okay? Don't say nothing to the other guys."

"All right, I'll leave it up to you to tell 'em."

"Well," Kicks began, "remember when we first found out Quantrill and his army of outlaws were here, and he'd thrown in with Bob Jensen? We told Mayor Harper and Judge Cleveland to wire Fort Harrison to send a troop of cavalry in to intervene? The fort ain't much more than ten miles away so they could be here in a matter of hours."

"Yeah, I remember," Muley said. "Mayor said they already wired Fort Harrison and they wrote back that the army couldn't get involved in civilian affairs, not unless the town was under siege. Seems to me they tried to wire them a second time and got the same answer."

"Yep, your memory serves you right, partner. Remember when I mentioned the Dragoon Soldiers? Told you I had a couple friends of mine who were at the fort."

"Yeah, the Dragoons," Muley said. "You thinkin' of asking them to come help us? Maybe I should go with you."

"No, I need you to stay here, make sure no one tries to break those outlaws from jail. You need to keep an eye on Cathy and the other women folk too. Those men showed they don't care about hurting a woman. Don't worry about me. I'll be fine."

Kicks and Muley sat back and smiled when Cathy came back with two heaping plates of food. "Here you go, fellas. Hope you're hungry."

"Always," Kicks and Muley said together.

Kicks finished his meal, then excused himself and left Cathy and Muley at the café.

It was still early by the time he got back to the livery to saddle his horse. There was no one in the office, but he found Whiskers lying in the corner of one stall, sleeping. Kicks watched the old man for a minute; he seemed restless and then started mumbling something about the Guardian of the Gulch. Kicks frowned, whispering, "Still havin' dreams about that, huh?"

He shook his head and turned from Whiskers, going into the office to retrieve an extra box of .44 cartridges from his war bag. Buck had finished up his hay by then, so he got the buckskin out and saddled him, stuffing the box of shells in his saddlebag. Kicks also grabbed his Winchester rifle and fit it in its scabbard. He hesitated, then went ahead and tied his bedroll to the cantle. Never knew when one might get caught out after dark. Best to be prepared.

It was just before dark when Kicks reached Fort William Harrison. The soldiers on duty were just closing the big wooden doors to the compound for the night. Kicks stopped just short of the entrance and identified himself. "I'm here to see Sergeants Sam Ford and Frank Mullen."

The soldiers escorted Kicks inside and finished closing the compound doors. "Follow us," they said. "We'll take you to the Sergeant's Quarters."

As soon as Sergeants Sam and Frank saw Kicks, they shook his hand. "Damn, Kicks, glad to see you," Sam said. "Where you been? Whatcha been doing with yourself?" Sam was a tall, lean-built man of about thirty years. Clean-shaven, he kept his dark hair combed back, the curly tips just above his collar.

"Doin' fine. Been around here and there." Kicks laughed. "Can't believe they haven't kicked you boys outta the army yet."

They all three laughed, and Sam said, "Uncle Sam's been trying to get rid of us for years, but we won't leave."

Then Frank said jokingly, "Actually, that ain't quite true. You see, we keep trying to leave, but being that we're the two best men they got, Uncle Sam won't let us." Frank was a little shorter than Sam with blond hair and a sturdier build. He kept his beard trimmed short, and his blue eyes tended to sparkle with a little more humor than Sam's.

The Sergeant's Quarters were two large rooms with plenty of space. The larger room held cots, their sleeping quarters. The smaller room was fixed up with a couple of tables and chairs. One table was used for writing letters and reading. The other was for relaxing with a cup of coffee, or just talking. In one corner of this room was a small woodstove for making coffee.

The three men sat and talked over old times for a while, and then Frank said, "We're sure glad to see you, Kicks, and I know you're glad to see us, but I got a feeling that you're not here just for a social call, right?" He ran his fingers over his moustache, smoothing the hair down.

"Yep, you're right as rain, partner. I got a big problem, and I'm not sure I can get myself or my friends out of it, not alone. Might need your help."

They sat and listened while he explained the situation to them.

Sergeant Ford asked, "So you think Quantrill was in on some scheme with Bob Jensen and the sheriff, this Cal

Tidwell. You say you and these six other fellas got rid of Bob and the sheriff, but you still got Quantrill and his army of outlaws to worry about. How many men you figure he has camped out there in the woods by the Gates?"

"Don't have an exact number," Kicks replied. "Cook out at the Running J, Bob's place, said Quantrill left with fifteen or twenty men late last night. I know he had some men holed up out at an old ranch house east of town. Don't know if they're still there. Bloody Bill Anderson is riding with Quantrill now, but I'm not sure where he is either. He killed a poor sodbuster in town a few weeks back. Think he might have been in on a bank robbery took place around then too. Could be Quantrill's got thirty or forty men all total."

"So," Frank asked, "You don't know what this whole thing's about? I mean, Bob and that sheriff calling in someone like Quantrill…" He paused, shaking his head. "Sounds like trouble, all right. Think Quantrill held a hand in kidnapping those two women?"

"Not sure about that one," Kicks said, having serious doubts. "Sheriff wanted information about some old map to the Last Chance gold mine. Might not have anything to do with the other stuff between Bob and Quantrill. Far as I know, the mine belongs to the town itself."

"Yeah," Sam said, looping his fingers behind his head as he sat back in his chair, long legs stretched out in front of him. "I'd say you're in a bit of a pickle here. Frank and me both got leave comin' to us. I figure we can probably help you out."

"Yep." Frank said, leaning his elbows on the table, "though I'm not sure what nine of us can do up against thirty or forty outlaws. Didn't you say two of your guys were just kids?"

"Yeah, but they held their own when the lead was flyin'. I ain't worried about them." Kicks took a deep breath and released it slowly, sitting back in his seat. "I shouldn't have come here, fellas. This ain't your fight."

"Now hold on a minute," Frank said. "We ain't never let each other down in the past. Ain't gonna do it now either, Kicks. You wait here a minute. I'll be right back." Standing, he motioned to Sam. "Come on; let's go talk to the commander."

"Wait," Kicks said. "We've already wired the post commander, twice even. Said the army can't get involved in civilian affairs, not unless the town is put under—" Before Kicks could finish his sentence, Sam and Frank were already out the door. "Okay then," he murmured, listening to the fading sound of their boots on the wood flooring.

Kicks paced while he waited. He, Frank and Sam had been in some tight spots together in the past, and they'd always come out with a winning hand. He didn't know if they could convince the commander to change his mind about helping the town on this matter. The commander had to follow rules, after all. But it would sure ease his mind if they could.

Sam and Frank returned about thirty minutes later, both men carrying big smiles.

Kicks relaxed some and grinned back. "I guess your commander said you could start your leave now, huh?"

They both laughed. "Better than that," Frank said. "We got a platoon of twenty-seven men compliments of Commander Wayne Churchill. And that's not all. We have the authority from the commander to take a Model Colt 1877 Bulldog Gatling gun." He shrugged, smirking. "Just in case we need it."

Kicks could hardly believe what he was hearing. "But in the wire he sent to us back in Helena, he said he couldn't take military action unless the town was already under siege?"

"Well, it's like this." Frank said. "We run a very tight and strict post here, but we're also like one big happy family. When one of us needs something, we usually get it."

"Kinda sticking his neck out, ain't he?"

"Nah, not really," Sam said. "He did give us permission to take the platoon and a Gatling gun. But if we screw up, he'll have to deny he authorized us to do anything. He'll just say we took leave, and he didn't know our plans."

"Wow," Kicks said. "I don't know if I can accept your help under such conditions. How you gonna explain it if some of the men get hurt or killed?"

"Kicks," Frank said. "We haven't had an injun uprising or any kind of a skirmish for ages. We, which are all of us here at the fort, are just aching for a fight. The commander himself said he would like to head up the platoon, but for obvious reasons, he can't. Needs to stay here and maintain the fort. You let us worry about explaining anyone getting hurt. Just tell us where you want us and when."

"Okay," Kicks agreed, nodding. "You know the area that's referred to as The Gates of the Mountains?"

"Sure, it's about twelve miles east of here, across the river and up the mountain."

"Great," Kicks said. "Day after tomorrow, you and your platoon meet us at the river where it forks. There'll be seven of us. We'll plan how we want to go in from there."

"Sounds like a plan," Sam said. "You gonna stay the night or ride back now?"

"Thought I'd stay the night. I can leave at first light, let the fellas know what's happening. It'll be a relief for them to learn we're gonna have help."

"Good," Frank said. "Let me grab a bottle of whiskey and we can play a friendly game of cards. It's been a while, Kicks.

Got some catching up to do, besides your troubles with Quantrill."

"Sounds good to me."

CHAPTER 28

Kicks got a little later start than he'd planned the next morning, having stayed up too late drinking and playing cards with the boys. It was midafternoon when he finally rode into Helena. Thirsty after the long ride, he decided to go straight to the Golden Nugget for a drink to knock back the dust in his throat.

Both hitching rails were already lined with horses. He had to squeeze in to make room for Buck, looping the reins around the post. Looking up and down the boardwalk, Kicks was a bit surprised by the amount of traffic out this time of day. Must be Saturday, the day sodbusters and ranchers drove in for supplies. Kicks tended to lose track of the days himself.

He smiled, recognizing the tune being played on the piano, someone singing 'Little Joe the Wrangler,' a song he'd sung himself many times while guarding a herd of cattle out on the trail. Kicks stopped a moment before entering the Golden Nugget, studying the brands on the horses tied at the hitching post. He recognized a couple brands as coming from the Running J outfit. Some of the others he'd never seen before. *Could be Quantrill's riders,* he thought. Hopefully, they weren't bringing the fight right into the middle of town.

Kicks stepped into the saloon and moved to the right of the doorway and stood there a moment, allowing his eyes time to adjust to the dimmer light. He nodded to Sammy as he walked up to the bar.

Sammy nodded back and immediately worked his way down the bar to him. "Muley and Stonewall came in a couple hours ago. They're back in the corner at your usual table." He put a glass on the bar in front of Kicks. "I assume you want to go sit with them?"

Kicks picked up the glass. "Thanks, partner, how's it been going this afternoon?"

"Sammy forced a grin. Business is good. But you can bet trouble will be coming before the night's over. I'm sure glad you boys are here."

"Why would you be expecting trouble? What's up?"

Sammy looked around nervously. "Muley can fill you in."

Kicks turned around and studied the room a little closer, a bad feeling coming over him. Trying to stay relaxed, he picked up his glass and walked over to the table where Muley and Stonewall sat with a bottle of whiskey in the middle of the table. On the way, he got a good look at some of the saloon's clientele. Some he recognized as locals. For the most he knew they were honest, hard-working men just trying to have a good time, drinking, gambling, and spending their money on the working girls here. A few others were strangers, hard, mean-looking men.

His chair creaked as Kicks sat his six-foot-two frame down and reached for the bottle. After pouring a glass, he drank it down in one swallow and poured himself another. "That hit the spot," he said. "What's going on here, boys?"

Muley sighed. "Glad you're back, Kicks. I think the lid is going to blow off this town tonight."

"Same thing Sammy said. So what's going down?"

Muley took three cheroots from his vest pocket. He offered one to Stonewall, and then to Kicks, placing the third one in the corner of his mouth. He struck a Lucifer on the edge of his chair and held it while Kicks and Stonewall got their smokes going, then touched the flame to his own cigar. "About two hours ago, me and Stony were on our way back to the livery when we decided to stop in and see how Sammy was doing. We sat here for a few minutes, having a quiet drink, when these two gunmen came in. Heard 'em say they rode for Bob Jensen. Or used to anyway. They don't look familiar to me, and I've met most of the men who rode for Jensen. Anyway, they started smart-mouthing Sammy and disrupting the customers in here. Think they mighta been drinking before they ever got here."

"What were they sayin'?"

"Talked about what happened out at the Running' J yesterday morning. Said how they was joinin' up with Quantrill and would make the people of this town pay for what was done to Bob Jensen and Cal Tidwell. Hell, man, they're talking about hunting down and killing the people of Helena. We can't let them get away with that."

Kicks rubbed his jaw. They must have been out tending a herd when he and Muley showed up at Jensen's place.

Stonewall continued the story as Muley paused to wet his whistle. "So we approached the two loud mouths and threatened them with bodily harm if they didn't leave, or at least behave. They settled down for a while, until two other gunmen came in and joined up with them. They drank together for a while, looking over at us while they talked. We just kept watching them real close. Then the second two left about a half hour ago. We're afraid they're going for reinforcements."

"Which ones are the troublemakers?"

Muley motioned by nodding his head at the two men. "That's them there, on the other side of the room, facin' us. They're playin' cards with those two other fellas."

Kicks narrowed his eyes but looked away before they took notice. He didn't remember their names but recognized their faces from wanted posters. They weren't cowpokes who worked for Jensen. These two were definitely part of Quantrill's crew. He suspected the two sitting with them, pretending to play cards, were too."

"You ever seen the other two?"

"Nope, they're all strangers," Muley said.

Sammy came over to their table with another bottle, using his rag to wipe the table as he said softly, "Overheard them say the two that left were going to get some of the gang and come back here to do some real damage."

Surprised, Kicks asked, "I better go get a couple of the other guys. We might need the backup if the shootin' starts. Who knows how many they'll bring back."

Muley grinned sheepishly. "Yeah, I figured me and Stony could handle these fellas, but you're right. This could get ugly real fast."

"You guys stay here," Kicks said. "I'll be back with help in a few minutes."

Kicks left the saloon and hurried over to the livery stable. As he entered the stables, he noticed the door to the office open.

Dave sat up straight when he entered, picking up on the tension. "What's wrong, Kicks?" he said. "Didn't know you were back yet."

"I'm okay." He explained what was going on over at the saloon as they walked over to the jail to pick up a couple shotguns. Kicks shoved extra shells in his pockets. Whiskers was keeping watch over their prisoners, so they left him there, suspecting Quantrill might try to bust them out. Their next stop was at the hotel where they picked up Seth and Kevin. He had

Tilly and Wendy close and lock the doors to the hotel, telling them to keep everyone inside for now.

"Kevin," Kicks said, handing the boy a shotgun. "I need you to run down and tell Cathy there might be trouble in town tonight. Tell her to shut down as soon as she can and stay low. In fact, she should go over to the hotel and stay with Tilly, Molly and Wendy. You stay with her until she's safe, then go on over to the jail and sit with Whiskers."

"Okay, Kicks," Kevin said, nodding. Then he sprinted off toward the Silver Spoon.

"You really expectin' trouble?" Seth asked.

"I am. Was kinda hoping to take the fight to Quantrill tomorrow, but we might not get that lucky."

As they approached the saloon, Kicks stopped at the hitch rail and double-checked the horses tied there. "There's only four here I don't recognize, so that means the rest of the gang hasn't showed up yet."

Kicks handed Seth the second shotgun. "Take this and go in the back way. Lock the door behind you so no one else can come in that way. Stay back out of sight in the storeroom. You can leave the door cracked open so you can hear what's going on. I'll let Sammy know you're there."

"You got it, boss." Seth hurried off towards the back of the saloon.

"Dave, I want you to stay out here and keep watch. Sit over in front of the general store there. No one will pay any attention to you. If you see a group of rowdy men ride into town, come in and tell us."

Dave nodded, his face pale but determined. "Okay, Kicks."

"Me, Muley and Stony will stay inside. We'll be at our usual table."

Kicks walked through the batwing doors and straight to the bar instead of heading over to where Muley and Stonewall sat. He moved down at the end, away from the rest of the men, where he wouldn't be overheard. At this point, Kicks didn't know whom he could trust and whom he couldn't. "Seth is back in your storeroom, Sammy," he murmured softly, accepting the glass and bottle from the bartender. "He's got a shotgun."

Sammy nodded, wiping the bar with his towel. "Thanks, Kicks. I'll do what I can to help if trouble hits."

"I'm counting on it. Let's hope we're just overreacting."

Kicks held his full glass as he turned to put his back to the bar, studying the room. Two of the four men sitting at the table were drinking heavily and making lewd cracks about the town's people. The other two were quieter, their postures relaxed, but with a sense of readiness. These were four of Quantrill's Raiders. Kicks would stake his last dollar on it. The rest of the men in the bar were cowpokes and sodbusters, come in to relax and blow off some steam after a hard week in the saddle or fields.

Twenty minutes later, Dave entered, his eyes wide, face pale as he made his way over to Muley and Stonewall. Kicks didn't need to hear to know what was happening. A few minutes later, the batwing door swung open and five tough-looking gunmen walked in. They stood in the doorway for a long minute, looking over the clientele.

Kicks narrowed his eyes, recognizing them by their wanted posters. John Thrailkill and the Wild Irishman were probably the most well-known. If memory served him right, the other three were Frank Coe, Bill Ryan and Tucker Bassham. They used to ride with the James brothers before they disappeared. Bloody Bill Anderson and their leader, William C. Quantrill, also known as Charlie Heart, wasn't among them. At this point, Kicks was starting to get mighty nervous. He had a feeling this was going to get bad. Real bad.

Three of the men made a beeline straight over to the other four who were playing cards. Thrailkill and the Irishman shoved their way in at the bar. After downing a shot glass full of whiskey, the two outlaws turned their backs to the bar. At the same time, the seven men at the table stood up, putting their backs to the wall.

"Shit, here we go," Kicks grumbled, nodding toward Sammy. Out of the corner of his eye, he saw the bartender reach for his shotgun.

"Better say your prayers, city boys," one of the men at the table said, his eyes stone cold as he drew his pistol.

At the same time, Seth stepped out of the back room, sliding the shotgun into the cocked position. He aimed at the two men at the bar. Surprising Kicks, Kevin pushed through the batwing doors, his shotgun pointed at the table where the other seven men stood. The kid must have been watching from outside.

"Sure you fellas want to go through with this?" Kicks asked, his Texas drawl loud in the suddenly quiet room.

The outlaws slowly looked around at the cocked shotguns covering them from two sides. When Sammy brought his shotgun up, Seth nodded as a silent message passed between them, then worked around so he could help Kevin cover the other seven men. The nine outlaws saw they were covered from all angles. If they moved the wrong way, it would be like shooting fish in a barrel, and they were the fish.

Tucker Bassham finally found his voice. "I reckon we made a mistake here, fellas." He slid his Colt back into its holster. "Reckon we'll just be moseying along now."

"Stay where you are," Kevin said, lifting the barrel of his shotgun toward the man. Though pale, the kid's voice remained strong.

Kicks stepped away from the bar, leaving only about ten feet between him and Bassham. "You and your friends unfasten those holsters real slow and lay 'em on the tables."

It was a nerve-racking waiting game, the outlaws obviously stalling for time while trying to decide what to do. They looked toward Thrailkill and the Irishman, those two obviously in charge.

When Thrailkill lifted his chin, Bassham chuckled. "What the hell you think you're gonna do … arrest all of us?"

"Yep," Kicks drawled. "That's the plan. It's your decision. You can lay your guns down and come along peacefully or you can be carried out feet first. You got about ten seconds to decide. Rest of you boys in here might wanna move outta the way. Don't want to hit you by accident."

There was a loud scrape of chairs as men got up and quickly worked toward the back of the bar. None of them wanted to get near Kevin at the door, whose finger was already putting pressure on the trigger.

The outlaw Bassham spit on the floor towards Kicks' boots. "Just who the hell do you think you are, the sheriff of this town? Heard that idiot went and got himself shot. Ain't nobody left here to arrest us."

Kicks grinned, and with his right hand reached for his vest, exposing the U.S. Marshal's badge that was pinned on his shirt. "I'm arresting you under the authority of this U.S. Marshal's badge. Muley over there is my deputy."

Bassham's upper lip curled back like a dog growling over a bone. He went for his gun. Kicks, never caught off guard, lifted his left-hand Colt with amazing speed. His right hand fanned the hammer as he sent four bullets into the outlaw's chest. Bassham flew backwards several feet and fell over a table, dead before he hit the floor.

The other outlaws quickly dropped their gun belts on the floor.

"Move over against the wall," Kicks said, motioning with the barrel of his Colt. "I'm talkin' to you two as well," he added, narrowing his eyes at Thrailkill and the Wild Irishman. "Sammy, Seth, pick up those pistols, would ya?"

Shaking like a leaf on a windy day, Sammy put his shotgun back under the bar. "I'm sure glad you boys got here in time. I'm deeply in your debt … again. I don't know how I can ever repay you."

Muley grinned. "Hell, Sammy, think nothing of it. This is what we do, but if you really want to reward us, just keep our whiskey glass full."

"Hear, hear," Kicks said. "We'll all drink to that. Soon as we get these here outlaws locked up."

"I'll do better than that," Sammy said, grinning "Free drinks and dinner all week, for all seven of you boys."

"Let's go, fellas," Kicks said, motioning for the nine men to head for the doors. He smiled as Kevin stepped back out of the way, though the boy didn't lower his shotgun. He had no doubt the kid would pull the trigger if one of the men made a move. Kicks knew they understood it too. Though they were angry, he saw respect in their cold eyes. At least most of them. He suspected a couple of them didn't respect anyone or anything, except maybe Quantrill.

"I'll get this dead crook over at the undertakers while you lock those fellas up," Muley said. "See you back here when you're done. I doubt Quantrill will send any more of his men down tonight, but you never know. We best be ready."

"You should go check on Cathy and the other women once you're done," Kicks said. "Tell 'em it should be safe to open up again."

Muley nodded. "Good thing that sheriff had extra cells built out back of the jail. Looks like we got a full house. Have to arrange transport out of here soon as this mess with Quantrill is taken care of."

Kicks nodded, hoping they could be done with it by tomorrow.

CHAPTER 29

Kicks arranged for the mayor and judge to assign trusted men to watch over their prisoners while they were gone. Dawn found the seven men on the road toward the Missouri River. They would meet his two friends, both Dragoon Soldiers, and the company of soldiers with them where the river split off into three different forks. They would cross there and ride through the Gates of the Mountains. Kicks hadn't told anyone but Muley about the soldiers coming along to help them. There was always a chance the commander would have second thoughts and he didn't want to get their hopes up.

As they followed the river, Kicks noticed a black woodpecker with a red top flittering along the branch of a juniper. Several startled deer jumped up from among the chokecherries scattered along the river's bank and bounded out of sight. The area was so serene and beautiful, it seemed almost impossible that in a short period of time it might become a deadly battleground, the dirt and grass discolored by the enemy's blood, as well as their own.

Muley rode his Morgan gelding next to Kicks, both men quiet as they contemplated the next few hours. "I pray God sees us come out of this as lucky as we've been so far," he murmured.

"Yeah," Kicks wholeheartedly agreed. "Me too."

"Maybe you should tell the other men about the soldiers," Muley said softly. "They're lookin' a bit dragged out."

"Yeah, a bit. Been a rough couple days." Kicks pondered on that a moment. "We'll know within the hour if we have help for sure. Let's wait a bit longer."

"Yeah, okay," Muley replied.

Dave rode up beside Muley and Kicks. "I know this area like the back of my hand. I used to come here and play when I was a kid. After we cross the river and get past those huge cliffs up there and enter the woods, we could come across Quantrill's men at any time. Or they could be watching for us."

"Thanks, Dave," Kicks said. "I appreciate the info. We'll make plans after we cross the river. A couple of us can scout ahead. We'll be okay." Especially with a platoon of twenty-seven soldiers, not to mention two Dragoon Soldiers. They would be better than that native at sneaking through the forest.

Kicks waited for Dave to fall back, then looked over at Muley and nodded up ahead. "They should be just around that bend. Supposed to meet us here this morning."

*   *   *

"So," Bloody Bill said as he sat across a makeshift table in Quantrill's command tent, enjoying a cup of coffee. "What's next? We've come all the way from a nice office at the Running J to this shit-hole in the woods."

"Wait for the Irishman and the others to come back. They should've taken out the do-gooders of town by now. All except that Gentry fella. I need to question him."

"What's the plan after that? We gonna head back to Kansas?"

Quantrill didn't answer right away. He rolled a cigarette and lit it. After taking in a puff or two, he took a sip of coffee, then continued to eat his breakfast of bacon and eggs.

Bill knew better than to push his boss. He waited patiently, understanding how eccentric the old man was. Hopefully, it wouldn't get them killed one day. He might just have to leave his mangy old carcass in the dust one of these days.

Finally, after Quantrill pushed his empty plate aside and refilled his coffee cup, he rolled another cigarette and said, "Bob Jensen had that idiot Cal Tidwell kill the old sheriff in Helena because he started asking questions around town that he shouldn't. Seems old Bob learned about a map to a gold mine in Helena, a mine that ain't been properly claimed yet. Family by the name of Gentry supposedly bought the rights to the claim from the four Georgians. You heard of them, haven't you?"

Bill nodded, his interest piqued.

"Bob killed old Isaiah Gentry and his wife, but he never could find that map. Apparently, it's why that dimwit sheriff kidnapped those two women behind our backs. The older one was the wife of the sheriff he killed. The younger one was their daughter."

Ah, so that's why he wanted to question the cowpoke named Gentry. "You think this Gentry is related to the couple Bob killed?"

"Don't know for sure but I suspect so. Might be what brought him to Helena in the first place. Not sure how yet, but we need to find that document, Bill. Need to stake our claim on that gold mine. Would get enough money from that mine to fund our cause, take proper care of our soldiers. We could own the town of Helena and everyone in it."

"What about the other cowboy, Kicks. Heard he's pretty fast with those twin Colts."

"Don't know anything about him personally. From what Bob said, I think those two just hooked up there in town. I know you're starting to get antsy about movin' on, Bill, but I'd sure appreciate you hangin' around until we can tie up this mine. I'll make it worth your while."

Bill nodded, chuckling inside. "Yeah, sure, I'm interested." Interested in taking the whole damn thing for himself.

"Good, then it's settled. Don't say anything to the rest of the men. Don't want any of them thinking they can get greedy and take the mine for themselves."

"Wouldn't think of it, boss."

"Good. Call the men to order. Time to make our plans. Thrailkill and the Irishman should be back any time." Quantrill pressed his lips together, looking pleased with himself. Standing, he stepped out of the tent and tossed out the cold coffee in his cup.

Bill stepped out beside him and yelled, "Meeting to order."

Within a few minutes, the men he still had left were gathered around, waiting for their leader to give them their orders.

*   *   *

As they rode around the last bend, Kicks breathed a sigh of relief, seeing a large group of soldiers. He smiled as the other five men pulled up, looking over at him with surprise.

"What's this?" Seth said. "The Calvary?"

"That's where I went the day before yesterday," Kicks said. "Got us a little help from the fort."

"Hallelujah," Whiskers said, rubbing his fingers down his beard. "That sure is a welcome sight."

They rode up to the large group and dismounted, shaking hands with the captain and some of the other soldiers. Kicks frowned as he looked around. "Where's Sam and Frank?"

"They went on up to scout around." He pointed to a crop of trees behind them. "Sam thinks we should probably set up here. They are going to try to lure old Quantrill and his Raiders down the mountain and we can ambush them here."

Kicks looked toward the covered wagon, suspecting that's where the Gatling gun was. He studied the landscape, the open area by the river, then the covered area back in the forest. "Yep, this will be perfect. The outlaws would be left out in the open if they tried to cross the river. No place to hide. As far as he knew, there wasn't another safe place to cross. "Captain, you get everyone moved over and set up. Me and Muley are gonna follow Sam and Frank up, just in case they get into trouble."

He chuckled, as if that would happen. "You go ahead. We'll take care of things here."

Kicks pulled his moccasins out of his saddlebag and exchanged them for his boots. He suspected he might be going part of the way on foot. The countryside was truly beautiful here, a place a man might want to settle down some day. They crossed the mighty Missouri River up ahead of where it split off into three different channels, then started the climb toward the twin cliffs that towered twelve hundred feet above the icy waters.

Kicks could see by the torn-up ground where Quantrill and his men had come through. They weren't even trying to hide. Too sure of their numbers to be worried. Still, Quantrill wasn't stupid. He'd surely have guards posted, especially through the Gates themselves.

"We'll need to leave the horses here and go the rest of the way on foot," Kicks said, glancing down at Muley's spurs. "Better take those janglers off."

"How you going to find your friends?" Muley asked. "The two who came up here scouting."

Kicks chuckled softly. "Oh, I ain't too worried about it. I 'spect they'll find us." Muley obviously didn't know the reputation of a Dragoon Soldier. There wouldn't be much Sam or Frank would miss.

After tying the horses to sturdy branches, Kicks started working his way through the brush and trees. He stopped once to watch as a huge white-tailed buck stepped out, counting twelve points on his rack. The buck's ears flicked nervously as it looked over his shoulder. A few seconds later, three does stepped out of the brush. Something behind them startled the deer and they all four went crashing into the timber.

Kicks stood still for a few minutes, Muley frozen behind him, until the birds began to sing their songs again, and the other forest creatures went about their noisy way. He suspected they were getting close to Quantrill's camp. He thought he caught a whiff of smoke in the air, signaling a campfire nearby.

A horse nickered, followed by several others. It sounded like they were just up over the next knoll. Kicks studied the land carefully, then crouched down and began to creep forward, pausing every now and then to listen for an alert that somebody had spotted them. He didn't know where Sam and Frank were but assumed the Dragoon Soldiers had him and Muley in their sights.

Dropping to his belly as they neared the top, he crawled closer, keeping his head beneath the brush as he peeked down. Kicks released a slow breath, finding more men present than he'd anticipated, especially since he'd already taken out a good number of them in town. At first glance, he figured there were around thirty-five or forty men.

They were actually close enough that Kicks could pick up most of what Quantrill was saying to the men gathered around him.

"As soon as Thrailkill and the Irishman get back, we'll ride in and take over the town. I don't care about anyone else, but I prefer to take the one called Muley Gentry alive. He has access to something I need. Take the bartender and his wife alive too. I'll be questioning all three personally. Are there any questions?"

"No, sir," came from most of the men.

"Good, then pack up and get ready."

Kicks and Muley exchanged a look, then began to work their way back down the hill.

"What does he think I have?" Muley asked once they were far enough away not to worry about being overheard.

Kicks frowned, shaking his head. "Not sure."

Kicks froze when he heard a familiar bird call to their left. He shook his head when Muley started to question him. A few seconds later, he heard the call again. Kicks offered Muley a hint of a smile, then cupped his hand to his mouth and returned the call.

A few minutes later, Sam pushed his way silently through the brush. "Hey there, partner," he said, holding his hand out to Kicks, then Muley. "Wasn't expectin' you two up here."

"Where's Frank?" Kicks asked.

"He's keeping watch over that outlaw gang."

"You been able to pick up what Quantrill wants around here?" Kicks asked.

"Yeah, overheard him talking to Bloody Bill. Quantrill says he's not leaving until he takes control of Helena and some gold mine. Said if he has to tear this town apart to get it, then that's what he'll do. Wants to use the money from the mine to fund his cause."

Kicks rubbed at his jaw. "Why would he think he could take control of the mine?"

"Might have something to do with Sheriff Durmhill getting killed," Muley said. "Maybe the sheriff found out something, and Cal and Bob had him killed for it."

"Yeah, maybe," Kicks said, his mind trying to work out the puzzle. "I don't know. It may be nothing, but the sheriff and Bob tried awful hard to get rid of you, Muley. I bet they recognized your name, and I suspect he didn't want you diggin' into the death of your parents."

"You think my parents were involved in whatever document it is they were looking for?" Muley asked, raising his eyebrows.

"Kinda lookin' that way, partner. Think there's any chance they coulda known something about this document?"

"I don't know, Kicks. I was just trying to find out what happened to them."

"Well, you heard Quantrill. He wants to take you alive. I bet the men he sent down yesterday were told the same thing."

"Well, we ain't gonna give him the chance," Sam said. "You fellas go on back. Tell the captain that me and Frank will follow these boys down the mountain. They're startin' to get antsy, so it won't be long. We'll pick 'em off from behind if they try to run back." With that, he shook Kicks' hand again, then disappeared silently back into the brush.

Kicks and Muley made their way down to their horses and mounted up, Muley quiet for about thirty minutes on the ride back.

"I think my parents mighta been killed over this mine," he finally said. "The only thing that makes sense."

"Yep, that's my thoughts too. Surprised we didn't figure it out before. We need to check into the records on the mine. See whose name the claim is recorded in."

"You think that's why Sheriff Durmhill was killed? He found out something about the mine."

"Would be my guess. Cal thought the old sheriff's wife knew something. That's why he kidnapped Tilly and Molly. It's starting to make sense now."

They were just about back to the river when four riders came up behind them.

Kicks and Muley jerked their horses around and both shucked iron, firing at the same time. Two of the outlaws flew back off their horses. The other two wheeled their mounts around, firing back behind them, but their shots went wild. It was over in seconds.

"Well," Kicks said. "Have a feeling Quantrill will be down here faster than expected. Better go tell the fellas to get ready."

Kicks was surprised when he and Muley crossed the river. He couldn't find a sign of their friends or the soldiers. They worked back toward the line of trees, Kicks smiling when Dave stepped out from behind some thick brush to greet them.

"You learn anything?" Dave asked. "I heard some shots."

"Yep, got a few more men up there than we'd planned. Course, they're two down now. Captain close?"

"Yeah, he's back a ways with the rest of them. We got the horses hid down over the hill there. They been busy diggin' trenches to take cover in here. Got a Gatling gun set up too." Dave looked scared, but also excited. "We're gonna be okay, aren't we, Kicks?"

"You bet, partner. They might have more men, but like my pappy always says, 'When you're outgunned by the enemy, you just gotta make yourself hard to hit. Pick 'em off one at a time.'" He motioned back toward where the soldiers were digging the trenches. "We make ourselves hard to hit. Better grab a shovel and get to helpin', son."

Kicks looked over to where a couple trees had fallen, then glanced over at Muley. "You thinkin' what I'm thinkin'?"

Muley grinned, loosening his lariat. "Sure am, partner."

They worked together, pulling logs over in front of the shallow trenches, giving them a bit more shelter. Kicks was glad to see the soldiers had created a three-sided shelter, just in case Quantrill and his men tried to sneak around and come in from the sides.

After filling all the canteens, everyone made sure all their guns were cleaned and loaded, and all the rifles and ammo were laid out next to where they would be standing or kneeling. Now all they could do was wait.

Kevin glanced over at his dad and grinned. "Dad, the way those logs are stacked reminds me of the first corral we built at our ranch."

Seth chuckled at the comparison. "Think you're right, son."

"What if they come in from the back?" Dave asked. "We're only covered on three sides."

"Trust me, son, the soldiers got their backside covered. They've probably been in tighter situations than this."

Dave nodded, though his expression remained tight.

CHAPTER 30

The attack from Quantrill's men didn't come until shortly after sunrise the next day. It started out with just a few random shots from behind trees. Some of them had obviously made it across the river without being seen. As suddenly as it started, it stopped.

"Is that it?" Kevin stated irritably. "Was expecting a little more firepower than that."

Seth reached over and put his hand on his son's shoulder, squeezing. "It ain't over, son. They're playin' with us."

Kicks could tell the rancher wished he'd never let his son get involved with this. "Don't worry," he said. "Everything is going to be fine. Quantrill ain't stupid, but he won't be able to get at us here." Kicks had confidence in not only these soldiers here, but also in his fellow Dragoon Soldiers, Sam and Frank. He knew they were keeping a watch over Quantrill and his Raiders. If they were planning something, they'd find a way to let them know.

Sam and Frank had kept watch over Quantrill and his outlaws throughout the morning, noticing Quantrill becoming more and more irrational as the day went on. Apparently, he'd been waiting for word from town, and his men hadn't shown up. Not long after Kicks and his friend left, two men came riding into camp hell-bent for leather, their horses lathered from a long, hard run.

Frank worked his way closer, picking up something about two cowboys killing a couple of their men. *That'd be Kicks*, he thought, chuckling to himself.

Quantrill ordered his men to saddle up shortly afterwards. They began to work their way down the mountain but stopped before they stepped out into the open at the river. Looked like they were going to hole up there for the night. A couple of the boys turned to the right and began to work their way upriver. Frank suspected they'd try to cross there and sneak in on Kicks and the others. Typical Guerilla tactics.

Frank waited until after dark, then motioned to Sam that he planned to sneak down closer and try to eavesdrop on Quantrill and his main man, Bloody Bill. There were guards set up all around, but they never grew suspicious. Frank, like his friend Kicks, could move through the woods with the sure-footedness of a native. When he got close enough to see the big tent in the light of the campfire, he deliberately broke a twig, then waited for the guard outside the tent to come over to investigate. Frank came in from behind and quieted him with his Arkansas toothpick. He eased the guard to the ground, then crept closer, listening. Sounded like Quantrill had a couple of his men inside the tent.

"We got those boys trapped in the trees on the other side of the river," Bloody Bill said. "Got a couple of our men set up on both sides to keep them there until morning. From what I've heard, there's only seven of them. And two of those are just kids. They don't stand a chance. We can keep seven men down while the rest of us cross the river."

"I'm done playin' around with these idiot cowpokes, Bill," Quantrill growled. "I don't even care if we can't take Gentry alive. Right after daybreak, I want you to attack with all your force. I want this ended. Now!"

Bloody Bill laughed. "You and me both, Chief. Should have taken care of this days ago, but you wanted to play with them."

"Well, I'm through playing. Bob's dead. That idiot sheriff is dead. They killed Two Bears, and I didn't think anyone could get the best of that injun. It's time to end this thing. You sure it's just the seven of them?"

"Yeah, had a man in town watching over them. He beat foot it back as soon as he noticed those seven saddling up before daybreak this morning. Nobody went with them. I gave my boys a couple sticks of dynamite. That oughta keep them down while we cross the river in the morning."

Both Quantrill and Bill laughed. "You're a good man," Quantrill said. "A good soldier. Glad to have you on our side."

Frank had heard enough. He made sure the dead guard wouldn't be found any time soon, then made his way back to Sam. Dynamite added a bit of danger to the problem they hadn't counted on. Might have to sneak into their camp late tonight and relieve them of it.

Kicks was glad the two boys were able to get some sleep. They both looked peaceful tucked away down in one of the trenches. He was too wound up to sleep, as were Whiskers, Seth, Muley and Stonewall. The soldiers were taking turns keeping watch, though things had been quiet once darkness settled in around them. Kicks knew that would change come morning.

Sometime after midnight, he picked up the hoot of an owl that seemed out of place. One of the soldiers stood up and walked toward the back of their camp, returning the call. A few minutes later, Frank walked into camp, his clothes wet from swimming across the river.

"Sam okay?" Kicks asked, holding his hand out to shake.

"He's fine. Keeping watch over their camp. Wanted to let you know that Quantrill's got dynamite. Or I should say, he had dynamite." He grinned. "Mighta relieved him of most of it tonight. I think a couple of his boys still have some, so be careful. I think they mean to take you out, or at least keep you down, with the dynamite so Quantrill can get the rest of them across the river." Frank held out four sticks. "Here, managed to get these across the river without them getting wet. Me and Sam will keep 'em busy with more on the back side." Frank held his hand out after Kicks accepted the dynamite. "I better get back. We've already taken out four of their men, and I heard you and your friend took out two more. Numbers are dwindling pretty fast."

"Appreciate your help," Kicks said.

"See you in the morning, partner." Frank nodded, then turned and disappeared back into the dark.

Kicks chuckled as he made his way over to the captain, filling him in on what was going on.

Muley met him over there. "What you got there?" he asked, his eyes widening when Kicks held out a stick of dynamite. "Holy hell, where'd you get that?"

The captain chuckled. "My guess would be Frank or Sam."

"You guessed right, friend," Kicks said. "Quantrill was planning on using it on us when he came over tomorrow. Think Sam and Frank relieved them of most of it, but they might still have a few sticks. Our boys mighta took out a few of their guards too."

After the excitement over the dynamite calmed down, Seth grinned at Kicks. "You knew they were going to pull something like this off, didn't you?"

Kicks returned the grin, "Well, it's like my Pappy always says, 'When a horse starts swishing his tail in the brush, there's no telling what kind of burrs he'll pick up.' Tomorrow, if the enemy gets too close, we can toss a few of these burrs back at them."

Right before dawn, Kicks, Stonewall and Kevin were sitting together when they heard a horse whinny across the river. Most of the soldiers were up and ready, though the camp remained deathly silent. They weren't rank amateurs here, most of them having seen a lot of combat during the war.

Kicks stood, putting his finger to his lips as he reached over and shook Muley awake. "Horses starting to move across the river," he whispered. He nodded at Stonewall. "Make sure the others are awake and tell 'em to stay low and quiet." He worked his way over to the trenches and watched through his spyglass through cracks in the logs they'd piled yesterday, though he wouldn't be able to see much until after sunrise.

Kicks ducked when a bullet pinged off the stump in front of him. *Here we go*, he thought. He picked up the shadow of movement across the river. It looked like Quantrill's men were splitting up. Then nothing. It grew quiet again.

"Can't see anyone," Kicks said as the sun finally started to shine its light over the mountain. "They must be hiding in the trees over there. We need to draw them out. The soldiers can easily cut them down with the Gatling gun then."

"Any ideas?" Muley said, settling in beside him. "Think they know we got back-up here?"

"Maybe."

An hour passed and still no attack. The captain worked his way down to Kicks. "Not sure what they're waiting on."

"What the devil they got in mind?" Whiskers said. He stuck his head up over the wall and yelled, "Come on, you yeller sons of hyenas. Let's get this thing over with."

From out of the woods to the left, Kicks caught sight of a stick of dynamite being thrown their way. It exploded in the air so didn't cause any damage, but sure woke everyone up. The cock of rifles and pistols was loud around him.

"Hell's fire," Seth hissed. "Good thing they weren't any closer with that thing. Bout deafened me."

"Hand me your rifle, Seth," Kicks said. He lay the barrel over the top of the trench and waited. He grinned as he saw a man step out, getting ready to throw another stick of dynamite. He squeezed the trigger, and the man crumpled to the ground before he could throw it.

BOOM!

"Damn, good shooting," Dave said, laughing. "You care if I get the next one?"

Kicks chuckled. "Help yourself, kid." He handed the rifle to Dave, grinning over at Seth. "I imagine they'll be getting plenty of target practice before this is over."

All was quiet for several minutes, and then the main attack finally came. About twenty men stepped out of the forest on the other side of the river and began firing. At the same time, two other groups came in from both sides on this side of the river. They were well organized; Kicks would give them that. "Cover me, boys," he lit the end of a stick of dynamite, then stood and threw it as hard as he could toward the group to his right.

BOOM!

When he peeked through, he saw the blast had backed them off, but didn't stop them. Kicks jerked back when a bullet pinged off the log in front of him, slivers of wood shooting back and hitting him in the cheek.

"You hit?" Muley said, aiming his Colt through the cracks in the logs and pulling the trigger.

"Nope, I'm good." Kicks wiped the blood away, knowing he'd have to get the splinters out later.

More shots were fired from the other side of the river, but these appeared to be farther away. Kicks grinned, pretty sure he knew what was happening. His grin widened when he heard the blast of dynamite come from several directions. Frank and Sam were pushing them forward.

"Here they come," Muley said.

The soldiers were easily holding off the two attacks coming in from the side. Kicks glanced behind him, seeing the captain pulling branches away from the Gatling gun. This is what they'd been waiting for.

As soon as the first outlaws hit the river, the captain gave the order to fire. The fight was over almost before it had a chance to begin. They put up a weak fight on the sides, but soon gave up when they witnessed the slaughter of most of their men.

"Quantrill and Bloody Bill Anderson," Kicks yelled. "You're surrounded. Give yourselves up." He glanced to the sides, seeing the soldiers gathering up the few outlaws to survive the massacre. "I didn't see Quantrill or Bloody Bill. Did you?" he asked Muley.

"Nope, but not sure I'd recognize either one."

When Kicks was sure the scene was under control, he went back for his horse. "I'm gonna ride over and see if Frank or Sam got them."

"Hang on," Muley said. "I'll come with you." He jogged over and grabbed his horse, swinging up in the saddle.

They crossed the river, trying not to step on any of the dead horses or outlaws. Kicks grimaced against the foul odor, the blood leaving a metallic taste in his mouth. It wasn't the first time he'd viewed such a terrible scene, but he didn't think he'd ever get used to it.

Not far into the tree line, they could see where Quantrill's men had holed up until daybreak. Kicks reached for his Colt, his heart skipping when he saw movement out of the corner of his eye.

"Hold on there, partner," Sam said, stepping out into the open. "It's just me."

Kicks dismounted and walked over to the Dragoon Soldier. "Any sign of Quantrill or Bloody Bill?"

"Those two cowards lit outta here as soon as they realized you boys weren't alone. They hightailed it back toward the Gates. Frank is going to follow them a ways, but I doubt we'll see 'em again."

"Then it's finally over," Kicks said, a statement, not a question.

"Yeah," Muley replied, "but I still don't know what they wanted or if it was connected to the murder of my parents." He blew through his lips, obviously frustrated.

"Let's head back to town," Kicks said. "We'll let the captain take charge of the prisoners. They can take 'em back to the fort. I'm sure they got a few good hangin' trees there."

Muley nodded, holding out his hand to Sam. "Appreciate your help, partner. Don't think it woulda gone so good for us without ya."

"My pleasure, Muley," Sam said, grinning. "Literally. I'm sure the other boys enjoyed it just as much. Was getting' kinda bored sitting around twiddling our thumbs back at the fort."

CHAPTER 31

When Kicks and his comrades rode into Helena, they were met by two happy town officials, Mayor Harper and Judge Cleveland. Sergeants Ford and Mullen, along with most of the fort's soldiers, rode into town with them, towing a couple of bound prisoners behind their horses.

"Dang glad to see you fellas," Mayor Harper said. "You can take those boys over to the jail and put them in with their friends," he said to Whiskers. "Hope we got room for them all."

"We regret to say that Quantrill and Bloody Bill Anderson got away," Muley said once they got to the mayor's office. "The cowards ran once they realized who they were fighting against." He glanced toward Sam and Frank.

"Let's hope they stay gone. We can't thank you boys enough," Mayor Harper said, shaking Sam and Frank's hands. Now, if you'll excuse us, we need to get back to the office and start on a mountain of paperwork."

The judge added, "Before you leave town, have Kicks and Muley take you and the other men over to the Golden Nugget Saloon. Tell Sammy to put all your drinks on my tab."

Frank laughed, "We'll be sure and do that, and thanks." Then to Kicks and Muley, he said, "Think you boys were given an order. Shall we leave these two fellas to their work?"

Muley grinned. "Yep. Kicks, why don't you take the fellas over to the saloon. I'll meet you over there in a few minutes."

Kicks chuckled. "Need to go check up on a certain young lady, do ya?" Seth and Kevin had been anxious to get back to the hotel to check on Em too, and Dave went with them, wanting to check up on his ma and grandma.

They ran into Whiskers outside the judge's office. "Got those fellers locked up, boss." He looked around, seeing only Kicks, Sam and Frank. "Where'd everybody go?" Whiskers said, laughing as he run his hand over his scraggly beard.

"Glad to be back with their families with their hides intact," Kicks replied. He grinned over at Sam and Frank. "Well, you heard the judge, boys. Let's go over to the Golden Nugget. Got a bottle over there with our names written on it."

"Not gonna argue with that," Frank said. "A might thirsty after all that hard work." He chuckled. They all three knew he'd loved every minute of it.

There was hardly any standing room in the Golden Nugget by the time they arrived. There were a good number of soldiers already there, but also a lot of townfolks, ranchers and sodbusters. There were even a few women present, both respectable and soiled doves. They were all appreciative of the help their town had received.

"Sorry about the crowd." Kicks told his friends. "Afraid you boys are heroes here. Whole town wants to shake your hands, not to mention buy you a drink."

Their faces reddened somewhat, but they were enjoying the attention. "That's quite all right, Kicks," Sam said. "We don't often get much praise. Besides, this might be good for public relations, you know?"

After getting a couple bottles of whiskey and glasses from Sammy, Kicks led his friends over to his usual table in the corner. The men already sitting there were happy to give up their seats. A few minutes later, Muley, Dave, Whiskers, Stonewall, Seth and Kevin straggled in and joined them. They had to pull another table over to make enough room for all of them.

"So, fellas, mind telling us what the difference is between a regular soldier and a Dragoon Soldier?" Kevin asked. "What do those insignias and arm patches represent?"

Frank chuckled. "Be happy to answer those questions for you, Kevin. As far as the difference between Dragoon Soldiers and regular cavalry, I'll try to answer as simply as I can. First, we have the infantry, sometimes called foot soldiers. They are trained to march and fight on foot. Then we have the cavalry, sometimes called horse soldiers. They fight from horseback and supports the infantry, or foot soldiers. Then we have the Dragoon Soldiers."

"Why are they called Dragoon Soldiers?" Kevin asked.

"Dragoon Soldiers are specially trained to fight on foot or horseback. The name Dragoon is derived from the Dragoon's primary weapon, a carbine or short musket called the Dragon. They were called dragon carbines because the injuns said they breathed fire. Dragoon Soldiers ain't organized in squadrons or troops like the cavalry, but in companies, like the foot or infantry soldier."

"So what do those insignias and arm patches represent?" Kevin asked again.

"First" Frank said, "See this badge?" It was a yellowish-orange, eight-pointed star with a black hawk standing on a gold and orange wreath. Inscribed within the black belt encircling it were the gold letters '*Amino et Fide.*' "It's called the Distinctive Badge. The tip of the hawk's beak and talons are red, symbolizing courage. The phrase *Amino et Fide* is Latin, meaning 'with courage and faith.' Courage in battle, faith in each other. Courage, Faith, Strength and Honesty."

Sam pointed to an insignia on this shoulder. A black disk within a yellow border with concave sides and a green scalloped circle bearing a white *fleur-de-lis*. Above was a green motto scroll bearing the inscription '*Toujours Prêt*' in yellow letters. "The yellow octagon simulates the eight-pointed star insignia worn by Dragoons. The green scalloped circle simulating a palmetto leaf. It represents the regiment's first action against the Seminole Indians in Florida. The *fleur-de-lis* is for combat service in France. It symbolizes the 'flower of the lily.' This symbol, depicting a stylized lily, or lotus flower, has many meanings. Traditionally, it has been used to stand for French royalty, and in that sense, it is said to signify perfection, light, and life. The motto '*Toujours Prêt'* means 'Always Ready,' and expresses the spirit and strength of the Dragoons."

Frank, beaming with pride, looked at Kevin and said, "There's a lot more to it than what we just described, but I hope that does justice to your questions."

The whole bar had grown quiet while Sergeants Frank Mullen and Sam Ford were talking, explaining to young Kevin Morgan about the Dragoon Soldiers. The quietness was broken when Kevin said, "Yes, sir, it explains a lot. The Dragoon Soldiers are an outfit I'll sure consider joining."

Then someone else said, "Set 'em up again for the Dragoon Soldiers, Sammy!"

Suddenly the Golden Nugget was alive with happy sounds and activity.

By the next morning, all was quiet and peaceable around town again. The Dragoon Soldiers had left early with all the prisoners. Kicks and his comrades were waking up after getting little sleep, meeting in Dave's office for coffee.

"Well," Muley said. "we got rid of the outlaw problem, but I ain't no closer to finding out what happened to my family than when I first came here."

"No," Dave agreed. "And I ain't no closer to finding out what happened to my Grandpa Frank either."

"Well, I ain't no better than you fellas," Seth said. "I s'pose we got the guys responsible for torching my house, but I still don't have a home for my family to go to. Gonna take me a week or two just to round up my scattered herd of cattle and horses, then I've got to rebuild my house."

"Now hold on there, you guys," Kicks said. "What you just said ain't exactly true."

"What do you mean?" Muley said. "How do you figure that?"

Kicks shook his head, a hint of a smile showing. "Like my pappy always says, 'Some people can't see the forest for the trees.'"

"You know, Kicks," Muley said, shaking his head. "I'll admit that most times you have a way of seeing all the trees in the whole blamed forest, but I gotta tell you, I can't see how you can tell where we're wrong about not being any closer to finding answers to our problems."

Kicks laughed. "*Amigos*, I think the answer to your problems is sitting right there in front of your eyes."

"Now what do you mean by that?" Seth and Muley said together.

Kicks laughed again. "In the jail; all your answers are sitting right there under lock and key." They all looked at each other, then at Kicks.

Muley shrugged. "I guess you'll have to draw me a picture, Kicks."

"Well, seems to me at least a few of those outlaws over at the jail has to know what Quantrill and Bob were up to. They wanted something in this town, something to do with that gold mine. We know Cal Tidwell hired a couple of them to help kidnap the women. Like my pappy always says, 'You might not be able to squeeze blood out of a turnip, but if you squeeze it real hard, you can get turnip juice out of it.'"

Muley grinned. "I get it. If we put enough pressure on those guys, they'll cave and talk."

Kicks nodded. "You got at least four weeks to put the squeeze on them. It'll take that long for Mayor Harper and Judge Cleveland to get the paperwork sorted. Judge Harper can hold court right here, but we can't leave town, being the only law they got left. It'll take time to arrange transport of the prisoners to the Montana State Prison up in Deer Lodge."

Dave and Muley both acted excited about finally finding answers to their many questions. Dave grinned. "As soon as we get breakfast over, I say we start interrogating those prisoners."

Muley agreed wholeheartedly. "The sooner the better." As they all walked out of the stable office to go to the Silver spoon, Kicks looked at Seth. "Well, it looks as if Dave and Muley might be a bit closer to ending their quest, so I'll make a deal with you. If you'll stick around just a little longer, let us get this wrapped up, I'll help you gather up your stock and rebuild your house."

"Hell, Kicks," Seth said, "you've already done enough for me and my family." He snorted, then grinned. "But I'm kinda short on help at the moment, so … it's a deal."

Kicks was glad that Seth had agreed to stay the course, because he wasn't so sure this fight was over yet. Sam and Frank didn't think Quantrill or Bloody Bill would be back, but he wasn't so sure. He suspected old Quantrill might try to break his men out of jail. He wasn't finished terrorizing this town.

Stonewall, who'd been fairly quiet up till then, said, "Hey, don't forget about me, I'm in this thing for the long haul too. I can help you with your house."

"I appreciate that, Stony," Seth said. "I can use all the help I can get." When they entered the Silver Spoon Café, they walked in and set down at a table.

Cathy, excited to see them, came over to take their order. "Morning, cowboys. What'll you have?"

*   *   *

For the next three weeks, the seven *amigos* took turns interrogating the prisoners. They questioned them all together, then one on one, then two and three at a time. So far, out of the twenty or so outlaws, only Tom Pickett seemed to know anything about Bob Jensen, Cal Tidwell and Quantrill, and he wasn't talking. It had something to do with a document concerning the Last Chance gold mine, but they couldn't figure out exactly what.

One day while Kicks was in the stable taking care of his horse, Whiskers came in to talk to him. "Morning, Kicks. If you ain't too busy, I thought we might chat for a while."

"Sure thing, Whiskers, I was just talking to Buck here. Me and this buckskin have covered a lot of miles together. So, what's on your mind?"

"Well, you remember those dreams I been havin' about the Guardian of the Gulch?'"

"Sure. That old fire tower outside of town. Right?"

"Yep, that's the one. But now … well, they been more like nightmares."

Kicks stopped brushing Buck and faced his friend. "What's changed?"

"Before, I used to just dream about the old fire tower. I'd get a message to watch the Guardian of the Gulch. Lately, I see myself as a part of the dream, but I don't understand it."

Kicks frowned. "What do you see yourself doing in the dream? What's the connection between you and the Guardian of the Gulch?"

Whiskers shook his head. "That's just it. I don't rightly know. As soon as I wake up, the dream gets fuzzy. I try to forget about it, but the dreams won't stop."

Kicks thought about it for a minute, then turned to Whiskers and asked, "You been drinking before you have these nightmares?"

"Nope, not a drop. I quit drinking a long time ago. Just have one with you fellers once in a while. I ain't been drinking, Kicks. That ain't it."

"Well then," Kicks said, "maybe you need to try harder to remember. Why don't you sit on the bale of hay over there. Lean your head back and close your eyes. Try to relax and let it come back to you."

Whiskers didn't seem too sure, but he did as Kicks asked. A few minutes later, Whiskers' facial muscles began to twitch, and his eyes moved back and forth beneath his closed lids. Suddenly, Whiskers opened his eyes, then he wiped the sweat from his face with his bandana.

"What did ya see?" Kicks asked.

"I seen two people at the fire tower. They was burying somethin' beside one of the leg supports of the tower. Then I saw myself."

"Who were the two people? Do you know what they were burying?"

Whiskers grimaced and turned away, as if embarrassed. "In my dream, I was dead drunk, so I couldn't tell who they were, or what they were burying. I used to be drunk all the time, so it wouldn't be surprisin'."

"Think, Whiskers," Kicks urged. "There must have been something there you remember or recognize."

Whiskers closed his eyes again, trying to remember. "I remember something shiny."

"A metal box, perhaps? What else?"

Whiskers tried to close his eyes again, but his shoulders slumped a few minutes later. "Nothing. I can't remember nothin' else."

"That's good enough, Whiskers," Kicks said. "Maybe the identity of the two people will come to you later."

Whiskers sighed. "You think it was real? A memory, not just a silly dream?"

"Maybe. Probably be a good idea to go out to the old fire tower and check it out, see what we find. Might be nothing. But first, I got something else I need to check out."

"Okay," Whiskers said. "Only … can we keep this a secret between you and me, at least until we get a chance to check it out?"

"You bet, Whiskers. I'll let you know when I'm ready to go out to the old fire tower and the two of us will take a look around."

"Thanks, Kicks." Whiskers looked around the barn. "Guess I'll start cleaning the stalls."

Kicks grinned as he watched the older man grab a shovel. He left Whiskers to his work and walked over to the judge's office, hoping he could gain a little more time to try to break down Tom Pickett. He found the mayor present too.

"I'm sorry, Kicks," the judge said. "I was just talking to the mayor about this. We can't give you any more time. The men with the prison wagons should be here in the morning."

"Well," Kicks said. "I don't blame you for wanting to get rid of those outlaws as soon as possible. You got the whole town to worry about, and they're a lot of trouble. Guess we just missed our chance."

"I just wonder," The mayor said, rubbing at his chin. "What with everything else going on, I clean forgot about them being after that document."

"What are you thinking?" Kicks asked.

"Well, did anyone ever think to check out the records room? Anything about the Last Chance mine should be documented there. Might find your answers were right under your nose the whole time."

Kicks cocked his head, frowning. "You know, I don't think anyone has. Might just clear up this whole thing."

"Let's go upstairs and check it out," the judge said. "No time like the present."

Kicks leaned against the wall as the mayor and judge began to look through their files.

"I don't get it," the judge said. "The document on the mine is not here?"

"Could someone have taken it?" Kicks asked. "Or maybe it was never recorded in the first place."

"Could very well be," the mayor said. He scratched his cheek for a moment, his expression thoughtful. "Bob mighta found out. Seems to me he used to run a faro table before he bought that ranch. I know the four Georgians, the original owners, used to gamble here. Bob brought Cal in to replace Sheriff Durmhill when he was killed."

"Or Bob had the sheriff killed," Kicks said. "Sounds more probable to me."

"Maybe Bob couldn't locate the original claim," the mayor said. "Maybe that's when he brought Quantrill into the picture. Could be how this whole mess got started."

Kicks agreed with the mayor's hypothesis, but they still didn't have all the pieces needed to fit the whole puzzle together.

"What do you suggest we do?" the mayor asked.

"Hang tight for now," Kicks replied. "Don't say anything to anyone. I got a couple of things I need to check up on. Everyone in town thinks the mine belongs to the town. I don't want to cause a panic if this turns out not to be true."

Mayor Harper and Judge Cleveland both agreed to keep it between themselves for now. "But you will let us know when and what you find out, right?" the judge said.

"That I will, gentlemen. That I will."

CHAPTER 32

Feeling relived, most of the town's people stood watching in the early morning as the prison wagons faded from sight. Among the watchers were Helena's town officials, and of course Muley and Kicks, along with their five comrades. When the wagon was no longer in sight, the crowd all yelled a cheer of goodbye and good riddance. And then they dispersed, each person going about their own affairs.

"Well," Kicks announced, "me and Whiskers have something to check out, and if I'm right, it may be interesting to us all. Right, Whiskers?"

"Yep. It's been haunting me for a long time!"

"Well, what is it?" Muley asked.

"Can't say yet," Whiskers said. "But I think it involves the fire tower." He glanced over at Kicks. "You all can come along with us if you've a mind to."

Kicks nodded in agreement.

A half an hour later, they were all mounted up and headed for the old fire tower. When they reached their destination, Kicks and Whiskers dismounted. "Here we are," Whiskers said, brushing his fingers down his beard. "Would be lyin' if I said I wasn't a little scared about this. Been botherin' me for years."

The rest of the men dismounted and secured the horses to sturdy branches. Kicks, knowing ahead of time why they were coming here, had brought along a shovel.

"Before we start digging, Whiskers, you have an idea of where to start?" Kicks asked.

"You bet your long handles I do," Whiskers replied. "Let's see," he mumbled, walking over to one of the legs of the fire tower. "In my dream, I'm always right here, only I'm sitting on the ground, leaning against the leg of the tower. I see two people buryin' something over there." As he talked, he pointed to the leg that was catty-corner from where he stood. "Right there." He took the shovel from Kicks and walked over to where he had pointed and started to dig.

After turning over only two shovels full of dirt, he heard the shovel hit metal. "I think it's a box." Excited, he finished uncovering the object. "I knew it. I knew I must have really saw something." Whiskers picked up the box and opened it. Inside was something wrapped in a piece of burlap. He removed the burlap and found another wrapping of thick leather. Inside that, he found three papers. He separated them and looked at the first one, and shouted, "You ain't gonna believe it. This is the document to the discovery of the Last Chance gold mine.'" He handed it to Kicks. "Here, look."

Kicks scanned the document over carefully. "You're right, Whiskers, but there's much more to it. The boundaries included in this document cover not only the gold mine itself, but every inch of the town. And," Kicks said, looking up at Muley, "guess who's named as owners?"

Spellbound, everyone asked, "Who?"

Kicks handed the paper over to Muley. "Here, I think you need to see this for yourself."

Muley took the paper and read the first written line of the document.

"July 14, 1864. This document and its contents are the property of ... John Cowan, D. J. Miller, John Crab, and Reginald (Robert) Stanley. Otherwise known as the four Georgians. Upon this date: July 1, 1867, we, the said owners of the Last Chance gold mine and all its boundaries, have hereby sold it to Isaiah and Geneve Gentry for the total sum of fifty dollars.

Muley stared at the document for several seconds, and then said, "I don't know what to say. I just can't believe it."

"That's your ma and pa's names, ain't it?" Seth asked.

"Yeah, that's their names, but how do we know it's them? Maybe it's someone else." All the color had drained from Muley's face.

"Here," Whiskers said, handing Muley another piece of paper. "Here's a letter written to you. It was with the other papers. I think this oughta clear a few things up."

Muley hesitated, his hand shaking a bit as he took the letter and began to read out loud,

> *To Muley Gentry*
>
> *Dear Son,*
>
> *We knew we wouldn't be around...."*

Muley's voice began to tremble, and tears flooded his eyes.

Kicks turned around and started to walk away. "Come on, men. I think the horses need tendin' to."

"Yeah," Whiskers agreed. "Let's go check on those horses."

None of the men looked at each other as they walked away, leaving Muley alone with the letter from his folks, because all of them had tears in their eyes.

*   *   *

Mayor Harper sat at his desk in the town's courthouse, scrutinizing the document and letter they'd found out by the Guardian of the Gulch. Finished, he handed the papers to Judge Cleveland, who also carefully examined the papers. All the while, the seven sidekicks looked on, patiently waiting for them to declare their assessment of the find.

The judge finished examining the documents and folded them neatly. He looked over the top of his spectacles at the seven waiting men, cleared his throat, and said, "Humph, this document has never been recorded, so it may not be valid. You understand that, right?"

Kicks understood what was going through the judge's mind. He and the mayor were probably afraid Muley, being named owner of the Last Chance gold mine, would try and claim full power of said document and all its contents. Therefore, he would legally own not only the mine but the entire town.

"Wait a minute, Judge." Kicks said. "I may not talk or act smart, but I did go to college, and I passed the Bar Examine. I'm a licensed lawyer. I too studied this document and I assure you that even though it was never properly recorded, it has all the necessary dates, names, and signatures. I say it is legal and binding. If you insist, we can call in another judge and lawyers to verify it."

"No, no," they both said. "Look, we can see this document is indeed legal, and we wouldn't try and swindle Muley. It's just that, legally, he owns this whole town, not just the Last Chance mine."

"Wait a minute," Muley said. "You think I want to claim this whole town, and all its gold? Look, fellas, I only came

327

here to find out what happened to my family. And now I know. I don't want your town. I don't want to cause hardship on any of its people. I just want what's fair."

Muley's humble attitude shamed the judge and the mayor so much that they both apologized. "Well, Muley," the judge said. "What do you consider fair?"

"Why, I always did want to be a rich gold miner, but I always thought I'd have to find the gold, and work hard to get it out of the ground. I don't feel right having someone else do all the work and just handing it over to me. So I guess I'll just sign it over to the town … or something."

"Okay, Muley, if that's what you want," the mayor said quickly. "I think that makes you a mighty big man. I feel the town owes you for being so generous. Is there anything we can do for you?"

"I guess not. Unless you want to pay Kicks here all the money I owe him. I been in his pocket ever since we met."

"It's a deal," the mayor said, coming to his feet and holding out his hand. "But there's one other thing I think we can do for you, if you're interested."

"Oh, what's that?" Muley asked, taking the mayor's hand.

"You see, about five or so years ago, Bob Jensen came to us." The mayor looked over at the judge. "You remember, right, Judge? He tried his best to buy that old, abandoned ranch house out east of town. Think some of Quantrill's men were staying there for a while during this last ordeal. Being the kind of man he was, we knew old Bob was up to no good, so, in the name of the town, we took the old ranch over for back taxes and wouldn't allow it to be sold to anyone. I kinda forgot about the old place after that. After everything you've done for us, I figure that old house and the property should belong to you. If you're interested, we could sign the place over to you, lock stock and barrel, as they say. How's that sound?"

Muley got excited, "Why sure, that'd be fine by me. I got my eye on a pretty little gal that I been thinking about a lot. Now I got something to offer her."

The mayor laughed. "Then that's what we'll do. It's really a great ranch, comes with about twenty-five-hundred acres, but that's a small price to pay for what you're giving us in exchange."

"I'll take it," Muley said, holding out his hand again.

"Well then," the judge said, "let's go upstairs to the records room and see if we can't find the deed to the old place."

It took a while to find it, but finally the judge said, "Here it is. I just have to look it over carefully to make sure all the paperwork is in order."

As the Judge was reading through the paperwork, he kept mumbling, "Hmmm, now that's interesting." Finally, he looked up. "Well I'll be, Muley. I believe you've hit pay dirt. This old ranch was originally registered as the Triangle G, bought and paid for by Isaiah and Geneve Gentry. Son, we are going to deed this, your ma and pa's ranch, over to you free of taxes."

* * *

Muley could hardly believe what all they'd learned. As he and Kicks left the courthouse and started to walk back to the office at the stables, he said, "Kicks, I never thought I'd live to see this day, and I owe it all to you, pal."

Embarrassed, Kicks laughed. "Well, I wouldn't go so far as to say that, but you're welcome, Muley. Glad I could be of some help. What's the first thing you're gonna do now that you're in your rightful place? I mean, owning the very ranch that your parents owned and lived on?"

Muley grinned. "The first thing I'm gonna do is ask Cathy if she'll marry me. Then, if she says yes, I'm gonna fix up that old house like new and move her into it. Then we're gonna have us a whole batch of kids." He paused for a moment. "Of course, I'll need a partner to help run the ranch. You'll stay and be my partner, won't you, Kicks?"

Kicks chuckled as he answered, "I'll sure give it some thought, Muley."

When they got to Dave's office, they were so involved in telling everyone Muley's good fortune that they didn't notice when two men stepped inside the big double doors. They were halted by a voice.

"Stop right where you are," a deep voice commanded.

Kicks narrowed his eyes, recognizing Bloody Bill Anderson. He had two other unfamiliar men with him, though he suspected they were part of Quantrill's Raiders. Kicks chuckled. "Last time we saw you boys, you were running with your tails tucked between your legs back toward the Gates. Where's Quantrill? Send you to do his dirty work? You're a might too late, fellas."

Bloody Bill laughed insanely. "You think I really care what that old fool does? You did me a favor when you took out his crew. Now it's my turn to even up the score." Bill sneered. "Heard you were supposed to be pretty fast with that Colt, but that's not the main reason I came back here."

"Oh?" Kicks replied. "What other reason would there be, Bill?"

"I want that note from the four Georgians, the deed to the Last Chance mine. I intend to take over this town."

"Afraid we can't oblige ya. The note belongs to the town. It's already been recorded. Look like you came back here for nothing."

"Oh, I have a feeling the townfolks will cooperate when they learn they're gonna lose their town heroes if they don't. They can sign over the mine to me, or the seven of you can die, then I'll take the deed anyway."

Kicks snorted. "Sorry to disappoint you, but you've gone to a helluva lot of trouble just to die in a horse stable with a bullet between the eyes. I s'pose the horse apples can soak up your blood." Kicks didn't know if it was the refusal to get Bloody Bill the gold mine, or if it was the invitation to die on horse apples, but the outlaws eyes twitched, his face turning red, then Bill and his two partners went for their guns.

Bill's gun hand was blinding fast, but Kicks' was a fraction faster. Kicks' bullet hit Bill right where he promised it would, between the eyes. Muley took a bullet across the right foot, but not before his slug punched a hole in one of the other men's heart. They weren't sure if it was Muley or Kicks' bullet that took down the third one. Looked like he had two holes in his body, one between the eyes, and one in the heart, which was the trademark of both the cowboys.

"Wow," Dave said, peeking his head out of the office door. "That was fast." He grinned. "Guess we got three more to plant in Boot Hill." He turned to Muley, glancing down at his foot. "You okay, partner?"

Muley grimaced as he sat down on a bale of hay. "Yep, I'll be fine once I get this hole in my foot sewed up." He reached down and worked his boot off, blood dripping onto the floor.

Luckily, things quieted down around Helena after that. They figured when Dave's grandpa, Sheriff Howard Durmhill, found out about Bob trying to get his hands on the old ranch, he started snooping around and likely learned about the four Georgians and the sale of the Last Chance mine to Isaiah Gentry. It wasn't a secret that Isaiah and his wife had ended up killed quite a few years before. Bob Jensen had Cal Tidwell murder Howard Durmhill, shot him in the back. Then through his influence, Bob had Cal put in Howard's place as sheriff. When he couldn't find the document needed to claim the mine, and he couldn't purchase the old ranch, he brought in Quantrill. A mistake all the way around. Whiskers had been the only one who knew where the deed to the mine was buried, and he'd been drunk at the time, the memory only returning through his subconscious in dreams. The deed and map might not have ever been found if not for Whiskers.

CHAPTER 33

A few months after everything was sorted out, Kicks and Muley turned their badges over to Stonewall and Dave. They were the law in Helena now and doing a fine job of it. Muley and Cathy were married and living out at the old, abandoned ranch house, now rebuilt and working under the original brand, the Triangle G Ranch. It wouldn't be long before there'd be a little Gentry running around the old home.

"Well, Muley," Kicks said as he led Buck out of the barn into the early morning chill, "I guess this is it. It sure was good having a partner like you. I'm gonna miss you."

"Then why don't you stay on here?" Muley asked. "I could use the help. You know I consider the Triangle G half yours."

"I appreciate that, partner, but I just can't stay idle for very long, Have to keep moving."

"Yeah, I know," Muley said. "But now I got something to stick around for, I sure am a lucky man." He held his hand out to Kicks. "I owe it all to you, partner."

"Aw, hell, Muley," Kicks said, chuckling. "I didn't do anything. You did all this on your own. All I did was tag along and keep you out of trouble."

"I want you to know that you always got a place here with us. You come back any time."

Kicks was touched that Muley thought that much of him. "I know you mean that, and I really appreciate it, but I own too much property already, and I'm really itching to move on."

"But you're coming back for a visit sometime, right?"

"You bet," Kicks said as he swung into the saddle. "I wouldn't miss a chance to see my friends for anything." He touched the big buckskin's side lightly with a heel, and he was on his way. He said over his shoulder, "*Vaya con Dios, amigo.* Say goodbye to everyone else for me."

Late that evening found Kicks and Buck a long way from Helena on a knoll overlooking a large, peaceful valley. As Kicks built a campfire and put some coffee on to boil, he felt a little sad for a moment. He had made good friends in Helena, and deep down inside, he kind of hated to leave them behind.

He laughed out loud. "Like my pappy always says, 'A rolling stone gathers no moss.'" Then suddenly, he felt the urge to make a trip back to San Angelo in West Texas to see his old pappy again. It was time. Already, Kicks Burks could smell the rich aroma of his mother's freshly baked bear sign.

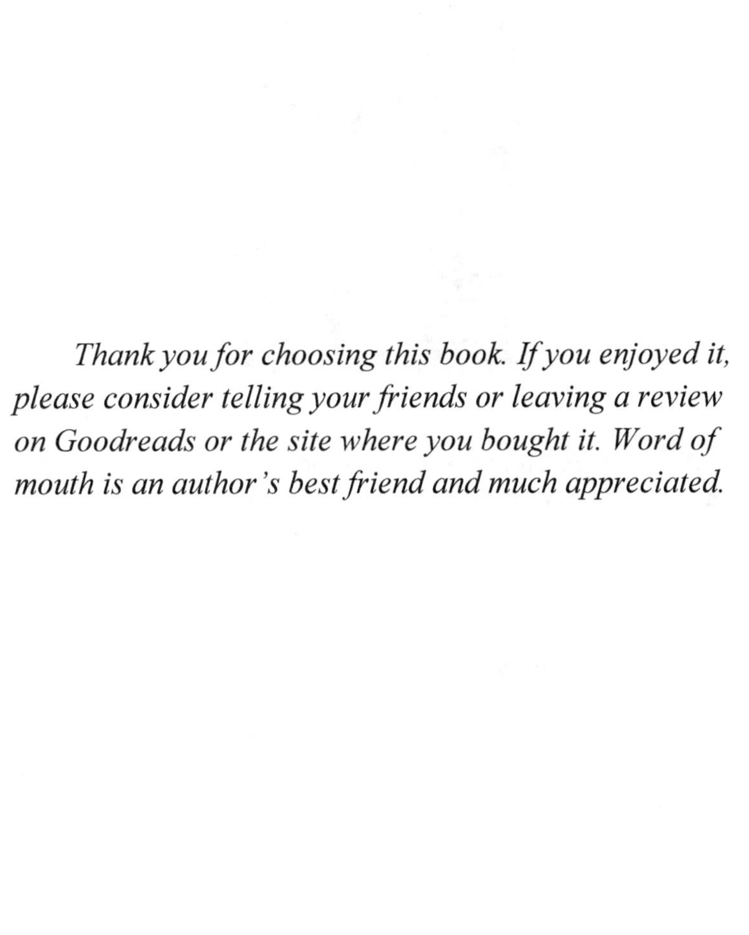

Thank you for choosing this book. If you enjoyed it, please consider telling your friends or leaving a review on Goodreads or the site where you bought it. Word of mouth is an author's best friend and much appreciated.

About the Author

Chuck Morris was raised on a ranch in the Midwest where he embraced a love for horses, cattle and firearms. As he grew, so did his love for stories of the American frontier. After completing his service in the Navy where he was a boxer, Chuck began wrestling professionally. After moving to California, he began a career in the trucking industry. During this time, he opened a horse stable, where he would board, breed, train and shoe horses. He also belonged to the sheriff's posse, was a minister and began his writing career. Chuck Morris is married with five adult children, two stepdaughters, numerous grandchildren and great-grandchildren.

Also by Chuck Morris

The Silver Concho

Jack Montana

Jack Montana's Quest